RADAR

INIQUUS CERTIFIED CERBERUS TACTICAL K9
BOOK 2

FIONA QUINN

THE WORLD OF INIQUUS

Ubicumque, Quoties. Quidquid

Iniquus - /i'ni/kwus/ our strength is unequalled, our tactics unfair – we stretch the law to its breaking point. We do whatever is necessary to bring the enemy down.

THE LYNX SERIES

Weakest Lynx

Missing Lynx

Chain Lynx

Cuff Lynx

Gulf Lynx

Hyper Lynx

Marriage Lynx

STRIKE FORCE

In Too DEEP

JACK Be Quick

InstiGATOR

Fear The REAPER

Striker

UNCOMMON ENEMIES

Wasp

Relic

Deadlock

Thorn

FBI JOINT TASK FORCE

Open Secret

Cold Red

Even Odds

KATE HAMILTON MYSTERIES

Mine

Yours

Ours

CERBERUS TACTICAL K9 TEAM ALPHA

Survival Instinct

Protective Instinct

Defender's Instinct

DELTA FORCE ECHO

Danger Signs

Danger Zone

Danger Close

CERBERUS TACTICAL K9 TEAM BRAVO

Warrior's Instinct

Rescue Instinct

Hero's Instinct

CERBERUS TACTICAL K9 TEAM CHARLIE

Guardian's Instinct

Sheltering Instinct

Shielding Instinct

Trusted Instinct

Acting on Instinct

CERTIFIED CERBERUS TACTICAL K9

Beowolf

Radar

Tank

CIA COLOR CODE

Red Line

This list was created in 2025. For an up-to-date list, please visit www.FionaQuinnBooks.com

If you prefer to read the Iniquus World in chronological order you will find a full list at the end

of this book.

RADAR

CERTIFIED

Cerberus Tactical K9

FIONA QUINN

THE PLAYERS

The Alphabets

- **Xander Belov – DIA and K9 Radar**
- Suko Hiro – DIA
- Anna (Anastasia Belov Senko) CIA
- Johnna White – CIA
- Dremonte Long – CIA
- Bill York – CIA
- Adele Gutterman – Mossad
- Steve Finley – FBI

The Scientists

- **Elyssa Kalinsky-Landers – Mechanical engineer**
- Eddie Baylor – Lab-produced proteins
- Claude Burns – Arctic squirrel hibernation studies
- Dr. Westergren – Lab-produced cheese culture studies

Iniquus

- Reaper Hamilton
- Halo
- Titus Kane
- Nutsbe Crushed and K9 Beowolf
- Sy Covington, lawyer
- Jerome (and his meatloaf sandwich)

AWG alum mentioned

- Scott and K9 Digger
- Tink
- Peter
- Jett

1

———

Xander
  Tuesday
  Bratislava, Slovakia

THE WARMTH of Xander Belov's exhaled breath formed a visible cloud as he stood under a lonely streetlamp.

He paused, assessed, then jogged across the road, jumping the ice-filled gutter.

There, on the corner, Xander paused again.

Something about this next stretch of cobblestones made his teeth itch.

Peppered with chained bikes, Xander noted how the residents parked their cars at an angle on the sidewalk, making the road passable for small vehicles. This configuration forced the pedestrians to hug the shadows of the building walls as they moved from Point A to Point B.

There were no pedestrians. There was Xander.

Who else would be out on a night like this?

Cold nipped at the tops of Xander's ears through his fleece

cap. It stabbed through the soles of his boots, piercing his thermal socks and reaching his bones, making them feel brittle and easily snapped.

This whole setup reminded Xander of the World War II film he'd watched on the plane ride in. The movie depicted people hauled from their homes, rounded up and herded at the point of a rifle, then sent on to a concentration camp with inadequate clothing. When they stood in formation for their daily roll call, the imprisoned people worked to stave off frostbite by stomping their bare feet.

This wasn't then. He wasn't them.

He had boots, good boots. And he was able to walk around freely.

Yeah, it was probably the sound of his footfalls moving in a habitual, military-trained cadence that was inventing ghosts in Xander's imagination.

"I'm a fortunate man," he said aloud as frigid air burrowed into the weave of his hiking pants to lay moist against his skin.

Xander reached behind his head to grab the collar of his wool coat, standing it up to cover the nape of his neck.

But it gave him little respite from the sensation of ice water in his veins.

As a whole, Xander had felt comfortable moving about the city of Bratislava.

He loved her history and music.

Loved the food—*my god, the food*!

Loved her architecture and the unexpected success of its May-December romance, marrying modern and ancient styles. Somehow, it worked beautifully.

The more opportunities Xander had to work in this Slovakian capital—to explore and learn—the more intriguing he found Bratislava's character.

Yes, as a whole, this was a wonderful city.

Just not *this* particular neighborhood.

Alarm bells clanged his nervous system awake. *Something's not right here.*

Tugging his hands from his coat pockets, Xander flexed his fingers against the frigid temperatures.

He didn't like this.

Tonight, fog crawled over the rooftops, prowled down the walls, and hovered just out of reach. It made the streetlamps dim by wrapping them, like a woman's shawl around her babe, hugging the light to her chest, leaving just enough illumination for Xander to move down the street, only semi-confident he wouldn't stumble over something lying in his path.

Above him came the plaintive strains of a saxophone as someone listened to the radio.

Other than that, the only sound was Xander's tread echoing off the cobblestones and ricocheting against the ancient walls made rough with curls of peeling paint.

Each step announced his progress toward the bar where he'd meet Anna Senko, CIA.

Maybe that was why his breath was coming heavily.

Maybe there was something about this meet-up that made his scalp prickle and itch.

Did he trust Anna and the information she was about to pass him?

Xander had been friends with Anna since he'd earned a place in the AWG—the Asymmetric Warfare Group, best known for its special forces' physical capabilities and its nerdy brains.

There, he and Anna discovered they were cousins.

With little effort, they learned they shared a Dedko Belov. Xander was a grandchild of his dedko's first wife (divorced). Anna was the only grandchild of Dedko Belov's second wife (also divorced).

That second wife, Anna's grandmother, was Olga *Zoric* Belov from the Slovakian-based Zoric family—a highly feared and highly successful crime family that had operated for generations behind the Iron Curtain. And even decades later, The Family was pissed as hell that when the Iron Curtain was raised to allow the former countries to enter the world stage, the Zoric family's power dimmed.

They meant to put things back the way they had been.

Since the fall of the USSR, The Family had worked toward reunification, creating chaos on a global scale decade after decade.

In fact, Xander had spent his entire AWG career trying to thwart them. He continued his efforts in the DIA—Defense Intelligence Agency—when the AWG disbanded.

At the AWG, Anna had worked on the Zoric case, too, but she had done it from inside the enemy camp. She'd used her name, her native Slovak language skills, and her cunning to snake her way in and bring information out.

After Anna fell in love with an FBI special agent, the Zorics asked Anna to be a double agent of sorts, and she had—with Uncle Sam's blessing—agreed.

Everyone seemed fine with her dual roles.

Everyone put up with it, Xander amended.

Should he trust this meet-up with Anna?

He shrugged his shoulders, getting himself primed and ready before he stepped off the curb between cars to jaywalk across the narrow street. Xander used the opportunity to seem natural as he looked both ways—as he was taught to do in preschool for traffic safety—as he was taught to do in spy school for bad-guy safety.

Casting his gaze to the right, out of the corner of his eye, Xander caught a shadow sliding up tighter against the wall just behind him on the sidewalk. Ahead on his left, Xander spotted an alleyway.

Xander slowed his gait, lowered his center of gravity, and kept himself off the wall. It was muscle memory from his time in Afghanistan that shifted his body into combat mode.

Then came the signal whistle, a light "Here, pup!" kind of tune.

Nope. This wasn't going to be pretty.

It was good that he'd crossed the street. It gave Xander a split second more time to adjust as a man leaped from the black alleyway and sprinted toward Xander's ten o'clock.

With the whistler racing up from behind, Xander had the wall to his right. Parked cars boxed him in on the left. Forward was the only way clear.

But forward felt like a trap. It felt like where a rat should run.

With his intuition telling him that advancing was a mistake, Xander swiveled to protect his back and square off before he discovered what was waiting for him up the street.

The two men spread their arms like linebackers, like cat herders, like barricades against escape. Xander wondered how fast they were and if he could simply pivot and dash for the bar, linebacker-style, plowing through any new roadblocks. He could burst through the door, and the bartender could pull out a protective gun. Then, Xander would be okay. He'd toss back a shot and feel like he'd dodged a bullet.

But forward felt perilous.

In most public attacks, the first line of defense was to get loud fast. Xander's Slovakian allowed him to excuse himself if he stepped on a toe, to say thank you when handed a key card at the hotel, or to ask for the bathroom. This wasn't a country where he frequently operated, so "Get the hell away from me!" wasn't something he could pull out. "Stop!" was the word he finally produced. "Stop" was as close to a universal language as existed.

The "stop" was shouted loudly enough that Anna should have heard it at the bar. He was only a block and a half away from the golden glow of what might be safety.

But the shout didn't produce any help.

No window flashed a light on. No one poked a head out the door and called out that the police were on their way.

A couple of dogs were barking, but they displayed their ferocity from the safety of a locked apartment.

Xander knew this mission was FUBAR because his brain had switched to adrenaline timing. When muscle memory and training weren't enough, the lizard part of his brain—the part that wanted him to survive—slowed everything down. It seemed like Xander had all the time in the world to process the scene as the bad guys moved in slow motion like they were running underwater.

Reality was the inverse; things hadn't slowed at all. His brain had revved to warp speed in order to save his life.

Yup, slo-mo was the tell. This was going to be the shit.

These two guys weren't big men. Yeah, yeah, two against one was problematic. In a hand-to-hand, his height and the length of Xander's limbs gave him an advantage. His years of combat experience would help. If this were a fisticuff mugging, he should come out okay.

If these two followed him because of his job with the DIA, that was a very different story.

Did someone send these men after him?

Shit, Anna! Did you set me up?

Most special forces men looked innocuous. Typically short and wiry, they were made of indefatigable steel. It was too dim out, and the men had on too many layers of clothes for Xander to decide if these guys were special forces types.

Xander hadn't seen the thugs reaching into their clothes to drag out weapons. But as he took a sidestep closer to the bar, he snatched up a trash can lid, holding it like a medieval shield to protect his throat and organs should the attackers pull knives.

It wouldn't do shit for him if they had a gun.

The men laughed and moved forward. Xander took another sidestep to maintain reaction space.

And another.

They were herding him, Xander reminded himself.

He stopped under an archway. He'd have to take his stand before he got to whatever surprise made them grin like that. As his back foot moved to fighting position, he thought that the men should focus on his shield—both protection and weapon— but instead, their heads tipped back, and smiles of delight spread wider across their faces.

Slowly, Xander tipped his chin.

Straight above him, in the archway, was a third man who pressed his hands against one wall and his feet against the other to make a human lintel over Xander's head.

It was so unexpected to see a man hovering above him that, even with an adrenaline brain, it took Xander a moment to understand what he was seeing.

By the time he processed the situation, the man had bent his knees. Without the tension holding him in place, his body—all hundred and eighty-ish pounds of him—dropped down onto Xander.

Knocked to the ground by three to one? Xander knew that, no matter his training, he'd be at their mercy.

Without a plan, Xander lifted his garbage shield to stave off the third thug, using both hands, thrusting outward to stay on his feet.

And to his surprise, it worked.

His adrenaline must be flowing at a higher velocity than theirs.

Xander tried to scramble backward, but the thugs quickly encircled him.

Now, only a block from the bar door, Xander yelled, "Stop!" This time, there was enough emotion in his voice that anyone who heard him would know that something bad was going down.

Fire, he thought. He should yell "fire." As a child, that was the word his parents taught him to yell if he needed help. Few came to answer the call for "help," but almost everyone came to the call of "fire."

I don't know how to say fire in Slovak. Xander lifted the garbage lid and stepped into horse stance, thinking that if he made it through tonight, "fire" would go on his short list of words he should know in every country he visited.

The men had their fists up, looking juiced by Xander's behavior.

If this were a mugging, he didn't have a single thing on him that would make them happy; his pockets were empty.

If these guys were Zoric goons, his lack of a cell phone to steal might just piss them off enough that he didn't survive their beating.

Xander wasn't coming out of this unscathed. That was all there was to it.

Now, it was up to his skills and fate to determine if he'd lived through the night and could feed himself in the morning.

As the first punch aimed toward his nose, Xander moved the trash lid for the block, pulling in a lungful of air to call out. He wouldn't yell for Anna. He wouldn't tie her to him or call her into danger's way. But he'd allow himself to try again with, "Stop!"

Before Xander released his word, the guy in front of him

perfectly aimed his uppercut, impacting Xander just below the ribs, knocking the wind clear out of him, leaving his diaphragm spasming.

He'd been here before. Both on the training mat and in the field, that punch was the go-to when the aggressor wanted someone to succumb but didn't want to break bones or knock them out.

Xander had trained for this scenario, spending plenty of time in the pool getting body and mind used to physical exertion without air. He'd practiced functioning through the panic.

It would take at least a full minute before he got his next breath.

In that oxygen-deprived minute, he'd be fighting for his life.

And through all his inner dialogue, Xander was aware that his brain was still functioning in adrenaline mode, slowing time to keep him alive.

That meant this situation still called for more than just strength and training.

With a well-placed kick to the back of his knee, Xander collapsed to the ground—the last place he wanted to be with three men standing above him.

Xander knew to roll once he hit the ground, dispersing the energy and lessening the impact. He'd learned to tuck his chin so he wouldn't knock himself out cold should his head bounce off the pavement. But he'd never trained on cobblestone, and the protrusions hit his vertebrae in a way that numbed his ass and shot fire down his legs.

Bystander attention still might save him, Xander thought as he kicked hard at the garbage cans, sending one flying. It landed with a clatter. As empty food cans bounced out of the yawning mouth, rolling and clanging over the cold stones, Xander pulled his knee to his chest and kicked out, clipping one of the men hard on the shin. The goon's leg gave way, and he dropped.

With a quick retraction of heel to ass, Xander rolled his hips to the side and kicked the steel toe of his boot into another goon's ankle.

The man bellowed from behind gritted teeth, hopping back into a doorway to recover.

When the third goon jumped on Xander, he sandwiched the garbage can shield between them. The rim was driving down into Xander's clavicle, a bone so thin that it was easy to break. It would be excruciatingly painful if it did snap and would make lifting his arms in self-defense all but impossible.

If circumstances were reversed, and it was Xander on top, he'd punch the can lid and break the goon's bone and feel good about it.

In this configuration, with the solid surface of the lid unyielding against Xander's chest, trapping him against the road, Xander's brain was at a loss.

He had no idea what to do from this point.

Xander was a panini pressed between two hard surfaces. If it were just the goon on top of him, flesh and muscles would allow at least a little flexibility, and Xander might be able to sip some air into his body.

Very soon, Xander was going to black out from compression asphyxia.

He'd grabbed the lid to protect himself, and that might have been a fatal choice.

The goon on top of him growled words that Xander didn't know.

Xander pushed out, "English," from the last reserves of his dimming consciousness.

"Where is monies?" The words were spoken with a heavy

accent and antipathy. Each word was pronounced with a shower of spittle that misted Xander's face. "Where phone?"

Xander shook his head.

The goon grabbed Xander's hair, yanking his head up until Xander was chin to chest.

Xander was about to have his brains bashed against the rock. Clenching his jaw, he hardened his neck muscles to stop any momentum.

"Where is these?" the goon growled.

In a surprise reprieve, the man jumped off him. His coconspirators jerked Xander to his feet, where they unbuttoned Xander's coat and dragged it down his arms. One of the men searched the pockets and seams while the others held Xander's arms in vice grips. They lifted his sweater and shirt, running hands over every inch of him, taking the opportunity to land punitive blows as they went.

Xander didn't feel any pain. Adrenaline was doing its job of masking in the moment so he could stay in the fight.

He'd feel it later.

The attack had been fast and violent despite the leisurely crawl his brain was taking him on.

This encounter was probably at the three-minute mark from the signal whistle to the rabbit punches he was bracing his muscles against.

The way they groped and rubbed every inch of him, Xander might have thought their intention was rape, but they'd asked, "Where is these?" This was a robbery, he reasoned—hoped.

Right now, Xander was rubbery on his legs, not yet able to hold his full weight. Not that he was trying all that hard. Holding him up made this—whatever *this* was—more complicated for the attackers.

Playing possum sometimes served a fighter well. In a

moment, Xander could just burst out with his special forces fighting skills and take down all three.

Joking. He was joking.

Okay, maybe not joking, Xander thought as he wrapped his hands around the scruff of two of the men's necks and banged their heads together in a violent blow. The hollow-sounding thunk of the heads crashing one against the other cast a nauseating echo.

Stunned, they dropped to the ground.

Xander raised his fist in the air and drove his elbow down behind him to break the grip of the man at his back and to feel for the guy's position. Nodding forward, Xander banged his head backward, impacting the goon's face just as a light flashed in front of Xander with such high lumens that he squinted his eyes tightly shut and ducked his head to protect his ability to see on this gloom-filled night.

The light lowered to his stomach, and a woman's voice, menacing and authoritative, said something incomprehensible; he supposed it was in Slovak.

The three men staggered back to their feet and shambled off into the shadows.

Xander fell against the wall, sliding down until he sat with his knees posted and his head curled over.

"It's Anna." She turned her light toward the street and did a sweep.

Xander realized she was breathing just as hard. She must have leaped up from her bar booth and raced to his aid.

He raised a hand in acknowledgment.

"Well, shit, Xander." Anna shoved her gun into her waistband and reached under his arms, dragging him to his feet. "You can't sit on the ground without your coat. You'll go hypothermic."

As he stood, Xander looked around him for where the thugs

had tossed his jacket. He noticed Anna didn't have a coat on either. Yeah, she'd jumped and run out into the subzero night to come to his aid.

That's how he remembered her from the AWG. If someone was in trouble, Anna was the first to plunge into the fray to help with zero thoughts of her own safety.

He should never doubt that her character was above reproach.

"They took the coat with them," she said. "Do you know who they were?"

Xander winced as he took a step forward. "Me? No. Did you recognize them?"

"Why would I rec—Come on." She pulled his arm over her shoulder, holding it in place with her outside hand as her inside arm snaked around his waist. "Walk."

Xander moved gingerly to the bar door.

Before Anna turned the knob, she said, "No one knows I'm meeting you. My good friend Tatiana lives in the apartment upstairs. I always hang out with her on Tuesday nights and have for years. Those men aren't associated with The Family, I can assure you. Why would you think that?"

"Because I'm here with you."

"We can talk it through when you've caught your breath. First things first." She looked up to catch his gaze. "Tell me truthfully, tough guy, do you need an ambulance?"

2

XANDER
Tuesday
Bratislava, Slovakia

ANNA GOT herself a club soda and ordered Xander a White Russian, just to be funny.

Belov comes from the Russian word *belyy*, meaning "white."

It was an old familiar joke they had shared, but tonight, Xander didn't find it particularly humorous. At this point, he needed something to take the edge off; he'd accept any port in the storm.

Xander thought his ribs were probably just bruised. Though it was possible the thugs cracked one or two. Something was making every inhale into a wince-inducing stab.

"You go to a doctor's when you leave here," Anna said with a schoolmarm's inflection.

He tapped his glass on the table before he threw back the

creamy alcohol as best he could with all the ice cubes. "I'll do that." He put the glass back on the table and used his cocktail napkin to wipe his mouth.

Anna turned to the bartender, calling out some word that Xander interpreted as "Shots" because she held up four fingers. Leaning forward, she scrutinized his face. "Street thugs," she announced. "They didn't hit you where the bruising would be evidence of a crime. It's always so much harder to convince the police that you just got the shit kicked out of you when your face is still pretty." Anna lifted her jacket from the table and draped it across the back of her chair.

"I thought they were aiming for my nose, but in retrospect, it was just so I'd use my trash can lid as a block, and I'd expose my diaphragm. They've done this a time or two." He pushed his glass to the end of the table, then caught Anna's gaze. "You think I'm pretty?"

"While you're rough around the edges, I can see the family resemblance, and *I* am gorgeous."

A teasing smile spread across her face, but Xander thought that it was accurate. She was gorgeous by almost any standard.

Her smile dropped off. "What did the thugs get off you?"

"Nothing."

"No phone? No wallet? No hotel key card?" she asked.

"I've gotten into the habit of carrying nothing on me when I can at all help it. I left the key card with the desk," Xander said.

"They didn't think it was strange that you did that? That move didn't make you stand out?"

"Let me be clearer. I left it in the plant beside the desk," he said. "I'll retrieve it when I crouch down to tie my shoe when I get back."

"Clever boy."

"I would have been more clever had I brought along a

broken phone and fake wallet, but the airline delayed my luggage, and I didn't have time to invent a substitute. The thugs said they wanted money and my phone."

Anna leaned in. "They asked in English?"

Xander rubbed his fingers on the scratched finish of the wooden table, giving himself time to think that question through, trying to remember the details that were so crystal clear during the fight but were getting fuzzy now. "They were commanding me in Slovak, and I said, 'English.' And the head guy asked, 'Where is these?' They said monies and phone."

She let that sink in with a slow nod of her head. "It's hard to come up with words in a foreign language when a) you're not expecting it and b) adrenaline is flowing."

"Agreed." Xander slid his hand forward and tapped his index finger in front of Anna. "How do you say 'fire' in Slovak?"

"*Oheň*. You can remember it because fires are orange, and if you drop the r, it sort of sounds like the first half of orange." She tipped her head. "Why?"

"Just something I thought during the fight." He licked his lips, then said, "Oheň." He waited for her nod, then repeated it again a few times to cement it in his mind. The orange mnemonic helped.

"I'm sorry that happened." She reached for his hand and squeezed it between both of hers. "I was looking forward to a nice visit with you—short-lived as this is going to be."

"I haven't said thank you yet."

"That's not a thing we say to each other. It's a given that we help when we can."

"Still." Xander swallowed as the bitter taste of bile slicked up the back of his throat. Fear was fear. They trained his team to feel it, deal with it, and do their job. But they could never train a soldier enough to make fear go completely away. "Thank you."

The bartender showed up with the shots on his tray and set two in front of each of them.

When he was back behind the counter, Xander said, "I haven't seen you since Peter was brought home. You know about that?"

"Johnna White got word to me, yes. His death has been hard," Anna admitted, pulling one of the shots in front of her and looking into the amber liquid. "Here in Bratislava alone and all. It would have been good for the team to get together." She lifted her gaze. "Have you seen Tink?"

"Tink is having a lot of mental health issues. She just wanted her husband buried at home, and the time it took the Kyrgyz government to repatriate him seemed to have broken her."

"God." Anna's face melted into grief.

Xander lifted his glass and waited.

Quietly, Anna intoned. "Peter, never forgotten."

"Never forgotten."

They tossed the whiskey back. The shot slid aggressively down Xander's throat, landing in his gut. As they sat in silence, each in their own head, Xander remembered Peter and Tink falling in love, getting married, and serving side by side. He wondered if being in the same fight, shoulder to shoulder, made the job easier or if it was a distraction and added burden.

Xander didn't have a good point of reference. He'd never been in love. He didn't even know if he had the capacity for the kind of devotion he'd seen between Tink and Peter.

Of course, with his job, Xander was never in a single place long enough to form those kinds of bonds. When Xander dated, he wasn't seeking out the type of woman who wanted a stable relationship. He dated busy women. Distracted women. It worked best for everyone. But, as he stared into his empty glass, he thought he was probably making a mistake.

Just not a mistake he knew how to correct.

Xander lifted the second shot. "This one is for f'ing Delta Force Echo and Jett finding and saving Scott and Tink."

"To Echo and Jett with gratitude." Anna downed the shot, then dragged the back of her hand across her lips to catch the drips. "Just say it, Xander."

"Say what?"

"You're always saying 'f'ing.' If you want to drop the F-bomb, have the balls to drop it."

Xander shook his head. "I promised my grandmother I'd never say the word again. It's stress relieving, though, biting my teeth into my lip and hissing out my frustration, so 'f'ing' is my compromise. Has been and will be."

Anna tipped her head. "How old were you when you made this promise to your grandma?"

He shrugged. "Six, maybe."

"Six," she repeated with emphasis, maybe some exasperation. "This was your Babka Belov?"

"Babka Belov swore like a drunken sailor. No. This was my Oma Meyer, my mom's side. A promise is a promise. I never go back on my word."

Anna rested her elbows on the table, leaning forward with a heavy sigh. "I know it's not me putting the world in danger. It's my family. But I still feel responsible for what happened to the AWG team in the Kyrgyzstan mountains, for Tink's pain and Peter's death. I keep thinking that if I had done my job better, I could have pinpointed The Family's damned doomsday machine and would have known exactly what they were testing out there and why." She frowned deeply. And Xander sat silently, giving her the space to say what she needed to say when she had so few opportunities to express herself freely.

The pause was long and poignant.

"While the team was roaming the Kyrgyzstan mountains and facing death," tears filled Anna's eyes, "I was fine dining and going to the opera in beautiful ball gowns." She shifted her gaze off into the distance, looking miserable.

"We each have our roles to play," Xander said. He understood that guilt. He felt it acutely. His AWG team needed him, but he was elsewhere doing his bit. This spring, though, he'd get his turn in the mountains searching for the Zorics' Machine Against Humanity.

"You're the first person I've seen from the old team. When White told me about Peter, she'd started to tell me about Scott getting injured, but we were interrupted before I heard the story."

"Here's the short version," Xander said. "When Peter and Tink were in trouble, Peter set off a flare, hoping his signal would get them help. Scott was up on the mountain alone with his AWG K9 Digger. Scott saw Peter's signal and raced up the mountain to see the trajectory so he could figure out the point of origin, and his foot went into a crag."

"Shit."

"Completely stuck, there was no way for Scott to save himself. Digger was indefatigable and mission-focused," Xander shook his head as he spoke. He still couldn't wrap his head around Scott's survival. "Day after day, night after night, week after week, that doggo was always doing the right thing until he was successful in saving Scott. If there is such a thing as a miracle of a dog, it's Digger."

Anna put her hand on her heart. "Have you heard much from Scott since then?"

"Not really. I don't think he wants the memories."

"Or the look of pity in your eyes," she said. "But he recovered?"

"They have him up on his feet again, but he'll never walk without a limp. When AWG shut down, they did right by Scott and his mental health by letting him keep Digger. Sort of."

"Least they could do is what I'm hearing in your voice. What does 'sort of' mean in this instance?" Anna asked.

"AWG wasn't all that benevolent. Digger was Army-owned."

Anna leaned back, crossing her arms over her chest. "So, what happened?"

"When they handed Digger's lead over to his new handler—or tried to—Digger refused to work. Wouldn't follow a single command, wouldn't even get up. They decided that since Digger seemed to have PTSD, it was time to retire him and—"

Anna nodded. "Per military policy, the last handler gets the first right of refusal."

"I swear Digger knew that and did what he had to, which would allow him to continue to save and protect Scott. Loyal to a fault. Smart. Yup, a miracle of a dog." Xander moved a hand to his side to support his ribs as he took in a deeper breath. The ache was growing more intense. "After seeing that, I bought myself a German Shepherd named Radar."

"Radar! Did you name him that because he was to be tasked with going into the mountains to find 'we don't know what, but it's bigger than a breadbox?'"

Xander blew a short, derisive breath through his nostrils and shook his head at the absurdity of it all. "I'd show you a picture of him, but—" He watched as her face hardened the way it did when her brain was churning. Xander waited.

"He's yours, right?" Anna asked. "You bought him and had him trained on your own dime?"

"Yes, well, Iniquus Security is doing his training, so I

wouldn't say 'dime'. When I get home, I'm going to pick Radar up for our regular bonding time."

Anna let out a low whistle. "Did you mortgage your home to get Radar trained by Cerberus?"

"They trained Digger, and Digger saved Scott. I consider it life insurance for when I go into Kyrgyzstan after the snow melts."

Anna reached for one of the empty shot glasses and twirled it between her fingers, avoiding Xander's gaze. "What would you do with Radar if you weren't assigned to the mountain search?"

"I'm not sure." Xander tightened his stomach muscles as if he were about to take another blow. "Radar's my brother. But if I'm not crawling all over the Kyrgyzstan mountains looking for *something,* I don't know what I'd do. If there was a Mrs. Belov who didn't travel, then Radar could be home when I'm not using him on field missions."

"That's the dream, isn't it? A home and family, a place to anchor." She paused with emotions storming in her eyes. "The reality is that it's hard to find love and solidity in our line of work."

"You did it." Xander nodded toward Anna's hand. "Finley's a good man."

"From the intelligence reports you've read on him and us?" Anna grasped her engagement ring and turned the diamond around and around her finger. "He *is* a good man. But he's in my life to the extent that The Family will allow him to be."

"For now, maybe that's true. But Anna, we'll figure out a way to take out the core of the Zoric enterprise. The Family will implode. Then you'll be free. We all will."

Anna held Xander's gaze without blinking. "We either succeed at that soon, or they're going to destroy the world as we know it."

"Wait." Xander angled forward. "The *whole* world? Not just targeted attacks?"

Anna whipped her head around to assure herself that the bartender stood on the other side of the room before turning back to Xander. "Have you rested enough from the fight now? Caught your breath? Because I need to get you up to speed."

3

———————

Xander
  Tuesday
  Bratislava, Slovakia

Xander clasped his hands, then leaned his weight onto his forearms, bringing his face closer to Anna's. "Spit it out."

"You're heading home to Washington?" she asked.

"In the morning." Xander eased back, crossing his arms over his chest. "Why?"

"Two things." She swiveled in her seat and reached into her coat pocket. "First, I have a message for Nutsbe Crushed in Panther Force." She held out a greeting card envelope with a quirk of her brow. "Do you think you can pass it to him without losing it in a mugging?"

"Not at all funny." Xander accepted the communication, looking down at the pink envelope. The Slovak accent marks that decorated the curly, old-fashioned script written with a purple glitter pen looked like confetti at a birthday party. "What does this say?"

"On the front? 'For my precious granddaughter.'" Anna tapped it. "I brought it just in case you had time to do me a favor and take this by Iniquus. It sounds like you're heading there, right? You said you're picking up Radar at their Cerberus campus?"

"That's right." Xander turned the card over to find a sparkly cupcake sealing the seam.

Anna turned her phone over to check the time readout, then twisted toward the bartender, calling out to him.

The bartender focused hard on Xander, nodded, and then walked away.

Xander tipped his head toward the door the guy disappeared through.

"I told him that a homeless guy with a knife jumped you on the way here and took your coat. That was what all the shouting was about when I rushed out. Then I asked if some drunk left a jacket in the lost and found that you could use to get home. You can't go out on a night like this without something warmer on."

"Thanks, cuz." Xander reached under his sweater, unbuttoned his shirt, and tucked the envelope away.

"If someone does get hold of it," Anna reached back into her coat pocket and pulled out a lip balm, "I wrote the card as if for a child and then included a letter written in English. It embeds the information that needs to go to Nutsbe and *only* Nutsbe; it reads like it's news for the granddaughter's mom. More importantly," she glanced over her shoulder, ensuring they were still alone. "I need you to meet up with Bill York." She mouthed, "C.I.A." silently. "York can give you the particulars of his assignment so we can coordinate with your D.I.A. team. There's no room for overlaps right now. York's been tracking a man named Orest Kalinsky."

"Orest Kalinsky," Xander repeated to memorize it.

"They fly to D.C. tomorrow."

"York and I were buds in Afghanistan. I have his contact information. This Orest Kalinsky guy, what's he doing in Washington?" Xander asked.

"Walking around without having a Zoric last name, mostly." She uncapped the tube and slicked the balm over her lips. "But he certainly is a Zoric. He's Medved's favorite cousin."

"Orest is new to me," Xander said.

Anna snapped the cap back in place and turned to slide the balm into her pocket. "He would be. His role is both intrinsic and somewhat peripheral. I'll tell you about it in a second. First, York believes Orest is going to visit the Zorics in their various prison cells to bring them up to date on the family happenings."

"Happenings plural?" Xander asked.

"We're not entirely sure what messages he means to pass because things are fluid right now, which I'll also touch on in a minute—So much to tell. So little time—But importantly, Orest planned this trip months ago. We speculated that Orest was adding a day to his itinerary to do the prison visits and perhaps explain how The Family has been working the back channels to see if they can't obtain pardons and releases since there's a rash of millionaires being pardoned for no apparent reason right now."

"Why not take advantage?" Xander deadpanned.

"Exactly." Anna wrinkled her nose as if the whole thing stank.

Which it did.

"Their releases are improbable, right?" Xander asked quietly. "They're going to stay out of the public sphere, tucked under a shoddy blanket on a prison shelf, right?"

"The Family has dangled carrots of possible rewards and raised their sticks for inflicting pain. That's not in my wheelhouse, so I'm not the best person to ask. I wouldn't say improbable, though. The D.A. only charged the East Coast Zoric family with trafficking minors."

"Only?" Xander's face clouded.

"The worst crimes weren't charged because who wants pundits on the evening news telling the world about the method the Zorics developed to kill people with neurotoxins that are legal to obtain, easily accessible, imperceptible, and without any known medical interventions?"

Xander released a breath. Yeah, there was that.

"At any rate, we speculated that Orest was taking an extra day in D.C. to update the imprisoned family members on the potential for their release. But now?" Anna paused to draw in a deep breath. "Now, something new is rumbling under the surface."

The same sensations that flooded Xander's system in the street before the thugs jumped him raced along his nerves. "Okay."

"The Zoric dinner table discussions have become extra bitter. The Family has put *decades* of effort, blood, and treasure into their project."

"Project is such a laughably innocent-sounding word," Xander said. "They're trying to upend world order so they can reestablish their beloved USSR."

"And," she leaned forward to whisper, "they're afraid that AI is advancing to the point that if they wait, they'll lose their chance because their systems will be obsolete. The sense I get is that it's now or never."

"F'ing hell." Xander threw his hands into the air. "That's what you brought me here to tell me? Doomsday is fast approaching?" He stalled and caught her gaze. "Wait. Why were you asking if Radar was mine?"

"The *thing* your team was looking for in Kyrgyzstan has moved, so you won't need Radar for that mountain trek. We don't know where the *thing* moved. Westward toward Europe is all I have right now."

"I—"

Anna held up her hand with a little smile and a shake of her head. "I'm going to take this conversation back a step and tell you that Russia's space agency sent up a rocket last week."

"With satellites, yes." Xander sat up straighter, stretching his arms out the width of the table and wrapping his fingers around the edge. "Two space weather monitors and then about fifty smaller satellites."

"Not just Russian satellites. It had two Iranian satellites that it put into orbit. Of the two Iranian satellites we identified, one is a communications satellite—that's the one we're going to focus on. The other is for high-resolution imaging."

"This isn't a first," Xander said. "Russia worked with Iran in the past on a satellite project. A couple of years ago, they put up an Iranian satellite that was legitimately there to help research Iranian topography. So, there's precedent. As I remember it, they got Russia to do it because the Iranians had had a bunch of failed launches." He let his focus shift away as he contemplated the regional fallout. "Israel isn't going to love that much, given the present circumstances," he muttered under his breath. When Xander focused on Anna, he asked, "Are the Iranian satellites driving more instability? The Zorics have taken advantage of unrest in the area in the past."

Anna turned to the window, conducting a practiced sweep of the street. "The Iranians are saying they need the images to monitor their natural disasters."

"Which is true." Xander's voice drifted off.

Anna brought her gaze back to Xander, offering him a weak smile. "Yes, while true, and therefore a plausible reason to have the satellite, the Iranians can also use it to gather other information."

"Also true. Realistically, though, how good are the images?" Xander asked. "What kind of pixels can they see?"

"Now you know as much as I do about the Iranian imaging satellite," Anna said. "Our concern isn't about the images. We'll leave that to others. My team is worried because the Zoric Family paid for the Iranian *communications* satellite."

"Shit," Xander whispered.

"Yup. Whatever The Family has going on down here on planet Earth, they needed a satellite where they had a door—not a back door—but a door they could legitimately walk in and out of whenever they wanted. Why? To do *something*."

"Right to do *something* with *some machine* that's bigger than a breadbox and is functioning in the mountains of Kyrgyzstan—"

"*Was* functioning there but no longer *is*," Anna reminded him.

"Right. Bigger than a breadbox and on the move toward Europe. But please, AWG alum, go find it and figure out what the Zorics are doing with it that puts humanity at risk." Xander bit down, making his jaw bulge as he looked at the shot glasses that represented the death of one team member and the lifelong injury of another. When he returned his focus to Anna, he said, "You've stopped blinking. There's more to it."

"Do you remember last year when Niko Popyrin's yacht was taken over by Somali pirates?"

"Vaguely," Xander squirmed in his seat as a new shot of pain traveled up his spine from his bounce off the cobblestones. "I read in the paper how the passengers were saved by one of the cruising bajillionaire's security forces that showed up out of the blue."

"McKayla Pickard's security. And it was Iniquus' Strike Force that saved them. It's a very small world, after all. Also, it wasn't East African pirates; it was a group of very selfish, very wealthy friends who bankrolled a rogue mercenary band in the hopes of becoming the Kings of the Earth. The friends group included one Karl Davidson."

"Karl Davidson, the oil guy that lost his leg in a big game hunting accident in Tanzania?"

"That's the guy, and that's the story. It's neither how it happened nor where it happened. And that really doesn't matter to what I'm telling you. Karl and his buddies had this new 'Rule the World Economy' scenario they were trying out. And honestly," Anna rolled her lips in, lifted her brows, and nodded, "if not for McKayla and her security, Karl and his buds could very well have succeeded. Instead, Karl is in prison in the Seychelles while he fights extradition to the U.S."

Xander shrugged. "His dad'll get him out of that. Billion-aires live in a different world than you or I do. In their world, consequences have no gravity." Xander leaned in a little farther, bringing his shoulders up near his ears to stretch the cramp in his back. That plane ride tomorrow was going to be hell.

"Not this time. Eastern European power players are upset with the Davidson family as a whole. Medved' Zoric, for example, is *pissed*. You don't need to know the palace intrigue. But the bottom line was that Daddy Davidson needed to make nice with Medved', and he did so in a big way. Daddy Davidson handed Medved' his private island, Davidson Realm."

"Where's this island?" Xander asked.

"Off the west coast of Sumatra in the Indian Ocean."

The location didn't surprise Xander. Until the team found a way to disable the Zoric core, world safety was at risk. To the extent possible, those working on the problem monitored every Zoric Family member with a connection to The Project. And to that point, Xander had seen an odd uptick in Zoric movements. "There have been an awful lot of Zorics flying to Singapore in the last week."

"There have," Anna agreed. "They're trying to get to Singapore nonchalantly so that when the Doomsday Clock strikes midnight, the group of two hundred fifty invited family members and friends, along with a sufficient number of, say fifty, servants, will take boats to the island. Even though it's a trickle, not a stream, it is apparent that a Zoric migration is occurring," Anna said. "Shall I tell you about the island where they'll eventually be landing?"

Xander looked up as the bartender came back with a ski jacket that had seen better days.

The bartender spoke to Anna.

"He says he thinks this might fit you," Anna translated. "There's also a woman's wool poncho in pink and purple that looks bigger and warmer."

"*Vd'aka!* Thanks." Xander reached out. "This will do nicely. I appreciate the effort."

The tone of his voice seemed enough for the bartender because he gave a slight bow and left to go to the other side of the room without Anna's translation.

Xander refocused on Anna. "The island?"

"First, you already know that Karl's dad is William Davidson, and William Davidson is not a good guy. He walks a tightrope between legal and not. Like the Zorics, he's highly protective of his family. Like the Zorics, he has no trouble working with terrorist organizations. And because of that, Daddy Davidson knows some of the things in the pipeline and is afraid for his family. Speaking of family," Anna popped her brows, "want to hear an interesting tie-in?" Without waiting for Xander to respond, she said, "Strike Force's Gator Rochambeau just married the Davidson daughter, Christen."

"Dirty DNA?" Xander asked.

"As much as mine is," Anna said softly. "She's a Night Stalker, so perhaps she's doing family penance like me."

Night Stalkers were the best pilots in the world. It was their task to move American special forces into and out of the gnarliest operations. Xander's life had been on the line a time or two when a Night Stalker flew through hell to get to his team. He had nothing but respect and appreciation for them.

"Anyway," Anna continued, "Daddy Davidson is afraid that the world is coming to an end. In the papers, we can read about how multimillionaires are buying places to survive a zombie apocalypse in New Zealand. Daddy Davidson took it further. He bought an island all for himself. He named it Davidson Realm because he's a narcissist." She reached up and scratched the side of her neck as she sighed her disdain. "The island is perfect as a sanctuary. It's close enough to different civilizations, so they could get back to a mainland if necessary. It's also far enough away from anything, so displaced survivors aren't likely to wash up on the shore. There's an ancient volcanic chimney on the island. In the chimney, Davidson built his family's survival bunker. And by family, it's large enough for—"

"About two hundred and fifty friends and family plus servants." Xander was getting the picture.

"Think cruise ship conditions for the family and fifty servants in bunk rooms. Johnna White, with the CIA Color Code, got on the island a couple of years ago and had a gander at it. And even at that point in its development, it freaked her out just a little bit."

"I have a meeting with White when I'm in D.C., so I can ask her about it. But on the surface, that kind of Davidson project comes off as eccentric, right?" Xander asked, but he knew where this conversation was going. "It's the kind of thing a billionaire like Davidson might do to flex for his friends."

"I think this goes beyond eccentric. Above the bunker is—hang on. Look at this." Anna pulled her phone from her pocket and queued up a photo. "This is a satellite photo of the island with its ginormous volcanic chimney before it became Davidson Realm. That's the hole there." She tapped the image.

Xander took the phone and looked at a satellite image of an island that stood high above the ocean. The cliff sides would be formidable for anyone trying to breach the area. On one end, the island was level. On the other, a skyscraper-sized hole was flush to the surface of the topography but was so deep that, even looking down from the satellite's bird's eye view, Xander couldn't see the bottom. "Who did Davidson buy it from?" Xander asked, handing the phone back.

Anna swiped the screen to queue up the next photo. "It was in disputed territory. So, Davidson solved the conflict by paying each of the countries' governments an unknown sum." Anna extended the phone back to him. "And now look at this."

In this photo, Xander saw an island with the same footprint as the last photo, but now, the entire surface was flat. There was an enormous mansion, along with what appeared to be a golf course, a beach, a dock, and a helipad, but no volcanic chimney. "The bunker is under the mansion?" Xander asked, handing the phone back.

"Right. So, underneath, there's everything that three hundred people would need to survive without coming up for a breath of naturally occurring air."

"Clothing. Food. Medicines."

"It goes beyond that." Anna ticked off on her fingers, "Air cleaning machines, desalination, water purification, sewage pipes that go out to the ocean. Power generators that get energy from wind and tides. Food storage that will support three hundred people for fifteen years."

"Fifteen." Xander let out a soft whistle. "You didn't say solar energy. That seems significant."

"It is if you think that debris in the air could block out the sun à la the extinction of the dinosaurs," Anna agreed. "Since

Davidson had the bunker prepped for fifteen years, I'm assuming he calculated the time to repair the ozone layer after a nuclear holocaust. And interestingly, Orest Kalinsky is the one who made it all possible. As a matter of fact, he's even been developing a vertical interior farm inside the chimney."

"This is the Orest Kalinsky guy that Bill York is shadowing?" Xander drew his thumb along his chin. "What's Orest's role in the Zoric family?"

"To be rich," Anna said. "He's the jovial uncle, much beloved. But he is as invested in the return of the USSR to world power as anyone else in the family. The Zorics need science to make their schemes work. As you know, their schemes rely on very advanced science applications. The Zoric murder weapon was kept from public scrutiny, for example. That scheme came out of their study of neurotoxins."

"Orest isn't doing the research. He's funding it?"

"Yes indeed. As the USSR started to break apart, Orest moved to Paris, where he set up a legitimate and internationally acclaimed foundation that funds young, cutting-edge scientists called the Carpathian Foundation for Scientific Advancement. To answer your question: 'What is Orest's role in the Zoric family?' It's Orest's job to find the right scientists to advance The Family projects and to own the intellectual property so that they decide what enters the public sphere and what they personally hold onto. About a decade ago, when Orest discovered that William Davidson owned an island, Orest showed up with science in hand and a strong argument for using the island as a lab to test his young scientists' theories as a global good but also to ensure the Davidson family's survival should the world catch fire."

"You mentioned energy systems and desalination, along with interior farming. That was all Orest's doing?"

"The science was developed under the Carpathian Foundation for Scientific Advancement umbrella, yes. But Daddy Davidson installed it on his own dime. The island with all of its updates was handed over to Medved' Zoric with a big red bow, along with a 'Please don't kill me and my family' after his son Karl attacked the yacht full of Russian elite, many of whom were close friends with Medved'.

"Okay. And again, *shit*. If the Zorics own their own nation, they make their own rules," Xander said. Medved' Zoric had his own tiny country? That was exactly the kind of crown jewel that the patriarch of the Zoric family would covet. Now that it was in Zoric hands, Medved' would probably rename the island and declare himself king. "When did that handover happen?" Xander asked to get a handle on the timeline. This was all news to him.

"About this time last year, right after the fake pirating debacle. I bet Medved' decided not to wait but just nabbed the island while the anger was ripe. The yacht incident, coupled with Karl Davidson's arrest and William's wife being shot in the head and recovering from a coma—Daddy Davidson was a beaten-down man. The wife thing was a separate incident and not pertinent here, except that it was part of Davidson's psychological stress. Yeah, from what I can tell, Davidson didn't put up much fuss when Medved' came a-knockin'." Anna pulled her lips tight. "Surely, Davidson Realm has terrible memories, and Daddy Davidson was glad to just hand it over. At that point, Orest took over preparations to make the island into a Zoric sanctuary. This year, the main event was the installation of a vertical farm, along with stocking up on pharmaceuticals and medical supplies. I've been keeping a close eye on Orest's progress as a means of calculating timing for their big event."

"And?" Xander realized he was holding his breath.

"From watching Orest get the systems up and going, in

particular his vertical farm, I *thought* our team had another two to five years to figure out this mess and stop it cold."

Now. It's happening now. We're out of time. Xander's blood thrummed at his temples.

"Interior vertical farming," Xander was struck by the decadence and luxury of a fresh tomato in the apocalypse.

"Food is a main priority. Orest is a food snob and doesn't enjoy the consistency of the freeze-dried foods that Davidson stored there. And I quote, 'I'd rather die than eat powdered eggs.' Orest's motivation in preparing the island is all about ensuring that he has a plentiful supply of fresh food. That and satin sheets."

Anna sounded nonchalant about all this. But she'd been processing it for a long time. To Xander, it was a blow. In his mind, the fact that the Zorics had to breathe the air and drink the water like everyone else constrained their plots.

This news disabused him of that notion.

The countdown clock on Armageddon was ticking.

"You're easily read," Anna said with a deep frown.

"How's that?"

"You're wondering how I can make light of our circumstances, joking about powdered eggs. I can assure you that I'm painted in hives and haven't slept for the last two weeks—not since I got my invitation to go to Singapore as the migration began." Her frown was deep. "At night, I wake up so terrified that I have to jump out of bed and pace my room with a pillow to muffle my screams."

Xander reached for her hands, and they were icy cold. "We're not out of the fight yet, Anna." He caught her eye and waited for her to focus fully on him and nod her head. "The other Zorics are going east, and Kalinsky is going west. Why?" Xander asked.

"I don't know. But I'm hoping Orest is the weakest link,

and we can get some information about what sparked the sudden migration to Singapore."

Xander didn't believe that for a minute. "Does it make sense in terms of role and personality that Orest is out there on his own?" Xander asked.

Anna looked off in thought, then said, "I think he's working on some task that supersedes his jumping on the first plane to Singapore. Since he's tight with Medved', we think—hope—that as long as Orest is out and about, things aren't imminent. It's one of the reasons we need to keep not just tabs on the man but eyes on to see if, in fact, Orest is finalizing things at the Realm from afar. When he heads to Singapore, zero hour is approaching."

It was Xander's turn to look out the window and scan. The street was as bleak and empty as it had been before the thugs had jumped him. Xander shifted his attention back to Anna. "Where is Kalinsky, the Harbinger of Doom, right now?"

"Home in Paris. He's flying to D.C. tomorrow and will spend the whole day in Washington. The morning after, he's flying to Alaska."

"Alaska." Xander scowled. "Alaska? That wasn't on my bingo card."

Anna flipped a hand through the air. "That's a nothing burger. He owns sled dogs as a hobby. They're competing in the Iditarod next week. The team's up there training now, and Orest wants to check in on their progress. It's his passion."

"So, Alaska has nothing to do with Doomsday," Xander said it as a statement.

"We have to assume he feels like he has enough time to—" Anna swung her head toward the click-clacking on the stairs.

Xander lifted his chair and turned it to the table behind him, scooping up all four shot glasses and taking them with him. He crossed his arms on the table and drooped his head down.

Anna used the sleeve of her shirt to wipe up the dew left by the glasses.

As a woman emerged from behind the door, she cooed as she approached Anna, "Here you are. Of course, you are. Always so punctual."

Xander heard the scrape of a chair followed by the smacking sound of traditional cheek kisses.

The woman continued speaking English with a Russian accent. "You are better than a clock."

"I'm always excited to see you, so tell me …"

4

———

"EDDIE!" Elyssa raised her hand and waved it excitedly. "Here we are," she sang out, standing as he approached to give him a hug. "Yay, that you were able to join us." She turned to the elderly man, pushed back from the table to make room for his copious girth, and held open her palm. "Eddie Baylor, please meet my uncle, Orest Kalinsky."

"The famous Uncle Orest." Eddie's hand shot out for a shake. "How do you do, Mr. Kalinsky?"

"I'm delighted for meeting Elyssa's dear friend, finally. Sit. Sit. I am not Mr. Kalinsky. I am Uncle Orest," he said with a pat to his chest. Uncle Orest waited while Eddie dragged out a chair and settled before pulling Eddie into the conversation. "As we look at menus, I speak to Elyssa about newest gastronomical fashion in Paris. They call it 'sustainable low-waste dining.' What they mean is portions for toddlers, and much of it is raw.

This is not for me. I prefer traditional French cooking. You will find menu here very good."

"Butter." Elyssa handed Eddie a menu. "What Uncle Orest prefers is copious amounts of butter."

"Butter makes life worth living." Uncle Orest moved his hand down to rest on his rotund stomach. "I say this to my doctor. He tells me, 'Orest, eat new Parisian style, and you will live a long life.' And I say back, 'Without butter, life is not worth living.'" He looked pointedly at Elyssa. "And chocolate. But I feel sure that you will find solution to this problem."

Eddie smiled as he scanned the menu. "I have to agree with Uncle Orest about the butter. Last night," he popped his head up to catch Elyssa's gaze, "Yum. Can I just say Yuuum!" he sing-songed. "So, so yum. I had fish simmered in butter." He focused on Uncle Orest. "I called my fiancé Ben, from the dining table, to regale him with the decadence and the delicacy. I believe I could live my whole life eating that for dinner every night." Eddie turned back to Elyssa. "Benny, poor thing, was spreading peanut butter onto sad, stale bread. What is it that they say? Give a man a fish, and he eats for the day. Teach a man to fish, and he eats for a lifetime. Same goes here, but with cooking. Ben definitely prefers that I give him a fish cooked and on a plate with sides rather than teaching him how to cook the fish himself, so he always has a decent meal. So, while I don't feel bad about his PBJ," Eddie smiled, "I did promise him I'd do my best to recreate the recipe when I get home. *Meunière*, they called it." He shut the menu and rested it on his lap. "Though I'm butchering the pronunciation."

"Ah, butter and lemon," Uncle Orest nodded with enthusiasm. "This, this is a man worth knowing. We will be friends." He tapped his fingers on Eddie's sweater-clad arm. "I feel that I know you already. I hear many stories about you and your adventures with Elyssa." He wagged his finger at Eddie. "Some of these adventures I am very glad I didn't know about until afterward. You had her on back of rodeo bull?"

Elyssa leaned in. "He's talking about the mechanical bull contest when we were in Dallas."

Eddie grinned. "She put the cowboys to shame."

"Very dangerous, I think." Uncle Orest gathered his napkin and pulled it across his lap. "But I forgive you because you take care of my Elyssa when she gets sick there—COVID, such terrible virus—and got her home again when she cannot get on plane." He shook his head. "How many hours of driving?"

"Ben and I tag-teamed the drive, so it wasn't that long," Eddie said.

"It took us around twenty hours with gas breaks and fast food, wearing N95s the entire time while I moaned in the back seat. They are saints," Elyssa said from behind her menu.

"For this, I agree." Uncle Orest held Eddie's gaze. "Family is of utmost importance to me. Family of the blood as well as family that we meet on our paths." He tapped his chest. "I consider you to be my family. It is one thing to do a day's service; it is another to stay beside Elyssa for weeks and months when she was trying to figure out the lingering illness after COVID. As you well understand, this has been a long and difficult road for Elyssa. But now we know what's wrong and can best support her." Uncle Orest leaned closer and said earnestly, "This is a gift you have given our family and a debt that I cannot repay."

"It was just a normal thing to do." Eddie's face pinked. "Elyssa and I have had each other's backs since undergrad."

"You've decided what you want?" Elyssa asked, hoping to change the subject. Eddie was the kind of golden friend who would do anything for you, and also the kind of humble person who hated his kind nature being spotlighted.

"I saw they have fish *meunière,*" Eddie said.

"You've tried this while in Paris, Elyssa?" Uncle Orest asked. Without waiting for her to reply, Uncle Orest lifted a finger into the air to signal the server, adding, "You must have it. We all shall. Butter will make us all feel satisfied with life. Full and happy, who could want more?" As the server approached, he said, "Les menus of *meunière,*" he held up two fingers and a thumb in the French style of signaling three, "and whichever wine the chef believes will enhance the flavors best."

"Les menus" indicated the multi-course meal, from appetizer to dessert, designed by the chef so that all the tastes complemented each other. It was one of the things Elyssa liked best about choosing a meal in France. She picked up the menus and handed them off with a "thank you."

"So, what is this chocolate problem that Elyssa needs to solve? Something to do with her big project?" Eddie leaned back, settling in for the conversation.

Elyssa laughed. "Eddie has been trying to wiggle information out of me since I started the Carpathian Foundation's project. I told him that your research recipients can't discuss their projects in advance of the papers going to peer review."

"And she's a vault," Eddie frowned. "Elyssa hasn't shared a thing other than that it has something to do with advancing her doctoral project."

"Yes, well, if you don't mind," Uncle Orest said, leaning slightly to the side to allow the server to set a bottle of still and a bottle of sparkling water on the table. "I would very much like to hear about your research, Eddie. Elyssa says to me that you have a machine that produces 3D-printed meat."

"That's right. After a biopsy from a live animal," Eddie stretched a hand wide and swept it through the air, "we never again need to use an animal. Ever. The cells are lab-grown."

Elyssa swept her long blonde hair over to one side and held it in her fist as a gust of wind blew in when a patron held the restaurant door wide. "Though, I'll add that there's a huge emotional component to Eddie's research. Granted, there are a lot of big-agro businesses involved in meat production, and I don't care about corporate feelings. I'm concerned with ranches owned and operated for generations and families where that's a way of life."

"Given the last polling that we did on consumer desire to eat printed meat," Eddie reached for the still water bottle and lifted it, waiting for Uncle Orest and then Elyssa to nod their ascent before pouring out three glasses, "I'd say we're not going to be putting anyone out of business for at least a generation." He lifted each glass and set it in front of his tablemates. "I figure we'll have our niche market—restaurants, for example, where the consumer has no idea they're eating printed meat—and eventually the ick factor will die down."

"Muscle is lab grown," Uncle Orest qualified. "But what kind of meat would this be? It would be too lean, even worse than ostrich for leanness."

"We can 3D print fat as well. The medium for printing is simply lab-grown fat cells. So, imagine how you might print a plastic object in 3D. All you're doing is shaping the object out of a material. In this case, fat cells and meat cells—there's a little more to it, but I'm putting this in its most simplistic terms—are arranged by the printer to correspond with the shape and the marbling that is perfect for the desired cut of meat." Eddie's posture shifted, moving from relaxed to animated with the change of topic. "On each machine, there's a selection the consumer would press—ribeye, T-bone, filet mignon, and so on."

Uncle Orest clapped his hands together. "Marvelous. Fat is everything to taste and mouth feel. Both are extremely important to a satisfying meal." Uncle Orest lifted his chin. "But how does this taste your printed meat?"

"Once the meat is printed, then it's aged, allowing the flavors to develop," Eddie explained. "In side-by-side taste comparisons—*if* our panelists weren't told that one of the pieces of meat was lab-produced—the traditional meat and lab meat are indistinguishable. That's true when we present the meat to chefs. They have no idea that it's printed and not the variety already available from the butcher."

"Advancements of science are wonderful things," Uncle Orest said with approval. "They are my lifeblood and give me energy. I am most enthusiastic about your work, Dr. Eddie. Now, I love my filet mignon wrapped in bacon. Can you print meats other than cow? Could you print bacon?" Uncle Orest tapped his fingers on Eddie's arm. "Island nations struggle to be food-independent. We need new ways to manage. And, in my mind, one of best ways to lift food pressure is by reducing or eliminating the need for domestic herd animals." He patted both hands on his stomach. "And people should not eat for survival. They must eat for joy. A perfectly marbled steak?" He kissed the tips of his fingers, then spread his fingers wide to release the love. "This is beautiful thing. In my humble estimation, filet mignon is king, but only when wrapped in bacon. So, you tell me, what meats can you print in your lab?"

"Beef, pork, chicken, and white fish." Eddie's face pinked. "The white fish isn't looking like it's going to be plausible. Its mouthfeel isn't …" He sighed. "Yeah, it just isn't good, and we haven't found a method that makes it a pleasant experience."

"No goat?" Uncle Orest asked. "No sheep?"

"I haven't tried that. There's limited commercial use for either in the United States. It's not widely sought after. I had to take my investors into consideration."

"He wanted to try alligator," Elyssa said with a grin. "Eddie comes from Florida, and he is a big fan of alligator sausage, but—"

"I couldn't find funding to produce alligator meat when demand is so limited now," Eddie finished.

"I see, but Elyssa, she calculates such things for her project, trying to provide protein." Uncle Orest lifted his chin toward Elyssa. "How many meals?"

"Two meals a week of meat and two meals a week of fish, shrimp, or shellfish. Four meals a week of eggs. The rest consists of plant-based protein, lentils, beans, and peas. We've balanced out nutritional requirements as much as we can. A healthy level of fats and proteins is a challenge in most parts of the world."

"But Eddie, you grow fat along with the meat." Uncle Orest said. "You can solve this problem."

"Working on it." Eddie smiled. "But at the beginning of this conversation, the problem was chocolate?"

"My Elyssa says that she cannot make chocolate a part of her calculations. I'm sorry to be cryptic, but we have contracts that say we must be so. Now, with little idea of what I could mean, I tell you anyway that I say to her, 'No, Elyssa, this will not work. People cannot survive without chocolate. How do you say? They scrape by?" He waited for Elyssa's nod before diving back in. "It's enough already she say butter is not possible."

"Oh, no, that's not true," Eddie said. "Not only butter but cheese. I know a lab in Seattle that can grow both."

"Grow, not print?" Uncle Orest asked.

"Exactly. They have the cheese figured out. It's bioidentical to what we make now in the old-fashioned way. It has the same melting point and elasticity. My friend's lab is just waiting for the FDA to sign off. They're working with mechanical engineers on ways to scale to commercial production."

"Delicious." Uncle Orest clapped his hands and rubbed them together. "Cheese is not just food of gods. It is also important for good digestion. Everyone should have a nibble from cheese plate and a little fruit at the end of a meal. This is why I am," he tapped his fingers on his belly, "despite outward appearances, such vital and healthy man. So," he tapped Eddie's arm, "your 3D meat machines can create on a commercial scale?"

"Mine? No, sir. Currently, our lab's production can only supply approximately thirty-six thousand pounds per year. It sounds like a lot, but it's only enough protein for about two hundred individuals if they consume an average American adult's yearly portion."

"And this is why I invite you to speak with me today. Given Elyssa's friendship with you and my enthusiasm for what you are undertaking, Dr. Eddie Baylor, I wish to invite you to be part of our 'Feed the World' effort. Your work with meat could naturally couple with what Elyssa is working on. This is good idea, isn't it, Elyssa?"

Working on a project with Eddie would always be a good idea. But Eddie's lab was very expensive. At scale, they could produce protein at a cost savings, but not on a micro level. The expense was an issue since one of the foundation's goals for her own project—once they were out of the gold-standard bells-and-whistles prototype phase—was to make her interior farms as cost-effective as possible.

Was adding 3D meat production a good idea?

Sure, easily procured protein that did little to harm the environment would be a boon to society. But at the same time, Elyssa didn't know the production requirements, and she didn't want to adjust her designs. Going back to the drawing board at this late stage could cost her years. "In the same building? I don't think so, Uncle Orest. We could possibly have two buildings side by side."

Uncle Orest focused on Eddie. "As Elyssa will tell you, I

compensate my scientists handsomely. Anything you are now receiving, I will make it more lucrative for you."

Deep, rosy-red crawled up from Eddie's collar. Like a thermometer, the blush spread up Eddie's cheeks to his forehead and into his hairline, making his carrot-colored hair look like flames in contrast. "Sir, you are incredibly generous. And I can readily see your love of food and your kind heart trying to help those in need, but I recently signed a contract with NASA, so I'm unavailable."

"You decided to do it?" Elyssa exclaimed, reaching out to hug Eddie. "That's wonderful news."

"3D meat for NASA?" Uncle Orest pulled his brows together. "Is this for the trip to Mars?"

"Mars, exactly," Eddie said as his color slowly faded to normal. "How would you guess that?"

"I'm losing a foundation scientist to the effort, Dr. Claude Burns. Everyone calls him Paca. He tells me this is short for 'Alpaca' for his hair," Uncle Orest held his hands to either side of his head and made a wiggling motion.

"What does Paca study?" Eddie asked.

"Squirrel hibernation in Alaska." Uncle Orest scratched his nose. "He tells me that China thinks they can get to Mars by 2033. And the United States is competitive country."

"That's true," Eddie said. "NASA had its sights set on 2050, but much like the moonshot, the US wants to get there first. They're pushing harder with scientists of all kinds. Some, like me, are looking into ways to produce food. Since the astronauts will be gone anywhere from months to years, for their psychological health, they occasionally need to have fresh food."

"Elyssa consulted for NASA when she was doing her doctoral research." Uncle Orest nodded toward Elyssa. "As I remember, that had to do with the International Space Station. I agree that fresh food contributes to well-being in ways that freeze-dried meals or pouch pastes cannot. Even if they are superior in nutrients, they are inferior in regulating stress and anxiety. I have seen powdered eggs, and I would rather die than subsist on them."

"I was just reading," Eddie said, "that NASA hired a team to work on social psychology. Of course, every group is unique with its own characteristics, but they have sent teams to places like Antarctica to test their capabilities in -60 °C cold, where no outside help can reach them for months. That must be a terrible anxiety in the back of your mind. Not only is no one coming, but you can't run away."

"Seems a brutal existence. I have no desire to experience any of that," Elyssa said. "I'm not knocking it for those who enjoy the challenge. Though there's that story about a scientist in Antarctica whose cabinmate would tell him the endings of his books before he could read them himself. The reader scientist snapped and stabbed the spoiler cabinmate to death." Elyssa's face showed her horror at the idea. "Personally, I like to know the ending."

"Are you one of those people who reads last chapter first?" Uncle Orest looked bemused.

"I read the last chapter second," Elyssa said. "First chapter is first to know who I should care about, and the last chapter is second to make sure everyone is okay in the end, because I can't handle the emotional pain of a beloved character not getting a happily ever after. Then, I read the middle to get the substance of their journey."

"Aww. You're so tender-hearted," Eddie teased. "After all these years, I didn't know that about your reading. Here's something you probably didn't know about me. I'm the opposite and can empathize with the man who did the stabbing."

Laughing, Elyssa lifted her water and took a sip. "I'm not

going camping with you." She took another sip, then set it down on the same wet ring that the glass had left.

"I think we'd be fine," Eddie replied. "We don't read the same books." He turned to Uncle Orest. "I'm curious as to why NASA hired the squirrel hibernation expert you mentioned earlier. And for that matter, why was the Carpathian Foundation interested in that work, sir?"

Uncle Orest pulled in a deep breath. "Things go very wrong. We push nature too far, and we stop the circulation of the oceans. Suddenly, we are living on a frozen planet. Or, a volcano blows, and the ash blocks the light for years, or there's an asteroid." He paused. "Events could even trigger nuclear war. And one must prepare. For survival, we must have systems in place in advance." He reached over and tapped Elyssa's hand. "My genius great niece has studied all of this with her many degrees and her brilliant—"

"Uncle," Elyssa whispered, hoping he'd stop his effusive praise.

"Hush, I speak." He turned to Eddie. "Her brilliant, creative mind is involved in averting catastrophe in case there are any of these events. For this, my family is grateful. Now, what does this have to do with NASA? Because my foundation foresaw a need, science was advanced, and now it will potentially be used by NASA. I'll explain. NASA wants to hibernate Mars crew for eight months each year of their journey to reduce the requirements for food, water, and air, as well as the accumulation of human byproducts. They will rotate people who are awake. This possibility has been an area of interest for my foundation for years now. We attempted to answer the question: Under dire circumstances, until nature became survivable, could we rotate people in and out of hibernation to reduce their needs? If a community could support three hundred people who were awake, would it be able to support nine hundred if they were cycling through sleep? Or take Polar reader stabbing the cabinmate. What if you had bad apple causing disorder? Ostracism is death. Could you just let them have a time-out, sleep it off, and avert a Lord of the Flies situation? Even medically, we see use. What if cure for disease is right over horizon? Hibernate patient, wait for cure, cure patient, all is well. And so, while my guy will no longer be working on squirrels in Alaska, he is taking the knowledge that my foundation proudly invested in and applies it with NASA. We approved this. We agree with these new circumstances, Paca will be better able to advance our studies, especially as we weren't clear on how to get the okay to hibernate live people."

"I was going to ask how that was going to work," Eddie said. "I mean, the FDA posed an enormous obstacle in even allowing people to taste our 3D meat."

"You know Elyssa and I fly to America tomorrow." Uncle Orest said.

Elyssa tipped her ear toward her friend. "Eddie is, too. He's on our flight."

"Very good," Uncle Orest said. "I have some meetings in Washington on Thursday, and then Friday, I leave for Alaska."

"That's right, the Iditarod is coming up," Elyssa smiled.

"It is, and my dog team is very strong. Very strong. We have good chance of winning this year." Uncle Orest looked from Elyssa to Eddie and back. "You know, yes, this is very good idea." He sat quietly for a moment. Then said, "Yes, this is what needs to be done under these circumstances. You both must clear your calendars this week and come with me."

"To Alaska, sir?" Eddie pinked all the way up to his ears.

"Yes, just so." Uncle Orest pulled his phone from his pocket and handed it to Eddie. "You put your contact information here. And also, please type out the name of your friend who grows the cheese and butter, and the name of friend's lab, I wish to contact this person."

The server brought a bottle of white wine, uncorked it, and poured three glasses while Eddie complied with Uncle Orest's request.

Accepting his phone back and looking over the contact information, Uncle Orest said, "Yes, I will forward this to my secretary to make your arrangements. My foundation invites both of you. All expenses paid." Uncle Orest took a sip of wine. "Delicious, just a slight citrus on tip of tongue to help butter taste rounder." He nodded his approval to the server. "Lovely."

The server bowed and went away.

Focusing on Eddie, Uncle Orest said. "In Alaska, I will introduce you both to my squirrel guy. And you get to meet my dogs and watch the Iditarod leave the starting gate. How many people can say they have seen such a famous thing as this race?" He held his wine glass out, "A toast to our adventure together!"

"Cheers," Eddie and Elyssa said as they clinked glasses.

Uncle Orest smiled broadly. "Dr. Eddie Baylor, 3D meat scientist for NASA, this trip will be perfect time to better know a man who understands importance of a good *meunière.*"

5

Xander
 Thursday
 Iniquus Campus

Yesterday's flight from Bratislava to D.C. was a groggy blur of tight confines and pain.

Back in his own bed for the first time in a month, Xander had a solid night's sleep. And though he wasn't a hundred percent, he could stand without wincing.

He was more than ready to go get Radar.

Xander had lucked out with warmer-than-usual weather. And even with the sun just creeping over the horizon, he was comfortable with a fleece pullover.

Edging up to the Iniquus guard station, Xander lowered his window and gave his name as he handed over his credentials. Now, he sat and waited as a Cerberus K9 sniffed his car for contraband.

Xander knew that Iniquus was a fortress masquerading as a

country club, much like the newly acquired Zoric island, Davidson Realm, but with polar opposite motivations.

If the Zoric machine let loose the dogs of war, he might call on his Iniquus friends to let him come and survive the apocalypse with them.

With the Zorics swarming toward their own safety, Xander had to at least consider where he wanted to be on Doomsday. He contemplated going home to protect his mom. But his mom would say, "I'm fine. Get out there. Do good. Come home safe."

"Do good. Come home safe." That was the little bird that sat on Xander's shoulder, singing the tune in his mom's voice when things got tough.

He'd promised his mom he'd do just that, and Xander worked hard to make his word his bond.

But in this fight, Xander wasn't so sure that his good intentions could beat the *machine*.

Precisely what did the Zoric machine do?

Hidden in the Kyrgyzstan mountains, aimed at the war zones to the south, it was hard to figure it out exactly. Though everyone on the hunt for the apparatus agreed that the war-torn landscape offered the Zorics the degree of obfuscation they needed to continue their testing, anything that the Zorics engendered was easily attributable to something else. Was that a machine or an insurgent attack?

Figuring it out was like trying to grab hold of a shadow.

What the IC community did know was that part of the Zoric capabilities included "smart spoofing," where the machine could influence GPS navigation by the tiniest increment, a measurement so small, in fact, that it was imperceptible to the navigator. In a short distance, it wasn't a significant factor; over a long flight, it could throw a pilot completely off course, sending them to a different country or so far out over the ocean that they became fuel-critical.

Then there were the unaccounted-for electrical outages over wide swaths of Afghanistan to the south of Kyrgyzstan, extending to the Chinese border to the east and reaching as far as Syria in the west, but never at the same time. The AWG had speculated that whatever the Zorics were doing meant they needed to move the machine between trial events.

If this were true, it meant the machine had to be a size that could be manipulated by a small group, if not a single person.

And whatever the Zorics were doing didn't just stop at GPS manipulation.

In fact, a dystopian reader would find a correlation between Zoric's machine and potentially society-destroying electromagnetic pulses (EMPs).

In fiction, a large solar storm could cause damage to power grids by overwhelming the transformers with an electrical surge.

Decades ago, it was an electrical grid attack that landed the Zorics on the CIA's radar (small r).

The Zorics had always had alliances in Iran. And because of that, The Family had held a grudge against Canada because the Canadian Embassy helped get Americans out of Tehran during the hostage crisis.

In 1989, with his freshly calligraphed graduate diploma in energy systems, Medved' Zoric was finally able to do something about his family's thirst for retribution. Medved' shut down Quebec's power for nine hours.

Public-facing, the electrical disruption was caused by a geomagnetic storm on the sun.

But the Royal Canadian Mounted Police, working closely with Langley and the FBI, believed that it was, in fact, Medved' Zoric sabotaging Quebec's hydroelectric power.

Okay, not *in fact*. In speculation.

The IC community couldn't prove the connection to Medved' Zoric.

"Come back to me when you have concrete evidence. Then we can get you funds and teams to make that go away," the heads of departments had said.

It was a catch-22.

Without funds and boots, how could Xander's predecessors get the proof?

Then, the Berlin Wall came down, followed by the collapse of the USSR and the end of the Zoric way of life. The family was fractured and flailing in their new reality.

It was Medved's ballsy attack on Quebec that helped launch him up The Family leadership ladder until he became Papa Bear.

Medved' was no longer a young revolutionary. He was silver-haired and lead-hearted.

In the years since the USSR broke apart, the Zorics wanted their pound of flesh for the upheavals they had borne. They learned to hijack satellite communications, shut down cell tower connectivity in ways that were subtle during the event but devastating in their consequences. Just ask Iniquus' Strike Force, which had almost lost their entire team because the Zorics disrupted their radio signals.

And the worst part of a dystopian landscape was the destruction of Syrian computer systems that handled everything from medical records to banking, energy to water, and food distribution.

Officers in the DIA and CIA working in the affected region began carrying their laptops and phones in Faraday bags to protect them from the effects, only taking them out for short periods to conduct their work.

Basically, the Zorics had proven in their reach from Kyrgyzstan that their machine could produce what amounted to the effects of an EMP.

And now, the Zorics were swarming to Singapore, preparing to go underground; it was the result of a concerted effort spanning nearly forty years.

As everyone knew, even the smallest trickle of water, over time, could erode the hardest of rocks.

Persistence was a tool for both growth and destruction.

Thwarting that destruction was the reason Xander was here at Iniquus.

Xander raised his hand to thank the guard who waved him through as the massive gates slid wide.

A short distance up the main road, Xander followed the curve east to the Cerberus campus, where he pulled into an open parking spot.

Still feeling the effects of his bruised ribcage, he climbed carefully from the car.

Slamming his door shut, Xander turned to saunter across the tarmac toward Iniquus' Cerberus Headquarters.

Today, Xander added a pair of knee pads to his outfit and changed out his regular hiking boots with a pair that had less ankle support, allowing his feet a wider range of motion.

Things were going to get kinetic.

Halfway across the parking lot, Cerberus's front door popped open, and the head trainer, Reaper Hamilton, emerged with Xander's magnificent German Shepherd, Radar, at his side.

It was funny how hard Xander's heart thumped every time he came to get Radar for their bonding time.

For Xander, Radar was home. He was family.

It was kind of interesting how this had all come about.

Digger was the first K9 acquired for their team.

Initially, Digger was trained to go into the field with the FBI and sniff out hidden thumb drives of child pornographers. As priorities and funds shifted, Digger made his way into the AWG fold. The Pentagon hired Reaper to further train Digger to find electronics in spaces where they didn't belong. In a house, Digger wasn't indicating on a fridge or television. But if someone dropped their phone in the woods, Digger found it easily.

Digger, being high-drive in the intelligence department, needed intellectual stimulation and lots of it. So, Reaper kept expanding his skills until Digger became the Swiss Army Knife of doggos.

That's what saved Scott.

That's what Xander needed—a nose that might find a cleverly camouflaged machine and a survival tool if things took a turn for the worse.

It was sheer luck that had brought Xander and Radar together.

Last year, a service dog training facility in Kansas conducted its testing and delisted some candidates from its program. Xander happened to be nearby and went to see if any of their dogs would make a good partner for his trek to the mountains.

With less than a year to get a K9 sniffer-trained and field-ready, Xander didn't have the luxury of starting with a puppy. He needed a working-line dog that had a good start to his training.

Xander had walked into the Kansas facility and sat to observe those delisted dogs having their playtime. Right away, Xander locked eyes with Radar. Radar trotted straight over and sat by Xander's side with a "Well, there you are, about time you got here" glimmer in his eyes.

They had been best buds ever since.

While Radar had excelled in his training at the service dog center, he was too high-energy for the medical alert service dog gig the team had envisioned for him.

Once Xander found and fell in love with Radar, he hired Reaper to go and make an assessment. Reaper said Radar had the character qualities that made him the right K9 for Xander's needs, qualities similar to Digger's.

Plans were made.

Training began.

How much smaller Radar had seemed back then when he was still an adolescent with paws too big for his body.

And here they were, a year later, Radar had filled out into his adult size; taller than average with a well-muscled physique. The glistening caramel-colored fur framed eyes filled with wisdom. Radar was an old soul. Radar seemed to carry an ethos of service much like the special forces brothers Xander had served with in war.

It was good to have a partner whom Xander didn't just love but esteemed.

But now that Radar was qualified and proficient, Anna said the machine was on the move, probably west toward Europe.

There was no Kyrgyzstan job to do.

No summer mission scouring the mountains.

The entire reason for finding Radar and having him trained had evolved.

Now, what was Xander going to do about Radar?

It would be impossible to integrate a dog—no matter the K9's masterful training—into Xander's current day-to-day.

Or even hour-to-hour.

Later that afternoon, Xander needed to meet with Bill York and find out if he needed to follow Orest Kalinsky to Alaska. And Xander would make a plan from there, whether Radar could fit into that picture or if Radar needed to stay here with Reaper.

Xander wanted to know what York had been chasing and what he'd learned in the process. Anna seemed to think York had hit on something important. And, in the bar, Anna could only say so much.

Xander had to push the ramifications of Anna's update, both global and personal, out of his mind. He'd focus on controlling the three feet around him, which included Reaper and Radar.

Blocked by the vehicles, Radar hadn't spotted Xander yet. But, as always, the first thing Radar did when he moved from one space to another was to do a thorough visual scan to get his bearings and gauge the vibe, then his nose went up as he did a secondary scan with his sniffer.

Today, the air current blew past Xander straight over to the team.

Radar turned his gaze on Xander.

A grin spread across Xander's face. "There he is! There's my good boy!"

As Radar stood politely beside Reaper, his entire body quivered with contained excitement.

Butterflies danced in Xander's stomach.

It was the same sensation every time he came to collect Radar from his training course to have some bonding time. It was hard to describe, except that it was like leaving a piece of him behind and not feeling whole again until they were together.

As Reaper stopped, Radar sat, but he couldn't quell the quiver.

"Xander," Reaper called out with his hand extended.

"You're being mean," Xander said, reaching for the shake.

"Just doing my job," Reaper said with a grin.

Xander knew Radar was facing a test—an important one—in the face of intense desire to break command and do what he wanted to do, could Radar exercise self-control?

Reaper looked down and caught Radar's gaze. "Radar, release."

A bit of warning might have been good. Xander needed a wider stance to brace against full-body contact with Radar.

Laughing, Xander crouched to rub and scrub and coo his welcome, "Hey, Buddy! I missed you, too."

When Radar had settled, Xander stood. "What have you got planned for us?" He looked at his watch, "I have to get back up to Iniquus Headquarters by ten-hundred."

"That should do it." Reaper pointed down the road farther back on the property. "We're about to sign off on Radar's training. To certify him, we've been gradually adding complexity to his evolutions. If it's okay with you, we're going to go at this like it's a day in your life. We'll start you dancing as you approach a shoot house. Once inside, you and Halo will clear it, then search it for a missing electronics component. And we'll let things unfold from there. You'll get directions as necessary, but we want the emotions to be true. If you don't know what's coming, there's no way you can telegraph those pictures to your dog."

"I'm up to the challenge. Complex, huh?" They were walking toward an SUV at the back of the lot.

"We recently brought on a dog named Mojo out of Etosha National Park, which is a game preserve in Namibia, Africa. Mojo's trainer had the same philosophy as Cerberus: we don't train to be pretty, to show off, or act badass on a field in front of spectators. We train to save lives—our own and those around us."

The truth of that hit Xander in the gut. "Digger."

"His actions saving his handler are a source of pride here at Cerberus," Reaper said. "It took the right combination of Digger's instincts, as well as our training methods. Since that incident with Scott on the mountainside and what we learned from Mojo's trainer in Namibia, we've focused on training our dogs' problem-solving skills. It's perfectly fine to have a working dog that is on point with his behavior. We need that in place as a baseline for safety's sake and for the air of professionalism that our clients expect. But now we're paying a great deal more attention to layering scenarios and making them as true to life as possible, so we can accurately predict how the dog will perform. I promise you, if we had only trained Scott's dog to follow a command, Scott would have died. Radar's ready to be your battle buddy in Kyrgyzstan."

Xander kept it to himself that it looked like time was up on that mission before he and Radar got a shot at finding the "Big and Bad" their team had been hunting.

Usually, these training sessions were a blast, just a hundred percent fun, jumping out of helicopters, fast-roping with Radar strapped to his pack, running and gunning through mazes and shoot houses.

And up until his Bratislava meet-up with Anna, Xander had looked forward to today richly.

Now it felt like he was fiddling while Rome burned.

There was nothing he could do but move steadily through his day. First, train with Radar, then deliver Anna's message to Nutsbe, and then meet up with Johnna White, his CIA counterpart, and Adele Gutterman, who was with the Mossad. He wondered if Adele wanted to chat about the Zoric-Iranian satellites that Russia had just launched. At least Anna had told him about them, so he wasn't blinking at Adele like an idiot.

He was interested to hear what the CIA and the Mossad thought of the sudden shift toward Singapore.

If the Zoric family was heading into a lockdown bunker with supplies for decades of survival, man, that was a bad sign.

Ice washed through Xander's blood, and Radar reacted by stiffening his spine and scanning for a threat.

"Radar," Xander pulled his attention around. "It's okay, buddy. I'll tell you all about it when we're alone."

"All right, here we are." Reaper lifted a hand, and a man dressed in Cerberus Tactical with a Team Charlie jacket jogged over. "This is your partner today, Halo."

"G'day," Halo said with an obvious Australian accent and outstretched hand. "I'm the guy who's got your six, yeah? You're going to lead since you've got the land shark with you. I'm just here to cower in the shadow."

"You know Radar?" Xander asked.

"Aw yeah, we're great pals, Radar and me. I've been working with him on his water skills. If you ever have to chase the bad guy into the drink, Radar can see that through."

"Okay," Reaper said, "today you're going to practice your dancing skills, Xander. Out there is a bad guy. If you find the criminal and take control, then we'll move on to the point where Radar needs to solve a problem that he's not been faced with before." Reaper pointed out. "Your bad guy is in that area. There's a shoot house that you will treat as lethal, though we're using laser guns today that release the scent of gun powder and sound like suppressed fire. Orange tip, no barrel." He pulled the weapon out of his pack and handed it over for Xander's inspection. "You're the only one with a weapon in hand during this scenario."

"Got it." Xander accepted the training tool.

"Nothing else on you? No knives, ankle holsters, anything?" Reaper asked.

"That's all I have," Xander said as he tucked the laser gun back into his belt at the small of his back.

"Very good, gentlemen," Reaper said, "have a productive evolution. We'll be watching and taping from the various cameras, especially the one on Radar's collar, so we can assess after."

Just like that, Reaper melted into the background.

6

———

Xander
  Thursday
  Iniquus Campus

Xander turned to Halo.

"Here's the setup. There's been a crime. The bad guy is hiding electronic information." We're going to get into your vehicle and drive to our training ground just over the hill. It's been reconfigured since Radar was last training there. It should look completely new to him."

"Got it."

Reaper had said dance. It was a skill set that they had discussed and decided would be useful. It was the flow of "Where I go, you go." Once they started, man and dog were in sync. Xander could use quick flicks of his hand to make his silent signals, or he could depend on Radar's attention and precision. Done well, it was glorious. Done poorly, it could trip Xander up when his life was on the line. He had to trust Radar to be unwaveringly on point.

It had been a while since he'd done this, and Xander felt rusty.

It was a short drive to the training site. There was a shoot house and various cars parked as if on the street. It was ghostly quiet.

Halo pulled up under a tree, hiding the charcoal gray car in the shadow. They exited in silence without shutting the doors all the way, crouching by the sides, keeping their heads from becoming watermelon targets in a shooting gallery.

Xander signaled the dance, and Radar snapped to.

It was good that Xander was so tall, or Radar's head would be dangerously close to Xander's crotch as Radar came between Xander's legs.

Pulling his training weapon, Xander held it in ready position.

When Xander stepped, Radar stepped.

When Xander knelt at the front of the vehicle to scan, Radar flattened himself to the ground, jumping up to match Xander's next pace forward.

Halo was right behind them, giving them space to maneuver.

Racing forward to the next car that would afford them concealment but not the protection of cover, gunfire sounded, at the same time, dust puffed beside them as they advanced.

Movie set gimmicks helped train for real-world experiences.

Xander knelt, paused, assessed, and was up again, racing for the shoot house, signaling Radar from between his legs to his side.

Radar made the pass without breaking Xander's forward momentum.

Xander knew Halo was at his back when he got a tap on his shoulder. They peeled off, going room to room in search of the subject.

To Xander's surprise, the house was empty.

Halo showed up. "He left something."

Xander followed Halo back to a room where a bandage lay on the ground.

A bandage. Interesting.

Well, you work with what you're given.

"Radar, scent. Scent." Xander instructed, pointing.

Dutifully, Radar snuffled the scent, then, when he had a good hold of it, he looked to Xander for his next instructions.

Xander pulled an evidence bag from Xander's working vest and retrieved the bandage in case Radar needed to refresh his memory later. "Radar, seek human."

Radar was hard-focused. Legs splayed wide to get his nose close to the ground, he trotted down the stairs and out the back door.

Over the field, into the woods, down a path by the river, Radar stopped at a rock where a digital camera lay, then sat in front of it. Radar turned as Xander and Halo jogged up beside him to see what he'd found.

Radar was looking down the pathway toward the edge of the woods.

"Radar, hold." Xander documented the site, then took another bag from Radar's working vest to keep hold of the possible evidence.

"Looks like the SD card is missing," Halo said. "That might be important. Do you think we should find it?"

Xander pulled his brows together. "Now? You want me to stop the human search and move on to the second?"

"The SD card is the priority," Halo said.

Well, this was a first. Xander had no idea how to pull Radar off one search task and put him onto a second. "Radar," he called, drawing his K9's attention around. Holding out the bag for him, Xander said, "Scent. Scent. Electronics."

Radar caught Xander's gaze, and Xander did his best to conjure up a movie of what he needed to happen here. He pictured the camera and imagined someone removing the SD card. Then he pictured the SD card, held it firmly in his mind's eye, and said, "Radar, seek electronics."

Radar's nose went down to the trail, and he walked around sniffing the base of trees and rocks, the tiny plants along the path.

Xander stood still, not wanting to interfere in the process, but also not a hundred percent sure that he'd conveyed the command to Radar.

A breeze ruffled Radar's coat, and his nose went up in the air as he swung his head.

The breeze died. And Radar stood.

The second time the breeze rose, Radar's nose went up in the air; he followed with a step, then another, and another, until he stood at a tree, looking up into the branches. Then, he sat and brought his gaze back to Xander.

"Looks like the bad guy tried to pitch the SD card and it landed up there," Halo said.

"Are you kidding right now?" Xander asked.

"I'll tell you what," Halo said, standing next to the trunk with a grin spreading wide, "How about I give you a leg up?"

"Serious? You want me to look for an SD card stuck to one of these leaves?"

"I don't want you to," Halo said, his grin just that much bigger, "Radar does."

"Fine." Xander turned his attention to Radar. "Good boy, Radar, let's see what's up there, okay?"

Halo laced his fingers and bent.

"Radar, stay." Xander put his foot in Halo's stirrup, and Halo hefted him up until Xander could catch hold of a sturdy branch. He had to do a muscle-up to get his hips to the branch, then move himself up farther. It had been a while since he'd played Tarzan, climbing trees. He scrambled up onto the tiniest of tree forts. A space big enough for Xander to sit, but that was about it. There were two manila envelopes.

And the SD card sat on the envelope marked "1"

SEND the SD card down to Halo. Praise Radar. Open envelope "2" before descending.

"RADAR! GOOD FIND," Xander called out in high-pitched praise. "Good find! Good boy!" He put the SD card into the empty envelope and tossed it down to Halo's waiting hands.

Halo took out the SD card for Radar to sniff, then pulled out a towel and played tug to reward Radar for his hard work.

Meanwhile, Xandar opened envelope "2." Inside this envelope was a screen. When Xander turned it on, he could see it streaming Radar's collar camera. Xander adjusted the volume to hear Halo say, "Good job, mate. Radar, sit. Radar, stay." Then there was the sound of crunching leaves as Halo moved away.

Xander read the message.

THIS IS what you really wanted to know: Can you depend on Radar to be your Digger?

You can't get down. You need help. Tell Radar to get help.

REAPER WAS CORRECT; that level of training was the why for Radar being here.

And Xander did need to know.

He needed to trust.

There was a sizzle of apprehension that skittered over Xander's skin. It came down to this test. Was Radar's training a success?

Here we go. "Radar, get help," Xander called.

Xander couldn't see anything from his tree house perch. But on the screen, he watched Radar looking up into the tree. He sat and barked.

"Radar, get help!"

He stood and leaped to put his paws on the trunk and barked. He dropped down, looked around, and barked.

That bark had an urgent call to it. A "Come here!" to it.

Radar's nose was on the ground, snuffling the place where Halo had stood.

"Radar! Get help! Get help!"

Nose to the ground, Radar took off through the woods. Xander thought he was probably chasing after Halo, who was the most likely person to be able to render aid. But once he got to the road, that scent disappeared. Someone in a vehicle must have picked Halo up.

Radar stood and barked, his gaze sweeping along the horizon. Off in the distance, the main Headquarters was barely visible. Equal distance was the guard station. From Radar's camera, Xander couldn't see the Cerberus campus.

Radar's nose went into the air, and he focused back on the woods. He stomped his foot as if in frustration, then he took off like a streak toward the guard station.

The twenty-foot gate was shut.

Radar paced along it, barking at the guard station. From what Xander could see on the camera, no one was there. Since that never happened, Xander imagined the guard was crouched in their guard house, aware of the training evolution.

After a few minutes, Radar turned and raced toward Headquarters.

A car was driving toward the exit.

Radar loped in that direction, then as the car approached, he stood square in the middle of the road, making it impassable.

Xander's handheld radio sizzled. "Reaper here. Jerome, stop. You just got caught up in a training evolution. Roll down your window so you can see our K9 clearly. We don't need any accidents today. Stay in the car. Ignore the dog. Look forward. Both hands on the steering wheel."

Radar barked, ran a short distance back toward Xander, then paced back to the car to stare at Jerome.

"Jerome here. I'm not a dog person. Especially not a giant war dog person."

"Reaper here. We have control of the K9. You're fine. Hold your position."

Over and over, Radar made the circuit each time barking with increasing frustration.

"Reaper here. Jerome, go ahead and carefully edge by the K9 and see what he does."

The next time Radar paced out, Jerome carefully edged forward, rolling toward the exit.

With the sound of the engine, Radar spun and raced for Jerome's car.

Suddenly, the camera jerked upward as Radar took flight, leaping through the window, stomping on Jerome's lap, and landing in the passenger seat.

Jerome slammed to a stop.

"Shit, man, he's in my damned car." Fear shook Jerome's voice. "I'm not great around dogs. I don't want to get mauled. What do I do?"

"Reaper here. Hands on the steering wheel. Face forward. Do not move."

"Wilco. No moving."

Radar barked at Jerome. Sniffed at him. Pawed at him. And Jerome didn't move other than a gentle quaking and a good deal of sweat.

Finally, Radar turned his attention to the inside of the car, assessing the interior, looking over the seat to the back.

He didn't seem to find what he was looking for.

Next, Radar tried threatening. He growled and barked, stomping his foot on the accessory box between them.

"Help." Jerome squeaked quietly as he white-knuckled the steering wheel, his whole body quivering.

Xander felt for the guy. Radar was intimidating as hell.

Finally, Radar bent his head, gathering something into his mouth, then he scrambled back over Jerome's lap and leaped through the window.

"Reaper here. Jerome, what did he pick up?"

"My phone and, goddamit, he took my lunch. That's *my* lunch, man."

Radar was tearing across the field while Reaper was laughing over the radio. "What did you pack?"

"My mama's meat loaf sandwich. I'll be *pissed* if he eats it. Reaper, there's gonna be hell to pay if he eats that sandwich."

At the edge of the woods, Radar dropped the bag and moved to the same spot he'd stopped before and stared into the distance.

From the camera feed, Xander couldn't make out what made that spot interesting.

A moment later, Radar was back snuffling the lunch bag.

Xander watched with interest. That meat probably smelled delicious. Was it enough to distract Radar from his mission? Xander could see the bag was wet from Radar's saliva. Radar's nose went into the top, and he snuffled the scents, but instead of pulling the sandwich out, Radar dropped the phone inside. He chomped down on the items and trotted into the woods and over toward Xander's tree.

Xander laid the screen down.

Radar was in view. He placed the items at the roots and barked for Xander.

Xander wondered if he thought the food was part of helping him.

Reaper was on the radio. "Xander, the only thing you can say is 'Radar, get help.'"

"Wilco," Xander said, then leaned out of the tree house. "Radar, get help."

Radar picked up the bag, dropped it, and barked.

Xander had to bite off the good boys and praise. He stuck to the script, "Radar, get help."

Radar picked up the bag and stood on his hind paws, lifting the items toward Xander. Xander lay on the boards and stretched long but couldn't reach it. So, he said again, "Radar, get help."

Bag in mouth, Radar trotted away.

The whole thing was genius. Radar had found food and comms. If he'd brought Jerome's water bottle, Xander would be set.

Xander turned back to the screen to see what Radar was up to.

Radar had once again dropped the bag, then picked it up again. Xander assumed to get it better positioned in his mouth because a moment later, Radar was hauling ass toward the tree.

Radar pressed his paws onto the trunk and was able to run two paces up the tree, release the bag into Xander's waiting hand, before falling back to the ground.

Xander immediately clambered down from the tree to give Radar whole-body scritches and high-pitched, enthusiastic praise.

But Radar wanted none of that.

He stomped his foot and ran out. Traced back and ran out again just as he'd attempted with Jerome.

Xander wondered if Radar was leading him back to Jerome's car. Which was fine, he needed to return the man's things.

About a hundred yards out, in the exact spot that Xander remembered Radar had stopped, looked into the woods, and stomped, Radar stopped again.

There, Xander found a woman curled up under a tree reading a book.

"Your bandage?" Xander called out.

"My bandage," she said with a wave.

Xander wondered why Radar had bypassed her when searching for help. And the only thing Xander could assume was that the "find human" command sent him on a search that fell into one of two camps—a victim or a perpetrator—and neither was suitable for the command, "Get help."

Could that be right?

The whole thing, from start to finish, was mind-bending. Xander knew some men on the battlefield who couldn't have juggled all the balls that Radar had during one of the most complicated training evolutions Xander had ever seen.

The radio sizzled. "Jerome here. I have a meeting. I need that phone."

"Yeah, yeah, come on over and get it," Xander said. "Oh my god, man, your mom is the best cook. I've never had a meatloaf sandwich as good as this one. No wonder you were ticked about your lunch."

"Dude, you'd better be kidding or we're going to dance."

"Mmm, sorry, can't hear you past my moaning. So good. Wow."

"Dude!"

"Gotta go." Xander put the radio back on his belt. He hadn't approached the woman with her book because he didn't know what role she was playing here.

A rescue team came up the mound with a soft approach.

Radar turned and braced a low rumble in his chest, warning the crew against advancing as he maintained control over the area.

Xander commanded Radar to allow the team to come forward with a "Radar, leave it."

The group wore jackets with identifying logos that weren't from Cerberus. Reaper must have wanted a crew that was new to Radar.

The men stepped in to perform mock first aid on both Xander and the woman with the book, laying "the victims" on stretchers, and moving them to the car where they were set down, all under the close observation of noble Radar.

That whole scene was beyond expectations. It was miraculous.

Reaper pulled up in his car. "Clear," he said. "End of evolution."

Xander was high-pitched praising Radar and playing tug, only coming to a stop when a red-faced man stomped over. "Hey! I'm Jerome. I need my phone. And I need my mama's meatloaf sandwich."

7

———————

Xander had showered at Cerberus and changed his clothes.

He would loosely describe his style as "always ready for a hike." Traveling from country to country, urban space to rural, bog to coffee house, this particular look let him slide into a space and slip by anyone's notice.

Camouflaged without wearing camo, Xander was an everyman except for his height, and there was nothing he could do about that except stand near a wall.

The kennel hand had spruced up Radar, so he wasn't tracking mud through the Atrium of Iniquus' main headquarters as they followed their escort to the tactical forces wing.

Reaching Panther Force War Room, the escort tapped on the door, and Nutsbe opened it, a giant bullmastiff at his side. Today, he was in his wheelchair.

"Oh man, who's this beast?" Xander asked as he followed Nutsbe into the conference room, shutting the door behind him.

"This glorious monster is my service dog, Beowolf."

"Awesome. I'm happy for you." Xander paused his forward momentum. "Is it okay to have Radar here? I can take him back to Reaper."

"These two are buds. They lived at Cerberus together." Nutsbe waved away the idea, then reached for his wheels to roll toward the conference table.

The two men, sitting cattycorner at one end, looked up from the file they'd been studying.

Nutsbe spun his chair and pointed to the black leather captain's chair beside him. "So, what did you need to see me about?"

"I brought you a card from Bratislava." Xander reached into his pack and handed him the slightly bent pink envelope with the purple glitter ink script and the cupcake sticker on the back that Anna had asked Xander to deliver.

Nutsbe accepted it in one hand and swept the other out to indicate the other two men in the room.

"Titus, good to see you." Xander leaned forward with his hand extended toward the Panther Force leader.

After receiving the welcome, Titus turned to indicate the man in a well-tailored suit who gave Xander a genteel nod. "This is Iniquus counsel, Sy Covington."

"Glad to meet you, sir."

Titus closed the file as Xander settled in his seat, gesturing for Radar to lie down under the table out of Beowolf's way.

Nutsbe glanced at the children's card, written in Slovak, and laid it on the table before unfolding the single handwritten page in English, also written in a curling purple glitter pen.

Who would send State secrets in purple glitter pen? Xander

liked everything about the subterfuge, and he stored the tactic in his memory bank.

There was a knock at the door, and Titus opened it to Steve Finley, an FBI domestic terror agent who had helped put the East Coast Zoric family in prison and was also Anna's fiancé.

Finley scanned the room, and apparently sensing something afoot, simply lifted a hand in greeting as he took a seat next to Xander.

"I saw Anna two days ago," Xander said under his breath. "You know about the movement to Singapore?"

Finley nodded.

"She got an invitation. The Family trusts her."

Worry clouded Finley's eyes. "How's she holding up?"

"Ignorance is bliss, and she doesn't have that luxury," Xander replied.

With one hand on Beowolf's head, Nutsbe read through the letter. Then he lifted his gaze to meet Sy Covington's.

Sy tipped his head, inviting Nutsbe to share.

Nutsbe cleared his throat, but that didn't quell a warble of emotion as he read: "Hey, sweety, I have some gossip about little Amanda Bradshaw. You remember her? She's leaving for an exchange program with the United States and is very excited about the opportunity. She should arrive on Friday."

"Amazing," Covington said with a smile and a shake of his head. "Not a done deal, obviously, but we had hoped all along that she'd be included in a Russian prisoner exchange."

"I wonder who they got in return," Titus said.

"Do you think her parents and her university know?" Finley asked.

"Brother," Titus said, "you're sitting in a sacred room. What you hear here—"

"I didn't hear anything here," Finley said. "Unless I'm

specifically told that I'm hearing something, I hear nothing in Iniquus, ever."

"Exactly," Titus said.

Nutsbe lowered his chin to read more. "Also, I have terrible news to tell you about Uncle Leo and Aunt Jo. The neighbors found their bodies in the McMahan family swimming pool. Not to bring terrible pictures to mind, but enough time had passed that any further investigation into their death isn't going to be possible. The neighbor, Darina Zoric—I think her name is— told the Belgrade investigators that, of late, Aunt Jo and Uncle Leo seemed to be drinking heavily. I know they were having their troubles, but I'm sorry for your loss. The Serbian police speculate that they might have been too inebriated to get out of the pool once they had fallen in. I imagine that this will be in the Serbian newspapers soon, and surely in the United States as well. So, I wanted you to hear it from me first. I'd look for an article sometime next week in New York. I'd imagine it would be a small mention in the obituary section as Uncle Leo's crimes might make waves at his old place of work. I know there were some concerns about your involvement with their affairs, but alas and alack, that is now in the past. Though I know the family will never fill the hole that Leo and Jo left with their deaths, any bad feelings or concerns go into the hereafter with them. I advise you to move ahead with your life. Your future is bright. Love to you!"

Whole-body shaking, Nutsbe handed the letter off to Covington, then he bent to wrap himself around Beowolf.

"Wait," Xander leaned forward, posting his forearms on his thighs. "Leo McMahan? This is retired FBI counterintelligence chief out of New York, Leonard McMahan, who went missing?"

"Cone of silence," Titus said.

"I was supposed to be on the lookout for McMahan when I

was in Albania a few weeks back as a favor for a different alphabet. Obviously, that was a dead end, no pun intended. My orders were to have a look around, observe, and report if I saw him, but I had no other information." Xander caught his chin between his thumb and index finger, processing that Darina, a known Zoric enforcer, was at least peripherally involved in the McMahans' deaths. The Zorics didn't work out of Serbia. Their intervention had to be a gift for one of the other crime families. Had to be, otherwise, it didn't make sense. "Dead, huh?" He pressed his hands on his knees and straightened his arms. "Good that it'll come out in the paper. When you see it, if you can let me know, I'll forward the article to my department so we're not wasting man-hours." Xander hated that the old families had been consolidating over the last few years. And this looked like proof.

"Will do," Titus said.

Finley patted Nutsbe on the shoulder. "Looks like you got a reprieve. I'm happy for you, man. Looking over your shoulder every second of every day for a Russian shadow to pop out at you is hell."

"Mostly I was worried about Olivia," Nutsbe's voice was gruff. "The idea of endangering a loved one, now that's true hell."

Xander had witnessed that. He had seen the power of love brandished as a weapon to destroy. Love was easily exploited with the threat of "do as I say if you want your family to stay whole and healthy."

Just look at William Davidson.

William Davidson had 'f-you!' kinds of money. He had the kind of money that meant he was beholden to no one under any circumstances. And yet, Medved' Zoric—who easily had the means to follow through—had threatened Davidson's family. Davidson handed over his whole Doomsday-prepped island, leaving his family without that security blanket. What Davidson might not have realized was that, by providing the Zoric family with a safe haven, he removed an obstacle from the path, shortening the attack timeline.

Davidson, hoping to protect his family, only pushed his loved ones further into harm's way.

Play in a cesspool, and you can't wash off all the shit when you go home. You reek of it as you track it through your house and into their lives.

Time and again, Xander saw the lesson played out for him —love was good and love was excruciating pain.

The utter joy of a loving connection, the comfortable banality of it, and then evil snaked its way in.

Just look at Anna and Finley and how wonderful yet, at the same time, painful that relationship was.

Look at Nutsbe processing his reprieve. Obviously, the man had been in hell.

It was one of the reasons why Xander never dated the kind of woman who might turn a dinner into something more.

Purposeful, busy women—that was the ticket to the relationship carnival ride Xander was willing to go on. Anything else was a liability.

A tap sounded at the door.

Johnna White, CIA, walked in with Suko Hiro, Xander's handler at the DIA, followed by Adele Gutterman from the Mossad.

CIA, DIA, and Mossad walked into a bar … It could be the start of a joke if this weren't all so deadly serious.

Similar to the Color Code for the CIA, the Mossad had a specialized group with a specific global target. Their members tattooed their left wrists, in the area where a thick watch strap could hide the telltale symbols. When Xander had crossed paths in the field, he'd seen the tattoos with multiple colors specific to their calling within the group, almost like a religious sect. Adele's tattoo was white ink on fair skin, all but imperceptible unless you knew to look.

A secretive group, Xander had limited information about them.

He knew Adele's activity centered on thwarting science experiments that endangered her country. He also knew that her team had been doing intelligence work in Northeastern Lebanon when they'd had their electronics and communications wiped, putting them in extreme danger, which led to the death of a teammate in the event.

And Xander knew that fatal mission was the catalyst for Adele's group joining the AWG alum on the hunt for the Zoric mystery machine that caused the Lebanese catastrophe.

Xander watched both Nutsbe and Titus stiffen as Adele passed into the room.

Tension always hid beneath the Panther Forces' professional demeanors when Adele showed up. While Xander didn't know the details of the story—didn't want to know the details—what he'd pulled from the wind was that Adele had been on a mission that sought to neutralize what the Mossad viewed as an existential threat.

The threat happened to be a Panther Force operator's now wife. And she had been the victim, not the perpetrator.

Once again, Xander heard the drum beat of perils when falling in love while working in a career like his.

Just don't do it.

"We'll give you the room," Titus said, gathering his file. "Your escort is standing outside the door, for your convenience." Titus and Nutsbe, along with Beowolf and Covington, left the room.

When various alphabets came together for exchanges that required plausible deniability, Iniquus often allowed the meetings to take place on neutral ground. Today, they were in the war room because it was effectively a SCIF. They had not just privacy here but security as well.

White and Adele moved to find seats around the table with Finley, Xander, and Radar. Hiro sat to Xander's right.

Xander had known Suko Hiro from Afghanistan, where his call sign was Super Hero, and he'd lived up to his name. After losing the toes of his left foot to an IED, he'd moved over to use his brain in logistics since his body was no longer able to keep up in the field. It was a good day when Xander realized that most of the AWG alumni would be under Hiro's command.

"White, I haven't seen you in a while." Xander was rubbing Radar's ears as Radar assessed the newcomers. "I heard your teammate, Red, was in a car accident in Morocco. How's she doing?"

"She'll never be in the field again," White said, her face purposefully wiped of emotion. "She's okay with that. She's had enough."

"Of course," Xander said.

"She has another surgery coming up. Did I hear correctly?" Hiro asked.

"Yes, tomorrow morning, actually. We're hoping it reduces Red's pain levels. She's in pretty good spirits, taking things day by day." White turned her focus on Xander. "That accident has a distant connection to you."

"Yeah?" Xander paused his Radar scritches.

"On the day of the accident, Red was traveling with a Delta Force operator, Nomad, who was a new guy on the same Delta Force Echo team I brought to Kyrgyzstan to find and extract Scott, Tink, and Peter."

"Small world. Nomad. You used his name," Xander pointed out. "Does that mean he's left Delta?"

"He took medical leave to stick with Red and help her

through. He's mostly healed from the accident. He gets migraines when there's bright light in his left eye. He can mitigate it by wearing a patch when he's out in the sun. But that's not compatible with Delta Force field requirements. I will tell you, he was heroic on the scene. If you're going to be in a car accident in the middle of nowhere Morocco, it's best to have special forces sitting by your side."

Xander said quietly. "Please let Red know that we stand in friendship if she needs anything at any point along the way."

"That's very nice of you. Thanks. I'll pass that on. Yeah, it's weird not having Red on the team. An adjustment." There was something hard and sharp in White's eye when she said that.

And Xander wasn't the only one to notice.

Everyone in the room knew that look; someone had stepped out of bounds to hurt one of White's team, and that person wasn't going to be allowed to go quietly into the night. White meant to extract her pound of flesh.

Xander silently wished her the opportunity to see that through.

But first, they had to stop the Zorics' retribution against the world.

"So now that we've settled into our seats and caught up a bit on the big news happening with our cases, the dog at my feet is Radar. He was trained by Cerberus to be my Digger as I continue to search for the machine."

Heads nodded.

"Let me tell you why I'm in town," Xander continued. "Anna Senko sent me to talk to Bill York," Xander said. "York has been tracking a guy named Orest Kalinsky."

"I know of an Orest Kalinsky, best buddies and cousins with Papa Bear Medved' himself," Adele said.

"What's his involvement?" Hiro asked her.

"He's rich. He uses his money and his fundraising skills for a foundation that supports cutting-edge science around the world," Adele said.

"York asked my team for help with this Orest's movements in the U.S. But I don't know Orest Kalinsky's background. What kind of science are we talking about here?" Finley asked.

Adele pushed her sleeves up to her elbows. "Mostly it has to do with communications and satellites, the kind that might inform their doomsday machine. Although their foundation has just released a study showing that warming waters create global security issues, as the hotter the water, the harder it is to find submarines. That study makes me nervous."

White leaned forward. "Now, why would the Zorics fund something like that, I wonder?"

Adele plunged on without responding to White's question. "But there's a wide array of science. Orest seems to have two pet interests. He's big into food security and naturally occurring neurotoxins like those found in the box jellyfish—box jellies and Palythoa." She turned to Finley. "You all had a murder here in D.C. using those neurotoxin studies, so you're well aware. Pretty much any time the Zorics need a little science to fuel their terror, Orest's got someone in a lab thinking they're saving the world, but instead they're helping it implode. He's a manipulative, jovial Santa-figure of a terrorist, swooping in with his rosy cheeks and bowl-full-of-jelly laughs, and death." Adele sniffed. "Unfortunately, Orest Kalinsky has created a public persona that is highly respected with connections to universities and labs worldwide. It's a formidable shield."

"I understand their use of neurotoxin and the communications pieces," White said. "Is food research interesting to us?"

"Anna explained that Orest is making sure the family can eat plentifully during the Apocalypse," Xander said.

"Davidson Realm," White posted an elbow and rested her cheek on her fist. "Yeah. That's problematic."

"I'm tracking his movements inside the United States," Finley said. "He's got tickets to Fairbanks tomorrow morning via Newark. Did Anna tell you why Orest is going to Alaska? Seems odd this time of year."

"Alaska to see his dog team participate in the Iditarod," Xander said, "so a little R&R before End Times."

"End Times," White said, "that's awesome." She turned to Adele. "Well, nice knowing you. Sorry, we didn't get that girls' weekend in Vegas we've talked about."

"Maybe we can meet up for drinks in the afterworld," Adele said.

White moved her hands to her lap. "I hope I'm going to the afterworld. I don't want to be one of those poor souls shivering around the fire during a nuclear winter."

"Yeah," Xander said, "that's not even funny right now."

Finley drew his brows together.

"Why 'right now'?" Adele leaned forward, concern lacing her brows.

"Zorics, as we all know," White said, "are aspirational world stage players, wanting a seismic shift on a societal level to force the world back to the fabulous early 1980s when the USSR was big and scary, and we were all jamming out to Madonna and Simple Minds."

Adele quirked a sardonic brow. "Right, well, what they want is a time machine, not a nuclear bomb."

"My understanding," White said, "is that if The Family waits much longer to deploy their machine, AI will be able to thwart their systems. And while we hoped that, in this case, AI could come to our rescue, The Family understands it's now or never. So, they may have to start their mission before it's a hundred percent ready."

"While the Zorics don't have nuclear aspirations," Xander said, "Sometimes when you push something over, there's a domino effect. The Family knows it and is moving to the environs of their fallout shelter."

"You saw the Zorics are flocking to Singapore?" Hiro asked.

"Yup," White and Adele said in unison.

"What are we doing about it?" Finley asked.

"We continue to try to work it out," Hiro said. "The problem is we've got a twenty-two-year-old over at DHS running the terror division who wasn't alive to experience the USSR. The idea of a return to that world-order isn't possible in his imagination. Since he doesn't think the Zoric family is a threat, he's closed the file, and everyone's been fired or reassigned."

"What is this now?" Adele leaned forward.

Hiro said quietly, "Priorities are being redefined."

"Color Code is unaffected as we have a carve-out and work independently," White said. "Luckily, the Zorics case fell to Color Code over on the CIA side. I don't think we're on anyone's radar." White looked down. "Not you, lovekins," and Radar laid his head back down. "Because of our special congressional mandate, we might be safe."

Adele turned her attention to Xander. "But the AWG alumni are still looking for the machine in Kyrgyzstan after the snow melt, aren't you?" Adele asked.

"Not anymore," Xander said. "AI was watching satellite images to see if there was odd foot traffic on the mountain for us to check out once the area was passable." He put a hand on Radar's head. "Radar and I were packed and ready to go. But when I saw Anna in Bratislava two days ago, she said the machine is no longer in Kyrgyzstan. She thinks it's heading west toward Europe, but she had nothing actionable, not even a solid idea of a compass direction."

"Do not be disheartened," Hiro's voice was adamant. "We

still have a shot at figuring this out. It's easier to find something out in public than tucked in a mountain cave. We find the puzzle pieces, we put them together, we come up with a response, we eliminate the threat."

"Sometimes," Adele said, "it's a—" She paused mid-sentence as Xander and White grabbed their phones as a surge of incoming messages blew them up.

Finley thrust forward, worry etched on his face. "What's going on? What have you got?"

$$8$$

Elyssa
   Thursday
   Alexandria, Virginia

Elyssa answered her phone on the second ring. "Hey, Uncle Orest, did you find your hotel comfortable last night? The breakfast was up to your standards?"

"Lovely." Uncle Orest said. "I have found that overnight flights from Europe are best when dealing with jet lag. And this will be much more difficult as we head on to Alaska."

"I take melatonin and try to sync with the new clock," Elyssa said. "Eddie, on the other hand, just finished brunch and is heading to bed. We'll see on the flight tomorrow who had a better strategy."

"My dear," Uncle Orest's voice was raspy with excitement as it came through her phone. "I have a delightful surprise for you. Big, big surprise."

"Oh?" Elyssa, standing in her night shorts, tapped the speaker button and laid her cell phone beside her on the sink.

Lifting the hamper lid, she began tossing in the dirty clothes from her suitcase.

"You are packing for Alaska?" Uncle Orest asked.

"I'm unpacking from Paris. I'll run a few loads of laundry and then start packing again."

"You must bring two bags. One bag with very warm clothes for Alaska and another for warm air of Singapore.'

Elyssa stalled. "Singapore? What's Singapore about?"

"I am excited to tell you that we set up a prototype of your enclosed vertical farm. It now has its bones. Planting systems are in place. Fishes have been brought in and swim about. Orchards are planted with seven-year-old trees. Bees buzz in their hives. Even farmers and protein ranchers have moved into their quarters ready to plant and—"

"I'm sorry, protein ranchers?" Elyssa stood with a handful of worn socks and undies suspended mid-air.

"I coined this term to identify the people who handle all of the animals from crickets for flour and animal food, to fish, to ducks, and the bees."

She tossed her things in the hamper. "It's in Singapore?" Elyssa pulled up a mental map, and to her, Singapore seemed an unlikely place to test the prototype.

"No, no. Though urban centers like this are indeed tests that need trying eventually, this is not where we began. I wished to try this on a small island to test wave power systems as our energy source. For this, I turn to maternal side of our family, Zoric side, My cousin, he owns an island in the Indian Ocean with a volcanic chimney. We built your vertical farm inside chimney. Genius! Now, to my surprise, Zoric family recently decide to go to the island for a family retreat. This is a beautiful opportunity. You can meet your extended family, and they can finally meet you after many years of my telling them your stories. I wish you to inspect this setup and see how your ideas transitioned from blueprint to manifestation. You will see your creation almost to fruition."

"That sounds amazing." Joy blossomed in Elyssa's chest. She just couldn't believe her good fortune. This was everything. "Thank you. But I'm … say it again, when you asked me to pack two bags, did you mean for me to leave from Fairbanks to fly straight there?"

"Yes, Alaska, then down to San Francisco and over to Singapore. Then family has a ferry boat, and we will bring everyone over together. We have pleasure craft that will go, too. This will be an excellent time for fun, not just for work."

Elyssa headed toward her home office to check the calendar on her computer. "How long will this family reunion go on?"

There was a brief stall before Uncle Orest replied, "Why do you ask this question?"

"Well, you might remember, when you invited me to Alaska, I was planning to accompany you out there and meet your dogs, but I can't stay for the start of the race. I have to be back in D.C. by Wednesday night. My dear friend, Anita, we've spoken about Anita, she's the one who is working on her PhD in nanotechnology?"

"Yes, I know this name."

"She's getting married. I'm in her bridal party. I'm not sure if you're familiar with that term. It means that I'm going to the church with her and stand beside her as she makes her vows to her soon-to-be husband."

"I see. Well, this is a very important occasion. So, you go to Singapore, and I fly you right back."

"Uncle, I am so sorry to say no to you, and it would be the opportunity of a lifetime not just to see my ideas in practice but also to meet my family. But I've made commitments that I simply cannot step away from. I'm flying home Wednesday night because there's the bachelorette party on Thursday, rehearsal dinner Friday, the wedding Saturday, then there's the send-off brunch as Anita and Tim leave on their honeymoon on Sunday. Now, if I fly out Sunday evening or Monday morning, I could be in Singapore by Tuesday. Surely, I can find some way to get over to your island from there. Hire a local boat or something. Even if it's a shorter time, it would still be very meaningful to me."

Elyssa could hear her uncle breathing, and it sounded like he was processing stress, perhaps anger. These weren't emotions she'd experienced from her gregarious and generous uncle, so Elyssa decided that she was simply distressed that she couldn't say yes to his request, that she was making things up. "Uncle Orest, are you okay?" she asked softly.

"Excuse me, my dear. Please hold. I need to get a glass of water."

"Of course. Would you like to call me back?" But she heard the phone tap down on the table.

She hated to disappoint her uncle after his years of generosity. Of all the scientific projects his foundation funded, Elyssa had always felt like hers had the most enthusiasm. It was his baby as much as hers, the one that Uncle Orest was most excited about. Food. He loved to eat, and his generous heart wanted that for everyone. He thought the world deserved fresh, healthy foods. That it was a right, not a privilege, to eat.

Elyssa knew that Uncle Orest had been developing a site to put up their trial. But when she asked where, he chuckled and said he would let her know when things were further along. Elyssa had thought that Uncle Orest had been trying to purchase land and navigate local red tape. An island? That was on their priority list, for sure. Many islands were losing land mass to rising sea levels. But for some reason, she'd always thought Uncle Orest would try desert areas first because, while he loved meat, he hated the deleterious effects of herds, especially in arid climates.

The island was a surprise.

Off Singapore was a surprise.

She opened her map app and focused on the area.

Well, there were plenty of islands of varying sizes, all not that far away from the city.

And there was Jakarta.

Now that she thought about it, Uncle Orest had gone off one day about Jakarta's deforestation and the plight of orangutans.

Once they'd proven their team's model, it was going to be exciting to see what the next steps looked like and how fast the food systems could be implemented. But honestly, Elyssa tried not to think about it. It felt too hopeful, too close to being within grasp. She thought about the fight that Big Oil had waged for decades to prevent the world from shifting to renewable energy. There simply weren't decades to fight Big Ag. The world needed systems to go in place as quickly as possible. The sooner the better.

In the grand scope of population survival, Elyssa felt keenly selfish for prioritizing a friend's wedding.

But a promise was a promise, and she couldn't imagine why a few days would have any significance at all.

As she thought that, Elyssa's pain and pressure were building up behind her sternum, and she was growing lightheaded. Looking down at her watch to check her heart rate and blood pressure, Elyssa reached for her bottle of electrolyte water and gulped down the salty solution before slinking to the ground with her back against the bookcase.

In these moments of vulnerability, when she was unable to react to dangers in her environment, human or not, Elyssa had to focus on her breathing as much as possible.

Anxiety made her heart race harder.

"I'm here," Uncle Orest said. Whatever had happened in the interim had lightened his voice, and he sounded like himself again.

"Uncle," Elyssa said softly, "I'm having an episode. I'll get back to you." Without ending the call, her arm dropped to her side as her body became limp.

9

———————

ANOTHER PING DROPPED into Xander's messages. This one was from Dremonte Long, Bill York's handler, with a desk at Langley.

LONG: **Moved York to private room. When you get to the hospital come up to 569.**

XANDER TAPPED THE CALL BUTTON. "Long, you safe to speak?"

"Yeah. Where are you now?"

"I left Iniquus as soon as the text message started dropping. I'm merging onto the highway now, heading to the hospital. I don't have a good ETA because of traffic, but I'm not far out."

"You're coming from Iniquus? Who was with you at the meeting besides White?" Long asked.

"Adele was there. She went running out as soon as the messages came in about York. She said she's checking on something with her team and will be in touch. My superior, Hiro, was there, along with Finley, FBI Joint Task Force. We were settling into the meeting but hadn't gotten far."

"I've been in touch with Finley," Long said. "He's heading to the Hoover Building now to handle York's effects."

"Have you got a tail on Orest Kalinsky?" Xander asked.

"Yeah, we do. He's at the women's prison, having a family reunion. It makes it harder that they're speaking in Slovak, but our interpreters will give us a readout and their impressions by end of day. Like any good crime family, they're well-practiced in talking about nothing while the real message is sewn between the lines. We'll do our best with that and get the report to the stakeholders, including Adele."

"Good. And York? What are the doctors saying happened to him?" Xander jerked his wheel to get around a car that came to an inexplicable stop in the middle of the road. His wheels hummed on the pavement designed to keep drivers from falling asleep.

When the cacophony stopped, Long said, "Doctors are running tests. Those of us involved think it's probable that Orest Kalinsky knew York was following him. York started having issues on the plane over the Atlantic. He'd sent us a series of texts, and we met at the plane with our toxicologists to find out if somehow Orest had been able to get the Zoric neurotoxins close to York."

"Was anyone else on the plane having symptoms? How about the people sitting near him?" Xander asked as he pressed the gas down and weaved through the traffic.

"No one complained of anything, and we made sure that the

paramedics interviewed them before they took off for their connecting flights, asking about heart palpitations or breathing issues."

"But no pathologist report yet on York?" Xander asked, thinking of Nutsbe and how Anna's letter gave him some kind of reprieve. Finley had said, "Looking over your shoulder every second of every day for a Russian shadow to pop out at you is hell." Wasn't that the damned truth?

"Nothing yet," Long said. "We had to keep this on the downlow. The hospital was counseled that York owns a coral fish tank and might have had a palytoxin exposure, not that they knew what that was. I think a lot of Google searches went on as I left the room. The nurses were in full PPE when they scrubbed York down. They took blood, we took blood. 'We' being the FBI tech who Finley sent over. I don't touch blood. York's clothes and effects were all put in hazard bags. I'm waiting on someone from Foggy Bottom to show up and take them to their lab. Knowing the neurotoxins have a short shelf life, Finley is meeting the special agents at Hoover, and he's going to go impress upon them the urgency of the case. He's hoping to move it into the number one slot."

"No one's going to find anything in York's blood if Orest poisoned him over the Atlantic. The half-life is too short. It does its damage and disappears. It's worth a try, but it's not a rule-in, rule-out."

"If it were easily identified, we'd have Orest Kalinsky face down with his hands cuffed behind his back instead of checking into his five-star this morning. Regardless, the medical staff is prepping the O.R. for emergency open heart surgery."

"Is York responsive?" Xander asked.

"He's aware. He's focused on breathing right now. I'm standing in an empty hall. The staff know they aren't allowed into York's room unaccompanied. As close as we are to the Capitol, this cloak-and-dagger shit isn't unfamiliar to them."

"He can't be left alone with what's in his head," Xander said, tapping on his blinker and sliding toward the exit.

"Nope, we can't have him muttering State secrets to the orderlies. I'm on duty for now. I want to be a friendly, familiar face for him. But as he's getting better, we can send some paper pushers over to hold his hand, which I think he'll prefer, leaving him to fart in peace. My understanding is that you were meeting with York for a handoff of Kalinsky?"

Xander stomped down hard on his brakes to keep from hitting the biker, who swerved out of the way of the person getting out of their car, in what could have been an escalation of bad outcomes if his brakes hadn't been as responsive. "I was advised to meet with York and be ready to accept the baton if he wanted to pass it. But neurotoxins, man, I need to think this gig through." Xander swung his head to check his mirrors as he popped his turn signal on, then slid into the hospital lot. "I'm here. I'm finding a parking space. I'll be with you in a beat."

XANDER TAPPED ON THE DOOR, then stuck his head in, sweeping the room. The bed was gone. Long sat in the blue Naugahyde guest chair, looking shell-shocked.

Xander's skin prickled with cold.

"He coded," Long said. "Damned violent what they do to bring a person back. Then they grabbed hold of his bed and raced him toward the surgical wing."

"Well, shit." Xander shut the door behind him, then stepped farther in so he could talk in low tones. "Where are we? What do we know? You said York sent you some texts?"

Long pulled his phone from his pocket and opened the messages before handing it off to Xander.

YORK: **I feel like I might be dying. Get an ambulance in place. Tell the docs about the Zoric secret sauce. This came on too suddenly. I may be getting up there in age, but I passed my physicals with flying colors.**

YORK: **If not me, and it's not going to be me, someone needs to follow this son of a bitch and see what he's up to.**

YORK: **Here's what I know about his itinerary. Arrived on my flight. Day in D.C. paying his respects to the jailbird side of the family. Heading to Alaska to see his puppy dogs— D.C. Newark flight XVC 921 Newark Fairbanks KNP 783**

YORK: **Things are stirred up. Channels popping. Zorics leaving their houses. Too many of them are leaving their houses and heading in different directions. Their biggest muscles are heading west, the rest of the family is heading east to island.**

YORK: **I swear these goddammed Zorics.**

YORK: **I don't think I'm going to make it back to the U.S.**
York: **This might be it, my friend. Thank you for our years. Love to all.**

. . .

"Jeezis." Xander ran through the texts one more time, then handed the phone back to Long.

Long spread his feet wider and leaned his forearms onto his thighs. "Yeah, it was a kick in the nuts. I still feel like puking."

"And the doctors said?"

"If it's his heart and nothing else," Long said, "that would be one thing. If it's the neurotoxins, there's zero the doctors can do. Palytoxins are a survival coin toss. I'm not giving up hope that this is a good old-fashioned blocked artery."

Xander leaned his head against the wall and stared at the metal structure that held the ceiling tiles. He stood there in suspension without a thought beyond the gray cloud that filled his mind.

A knock sounded tentatively, then a head poked in. "Sir?"

"Hey, come on in." Long stood and picked up the bags. "You have a partner?"

"In the hall."

"These go to the labs, Code Orange. Do you understand me?" He tapped a bag with his index finger. "You protect this one with your life. You get to the lab straight as an arrow. Special Agent Steve Finley, terror—do you hear me?—Steve Finley, *terror,* will be waiting for you."

The guy audibly gulped as he bobbed his head.

"Finley will take charge of the clothing," Long said. "The contents of the phone and laptop are priority one. I need a full duplicate, and a printout will be on my desk by evening. You will stand there and glare at the investigation team and make it happen."

"Yes, sir." The man blanched as Long signed the chain of custody paperwork. Tucking that away, he took control of the bags, then he turned on his heels and hightailed it out of the room.

"Everything?" Xander asked.

"That computer is new and only has information about York's Orest mission. I'm looking for clues beyond the Zorics are swarming out of the nest."

"Anna Senko said they're heading to Singapore," Xander said, shoving his hands into his pockets and pressing a shoulder into the wall.

"York said island. That's not an island. Why are they moving?"

"Medved' Zoric took over William Davidson's island, Davidson Realm, and now has a fallout shelter for three hundred over the long term, read that as years to decades. Singapore is close enough to ferry the family to the private island in the Indian Ocean." Xander took a moment to explain the importance of William Davidson's setup on Davidson Realm and how Medved' took it over.

"Goddammed Zorics." Long swiped his hand over his face. "Did Anna have any other insights?"

"She received an invitation to Survival Island. They're supposed to get there this week."

"Like rats jumping the ship before Armageddon." Long blinked and brought his attention back to Xander. "We only have a handful of people working across the agencies on the Zoric problem. We're going to be running on all cylinders. What's your next move?"

"Me? I'm getting my dog, Radar, from Cerberus and packing our snow boots. Friday morning, I guess I'm heading to Alaska to see what Orest Kalinsky is up to."

10

ELYSSA
Friday morning
Newark, NJ

ELYSSA LOOKED over at Eddie as he slid his phone out of airplane mode and accessed his airline app. She lifted her brows and waited.

"It's still on the ground boarding."

"Possible then?" Her face brightened.

"Possible, I guess. I mean it should be in the air. But if one flight is off schedule, it's reasonable for others to be off theirs, too. I'm just looking here, it's asking me if I want to change my tickets, and the next one out is tomorrow afternoon, getting in the next morning."

"We'd miss everything. Well, I would. I need to fly back Wednesday, so I'd basically be landing, running down to the park to see Uncle Orest, pet his dogs, and driving back to Fairbanks for my flight home." She reached under her seat and grabbed her backpack, setting it on her lap, ready to stand when it was her turn to disembark. First class was the first to deplane. That might just make the difference in making it to their connecting flight.

"Short window for a cross-country trip," Eddie said as he leaned over her lap so he could reach his own bag.

"Yeah, but you saw how cute Uncle Orest was when he was talking about his puppies and how much he wanted us to see them. Food, science, and his sled team—and at the top of that list is his devotion to family. You can't say that's a bad way to live or that he's got his priorities messed up." Elyssa stood and took a step back to protect Eddie as he clambered out of their row and reached up to the overhead bin for his roller bag and their coats. "How could anyone say no to that little pout of his?"

"Adorbs," Eddie agreed. "But also, he was feeding you chocolate."

"We're in agreement, right? We're going to make a mad dash and see if we can't get there on time? Otherwise, you need to head on to Fairbanks on the next available flight, and I'll just catch a flight back home."

"Would that be weird?" Eddie asked. "That would be weird. I'm the tag-along friend. I can't show up all by myself as a guest. I've shared two meals with the man. You're the connector. You need to be there to do the connecting in order to make this work without being uncomfortable."

"My uncle has wanted to meet you forever. France was the first time you both were in the same place at the same time. He specifically told me," Elyssa lifted her chin to tell Eddie he could move forward, "that my friends were my family, and my family was his family."

"Big heart. I love that. Speaking of big hearts," Eddie said over his shoulder as he hustled forward past the "Buh bye, buh-bye" from the attendants, "I don't think your running through an airport is safe or sane. You shouldn't run."

"Any other ideas?" Elyssa asked. Thinking that Eddie was right, but it was such a mess not to have better options.

"I could always piggyback you," he offered, striding across the metal lip onto the skyway.

"Piggyback a grown ass woman with my backpack on my back, and you're also pulling your roller case with your backpack on top. Do you think security would allow such a thing?"

"Okay, you're right. I didn't think it through," Eddie said. "But listen, if there was an extra wheelchair sitting out there, like there are sometimes. I say we put you in it. Pile the bags on your lap, and I push you along at a solid trot."

"Putting the cart in front of the horse." Elyssa grinned.

"Or, if we see one of those tram things, the thing that makes that terrible pinging noise." They moved through the door across the carpeted gate waiting area onto the walkway. "How are you?" Eddie looked down to check. "You look okay. Just a fast walk, right? Stretch your long legs. We'll do our best, and if we don't make it, it's fine. It will be fine. But if we didn't have these carry-ons with us, I'd give you a piggyback."

"You're the best." Elyssa tried to manage her anxiety. She really did want to make this flight. If Eddie could bolt, she was sure he'd make it. She was the one complicating the issue.

"Oh, hey!" Eddie let go of her hand and ran toward a tram that was sitting in the corner.

The driver looked like she was taking her scheduled break.

"Hey!" he waved his hand in the air and dodged through the crowd of highly focused passengers beelining it to their own embarkation points. "My friend, her," he said, reaching for Elyssa's hand and dragging her over to his side. "She's disabled." He lifted her wrist to show the driver Elyssa's medical alert bracelet. "She's not allowed to run. And we're about to miss our flight."

The attendant glanced briefly at Elyssa's wrist without reading her diagnosis, then looked at Eddie's phone, where he'd queued up their ticket and was holding it up for her to read. "They changed gates, and we won't make it." Then he added, "We have first-class seats."

That last part, Elyssa thought, could go either way. First-class seats might mean this woman wanted to give them first-class treatment because they had paid for it. Or, it could mean that this woman, who probably had a second job waiting for her at the end of this day so she could put food on the table for her family, was unimpressed or perhaps bitter enough to need a dose of schadenfreude at the rich folks' inconvenience to give her morale a boost.

"Yes, ma'am," she said, looking straight at Elyssa. "I'll do my best, but this plane looks like it's ready to close its doors."

"Thank you." Elyssa let her pack slide down her arms, then Eddie piled it on the seat beside her as she climbed into place, and he scrambled his long, thin frame onto the plastic seat beside her.

Elyssa would admit, as obnoxious as these trams were with their blinking lights and their cacophonous bleats, it was a much better way to race for a gate than trying to run with a heavy sack banging against your back.

The tram driver could only get them so close. The ticket attendant was reaching out to close the doors.

Eddie leapt from the tram. "No! Don't shut them. We're here! Two seconds!" And then he threw it out there, again, like it was the open sesame for the airline industry. "We have first-class seats!" With her bag over his shoulder and his bag over the other, he grabbed Elyssa's hand and dragged her behind him along with his roller bag.

Elyssa turned and called over her shoulder, "Thank you, ma'am. I appreciate your effort." Then she pulled out her phone and swiped to find her ticket.

As they hustled toward the plane, Elyssa pulled her pack off Eddie's arm and took the weight herself so he could maneuver into the cabin.

Panting and laughing, they rushed into the aisle just before the attendant shut the doors.

"Made it!" she announced victoriously. With a glance at her ticket, she made her way to her seat. "Hello, Uncle. We thought for sure we were going to miss the plane. We were late leaving D.C." Eddie was lifting her carry-on into the overhead bin. "Our luggage won't be able to catch up with us." She reached for the water bottle Eddie pulled from the side pocket. "Thank you." She smiled at Uncle Orest. "Electrolytes and compression hose. It should be a good flight."

Eddie was maneuvering into his place.

"Just a second," Elyssa said. "I want to give Uncle Orest a hug." She put a knee on the seat and leaned in to give him a squeeze. "What an adventure! Are you all right? You look stressed." Stress might have been close to what she saw on his face, but it wasn't the whole picture. He was a little pale and a little sweaty. And there was a distraction in his eyes that wasn't typically there. Her uncle was jovial and let life flow past him, finding something to fill him with awe at every turn. As a matter of fact, the only time she ever heard scolding or disappointment in his voice was over food.

Orest glanced down at his watch. "No, no, right now all is good. I had anticipated a slight delay. Perhaps not this long. But we benefit as you were able to make plane."

"Ladies and gentlemen, if you would take your seats. I've put on the seatbelt sign. We've been cleared for takeoff. It's a busy day here in Newark, and we want to take advantage of the window of opportunity. Attendants prepare for takeoff."

"Eddie is sitting next to you for the flight. I'm so glad you'll have a chance to chat. Your mutual love of food and food sciences will be very entertaining. I'm just in front of you." She edged out of the seat and accepted her pack back from Eddie. She took a step forward and smiled politely at the man in the aisle seat. "Hey there, I'm the window seat."

The guy shuffled out of her way, and Elyssa quickly arranged herself. She wasn't used to flying first class. As a matter of fact, Uncle Orest's invitations were the only time it had happened, and then it was first class for everything. A girl could get used to a little pampering.

"May I get you a beverage?" the attendant asked.

"Cranberry and soda, please." Yeah, it was nice. These little touches were nice. But they weren't something Elyssa strived for. She liked to keep things simple. She enjoyed second-hand. Going to a shop and buying things from a factory-stuffed box felt too impersonal to her. She preferred thrift shops, where she found clothes and household items that needed a little love and a little creativity to make them her own. She liked a reason to exercise her creative muscles.

The attendant appeared with Elyssa's mid-morning mocktail in a crystal glass.

Accepting it, Elyssa would admit that a little luxury as a gift here and there was very pleasant.

The attendants swarmed the aisles, checking that electronics were properly secured, that seatbacks and trays were up, and that belts were securely in place.

As they taxied toward the runway, the attendants stood at precise points in the aisle and moved through the safety instructions.

Up, up, up into the air. This was the part of the flight that

Elyssa disliked the most. The part where she was most afraid of how her heart would handle things. So far, she'd been fine with the changes in altitude. But that didn't mean that she wasn't afraid of having a mid-flight event. In her nightmare scenario, the staff wigged out and instead of just letting her regain her equilibrium on her own and take care of herself, they'd insist on landing and pulling her off the plane. In this scenario, she imagined herself in Indiana, somewhere between her destination and home, and denied the ability to get back on a plane.

She wasn't cleared to drive.

Elyssa wondered how much a car service would cost to drive her from Indiana to Washington, D.C.

Behind her, Elyssa heard her uncle release a great exhale followed by a rich chuckle. He probably felt the way she did about takeoffs.

Whatever had been stressing him just moments earlier seemed to have passed.

"Look below us, Elyssa, do you see beautiful farmland?" he said in a voice loud enough to carry to her. "Now, imagine that this is all returned to Mother Nature and wild beasts because it is no longer necessary for farming, no more cow methane to increase greenhouse gases. You and I will save this world."

"That's the dream, Uncle."

11

———

XANDER
Friday
Newark, NJ

XANDER SWIPED his phone open when he saw Hiro's name.

"Where are you?" Hiro asked without a hello.

"I'm in Newark. I just watched Orest Kalinsky get on the plane. He's got a straight shot to Fairbanks, so we know where he'll be for the next few hours."

"You're not on it with him?" Hiro asked.

"They were overbooked. I'm flying to Chicago, then on. If the flights are on time, I'll only be a couple of hours behind him." Xander found a seat in the back corner and sat, signaling Radar to curl up beside him. "Maybe get someone from FBI Fairbanks to keep an eye on him until I can get there."

"I'll have Finley reach out. You brought your dog didn't you?" Hiro asked.

"Radar? Yeah, I'll be able to do a thorough check on Orest's rooms for hidden thumb drives. So, it's good we're on separate flights from Orest. It would be hard to keep my profile low if I flew from Newark and showed up where he is. Orest didn't get to his place in the family by being a dumbass."

"What are you doing now?"

"After Orest climbed aboard, I moved to my gate, then watched his flight take off from the window. And now I wait. And wait. And wait. It's a good test to see how a working dog line of German Shepherd does with a whole lot of boredom and sitting still."

Xander could hear Hiro crunching and could imagine him talking while downing a bag of chips. "What's the strategy?"

"For Radar's energy?" Xander clarified. "This morning, break of dawn, Cerberus put him on their running apparatus until he was tuckered out. They put a Malinois named Voodoo next to him. This machine lets the dogs run as fast or slow as they want. They took off like they were rocket fuel. They were racing for the gold, and it was a sight to see. Goose bumps."

"Did you take a video?" Hiro asked.

"Not allowed in their facility. Tight security."

"Tightest," Hiro agreed. "The I is always dotted. The T is always crossed. It's why we put such faith in their professionalism. Mistakes cost lives. Do you have the information about Orest's overnight stay in Fairbanks?"

"Upscale. To stay out of their sight, I have reservations at the hotel next door. Considerably less posh, but I was able to book a room straight across from his. Depending on his application of trade craft, I might be able to get something."

"He's staying in Fairbanks a single night tonight," Hiro said. "He'll spend the bulk of Saturday in Fairbanks, then at fifteen-hundred, a car service will pick him up. He's heading to a lodge in Lumberjack."

"That's where Orest's dogs are training?" Xander asked.

"Exactly. His trainer has a cabin out that way. It's two hours due east."

"Any ideas about what he's up to in Fairbanks?" Xander reached into his side pocket for a protein bar. Hiro's chewing was making him hungry. "Is it just a layover?"

"I don't have any direct communications on it. But Orest is funding an arctic animal study there. I'd imagine he'll stop by the lab."

"Arctic animals, that's a hobby project, right?" Xander asked. "Nothing to do with this case?"

"I can't imagine how arctic animals could or would have anything to do with the machine. But I'll dig in deeper. Okay, back to Newark. We checked the tapes, and Orest has the carry-on and checked only one suitcase. When you get to Fairbanks, you'll want to go through both. You'll find all of the search warrants in your file. But Finley sent a search order to FBI Fairbanks to pull the checked bag and give it a quick look-see. They'll be checking the bag for any substances that might be the Zoric neurotoxins, and then it will be put on the conveyor with the others. The inspection should go unnoticed."

"Did York come up positive for neurotoxins?"

"Long's here with me." Hiro crunched. "He said too much time went by. But York's oxygenation levels were wonky even for a heart crisis, so we're working on the assumption that he was poisoned. Watch yourself."

Xander stilled. "Go back. Say that last again? Orest checked a suitcase?"

"Correct."

"And he had another bag?" Xander asked.

"Carry-on."

"He didn't carry anything onto the plane."

"Are you sure?" Hiro asked.

"I'm sure. I wondered how someone could go on such a

long flight without a bag of things to support him and wondered what he had in his pockets."

"Okay, before there's a freak out. I'm going back to review tapes. Sit tight, I'm moving the video to your feed." There was a pause. "Okay, you should have it now."

The crew sitting near Xander had their heads down, scrolling on their phones. One by one, they popped their heads up, their eyes wide, their postures rigid. Then, as a group, they rose and turned to look out the window and up into the sky.

Xander put a hand on Radar's head as he watched the grainy security feed. There was Orest in a crush of people. Xander could only see him from the shoulders up.

He paused the screen and went back. "I think I have it. Hang on."

Xander moved back through the tape, and yeah. He hadn't made a mistake. Pressed by the flow of humanity, Orest had been shoulder to shoulder with another man, but when he peeled off and went into the men's room, he had a sizeable briefcase in his hand. "I'm taking a still shot of what I'm seeing." Xander took a screenshot, then spread the view wider. "Silver bag. Right hand."

"That would be it."

Xander kept watching. Orest went into the men's room. Moments later, Orest came out empty-handed.

"I'll get back with you." Xander ended the call, snatched up his backpack, gripped Radar's lead, and tapped his thigh to shift Radar to work mode.

Radar jumped to his feet and glued himself to Xander's side.

Sliding through the crowd, Xander put Radar protectively against the wall. They moved, salmon-like, against the flow toward the restroom.

Stepping through the opening into the men's room, Radar

did what Radar always did in a new environment: He cast his gaze around the room, then stuck his nose in the air. Xander took a survey of the area, loath to get Radar's sniffer going and letting people know a search was underway. They moved past the row of urinals and sinks to the stalls down to the far wall, where Xander gave Radar the slightest hand signal to search for explosives. Then, Xander slid his hand down Radar's lead to keep him close. In this configuration, they paced the bathroom.

No hit.

Xander felt zero relief.

Glancing around, he saw a man watching him in the mirror, a slight frown between his eyes.

The stalls were full, and Xander wasn't about to whip out his dick and take a leak as a cover. That seemed too vulnerable a position to put himself into, so he opted to wash his hands.

To keep Radar's tail free from being trod upon by men's feet, he signaled Radar under the counter. Soaping up and scrubbing his hands together, Xander used the time to scan for any place that Orest could have put a case that would have gone unnoticed. Just as Xander came to the conclusion that it had to be under the sink, Radar was tapping his foot.

Xander bent down and saw the case. Horror slid up his thighs into his ass, where he clenched it tight to keep it from rising higher into his system.

He messaged a picture of his findings.

There was an immediate ping in return.

HIRO: **Sit with it and see if it's a pass. I'll get someone there in the next 90 minutes.**

XANDER: **I'm not cool with that timeline.**

.   .   .

HIRO: **Is it ticking?**

XANDER: **Funny.**

HIRO: **What does Radar say?**

XANDER: **Electronics. I should walk this out to a big field somewhere. We'll stay with it, but I can't have a Zoric family briefcase anywhere near a population center. We need a bomb team that can try to keep this thing intact and not blow it up. I doubt it's a bomb. Radar isn't picking up any explosive scents. But if it's got some component of the machine, we can't lose the opportunity.**

HIRO: **Or it's neither bomb nor death machine. But it can't be nothing. They could have planned a brush past, and the person's plane was late. If that's the case, I'd like to know who the player is. Sit tight.**

XANDER: **Risk too high. What's inside could look innocuous enough. He did get through security with it. With York in the hospital, reasons undetermined, I'm not leaving this out for the public to find.**

.   .   .

Hiro: **Yeah, Orest could assume that if someone other than the intended recipient saw it, they'd call security. Security would take it out to the field and explode it without investigating the contents.**

Xander: **Plausible.**

Xander wished this were a phone conversation because texting took time. And time didn't feel like it was on their side here.

Hiro: **Sending you a map. Get to this door. Security will meet you and take you to an empty field. Good luck.**

Did Xander want to pick up the case? That would be a resounding "Hell no." If he were Orest Kalinsky, he would have smeared the handle with neurotoxins—not that Xander knew how that all worked.

Xander pulled a poop bag from Radar's vest and slid his hand in like a glove, then reached for the case.

With Radar at his side, his lead draped over Xander's shoulder to give himself use of both hands, they moved into the swarm of humanity coursing toward their destinations.

Xander followed the red line on his GPS. It took him the long way, but it kept them off the main arteries.

Xander's deodorant was failing him. His hair prickled as it stood on end.

Was he carrying death?

What the hell was in this bag?

Radar was picking up on Xander's anxiety. His ears back,

his eyes wide, with quick flicks of his tongue, he lowered his stance and trotted next to Xander, maintaining zero space between the two. What happened to Xander would happen to Radar.

When he reached the stairs, Xander tore toward the door, taking two steps at a time. He slammed his hip into the bar release and barreled out into a blast of frigid air.

A man stood with his walkie-talkie crackling, as he scanned the sky with binoculars.

"DIA." Xander held up his credentials. "Are you here for me?"

"Guy with a dog and silver bag is going to burst through the door, run him over to the field," the guy repeated his orders.

Xander looked around for a golf cart-type deal and saw none. "Guess we're going to actually be running," he said, lifting his chin to ask for a direction.

The guy pointed northwest, and they broke into a fast-paced jog.

"What's going on with the binoculars?" Xander asked, remembering how the flight crew had all lifted to their feet and looked out the window.

"The tower lost communications with the planes," he said breathlessly.

"The planes? All the planes? There's no contact at all?" Xander looked down at the briefcase.

Orest, you son of a bitch.

If this were a Zoric play, could it be *the* Zoric play?

Or maybe there was something bigger and they needed a distraction. It would, for sure, cause all hell to break loose, and everyone's eyes would be focused here.

Loss of communications with the pilots at this hub of activity was beyond disastrous. At that moment, thousands of lives were at risk.

This could be another 9-11.

Would there be a war?

Damned straight there would be.

As they got to the end of the macadam, and Xander had his foot on the grass, he yelled, "Don't follow me. Find shelter."

The guard didn't need to be asked twice. He bolted as if he were on fire.

As Xander stepped off the macadam, the air around him became acrid. "Radar, down stay."

Radar slammed to a stop, lying on his belly.

With his elbow pulled across his nose and mouth, squinting his eyes to protect them from whatever was seeping from the case, Xander raced full out to get as far from humanity as possible.

In the middle of the field, Xander dropped the case, stepped back, and, crouching low, called Hiro, giving him a quick sketch of what was happening.

"Acid? Can you open the bag without burning yourself?" Hiro growled.

As soon as Xander popped the locks, he jumped back.

So far, nothing blew.

Radar yipped and barked but stayed where he'd been told.

Using a tactical pen from the side pocket of his own backpack, Xander lifted the lid, but he already knew what he was going to find. He told Hiro. "I'm watching everything melt."

There was nothing to be done about it.

This was the same technology that child porn collectors used on their computers and thumb drives. If the password was entered incorrectly three times, the acid was released, and everything was obliterated as it melted into a gooey mess that quickly solidified.

Xander glanced at his watch.

Now here was the question: was the communications glitch

between the tower and the pilots caused by Orest Kalinsky? It fit right in with a typical Zoric style of attacks. If this was the apparatus causing the problem, Orest might have cut that operation very close. After all, he was one of the planes in the sky.

Walking far enough away that neither he nor Radar breathed in the unknown chemicals, Xander lay down, resting his head on Radar's haunch. Waiting for the FBI to show up and collect the carry-on remains, Xander kept an eye on the clouds to make sure that if planes collided overhead, he and Radar weren't hanging out on the crash site.

12

Xander
 Friday
 Newark, NJ

The phone rang. It was Hiro. "How are you holding up?"

"I'm having a pleasant nap in the meadow," Xander said.

"All hell was breaking loose at the airport. They had the emergency vehicles out and ready to respond in case the planes started falling out of the sky. But we've finally got support heading your way."

"It's over? Comms were reestablished?" Xander asked.

"Correct," Hiro affirmed. "I'm having the various timelines and video feeds run through AI. I'll have a readout soon," Hiro said. "Hey, six-million-dollar man, I watched you running on CCV. You're in pretty good shape."

"Surprising how a body responds to existential threat," Xander said. "What's this about six million dollars?"

"A seventies TV reference, let it go," Hiro said. "Listen, even if the contents of the case melted, there was obviously something there that the owner, supposedly Orest, didn't want seen. Good find. Radar gets a steak from me next time you're in town."

"I'll tell him. I didn't hear anything that sounded like a crash. Did all the planes make it down okay?" Xander asked.

"The planes are all safe. The FBI is headed your way to collect the carry-on's remains. I need you to sit tight."

"Well, I'm lying tight." Xander reached up to scritch Radar. "That's the best you're going to get from us right now."

"Fair."

"What was the reach of the communications outage?" Xander asked.

"Just the Newark tower. Cell phones and computer systems in the area were unaffected throughout."

"Interesting. I don't remember the machine doing anything like that before. It only affected air traffic control? And it hit Newark, New Jersey, but didn't hit Manhattan, NY? How is that possible?"

"I don't know," Hiro said.

Xander sat up. "How?"

"I *don't* know."

"Theory: The Zorics were testing their ability to cause a mass casualty event, specifically in a high-traffic hub. They meant to turn on the machine, test it, and shut it down once they had verification of efficacy."

"Okay. Possible," Hiro said.

"Theory: Occam's Razor."

"Your favorite," Hiro said with a crunch.

"Because it's true. Usually, the simplest answer is the correct one. Are you eating again?"

"I'm shoving carbs in my face at a distressing rate. I'm getting too old for battlefield nerves. Back to your Occam's Razor. In this case, the simplest solution is that the briefcase and the tower communications issues are unrelated and just happened to transpire in a tight time frame."

"Simple," Xander said. "But so is sticking your head in the sand and not seeing anything that's going on around you."

Hiro didn't respond.

"Let's wait to see what AI pulls up before we speculate," Xander finally said.

"In the meantime," Hiro said. "I have some answers as to the question, why is Orest Kalinsky spending a whole day in Fairbanks, Alaska? His foundation has been sponsoring a researcher who studies arctic squirrel hibernation."

"Say again?"

"Arctic squirrel hibernation. A guy named Dr. Claude Burns."

Xander pulled his water bottle from the side pocket of his pack. "I'm trying to see how that would help The Family."

"I've been trying to figure it out myself, as a matter of fact, we round-tabled it to brainstorm ideas. We've landed on one that was pretty farfetched and one that might be reasonable given Orest's obsession with food."

Reaching into Radar's vest, he pulled out a collapsible bowl. "Squirrel meat?" Xander poured water until the bowl was half full and dragged it toward Radar. "Let's start with reasonable as a warmup for farfetched." He took a swig and spun the cap back in place.

"Reasonable," Hiro said, "he wants to know how to hibernate animals so he can use them as fresh food."

"If you can hibernate a squirrel, why not a cow? So instead of just freezing the meat, he hibernates the animals, then brings them back to life—well, reanimates them and eats them fresh?" Xander asked. "Something about that is wholly unappealing."

"Agreed," Hiro said. "Our records indicate Orest isn't just a foodie, but his focus on food might be a manifestation of an obsessive-compulsive disorder. He dislikes any kind of preserved food. Orest insists that everything be fresh. Freshly caught, freshly picked, freshly butchered."

"What's the farfetched idea?" Xander asked, wondering if he really wanted to know.

"What if Orest was considering the possible outcomes of what the family was about to attempt. He wanted to make sure the family was safe."

"Okay, stop," Xander said as he checked his watch. His flight to Chicago had just left. He'd have to figure out a new path to Fairbanks. "If you're about to tell me that Orest was going to deep freeze the family, I don't need that insanity in my head."

"Except that it might be a real-life possibility," Hiro said.

"Are you being serious right now?"

"I am," Hiro said. "This Claude Burns guy was just hired by NASA to work on their Mars project."

"Like they think that it would be a good idea to hibernate the astronauts?" Xander ran that thought through the lens of all those sci-fi books he enjoyed so much. He enjoyed them as fiction, Xander clarified. He didn't like them so much when they might be coming to fruition in the here and now. "I can see why NASA would want to try it. I mean, they're talking about a possible three-year stint in a very small space. It would, in fact, solve a lot of problems. Food and water consumption, fecal production. Speaking of shit situations, I'm switching subjects." Xander crisscrossed his legs. "What's happening with York?"

"He's out of critical care in a step-down unit. But it was a sixteen-hour surgery. He's still in the 'anything can happen' window. Watch and wait."

"But his heart is pounding, and he's breathing on his own?" Xander pushed.

"Fortunately, he's at the same hospital where they took

Finley's ex-girlfriend. Grace Del Toro, who was Lacey Stewart back then. Finley met her at a car crash when she was overcome by palytoxins. The hospital had her medical records and was able to do a comparison. HIPAA, so that's all I have on that unless and until someone can produce a warrant or York and Grace sign off on it. I do know York's on oxygen but breathing on his own. We've got people sitting with him around the clock, checking credentials when anyone comes in, and closely monitoring what they do. The secrets that man holds in his head are of vital importance to the U.S. government. They're not cutting corners on his security. Speaking of security," Hiro said, "We don't have access to the code words to figure out the surveillance that York put in place when he was tracking Orest. We've got some high school hotshot code breaker who works for us after school and on weekends, trying to figure it out."

"Funny," Xander said.

"Our mission isn't ranked as critical," Hiro said. "Don't hold your breath. In the meantime, a judge gave permission to tap Orest's phone. That's how we know about the car to Lumberjack."

"He's traveling alone?" Xander saw a car pull up and three people with FBI emblazoned windbreakers get out.

"The car stops at Orest's address at the hotel, and then at the apartment building where Claude Burns lives. I have Burns's picture. I'm sending it over now."

Xander stood and lifted a hand to identify himself to the special agents before opening the message and blinking. "Serious?"

"What?" Hiro asked. "Do you know this guy?"

"Yeah, he's every squirrel that's ever run in front of my car. Bushy hair pulled back into a ponytail, big liquid brown eyes, and a pointed face. This man looks like he's in the same general family."

"Once seen, it cannot be unseen," Hiro sighed. "But Claude is a terrible name for a squirrel."

Xander watched as the FBI agents took safety equipment from the trunk. "Moving back to the question at hand. Claude is working for NASA? That means he's no longer working for Orest Kalinsky."

"Claude works for Orest's foundation until the end of the year's hibernation," Hiro said. "At any time in the next few weeks, the squirrels should wake up. That's what NASA told me when I stuck my thumb out and got a heli lift down to Hampton with a colonel who had a meeting. I flashed my badge at their human resources folks, got the information, and came back. I'm not saying that those helicopter rides aren't one hell of a perk and make life that much more interesting, I *am* saying that we didn't tell the tower about the flight."

"How do they get away with not telling the tower?" Xander asked.

"There's an exception in the airspace above Washington that allows some military flights without broadcasting sensitive information to the public."

"Lesson learned. I guess I can fly in and out of Richmond, Virginia, and drive a bit," Xander said. "It's inconvenient, but I like staying alive."

"The brass is taking advantage of the program. Military helicopters are clogging the skies, risking more helicopter-driven accidents. Did I take advantage, anyway?" Hiro asked. "Yes. Does that make me a hypocrite to be bitching about it now? I get that sometimes my moral fabric is frayed. But in this case, it was in service of humanity, so I don't feel bad."

"Is NASA going to give Claude a heads up that the DIA interested in him?" Xander asked, putting a calming hand on Radar's head, as he watched the FBI pull on their safety suits.

"I doubt it," Hiro said. "I shook my finger at them and gave them a stern warning."

Xander was looking at Claude's photo. "I think I'm about the same age as this guy. Do we have a file on him? I want a solid approach if I need to make him my bestie."

"We did a basic workup of his education and employment," Hiro was crunching again.

Xander had tossed his earlier protein bar without even a bite. As the adrenaline receded, he was starving.

"Basically, he's been with the Orest's foundation since he started his doctorate. From his social media posts, it appears that Claude hangs out with nerd friends playing board games. Wife. Three young kids. Every year when Orest comes to see his dogs, they hand out together in Lumberjack."

"It's the same pattern this year?" Xander asked.

"Exactly the same," Hiro confirmed. "I'm interpreting this trip as a normal behavior pattern for Orest Kalinsky. From Claude Burns's posts things are the same as they ever were. Claude posts nothing alarming, concerning, dark, ominous, or impending or doom-like. There's nothing political or ideological sounding. It's cosplay and kid pictures."

The FBI had finally gotten themselves together and were waddling toward Xander in their PPE.

"The squirrel guy's pretty laid back," Hiro concluded. "It's Orest who's the monster."

13

———

Elyssa

   Saturday

   Lumberjack, Alaska

"There she is," Uncle Orest said, looking over his shoulder, then shifting around in his seat to see Elyssa better.

"I'm here." Elyssa moved over to the dinner table to join him, dropping a kiss on her Uncle Orest's cheek and squeezing his shoulders affectionately.

"Did you have a good nap?"

"I rested. I wasn't able to sleep." She pulled out a chair and slid into the seat, taking in the single empty plate on the table. "Where are Eddie and Paca? Did you eat alone?"

"No. No. I ate with our friends. I am about to enjoy blueberry cobbler with homemade maple ice cream. This is a must. I quite insist you shall try this while you are here. As a matter of fact, every year I look forward to spending a delightful evening eating and reading." He held up a book in French. "I enjoy this dessert so much, I always order second bowl." He lifted his chin toward the door. "This evening, our friends go mushing with team for night practice."

"I read that mush comes from French Canadian '*marche*,' which is 'walk' in English. I guess it was like the horse driver calling out 'Walk on,' but people heard 'Mush.' That's kind of interesting. How do you say it in Slovak?"

"*Psie preteky.*"

"Beautiful. Someday I'd like to be able to speak Slovak, too." She laced her hands and dropped them between her knees. "Uncle, I need to talk to you about something."

He put his forearm on the table and leaned his weight onto it.

"I was just on the phone with the airport. They said that because the first leg of Eddie's and my trip arrived late at Newark and a subsequent airport glitch affected all the planes there, our bags ended up on the wrong plane. And while they were finally located, Eddie's and my bags won't get to us before Tuesday. Since I was originally scheduled to leave Alaska on Wednesday, I told them just to deliver them to my house in D.C."

"My dear, I'm so sorry this would all have been averted had my secretary been able to get tickets on my plane out of Washington."

Elyssa waved a hand in the air. "This was a last-minute adventure, and even under the best of circumstances, bags go missing. It's part of traveling. But even with the warm clothes I bought in Fairbanks to tide me over, I'm going to have to admit to myself that these frigid temperatures are too much for me. I am having a lot of trouble with heart pain."

When Uncle Orest scowled, Elyssa laid a soothing hand on his arm and continued. "Out here at the lodge, so far from a proper medical facility and the unpredictability of the weather, I have to tell you, it's adding anxiety to my heart issues. This climate just isn't something I can handle." She exhaled. "I don't want to disappoint you, but I spoke with the airline and was able to get them to change my ticket to tomorrow. I am so sorry to leave the adventure, but I need to go home in the morning."

"My dear, will a very few days more make such a difference?" Uncle Orest asked. "I'm thinking of Eddie. Of course, he is my guest. All arrangements are in place. He is, as ever, welcome. He seems to be having a marvelous time with the dogs."

"He is. I think you have him hooked on traveling by sled dog, which is not very practical where we live." Elyssa looked up as a server extended a menu toward her. "Thank you, but I ate earlier. Perhaps some water?" After the server retreated, Elyssa said, "I'm nervous about even waiting until morning to leave. It's the soonest I could arrange things. I hired a car to come pick me up. Because it's almost two hours to the airport, and you like to sleep in, I need to say goodbye to you now."

"What time is your plane leaving?" Uncle Orest asked.

"My car comes at seven. The plane leaves just after ten."

"And you fly straight through to D.C.?" Uncle Orest asked.

"I have a layover in Chicago, but it's a good one. Long enough that I shouldn't have to worry about delays and short enough that it's not difficult to manage."

"Ah, in Russian, there is an idiom that translates to say, 'The plan has no wealth.' We make plans and hope for best. This adventure worked for neither you nor for me. I received a phone call telling me of an urgent matter that needs my immediate attention with our family who visit Singapore."

"Oh dear. I'm so sorry."

"It is precautionary that I go and lend my wisdom." He chuckled. "I think there is something about me that our family finds calming. I'll go, give them lots of hugs and advice. Usually, they accept hugs and ignore advice."

"Shall we go to the airport together then?" Elyssa asked.

"I will be up before the cock crows. My car picks me up at 4:20 tomorrow morning. Now, as to driving together, I would ask you to join me in my car, but you've already made your arrangements, and I plan to sleep stretched out in back seat."

"Have you spoken with Eddie and Paca?"

"I have. Our friends are aware that they should continue with their schedule as planned and enjoy this time. They seem to be companionable. Perhaps when they work together at NASA, they will become good friends. But perhaps you prefer for Eddie to come with you, so you are not traveling alone?"

"No, sir. There will be plenty of people around me. If I need help, honestly, there is little Eddie could do."

"Well then, with lodge paid for, all is arranged. Our friends have met my dog team. They should enjoy watching start of Iditarod."

"That's very generous of you, Uncle." She laid a hand on his arm. "Thank you for being so kind to Eddie. And you know, Paca is really lovely as well. It was wonderful to meet him and spend a day having him show us Fairbanks and his lab. His squirrel stories are hysterical."

Uncle Orest pursed his lips and stared at her for a long moment with an expression that Elyssa couldn't decipher. "I really must press you, my dear. Is there anything I can say that would encourage you to get on my plane with me? In Singapore, surely there will be shops where you can find warm weather clothes to wear."

"The wedding." She reminded him. "I'm still coming to Singapore next week, and then the family retreat on the island. Your secretary booked the flights for Monday." She paused, a frown forming between her brows. "But you said that there's an urgent matter? Is there anything I can do to help, or will my presence be a distraction or a burden? I can arrange a different time."

"I think our new plans will be best. Come give me hug. I will see you when you get to our family island." Uncle Orest rose to receive Elyssa's embrace.

Adjusting her backpack on her shoulder, Elyssa felt a strange sense of dread creep through her system.

It was probably her fear of walking out into the bitter cold and its effect on her blood pressure as she walked to her room.

Yes, that had to be it.

Right?

14

XANDER
　　Sunday
　　Fairbanks, Alaska

"ALL RIGHT, Hiro, I'm in Fairbanks." Xander was about done with planes and airports. "I'm grabbing my bag, then heading toward the car rental."

Xander strode along the corridor toward the luggage claim with the rest of his flight's passengers.

After the Newark mess made him miss his original connection, Xander had been hipping and hopping from airport to airport like a child in an Easter egg hunt, trying to get to Fairbanks.

Orest Kalinsky got in almost twenty-four hours before him.

Orest's bags had not, in fact, been searched upon landing, and Orest had spent his day unencumbered by the Fairbanks FBI because their supervisor was disinclined to do the DIA or the CIA a favor. They even gave Finley's supervisor, Frost, a cold shoulder.

The play of words in that thought brought a momentary smile to Xander's lips.

Throughout his career, Xander had learned the importance of keeping things light along the trail. The dark was a burden that wore a man down.

Gallows humor was a survival technique.

Xander conscientiously looked for a reason to smile or laugh along the way. And, too, Radar was with him. Cerberus drummed it into Xander that Radar thought that work was play. And Radar would hardwire with Xander's emotions. If Xander wanted a working dog that actually worked, Xander would have to embrace the idea that work was play for himself as well.

And so Xander practiced keeping things chill as the dangers heated up.

Once he had his bag, Xander would head to Lumberjack, Alaska, a town with a population of 129.

Lumberjack was a dot on the map, so small that Xander had a hard time convincing the GPS search mechanism that it existed at all. Lumberjack was, in fact, two hours out in the pristine nothingness of Alaska. That's where Orest had kenneled his dogs for the last number of years.

With nothing there but trees and snow drifts, why else would Kalinsky be here but to see the dogs?

Here was the big question: Was Orest there, or was he in the wind?

"Once I have the car," Xander told Hiro. "I'm heading right for the lodge. You got me reservations, right?"

"Yeah, about that," Hiro said. "We had to hack in and remove a different reservation to get you in at all. Why it's so popular at this time of year is a mystery to me."

"Wait, did you say you *hacked* the system?" Xander asked.

"Not me, I used that high school hotshot code breaker who works for us after school and on weekends. Look, I did what was necessary to get you a place to stay. It's too cold to camp in Alaska this time of year. It's a six-dog night, at least, and you only have the one," Hiro said. "I was looking at the weather forecast, and you're in for nippy weather. I hope you brought mukluks with you."

"First thing I packed." Xander wished he had a good pair of indigenous seal-skin mukluks. The best he could do, given the spur-of-the-moment assignment, was to throw some extra thermal socks in his bag. If that didn't work in Slovakian temperatures, he knew his boots weren't up to double-digit negative numbers here in Alaska. At least he had a Russian fur hat with flaps that kept his brain toasty.

"In order to find you a bed," Hiro was saying, "we had to find a new arrival, someone you could beat to the registration desk. I wasn't able to get you right next to Orest. There are two rooms between you and him. Burns and Orest have signed in. Burns is first in the row. Then Orest, two rooms, you. Best we could do, but it makes surveillance harder."

"I'm not worried about that," Xander said. "Tell me more about beating someone to the desk."

"Get your bag, grab the car, pick yourself up some fast food, and book it to the lodge. The couple coming in has a note on their registration saying they'll be coming straight from Fairbanks Airport and will be late checking in. If everything goes to plan, you'll be tucked in bed. And according to the law, that means you win the race."

"Thanks, I appreciate the effort. But I hope something opens up for those people I'm displacing. That's not cool."

"But a nuclear winter sure is," Hiro said. "Think of it this way, Xander, while they may be inconvenienced, their sacrifice might prove pivotal to the continued existence of the human race. Man, I gave myself a chill. It's almost like I can hear the Doomsday Clock ticking in my ear. I'm eating a peanut butter and potato chip sandwich, pretending that the good guy always wins in the end."

"You and me both, brother." After Xander ended the call, he worked the plan.

He liked to think it was a good omen that everything was going smoothly. The car was ready. Radar was being his best-boy self. The food was tasty, the coffee hot, and the drive was interesting enough that Xander wasn't forced to sing along with the radio to stay awake.

But it was winter in Alaska, so now that it was dinner time, it was dark out.

The front desk lady handed out his key card with a "Welcome, Mr. Belov, enjoy your stay. The lodge staff lights the evening fire at seven. We allow dogs if they're on leash and under supervision."

"Thank you, ma'am." Xander pocketed his key card while taking another look at the map, protected under glass on the check-in desk.

The apple-cheeked woman put her finger on his room. "Just out the door and turn to the right. The numbers are visible. You're down toward the end there."

"Thank you, again."

In his doggie shoes meant to protect his paws from frostbite, Radar comically high-stepped by Xander's side. Together, they moved along the boardwalk past the dining room. There, sitting alone at a four-top, was Orest Kalinsky. Xander had only seen the man in photos and videos, but he knew it was Orest by the way Xander pressed his weight into his heels and his perception expanded, preparing him for a fight.

Here was the enemy.

And yet, he looked like a jovial old man kidding around with the waitress as she picked up a large empty bowl and set an identically large bowl in front of him. It looked like cobbler and ice cream, and Orest was clapping his hands and rubbing them together like an excited child. The waitress was laughing at what he said and looked delighted as she left.

As Orest dug into his dessert, Xander thought he had at least ten minutes to act.

Hiro had said that the squirrel-guy's room was at the end, and Orest's was the second cabin room in the lineup. After a quick scan to ensure he was alone, Xander used his universal entry device, which gained him access to any carded door. Leaving his suitcase outside against the wall, Radar followed Xander into the room.

A quick check of Orest's luggage tag told Xander he was in the right place.

"Radar, give warning," Xander said. He'd seen this skill on video but had never practiced it. If someone were to come into view, Radar should whine to alert Xander.

Radar knew what he was doing. He sat at attention at the door that Xander had left partially open. Radar's whole body was tense with concentration, giving Xander confidence he could focus on the list of tasks he needed to accomplish.

Over a decade of practice made these next steps fluid and efficient as he searched Orest's belongings and used the equipment in his backpack to wire the room for sound and place hidden cameras.

"Test. Test. Test," he said, looking at the readout on his phone to ensure the mics were operating properly.

Gathering up his bag, Xander was back by Radar's side. "Radar, release." He opened the door, scanned for any onlookers, then turned to give the room a final check to confirm everything was in order. When he closed the door behind him, he listened for the click that ensured that it locked properly.

He didn't need Orest's suspicions aroused.

Xander took hold of his suitcase handle. He and Radar

paced past the two rooms that made his surveillance a bit less efficient, and at that third door, he swiped his card and went in.

It was everything he could have imagined an Alaskan cottage room to look like, right down to the cheery red quilt that seemed hand-sewn and the wooden carvings of black bears.

Xander loaded Radar onto the bed and opened his computer, testing the surveillance cameras, checking the volume, and then lying back to wait and see.

The Bureau was tapping Orest's phone. That put the information in a chain of custody that might or might not filter its way to Xander.

Claude Burns, squirrel doctor, wasn't at the table with Orest. Xander saw Claude as a potential resource. He planned to befriend the man while they were in Lumberjack. If nothing else, he could put surveillance in Claude's room once Xander knew where Claude was and that the coast was clear,

Lying on his bed, booted feet hanging over the edge, Xander waited for Orest to go back to his room. Xander wanted to observe the man's behavior to ensure his surveillance work went unnoticed.

Radar stretched out beside him. His head rested on Xander's stomach as they relaxed together.

The mics in Orest's room picked up the click and swish of the door, followed by a great moan, and shuffling.

Xander tapped on the camera feed.

The room itself was empty, but Xander heard piss going into the toilet and a flush. There was no water at the sink. "Note to self, avoid shaking the man's hand," Xander said under his breath as he adjusted the angle of the camera set to watch the door.

There was an oof and another groan, and Xander toggled his switch to direct the mid-room camera to take in the bed, where

Orest Kalinsky stretched out wearing a t-shirt with his belt unfastened, and his pants spread open.

Orest reached into his pocket for his phone and tapped.

...

"WE ARE ALL HERE, but I am leaving very early in the morning. The team is in place? Planes? Boxes?"

...

"Good. Good."

 OREST'S WORDS came through the AI translator almost instantaneously. When the computer spoke the conversation in English, it retained Orest's Slovak accent.

Listening over the computer, Xander only had one side of the conversation. In the quiet spaces, Xander was guessing what might be said on the other end.

Frustrating? Absolutely. But the FBI was collecting the entirety of the back-and-forth.

And that was the fingers-crossed part of the operation. Could Finley get clearance to hand that file to Xander since Xander was in a different alphabet, or would the Bureau clutch it to their chests? Xander put his questions on a mental list as he continued to listen to Orest.

"DR. TAPPER IS PRESENT THROUGHOUT?"

...

"The pilot?" Orest asked. "He's one of ours?"

...

"Will be?" Orest sniffed deeply. "Good enough. Sadly, we must add the extra box. I had hoped to avoid shipping. Make sure Tapper has the file. This last box is the most important. There are to be no mistakes."

...

"My dear boy, I have an upset stomach. The cobbler was so delicious that I ate too much. The homemade ice cream? Sublime. Mastery. I almost wish for another cargo box, so I might have this always."

...

"I know, not in this shipment. The planes are too small. Still," Orest sounded wistful, "it was an appealing thought. Listen, tonight, I ate something new. They had moose on the menu. Very interesting taste indeed. I have never eaten moose before. Gigantic creatures. As big as a house, if you can imagine. Enormous. I wished to eat it tonight as I was angry at even the idea of a moose and wanted my vengeance."

...

"This is not for laughing, boy. I was traumatized. There was moose on the path when we were out with dogs this afternoon. We had to bring the team to a complete stop. It was frightening because we couldn't get the dogs to rest quietly, and we couldn't turn the team around as we had all fourteen on our line. Had the moose so wished, he could have trampled my entire team. And I would have seen it. Horrific. Nightmarish images. Oh, my stomach is too full of yummy things for such ugly thoughts. I need to sleep this away."

...

"Yes, it is quite early in the evening here. But as I said, I head back to Fairbanks early morning."

...

"San Francisco? Yes. Yes. Beautiful views and delicious wines. It's a shame I won't be there longer. I say goodnight then. Bye-bye."

· · ·

WHEN THE CONNECTION ENDED, Xander sent the readout back to Hiro for immediate assessment and a heads-up that he needed to speak with Finley's team.

This was news; Orest was heading to Fairbanks in the morning.

Xander would love to know what was said on the other side. It sounded like an upcoming trip would move him through San Francisco. But was that sooner or later?

Could that be part of the conversation about the boxes?

Where did the boxes originate, and where would they end up?

Mostly, Xander wondered what they contained.

The conversation didn't necessarily have anything to do with the doomsday machine.

It might, in fact, have to do with one of Orest's foundation's research studies.

Orest needed a doctor to be present with the boxes. What kind of doctor? What discipline of expertise?

At least they had a name that would be traveling with the shipment, Dr. Tapper. The systems could search for the name. But practically, Xander didn't expect anything to come of it. Worldwide, how many Dr. Tappers were there?

Xander followed up on his file share with a text to Hiro, asking him to check if Orest was taking a flight out of Fairbanks to San Francisco the next day. And if so, was there anyone working on the Zoric mission who could meet Orest's flight in San Francisco to see what he did next?

Xander couldn't go. There were so few people at the lodge that it would be evident that Xander was shadowing Orest. And, honestly, if Orest had used a Zoric neurotoxin on York to shake the tail, it was best to move the rabbit along to another set of eyes and keep everyone safe. Safer. He texted Long.

· · ·

XANDER: **Any word on York? How's he holding up?**

SINCE OREST'S phone call ended, there was silence in his room, followed by deep, resonant snoring.

Xander caught Radar's gaze. "We should go see if we can find Dr. Claude Squirrel-guy and make friends. There's nothing for tourists to do here at night but hang out at the lodge, so I can probably catch up with him there."

Xander figured that even if Claude didn't know who Dr. Tapper was or why Orest was talking about boxes and small planes, he might have heard Orest say something helpful along the way. Perhaps Orest dropped a breadcrumb that Claude could point to, allowing Xander to stop the machine that seemed set to go off on an expedited timeline.

15

THE WIND BLEW Eddie and Paca through the door into the lodge. They were laughing as they stomped their feet on the mat and made their way over to Elyssa, sitting at the bar.

Pulling off his coat and draping it over a stool, Eddie said. "Uncle Orest was looking a little gray when I saw him go into his room." He climbed onto the seat. "He said that two bowls of cobbler and ice cream were too much, and he needed to go to bed."

"There are worse ways to go than death by cobbler," Paca said as he sat on Elyssa's other side. "He does this every year. And every year, it's the same dessert and the same bellyache. He'll be fine tomorrow."

"I hope that's right," Elyssa said. "He's leaving out on that early flight."

Paca lifted his chin when the bartender came over. "Rum-spiked hot chocolate, please." As usual, Paca had left his hat on his head and his scarf wrapped around his neck.

Elyssa wondered if that was an Alaskan habit or a Paca habit.

"Same," Eddie added.

"A glass of sparkling water for me, no ice, please," Elyssa ordered.

"Orest flying again does make me a little worried," Paca said. "Orest isn't getting any younger, and he traveled from Normandy to Alaska, which was already a lot. And now he says he's flying to San Francisco and on to Singapore, that's hard-core even if he has a sleeping pod and first-class care."

"Mmm. I'm not sure I can blame the look you saw on Uncle Orest's face wholly on a maple ice cream upset stomach," Elyssa frowned. "I think it's something else. He's been pale and distracted since he was on the phone this morning," Elyssa said. "As Eddie will tell you, I'm not one who minds doing a little eavesdropping on loved ones, but Uncle Orest was speaking in Slovak. When I asked, he said he had everything under control, and I shouldn't worry so much."

"Eat. Eat. Look at the beauty. Eat." Paca laughed.

"That's Uncle Orest for sure," Elyssa said. "I think what-ever is taking him to Singapore is a concern for him. There's something that's happening in the family. But he didn't share, and since I don't know anyone else from over there, I thought it was rude to pry."

"It was nice of him to allow us to continue with our plans. Tomorrow is going to be a blast out on the sled." Eddie grinned. "Are you excited?"

"Hey, yeah. Eddie, listen," Elyssa said. "I'm not doing great in this cold. Circulation for me is already hard. This is just a bad combination. It was worth a try, but I know my limits."

Eddie ran his fingers down her arm and grabbed her hand.

"Do we need to go?" He swung his gaze to the window where the flutter of snow was picturesque against the dark of night. "We should go."

"I should go," Elyssa corrected. "You should stay. I have a car coming around first thing in the morning. I booked the first flight out."

"You can't leave without me," Eddie said.

"Of course, I can. You're going to watch the race start with Paca. He knows the ropes." She turned toward Paca. "You'll take good care of Eddie, won't you?"

"You'll get to meet the wife and kiddos," Paca said, looking up from his phone. "Hey Eddie, this is the site you were asking about with the different sled teams."

Eddie rounded to stand between Paca and Elyssa, and the two men lowered their heads over Paca's phone.

Elyssa turned as a guy walked through the main door with an enormous German Shepherd by his side. Frosted with snow, the German Shepherd shook his fur clean as the man stomped his boots, then shrugged off his coat, hanging it along with his fur hat on one of the many hall trees.

Something about this guy pulled Elyssa's full attention, and she forgot, for a moment, that she was an adult woman in an adult world where manners and social norms should be followed.

Instead, she just let herself gaze and speculate.

He was a reasonable looking man. Giant. He was reasonable looking for a giant. Not a lumberjack giant, though he looked like he was fine in the woods. Not a corporate giant, though he had reasonable hair that could be interpreted as "office clean cut" or maybe a busy guy who didn't like the fuss. Easy to go to the gym in the morning, take a quick shower—no, a nice long wash off with lots of rubbing and suds that smelled of warm spices—and head off for his day.

She imagined that he'd go to his meeting in a bespoke suit. Not that he looked hyper-monied, but did they make suits that big? The suit would fit him beautifully, Eddie-approved beautifully. He'd have his briefcase in one hand and a coffee in the other. Black. A medium black coffee—a very reasonable amount of coffee without any frou-frou about it.

Just *look* at him.

He bypassed any plaid flannel cosplay and wore a rust-colored Henley with an unzipped brown fleece. The Henley looked like it had been around long enough that it was probably buttery soft from all the washings. It was exactly the kind of thing that she loved to sleep in.

Yes, he wore reasonable clothes for an Alaskan lodge.

They looked expensive but not over-the-top. Upper-middle price range because he invested in quality and was not concerned with labels, but more about long-term functionality. Reasonable colors, not bright, not camo. Just an everyday guy-giant with an absolutely beautiful dog.

Blendable.

Forgettable.

Well, his body wasn't exactly forgettable, she'd admit. He hit the gym, but not in a gym-bro kind of way that she hated. He was doing something to build functional muscles. Handball. Tennis? No. Lacrosse came to mind. Violent enough, aggressive enough.

Yes, he was too developed—what she could see of him and what she could imagine—not to play some kind of competitive sport. Elyssa pursed her lips together as she contemplated him.

"He is a good-looking guy," Eddie said, leaning in.

Elyssa startled. "What?"

"That guy with the dog? And I agree, he wears those pants just right around his hips and thighs."

"Eddie, stop!" Elyssa hissed, shooting a glance toward Paca and feeling relief that he had his attention fixed on texting.

"It wasn't me staring at his package with those 'let me unwrap it' vibes." Eddie's eyes twinkled with mischief.

"I wasn't!"

"Weren't you?' Eddie raised his brows. "Okay. My bad. From my angle, it looked like you were interested."

"I'm horrified," Elyssa whispered. "How long was I looking like that?"

"Long enough, girlfriend. I'm surprised he didn't wander over and say, 'I'm game. Let's go play.' He must be very dedicated to someone back home. A lesser man would have pounced."

"I might not be his gender of choice." Elyssa forced herself not to look back over at the guy.

"Oh, sweetheart, that man is a hundred percent not gay."

"Okay. I'm not his type."

Eddie rolled his eyes. "You're everyone's type. You tick all the boxes. Nope. He's got to be married and very dedicated. It's the only thing that makes sense right now."

"He does have a good-looking dog." Elyssa, losing the battle with herself, glanced over her shoulder. "Beautiful." And she kind of got stuck there, taking in the picture. Giant sprawled on the leather couch, book in hand, dog curled at his feet, roaring fire to the side. She breathed in and let out a heavy sigh.

"Mm hmm." Eddie leaned in a little farther. "You're still staring."

"Lost in thought," she countered.

"You're drooling."

She rounded on him, swiping at her mouth. "I am not."

Eddie laughed. "Be brave. Invite him for a drink or some dessert," he gave his brows a double flick.

"Do you think?" Actually, a little dessert would feel very satisfying.

"Why not?" Eddie turned as Paca slapped a hand on his shoulder.

"That guy that just pulled up?" Paca pointed toward the window. "That's Dan. You need to meet him," Paca said, swinging his parka on.

Eddie stood and reached for his coat while Elyssa poured electrolytes into the glass the bartended set in front of her, then gave it a swirl. "I'll wait for you two in here. The cold is too hard on me."

Eddie turned to her. "We won't be long. It's too cold for me, too, if I'm out there for more than a couple of minutes." Eddie flicked a glance toward the giant on the leather couch. "You're okay?"

"I'm fine."

Eddie bumped into her. "If you need company, you could always wander over to warm yourself in front of the fire and give the guy an opportunity to say hi."

She waggled her fingers as they headed out the door. "I'll consider it."

She didn't have time to consider it.

As soon as Eddie and Paca moved away, a new guy stepped forward, picking up a stool and setting it back down in such a way that Elyssa felt like he was boxing her in.

She turned away from him and reflexively rested her hand over her glass. "Can I help you?" Elyssa asked as the man sat down, facing her. She'd pitched her voice to shut him down before he even got started.

"Thought I'd be friendly," he said with a slow smile that looked like it had been practiced in the mirror, perhaps refined for social media. She imagined he was one of those men who pulled off his shirt and chopped wood with his well-oiled and meticulously trimmed beard. He was looking at her hand on her drink. "Welcome to Lumberjack, Alaska. You're new here." He lifted his chin toward the bartender. "Beer."

"I'm with friends," Elyssa said.

The beer guy looked around. "I don't see anyone."

"I'm not interested in a conversation with you," she said more directly.

"Listen," he leaned in, "I know that you're not from around here, and it's cold out and all. But the frigid bitch act doesn't do well in this part of the country."

Elyssa leaned in, too, so he knew she wasn't intimidated. "Hey, Gaston, you have a bit of something caught in your teeth, just there." And with her teeth clamped down, she spread her lips wide, digging her nail beside her eye tooth.

16

———

XANDER
Saturday
Lumberjack, Alaska

HAD he noticed the blonde-haired woman with the delicate features and the men flocking around her at the bar?

He had.

Had he pretended to read his book while he watched her watch him?

Yup.

Did he notice the new guy's approach went over like a lead balloon?

Yeah, and whatever she said to him, dropped the guy's testosterone through the floor to the basement. It had Xander grinning behind the pages of his book.

Now did he see her, drink in hand, heading his way?

Absolutely.

So did Radar. Radar lifted himself to a sitting position, striking his most regal pose.

Xander looked down to catch Radar's gaze, and he would swear Radar was telegraphing the message that he was doing his best to be a good wingman.

"Good job, buddy," Xander said quietly, giving Radar a scritch.

She was definitely heading his way. Xander let his focus drift up to catch her gaze. Did Xander think this woman was interested in him?

Could be.

But according to his female friends, Xander looked safe, especially when Radar was around. After whatever tension just happened at the bar between the local stud and her, she was probably heading this way because he was a—

"Hi," she stopped next to the lounge chair. "I don't know you. But you look like a nice guy. I'm wondering if you would mind if I just hung out over here for a few?" She smiled.

Yup, he was a safe harbor.

That smile. *Wow.* Xander's blood raced through his veins. He wasn't sure he could catch his breath. "However long you need," he managed as he closed his book.

Xander shot a look at the guy on the bar stool and back to her. "Are you shaking?"

"Maybe a bit." She came around the chair, setting her drink on the table, and lowered herself into the deep cushions.

Was the shaking from her interaction with the guy or the cold? Xander started to take off his fleece to hand it to her.

"No, thank you, if that's for me, you're kind, but I'm just … I don't enjoy those kinds of interactions."

"Bear in the woods," Xander said as Radar moved to sit between his knees.

Having Radar there was grounding. It helped.

This woman was doing something to Xander's circuitry, and his cheeks had gone numb.

Radar looked up at him. His eyes said, *I mean, what the hell, man? Get it together.*

Xander patted Radar's side to reassure his doggo that he was doing his best under these unprecedented conditions.

"Ha! Yeah, well, if you're referring to the viral question of whether I would prefer to be with a man or a bear in the woods," the woman said, "that whole thing takes on a different meaning here in Alaska. I usually answer that with black bears in mind, since I'm from northern Virginia. I might need a little more research about grizzlies and polar bears before I answer that, while out here in the middle of nowhere." She leaned forward, stretching out her hand. "Elyssa."

And before Xander could shake, Radar lifted his paw and slipped it between her fingers.

"Hello, handsome. Aren't you the best dog ever?" she asked, then looked up at Xander with a smile even more radiant than before.

"This is Radar."

Xander followed Radar's gaze and saw the man Elyssa had fled, putting his arm out on the wall, capturing a woman. The bartender called out the guy's name, barking a warning, and the guy dropped his arm and stood up. The woman slipped to the side and hustled to her group.

Elyssa had taken in the scene as well. "Research complete, I'll chance the grizzly."

"That guy is terrible."

"If you're about to say, 'that's not me' or 'that's not every guy,' it's a poor answer. While I wait for my friend to get back, I appreciate the safe-feeling harbor, but—"

"But you're monitoring to see if your gut kicks in telling you that you made a poor choice, thinking I was harmless?"

"To be clear, I chose your dog." The return of a warm smile

took the edge off and made this exchange feel flirty rather than tense.

Xander liked the saltiness of it. Johnna White sprinkled salt on her melon, telling him that it made it taste all the sweeter. And now Xander understood that it could be true. "Radar's a great dog. Now, back to the terrible guy at the bar thing, it's a tough one for a man to navigate. I've had to come up with strategies."

Radar stood up, walked over to Elyssa, staring at her, his body rigid.

"Hello to you, too, sweetheart." She reached toward his neck and wriggled her fingers in his fur.

"Radar, come here," Xander said.

Elyssa reached for her drink, and Xander noticed she was wearing a medical alert bracelet. As Radar moved back between his legs, he whispered. "I got it, buddy, thank you." Xander stroked down Radar's neck and chest as he nodded toward Elyssa's glass. "What are you drinking?"

"Electrolytes." She lifted the glass. "Gotta stay extra-hydrated in the cold."

Xander raised a finger in the air. "Nachos with salsa and a shaker of salt," he called out. Then focused on Elyssa. "Will you eat some nachos?"

"Yes, thanks." She gulped down her drink, then pulled her purse around, drew out a bottle, and filled her glass again. "You were telling me about your strategies. Is one of them sitting off to the side, looking calm and capable, but also like you're in a steady relationship, and then the women flutter toward your light for safety?"

"Couple things there." Xander pulled his brow together, the shadow of a smile winking at the corners of his mouth. "That isn't a bad play, to be honest. Second, I look like a man in a steady relationship? I think I might like some more information on the last one, mainly because I'm not seeing anyone right now."

Xander paused as warmth spread across his chest, and he felt like he could, in fact, be a light that a woman could flutter to for safety. And then he thought he had lost his damned mind and wondered if he hadn't touched palytoxin in Orest Kalinsky's suitcase. After all, one of the weirdly dangerous effects of palytoxins was a sense of euphoria.

And euphoria was a pretty good word to describe these sensations he was experiencing.

Elyssa turned at the sound of the lodge door and signaled as a guy stomped the snow from his boots, looking her way. "He's not in a relationship," she called.

"Seriously?" the guy asked, shucking his coat. He focused on Xander. "You totally give off contented at home vibes."

Radar wandered back over to Elyssa, but this time, he booped her on the leg. He looked Xander's way, then booped her in the leg again.

"I've got it, Radar. Come here," Xander said.

A second man shuffled in and shut the door behind him.

"I am content at home," Xander said. "Is that something that's tied to being in a relationship?" He was laughing now. This was an absurd conversation, and it was fun.

"Well, okay, let me say it doesn't look like you're on the prowl. I'm Eddie, by the way."

"Ender," Xander replied. "And you're right. I'm not prowling out of self-preservation."

"I'm Paca." The other guy said as he joined them, pulling off his hat and loosening his scarf as he sat in front of the fire. "What's this now about self-preservation?" This guy showed up with his pointy face, huge liquid brown eyes, and a head full of crazy hair.

He may call himself Paca, but this was most definitely Dr. Claude Burns, squirrel researcher.

Xander's mark.

The bartender came over and set mugs of hot cocoa in front of Eddie and Paca, then placed the nacho platter and shaker on the table in the middle of the group. Xander gave his room number as he pushed the salt in front of Elyssa.

"Please help yourselves. I got the nachos to share," Xander said. "Okay, on the topic of self-preservation, I'm a visitor in Alaska. The danger is that if I were looking for someone whose company I would enjoy," Xander made a concerted effort not to flick his gaze toward Elyssa because that would have been over-the-top junior high shit, "it's very possible that I could make a significant connection here in Alaska. There are only three outcomes, and all of them are terrible."

"Truly?" Elyssa slid her boots off, then curled her long legs into the chair. "How do you figure?"

"If I make a romantic connection, first, she might just sever the connection, and I'd be left brokenhearted. Second, I leave Alaska with the intention that we hold something together long distance, and I go to bed in Virginia every night sad and alone."

"Pitiful," she said with laughter in her eyes.

Yes, Xander had heard Elyssa say she was from Virginia. Yes, he wanted her to know that he was, too. He thought he'd done that smoothly.

"Or third?" Eddie asked.

"Third, I leave heartbroken and decide I can't hold it together for a long-distance relationship, so I move here to Lumberjack, Alaska, to be with her. It's lovely, don't get me wrong, just, I can't with the cold."

"Before you came in, we were speaking of bears." Elyssa flicked her head in bar-guy's direction.

"Oh, sorry, kid," Eddie said. "I didn't mean to leave you to the wolves, bears, wildlife in general."

"I found safe harbor with Radar." She pointed to Xander's dog.

"Gorgeous puppy," Eddie said, then turned to Elyssa. "So, bears?"

"I was about to hear some 'dealing with women strategy' when you came in."

"Not so much a strategy as an awareness," Xander said. "I've spent a lot of time listening to women explain why they prefer the bear. I get that just my physical presence on a hiking trail, for example, can terrify women who don't know me from Adam. Adam, by the way, is my brother, and we do look alike."

"Boo." Elyssa wrinkled her nose. "You use that joke a lot ." She lifted the saltshaker and caught Xander's gaze.

"Guilty," Xander said. "And salt away."

Elyssa sprinkled the salt heavily on the far side of the platter, leaving the rest for others to decide how salty they liked their food.

"So, how do you keep women hikers from being terrified?" Eddie asked.

"Usually, I talk to Radar about how he's a good boy. I crouch down to rub his scruff, and he makes those deep guttural sounds of pleasure, so the woman knows my dog is relaxed, that means my dog doesn't feel tension in me, I'm not revving up for something."

"True if she knows dogs," Elyssa said, with a shifting light in her eye that made Xander think that she was settling deeper into the conversation, growing more comfortable. "I think it's a gut knowing that if a dog is blissing, there's not a lot of danger."

"Yeah. If I don't have Radar with me, and I see a woman, I just say, 'I see you coming up the path, how do you want me to handle this, so you feel safe?' That's usually enough to get a raised hand and a 'you're good.'"

"I get that," Elyssa said, "It means you understand the danger, you know the lingo, and you're comfortable with consent. And it means some woman or women educated you about their experiences, and you took it to heart and modified your behavior. I know for sure that whatever you wanted to do to me, you could do it. I have only your moral compass and integrity keeping me safe. That and your dog." She stared at him for a long moment and then asked, "Did you say your name is Ender?"

"Ender Belov." Xander didn't use a cover in the field. His work, so far, hadn't required him to develop a secondary persona. Being two people was time-consuming and mind-bending, so he preferred it that way. But to keep himself as unsearchable on the Internet as possible, Xander used his call sign, Ender, in the field as a layer of anonymity.

"Ender?" It was as if Elyssa was tasting it to see if she liked it in her mouth.

And that thought sent Xander's hormones flooding through his system. "It's a nickname I got in the military," he said evenly.

"Ender. Like you ended things?" Her brows pulled together. "Ended *people*?"

Huh, no one had asked him that before. It was a reasonable question, especially given the topic they'd started with. Her facial muscles stiffened as she grew wary.

"I ended conflicts with analysis," he said to wipe away the images she might be conjuring. It was true enough if he was malleable with the definition of the word 'analysis.' It was interesting, though, that while Xander trained to say what was necessary to get a job done, he felt uncomfortable obfuscating when answering Elyssa. "My given name isn't much different –

It's Xander Belov." He smiled. "You can call me Xander if you like it better."

Did it matter that Squirrel-guy knew his name?

"Ender from Xander," Eddie lightened things back up. "At least they didn't go with Dander."

"Are you calling him flaky?" Elyssa asked with a laugh. She turned back to Xander, "They could have gone for your last name instead, Belov could easily morph into 'Beloved.'"

Did she turn pink when she said that? Was that a blush?

"Can you imagine trying to get through boot camp called Beloved?" Paca snort-laughed.

"No one ever suggested that before?' Elyssa asked.

"Never." Xander let a slow smile spread across his face. "Well, my grandmother called me beloved, but I was about five, and it came with a cookie."

And as fun as this conversation was, there was humanity to save, Xander reminded himself.

XANDER
 Saturday
 Lumberjack, Alaska

IT WAS time to let the squirrel guy bring up Orest Kalinsky's name. "What's the connection? How'd you all meet?" Xander asked. They were obviously here together, and he needed to know if Eddie and Elyssa were involved with Orest, too.

"We just met Paca today," Eddie said. "But I conferred bestie status on Elyssa the night she threw me over her shoulder and sprinted with me out of a party, popped me in her car, and drove us into the sunset."

Xander waited for the punch line.

"Dude, what?" Paca leaned forward.

"I was at this cocktail party barbeque thing. Let's just say I was on the wrong side of the tracks, and it wasn't a safe zone for someone of my delicate stature."

Eddie was as thin as a bean pole, but he was about as tall as Xander, and Xander was six feet three. Eddie was hardly delicate. Granted, Elyssa was tall, too. Five ten maybe five eleven? Hard to tell with boots on.

The image of her walking across his lodge room, bare feet, long legs, his T-shirt just brushing the tops of her thighs, slid unbidden through his imagination.

Eddie was perched on the arm of Elyssa's chair as he told the story. "These frat boys, smelling strongly of beer, surrounded me. And they had a lot to say about people 'like me.'" He threw those last two words into finger-flexed quotation marks. "And how they were going to punish me for daring to be different from them. Now, I had never been in a fight before. I mean," he spread his hands wide, "I'd have no idea what to do in a fight even today. I am of the strong belief that everyone should just chill out. So, this boy-circle starts to edge closer and closer, like someone was pulling a lasso around a poor little calf. And all I can think to do is cover my face to protect my eyes when I hear. ''Scuse me. 'Scuse me coming through. He's mine.'" Eddie was animatedly miming this sequence. "Then Elyssa—I had no idea who she was at the time —grabs this guy's shoulder and tears him out of her way. I mean fierce! She goes, 'Yup, he's mine.' Then she bends at the waist, shoves her shoulder into my midsection, grabs me by my thighs, and stands. I am both confused and *incredibly* impressed. And also, all the blood was running to my head, so slightly dizzy. Anyway, she powers through the other side of the circle, through the party, and sets me down outside by her car and says, 'Can I give you a ride somewhere safer?'"

"What?" Paca was grinning hard from his cross-legged seat on the floor.

"Oh, Elyssa here was on our university rugby team. She is a warrior." He gritted his teeth and pulled his lips back, making his eyes fierce. "She does that on the field," he relaxed his face. "I'd say she was trying to terrify her opponents, but they're all doing it. Just this side of berserker. Just raw, brutal aggression. Women rugby players scare the living crap out of me."

Elyssa sighed and shook her head at him.

"You?" Xander couldn't keep the incredulity out of his voice. Elyssa presented as warm and soft but also forthright and intelligent. He couldn't imagine her as fierce, though.

"Elyssa," Eddie insisted. "My warrior angel saw I was in trouble and did what she'd trained to do, grab up the opponent who was clinging to the ball and put them down where she wanted them."

"Elyssa for the win!" Paca laughed with victory fists in the air.

"Years ago." She waved a hand through the air. "Back in the day, as they say."

"Wanna see?" Eddie pulled out his phone and started scrolling through his photo album.

"Please don't," Elyssa said quietly. "That was a long time ago." There was just enough wistfulness that caught the edges of her words that Eddie immediately looked contrite and slid his phone away. He followed up with a side hug.

Xander read that as Elyssa was an athlete benched by events. He'd watched it happen to friends and family alike. Some of them came through the change of circumstances okay, but different, some people became so uprooted that they wilted to the point of being unrevivable. Elyssa was obviously resilient in her effort to make a meaningful life for herself, regardless of what had happened.

"Rugby," Paca said. "How did you get interested in that sport?"

"I was a wrestler in high school. There wasn't a girls' team, so I was allowed to compete with the boys' all the way up to the State Championship."

"That means you made State Champion, and they wouldn't let you participate?" Paca asked.

"Exactly. My read on it was that the parents who wanted their boys to get college scholarships were putting up a fuss because they were afraid their sons would miss their opportunity if I showed the males up. But I tell you, a woman's leg strength is formidable."

"It's the truth," Xander said. "When I go to the gym, the women are deadlifting three-fifty-four hundred pounds. The men won't go near that. Arms, shoulders, and skip leg day."

"Butts are the powerhouse." Elyssa had a look of curiosity glinting in her eyes as she looked at Xander, then she blinked it away. "After an article about the situation showed up in the local paper, my future university's Rugby coach contacted me. She said that since there weren't a lot of high schools with girls' rugby teams, they recruited athletes from track and field, and when they could, wrestling. I'd never heard of rugby. The coach showed me a Māori women's team performing the Haka before a match. To me, the utter power they displayed was so antithetical to the messages I had heard growing up. There was such conviction in their power."

"What you're saying is that you were a rebel?" Paca asked.

"You would rebel, too, if your mother wanted you dressed in ruffles and bows and sat you like a doll on a chair."

"True," Paca said. "But I was a boy."

"Your mother didn't do that!" Eddie said to Elyssa.

"She did," Elyssa countered. "I can show you pictures. But soon enough, she learned that life was easier when I ran off my energy. The bigger the girl, the bigger the energy, so when I said wrestling, she adapted."

"I have three kids, and I know for certain that a child shows up with their own personality," Paca said. "I was an early disappointment to my father, who would have reveled in having a child like you, Elyssa. Instead, I wanted to stare at animals through binoculars all day long. Poor dad."

"My mom and dad wanted me to be a musician," Eddie said. "But I was told I have a tin ear. My piano teacher said they shouldn't waste their money."

"Oh, Eddie!" Elyssa exclaimed.

"To be fair. I was actually pretty good. But when anyone was home, I banged around like an elephant trying to play the keys because I said electric guitar, and they said piano. And I was a shitty little kid."

Elyssa turned his way. "Xander, did you disappoint your parents?"

"Every single day. Mostly, I think that I left them feeling lonely because I spent so much time with my nose in my books. I read everything and anything. I wanted to know it all. When I got uncomfortable because I was growing faster than the different body parts could keep up, my doctor suggested going to the gym and lifting weights. And she was right. Lifting and exercising hard took away the aches. I became a book-reading gym rat."

"And when you graduated from high school, what did you do with your brains and brawn?" Elyssa asked.

"I became an analyst." Shit, he hated not giving her a more honest answer. Not telling her the whole truth physically hurt. Now, wasn't that a revelation?

Xander reminded himself that, in this situation, Elyssa was a siren, drawing his attention away when he needed to focus on the rocks around him.

Though thinking of Paca as dangerous was hard for Xander to do with any level of seriousness.

Still, Xander's job wasn't to flirt with an amazing woman.

He was here to thwart Orest Kalinsky, and that meant figuring out why Orest was interested in Paca and his squirrels.

"So, how do you find yourselves in the wilds of Alaska?" Xander looked directly at Paca.

"Me? Oh, I live here. Well, in Fairbanks. I come out to Lumberjack every year to play with sled dogs."

"What kind of work is there in Fairbanks?" Xander asked.

"I'm the only one of us from Alaska," he said. "But we're all scientists. Eddie is in meat."

"Meat?" Well, Kalinsky did have a thing for food. Was that a link? Was Eddie another Carpathian scientist? "Like ranching?" Xander asked.

"No." Eddie shook his head. "No. I produce it in a lab."

"Lab-grown meat?" Xander made a face.

Eddie turned to Paca. "See? Every single time. I'm trying to save the environment. But when I say how I'm doing it, it sounds like I want to make soup out of their old running shoes."

"That's not how you should tell someone what you do," Elyssa scolded.

Eddie tipped his head. "Then how would you do it?"

Elyssa turned to Xander. "Eddie is a NASA scientist."

"Bovine in outer space?" Xander grinned. "Gives a whole new meaning to 'the cow jumped over the moon.'"

Elyssa was laughing.

"NASA has a goal of sending humans to Mars by 2050. Eating solely freeze-dried foods for years on end would be difficult psychologically. They thought," Eddie nodded toward Elyssa, "a fresh salad once a week or so, or some fresh chicken or fish."

"I see," Xander said. If Eddie worked for NASA, he wasn't a Kalinsky fellow. Turning to Squirrel-guy, he asked, "You work for NASA, too?"

"Not until next month."

"And your specialty is?" Xander asked. *Come on, Paca, tell me what you know about Kalinsky's goals.*

"Uhm. Squirrels," he said.

"Squirrels," Xander repeated slowly. "For … for food?"

"Oh no." Paca laughed. "Not for food. You'd starve."

Okay, this was moving too slow, and his getting mini chunks of information would start to sound intrusive. Xander was going to push. "I thought the only squirrels around here are arctic squirrels, known for going into—Wait. Does NASA think they can put the astronauts into hibernation so they can sleep through most of the flight?" He opened his eyes wide, and with his lips held tightly together, he dropped his jaw as he nodded. "Genius if it works. No food. Less air. Less shit." He turned to Elyssa. "Excuse me."

"Don't excuse yourself to me," Elyssa said. "That's a biological consideration the teams need to think through."

"She shits, too," Eddie said.

"Thank you, Eddie. While true, perhaps not a topic for conversation with our new friend."

Xander grinned at her. Yeah, he heard Elyssa add him to their circle. This was good. Tomorrow, he'd hopefully get another shot at trying to find his breadcrumbs, unless, of course, Paca was heading back to Fairbanks in the morning with Orest. "I've always loved reading science fiction. It seems to me that a creative person imagines something, describes it, and then it becomes a possibility in the minds of the scientific community. They start to talk amongst themselves, wondering if that something were feasible. They begin to ask the question, how would you get there? And in their wondering, the baton is passed, and the idea comes to fruition."

Paca closed his eyes and took a breath. When he opened them again, he said, "That was poetic. And so very true."

Eddie clapped his hands on his thighs and suddenly stood. "All right. That's it for me. I was in Paris a couple of days ago, then D.C. to Fairbanks yesterday, and in Lumberjack, Alaska tonight. This has been very hard on me, as I am a man who adores his sleep. And so, I bid you all a good night." He gave a kind of jovial bow. As he came back upright, Eddie shot Paca a look.

Paca obviously understood the meaning because he immediately stood, too. "Time to call home and read the kiddos their bedtime stories, or something. I'll see you all in the morning."

Elyssa stood. "Nope. I'm going to say goodbye to you now, remember? I hired a car to pick me up pretty early. I hope you guys have a cozy night and a lot of fun at the races."

As she hugged them both, Xander thought that, intelligence-wise, he was walking away empty-handed, having learned nothing from Paca. Honestly, he didn't think there was any intel to mine. It didn't seem that any of the three were involved with the doomsday machine, or they wouldn't be this relaxed and convivial.

Once the friends left, Elyssa turned to Xander, who stood to the side. "I should get to bed, too." She reached for her purse. "I heard you give your room number to the waiter. I'm in the room next to yours. And I was just wondering if your cottage is as cute as mine is."

Xander bent to gather Radar's lead. "Why don't you come take a look and tell me what you think?"

They pulled on their coats, and Elyssa tucked comfortably and naturally under his arm as they walked to his room.

What are you thinking, Xander? he asked himself. *I'm thinking that if these are my last few days on Earth, I deserve a taste of heaven.*

18

———

Xander
Sunday
Lumberjack, Alaska

Xander lay on his back, his arms splayed wide, his chest heaving, and he felt sublime.

Euphoric.

Was there even a word to describe this sensation?

Being with Elyssa had been a drug.

"Holy shit," he chuckled, then swept Elyssa's long hair into his hand, lifting it off her face, and bent to kiss her. "Shit." He dropped back down and ran his hand down his face, letting it fall off to the side.

She tipped her head to kiss his chest. "Same."

And as with any new addict, Xander had to make sure he had a way to get his next hit.

"Elyssa, I wanted to talk to you about something."

She eased back on the pillow, so they were looking into each other's eyes.

Xander reached down and laced his fingers with hers. "When we were talking at the Lodge, I said that I wasn't looking for someone while I was here because there were only three scenarios, and all of them had bad outcomes."

She rolled her lips in and seemed to hold her breath.

He lifted a strand of her hair and rubbed it between his fingers. "There's a fourth that I hadn't envisioned. And that was meeting someone with whom I felt a connection, and who might live near me. You said you were from Virginia?"

"Alexandria."

"I'm north of you in Arlington near the Pentagon."

"Close then," she said.

"I'm working away from home for the next bit. But I'd like to stay in touch. And when I'm back on the East Coast, I'd very much like to spend more time getting to know you. But if your job is like mine, that might become a challenge." He gave her an out that would suck, but might leave his heart intact.

"I'd enjoy getting to know you better, too," she said. "I only travel for random conferences and for vacations. Otherwise, I'm at the lab."

Xander reached his arm over her, rolling to grab his phone from the side table. "What do you do in the lab?"

"I do engineering."

"Yeah?" He opened his contacts, tapped the plus sign, and handed his phone to her. "A geek-girl, huh? What kind?"

"I'm a food systems engineer." She paused as she entered her information, saved it, then placed his phone back on the nightstand. "I design interior farming solutions."

Xander's heart pounded against his sternum. A sheen of perspiration salted his skin. He modulated his voice to sound sleepy but interested as she tucked back against him. "How did you, Eddie, and Paca end up out here in Lumberjack?"

"My great uncle invited us," she said, pulling her knee up so her leg sprawled across his hips.

And while his dick danced to attention, the only thought in Xander's mind was, *shit.* Finally, he managed, "Is he here with you, your great uncle?"

"Yes, well, for the moment. He's leaving before I do in the morning. We came because Uncle Orest has a sled team, a hobby that he's passionate about. He comes every year to see his team start the Iditarod."

Shit.

Shit. Shit. Shit.

"The Iditarod is next week. He's leaving?" Xander asked.

"Family crisis, unfortunately."

"I'm sorry. I hope things resolve. And your Uncle knows Eddie and Paca?"

She pushed herself up, straightening her legs, and rolled away from him.

"Where are you going?" Xander's arms wanted to pull her against him and protect her from … from her family. *Shit.*

"I'm coming back to bed with you." She kissed his shoulder before she squirmed out from under the covers. "I need the bathroom."

Xander took the opportunity to pull off his spent condom, knot it, and toss it into the trash, then he reached the end of the bed for his boxer briefs and tugged them on as some kind of shield between them when she came back.

Reaching for her phone, he found her driver's license in the back sleeve. There it was, *Elyssa Kalinsky Landers.* He snapped a picture.

Kalinsky.

He'd slept with the enemy. He was always going to have to call it in and report his sexual activity. But this was not going to go over well.

Xander listened to Elyssa's progress in the bathroom. As she washed her hands, he swiped his encryption app open. Sooner was better than later, he thought as he texted Hiro.

XANDER: **I had a sexual encounter. Forwarding a picture of her driver's license. Dig up what you can. I'll call in as soon as I'm able.**

WITHOUT CALCULATING the time zone or worrying if Hiro was sleeping, Xander pressed send, waited for delivery, then erased the message from his phone.

When Elyssa emerged from the bathroom, she picked up the shirt he'd been wearing earlier and tugged it over her head.

Something about seeing her dressed in his clothes made him feel–well, it was a new sensation, animal in nature. It was as if he wanted to stand in front of her and claim her as "mine."

When he turned the sensation into mental words, he remembered a conversation with his female friends. They said they loved to hear the growl of "mine" when they wanted it in a relationship. It made them feel safe and cared for. But they found it abhorrent to them when it came with the feeling of being owned and manipulated.

Those kinds of conversations had fallen not exactly on deaf ears but certainly on unfertile soil. There was no way for Xander to understand the nuance that his women-friends explained to him because Xander had never in his life felt the word "mine" or anything even close.

Now, it was a boulder of a thought, massive and heavy.

This sensation was unimaginable to him yesterday morning.

And yet here he was.

What *was* he thinking?

He was thinking … well, he was thinking that what he felt toward Elyssa right now was the look in Nutsbe and Finley's eyes when they talked about their partners. Sorrow that their loved ones were in danger's way and an utter conviction that they would throw themselves bodily in front of anything that came against them.

Those thoughts were all well and good if the loved one lived on the same side of sanity and morality.

It was devastating to think that not only could he not intervene to help Elyssa, but he was going to be one of the people working to bring her family to justice.

If she was involved in wrongdoing, Elyssa was their target.

He couldn't believe that Elyssa had anything to do with hurting people.

And if that was wishful thinking on his part, just look at how Radar stood as her protector.

Okay, sure, Elyssa could be a sociopath for all he knew, acting one way with him and turning around and advancing her evil family. He could choose to believe that he'd made a hellacious mistake, or he could trust his dog.

From the end of the bed, Radar opened his eyes, and in the dim light, he lifted one brow then the other.

"It's okay, buddy. We'll figure this out."

When Elyssa snuggled back into his arms, pressing her round ass up next to his hips, his dick stood at the ready. He ignored it.

He *tried* to ignore it.

This was such a mind-bender.

In the dim light of the side table lamp, he lifted Elyssa's hand and read her medical band, POTS. It was just as he suspected from Radar's boops back in the lodge. Radar only relaxed his vigilance after Elyssa curled herself into the chair, pulling her legs to her chest, gulped her electrolyte drink, and ate the salty nachos with a heavy-handed sprinkle from the salt shaker.

With his finger on the bracelet, Elyssa started to contract her muscles and pull away. Her medical condition was obviously not open for discussion, so he slid his finger along the script-written tattoo that decorated her wrist. "'My little bit,'" he read. "Is that a special someone?"

She relaxed her muscles. He'd been right. Her diagnosis was a topic that she wasn't open to discussing. And she was entitled to her privacy.

"That's my Desmond Tutu reminder that there are situations around me that I can ease."

"That's very sweet." He licked her lips before kissing her. "*You* are very sweet."

Settling back on his pillow, he said, "Little bit," as he rubbed the words with his thumb, trying to find a way to understand what was happening. "How does that work its way into your world?"

"I'm a scientist, and I hope that my work goes on to benefit humanity. I'm not in a position to do something grand. Desmond Tutu had a world stage when he asked us to do our little acts. Anything big I might accomplish is years away. So today, this minute, I can make something a little better. A smile. A helping hand. A design that feeds a hungry child." She turned to catch his gaze. "That's such an interesting glimmer in your eyes. Confusion?"

Torment, to be honest.

"Not necessarily confusion," Xander said. "But you really do present as a contradiction. The way you handled the Gaston guy was," he kissed the tips of his fingers and spread them wide to release his appreciation into the wind, "chef's kiss. Not a waver. You had it all handled. You are graceful with your strengths." And because he really meant it, he put his finger back on her medical bracelet. "I'm sorry about the POTS—it's obviously a touchy subject. It must be a real challenge. I don't know much about the condition. Is it genetic?"

"Can be," she said, and this time she wasn't pulling away from the subject. "In my case, I became symptomatic after a bout of COVID. It's possible that it will go away. And it's possible that it's here for life. Fingers crossed for the go-away prognosis."

"Absolutely," Xander exhaled. "How are you feeling right now?"

She answered by lifting her chin and smiling the most come-hither, wanton smile he'd ever been gifted.

What an f'ed up world this was.

Did he want her? Every cell, every atom, every pulse of energy in his body said, yes!

Instead, he reached for the light and clicked it off before wrapping her in his arms and tucking the blanket under her chin. He tried to signal that he wasn't going to follow through, but that wasn't meant as a rebuff of any sort.

She shuffled around, moving a hand down to rest on Radar's head, and with a sigh that sounded like contentment, Elyssa stilled.

19

Sunday

Lumberjack, Alaska

WHEN ELYSSA SLIPPED into REM sleep, Xander reached for his kit, pulling his throat mic into place around his neck so that he could speak silently and the technology could pick up his words from the movement of his larynx alone.

Xander spent a moment typing up a report on his encounter with Claude, Eddie, and Elyssa at the lodge, listing the details that were significant to the case like the fact that Eddie had said they'd just met Paca that day, Xander had no clue that Elyssa was in the Kalinsky family until she brought up her great uncle in a post coital discussion. He pressed SEND, then waited for Hiro's RECEIVED.

Giving Hiro a moment to read it over, Xander dropped magnetic comms into his ear canals so he could hear without visible technology.

Then he made the phone call.

"Xander, checking in."

"Xander, you're on speaker phone in my office," Hiro said. "White's here with me."

"You're sounding robotic," White said. "Is she sleeping next to you, so you have to use the voice amplifier?"

"Affirmative. Hey, White, you're working late." Xander was forcing himself to keep this word choice light. Tone couldn't be discerned over this type of communicator.

"Here it's early," White said. "I'm having my second cup of coffee. Listen, a report was forwarded to me. I have an update on the Zorics' machine's movement. Satellite imagery captured images of the Kyrgyzstan mountains. With the newest advances to the system, AI was able to find recent movements. The AWG team wasn't far from the site when the team was in the mountains. It was in Scott's search area, in the northwest quadrant. If Tink and Peter hadn't been captured—I'm not blaming them, please, don't hear it that way—just had they not stumbled into the wrong place at the wrong time, your team would have found the machine. But life happens, and here we are."

"Which is where?" Xander asked.

"A van moved in," White said. "A van moved out."

"It's not very big, then." Xander knew the technology had to be on the small side if the Zorics were moving it around and testing outcomes between different countries. But still, it would have been nice if the machine were bigger than an elephant and not small enough to fit in a van. "Crap."

"Agreed," Hiro said. "In this case, bigger would have been better."

"Were the images clear enough to make out specifics?" Xander asked.

"It looked like a machine," White said.

"Helpful." And because he knew the comms didn't inflect to show sarcasm, he labeled it for his team. "Sorry, sarcasm isn't warranted." He took a breath. "White, did you have a chance to read the report I just sent Hiro?"

"I did."

"What are your thoughts about this Lumberjack, Alaska situation?" he asked. "Why would Orest be talking to a squirrel person, a meat guy, and a food engineer?"

"I'm just now being apprised of how this contact proceeded," White said. "Do you think you have an in with this great-niece, Elyssa?"

Xander's whole body stiffened. "Well, I slept with her."

"Not the kind of 'in' I was referring to, but alright." That was White's sardonic humor.

Xander knew she didn't mean anything by it. Under any other circumstance, he'd mark the clever play on words. But when it came to Elyssa? "Not funny. Can we be respectful, please?"

"Do you have emotional ties to her now?" White asked.

"She's interesting, intelligent, and kind. Am I ready for her to have my babies?" When Xander asked that, he was surprised that he felt a momentary bubble of joy. Then he mentally popped it. Xander decided to keep things neutral with the team again, choosing to keep his words light. "I wore a condom, so that would be a no."

"Let me ask again," White said, the mild ribbing having fallen away. "If you had to target this woman, could you do it? I mean, an 'in' is an 'in,' right? Can you exploit the situation, or should we send someone else to take your place? Someone who didn't just bang the enemy?" Yeah, White was pissed with this turn of events. As she should be. He was angry with how this was playing out, too.

"Bang isn't ... please don't," Xander said.

"No, I'm sure it was a magical moment," White said dryly. "But in case she's about to destroy the world in some crazed terror attack, I'm going to say this as plainly as I can: Don't get emotionally involved."

"Noted," Xander said. "No problem there. Let's move past this."

"To your question about the four people in Lumberjack, this is what we have," Hiro said. "We'd already been working on Orest's movements into the United States. Eddie Baylor and Elyssa Kalinsky-Landers were on the same plane as Orest, flying out of Newark. We'd also noted that they each had a room at the same hotel as Orest when they stayed overnight in Fairbanks."

"I videotaped Orest boarding alone," Xander said. "Did they all come out of D.C. together?"

"Negative, Orest flew up earlier in the day. In the couple of minutes since you sent your report, we were able to check the date that Eddie and Elyssa got their tickets. That was done this past Tuesday. At that late date, I'd imagine they took what they could get by way of flights. Their layover was skin-of-the-teeth."

"Okay," Xander said, looking down at Elyssa's peaceful silhouette and pulling the blanket up to cover her back.

"We did a dive into the connections between the four. Claude is Orest's researcher in Fairbanks. We'll set him aside for the moment. Elyssa told you she has a familial connection to Orest Kalinsky, and you said Eddie is Elyssa's friend. Before the flight to Alaska, Orest, Elyssa, and Eddie were in Paris together—or at least they all passed through customs at the same time."

"Elyssa calls him Uncle Orest," Xander said.

"Yes, we're looking into which branch of the family tree she's swinging from," White said. "More on that when we have it."

"I saw her picture," Hiro began, "I—"

"Not a single other word about Elyssa that's not case-related." Xander's newfound protectiveness became a growl in his chest. "There are boundaries."

"Case related," Hiro said. "Chill out. I saw her picture, and she doesn't have the Zoric coloring."

"Going back to my earlier question to you about your emotional proximity to this woman," White said, "by making an intimate connection, you have a foot into the inner circle."

"Inadvertently. I had zero idea," Xander said. "I wasn't using her."

"Serendipity, then," White said. "Xander, I'm serious here. I'm listening to you and, damned, man, it sounds like you've fallen over a cliff."

"Nope. The comms must be playing with my voice. I'm good. I've got this," he lied.

"Okay," Hiro said, "play it cool while the profilers do their work. We'll get back to you as we have insights." There was a smile in Hiro's voice when he said, "Want to hear some shit?"

"You weren't already giving me shit?" Xander asked.

"Not even close to this. I was conducting AI analysis that included Orest's and your routes at Newark Airport. We tracked Orest by CCV cameras. I included the track we have from your phone. His, you already know about. Nothing new there. Yours is the interesting one. During the stretch when you were moving the acid box from the men's bathroom to the field, when you got exactly a hundred meters from the tower—and I mean *exactly* a hundred meters—tower communications came back online."

"Let's talk that through," Xander's heart was racing again. Ever since he talked to Anna in Bratislava, he felt like he'd been running a marathon. He remembered what she said about having to pace her room at night with a pillow to stifle her screams. He got it. This was unlike any battle he'd fought in the war. This was an existential threat to humanity that seemingly left the heads of intelligence unperturbed when it should be a five-alarm, all-hands-on-deck event.

Xander rubbed his thumb along the fine bone in Elyssa's arm where she'd tattooed her good intentions. "I'm listening," Xander brought his focus back to the conversation. "Was that when I moved off the tarmac onto the field? Because that was the moment when I smelled the acid."

"A few strides before that," Hiro said. "Which tells me it's probable because it would take a few strides before the scent wafted up to your nostrils."

"What I'm hearing about the exact one-hundred-meter point," Xander said, "is that as long as the bag was left unfound in the airport, it could potentially continue interfering with tower communications with the planes, and those planes would have remained at risk?"

"Either that or it's a strange happenstance," Hiro said. "The timing is why I think that the carry-on was involved in the communications crisis. But there's no way we'll be able to prove any of that."

Xander's phone buzzed. "Incoming from Orest's room. I'm looping you in."

Xander made out the sounds of someone getting out of bed. A pee stream hit the toilet. There was a flush. Some heavy breathing and the zipper on his case.

"He didn't wash his hands," White whispered.

Xander was about to switch the surveillance to videotape when English was spoken over what must be Orest's phone, set on speaker.

"You have everything set up?" Orest asked, then he coughed up some morning phlegm and spit it out.

"We're a go. I've got it handled," an unidentified, American-accented male said.

"My car arrive early. I leave now," Orest replied, ending the call.

Xander glanced at the clock; it was zero four hundred.

Over the room surveillance, they heard shuffling and banging, followed by a click of the door.

There was nothing else.

"He's on the move," Hiro said.

"Hiro, does Xander need to shadow him?" White asked.

"We've got access to his phone. We can track him that way," Hiro said. "Better that Xander stays in Elyssa's good graces."

"It would be odd if Xander kicked her out of bed in the middle of the night, then packed and drove away," White agreed. "Elyssa would mention it to her uncle. I would, anyway."

"Look," Hiro said, "it's been a stressful couple of days, and you're still recovering from getting jumped, Xander. Get some sleep. I'll listen to his phone and mark anything that comes up. It's a two-hour drive to Fairbanks with no side roads."

"Wilco. One other thing, though. Did you figure out why he's heading to San Francisco?" Xander asked. "I'm worried about the boxes he mentioned. Specifically, I'm thinking about when Russia planted magnesium incendiary devices at logistics hubs in Germany and the UK. While they were found because they accidentally went off before the cargo was loaded, if those devices had lit up over the ocean, with as hot as magnesium fires burn, it would be a conflagration. Is it at all possible that the boxes might be caught up in something like that?"

"Washington sent a backchannel message to the Kremlin to knock it off," Hiro said. "They said if a flight went down, it was an act of war, and we'd act accordingly. If war was the Zoric family's aim, why not just blow up a plane so everyone understood their game? Why mess with the system to drive a jet into the ocean? The same number of people are dead. But in the act of exploding a plane, there had to be retribution. In the case where a plane simply disappeared, there was only confusion and grief."

"They want something big enough to dial geopolitics back to the seventies and eighties, putting the USSR back on the map," White said. "But that something has to be just under the threshold of war. That's a fine line. They've spent considerable time and resources trying to perfect their balancing act, but they're also hedging their bets by heading to an escape hatch on Davidson's Realm, in case their calculations were wrong."

"What did the back channel communication produce?" Xander asked.

"Poland arrested four people over that," Hiro said. "We're pretty sure that Russia handed the names and evidence over to smooth the waves. Russia denies that it was involved in any part of the events."

"And they're right," Xander said. "Russia herself didn't do it. It was the families with whom they had a wink-wink, nod-nod relationship. The families are doing the things that Russia wants done but also wants to keep at arm's length. Russia invokes plausible deniability—as unplausible as it actually is—and everyone is grateful that we can pretend that it's okay because otherwise, an allied leader might have to push a nuke button or two."

"Dangerous times," Hiro said.

"Dangerous, indeed." White sighed. "Xander, rest so that when you put on your thinking cap tomorrow, you don't fry your electrical system. Sleep, that's an order."

"Not in your chain," Xander said.

"I am," Hiro said. "Sleep. That's an order."

20

───────

Xander

Sunday

Lumberjack, Alaska

Sleep, for Xander, was impossible.

His body buzzed from head to foot.

Even Radar's rhythmic snoring, which was usually the soft rumble of white noise that put Xander out, couldn't distract Xander from his racing thoughts.

Phone in hand, the light dimmed, sound playing in his earpiece, Xander conducted his own Elyssa research on social media. The whole time he searched, his gut clenched.

He didn't want his esteem for her to be disabused.

But he wasn't naïve.

After navigating the typical social media landscapes, Xander came up empty-handed. He wasn't that surprised. Many of his female friends chose avatars and nicknames to connect with friends while maintaining their anonymity.

But there was a simple way around that.

Xander went to Eddie's to see if he could find her name in his friendship list. And when that failed, Xander remembered that Eddie was bringing up a video when Elyssa asked him not to.

Scrolling back in time on what looked like an abandoned Facebook timeline, Xander found pictures of Eddie's college days.

And there she was on the rugby field.

Mesmerizing. Fluid. A powerhouse. A team player.

She took the hits and was back on her feet.

Those observations seemed to have played out both on the field and in her personal life, Xander mused.

Elyssa's grit and determination weren't a facial expression practiced in the mirror. It was sweat and dirt. It was straining muscles. It was pelting forward at mind-bending speed as she clutched the ball protectively to her chest, palm-fisting her opponents and sending them sprawling to the ground.

Video after video.

In this last video, like in the others, the crowd roared, and Eddie was screaming encouragement her way from the stands. She was in the scrum. She was bending, lifting, and running with a woman hanging over her back, as her opponent still desperately clutched at the rugby ball.

Honest to god, he'd rarely seen men as fierce and powerful as these women.

Xander could completely see Elyssa bursting into a ring of violent men, pushing her way into the center, grabbing up a stranger in need, as Eddie hid behind his palms, and taking him to her car.

Elyssa would probably just say she'd done her little bit of good.

Xander lifted his attention as Radar bounded off the bed. Radar stood stiffly at the door.

Xander figured Radar was sensing animals in the woods, and he went back to his scrolling.

Radar was softly growling at the door, and Reaper had told Xander in no uncertain terms that he was never to dissuade Radar from voicing what was going on around him. Radar might not get the distinction and fail to alert when it was imperative.

Radar kept on with his guttural growls, edging up to put his nose on the door.

Xander wondered if there was a bear outside. He'd get up and look, but he was loath to wake Elyssa. He had these few minutes of bliss with her in his arms—conflicted bliss, but bliss, nonetheless. Xander didn't want to wake Elyssa if it meant she might go back to her own room.

But suddenly, Radar's growling changed. It was no longer an awareness; it was a warning.

Xander edged out of bed, reaching for his pants and pulling them on as he moved toward the window to look out.

There was a man at Elyssa's door, fussing with the lock.

"Radar, dance," Xander commanded, and Radar was between his legs in a snap.

Opening the door only as much as necessary to keep the frigid temperatures out. Xander pitched his voice to his "I take no shit from anyone" combat tone when he said just above a whisper, "Do you need something?"

The man swung around, startled as he stood at Elyssa's door. "No. I was looking for a friend of mine."

"Which friend?" Xander asked.

"I—uhm."

Xander glanced at his watch. "It's 4:30, dude, and no one's around but me and my dog," he lied. Why did he lie?

"I'm sorry. Is it that late? I've," he looked over his shoulder. "We've been drinking and wanted to check on our friend."

"Wrong door, buddy. The woman who was staying there left with some old fat dude about thirty minutes ago." Xander had no idea why he said that. "Move along. My dog is paying attention."

As if on cue, Radar, the magnificent, softly rumbled a warning in his chest.

The man focused on Radar, then lifted an arm. "Yeah, no, just confused. Too much to drink." Then he stumbled up the path with the gait of a sober man, trying to feign inebriation.

Xander shut the door, threw the bolt, and watched through the window until the man was out of sight.

And only then did he process how damned cold he was.

"Good job, Radar." Xander gave his dog a thorough belly rub, then pointed to the bed. "Radar, load."

Elyssa was out like a light. She was wearing his shirt, and his suitcase zipper was loud, so Xander rubbed his hands over his bare skin to warm himself before getting back in bed to keep from startling her awake.

It was good that one of them was getting some sleep.

21

ELYSSA
Sunday
Lumberjack, Alaska

HER WATCH, buzzing on her wrist, woke Elyssa.

That alarm meant she had thirty minutes to get out the door and over to the parking lot where her ride would pick her up.

It was too soon.

Elyssa wanted more time to get to know Xander Belov. He made her feel special, cared for, and most of all, respected.

She'd spent a wonderful night with him—yeah, everything about their time together was incredible. She felt amazing.

Elyssa could use more nights like last night in her life.

Couldn't every woman?

Lying in Xander's arms with Radar at her feet had a magnetic pull, keeping her in bed, clinging to every moment she could stay here, and regretting the medical condition that was forcing her onto an early flight home.

Despite her POTS condition, Elyssa was *not* a dainty flower by any stretch of the imagination.

Yes, she had a delicately featured face, and she preferred romantic clothes and long hair. But for real, Elyssa had never led a rose-petal lifestyle.

She was, even after the sunset on her athletic career, a woman with defined muscles, and muscle was heavy. That, coupled with her height, which was the same as the average U.S. male, gave her privileges her smaller friends didn't enjoy. She felt safer doing things like declining to fawn and pet the Gastons of the world. There were, after all, only so many men who could physically lift her. Especially since, as Xander had pointed out during their chat in the lodge, men often skipped deadlift-butt day.

Xander could lift her with ease.

What an amazing sensation Elyssa enjoyed when he tossed her around the bed like she was a rag doll.

It was glorious! And fun. And weirdly freeing.

Up until her sexy time with Xander, Elyssa couldn't imagine the appeal. But now, she understood why her friends raved when they found a man who could manhandle them (in the best sense of that word).

It had set off something primal and wild in her psyche.

Exquisite, what other word could she choose?

Addictive. *If Xander is a drug, shoot it straight into my veins.*

Her watch buzzed her again. *Ugh.*

Decisions had been made when hitting the snooze button. Possibly poor decisions, but Elyssa had now waited until the very last minute before she needed to leave Xander's arms.

"If it's okay," Elyssa said, sliding from under the covers, "I'm just going next door to grab my bag, then get dressed here?"

"Whatever works best for you." Xander came up on one elbow as he watched her wrap herself in the extra blanket that had been draped over the foot of the bed.

Instead of bending over and risking a racing heart, Elyssa curled her toes into the fabric of her pant leg, pulled her knee to her chest, and passed them to her hand.

As Elyssa rifled in the pocket for her key card, Xander climbed out of bed and came to her side. She noticed Xander was already wearing his hiking pants. Had he gotten cold in the night?

She felt like she should say something about last night, and that she was glad they'd met, she edited the *finally* from her thoughts.

But what could she say? "That was memorable in every good way, thanks." Nah.

Elyssa ended up choosing. "The Pentagon area is a subway ride from my place. I'm looking forward to seeing you again."

"Elyssa, it's freezing out. And that's too hard on you." Xander took her key card from her hand without asking for her permission. Bare-chested, because she was wearing his shirt, Xander pulled on his coat, shoved his feet in his boots, and went out the door.

Luckily, Elyssa hadn't unpacked anything from her backpack. Her purse was sitting on the desk in Xander's room.

She was glad Xander went. Despite her efforts, her chest tightened in pain as her heart went into hyperdrive, trying to move blood around her body.

Elyssa sank to the floor, and Radar came over to lie across her outstretched legs.

The pressure helped improve her circulation, and by the time Xander came back with her pack, her chest pain had subsided.

"Arc you okay?" Xander asked, squatting beside her and

lifting her wrist to check her pulse. He reached up for her purse and handed it to her so she could get to her bottle of electrolytes.

How did he know how to take care of her?

How did Radar know, for that matter?

"Better," Elyssa said, after gulping down the entirety of the bottle.

"I only found the backpack," Xander said. "Nothing was lying out. No suitcase."

"The airline lost my luggage, so that's all I have."

Xander's focus was on Radar. "I think you have a new friend. He's going to be sad when he's left with only my company."

Dog and man locked gazes, and Elyssa would pay good money to know what they were communicating to each other.

It would have been nice, she thought, if Xander had added that he was going to miss her.

Instead, he said, "I'll set this in the bathroom." He stood and moved her pack to the other room.

Radar must have sensed that the dizzy sensation had lifted because he climbed from her lap and gave her a lick. "Thank you, sweetheart. That helped."

She moved slowly to get up, so she wouldn't retrigger her symptoms. Time was ticking, and Elyssa couldn't afford to have a full episode.

Xander was back, reaching for her hand to help her up. Then, he pulled her to his chest, but instead of kissing her, he took her face between his hands, looking deeply into her eyes. Something about her seemed to confuse him.

And his behavior this morning, while chivalrous and caring, was nothing like the energy between them last night. He confused her, too.

"I need to get dressed," she said.

In the bathroom, she pulled on her bra, then decided to pull his Henley back on. Yup, it was hers now. It was as warm and soft as Elyssa had imagined it to be when she'd first seen Xander.

Wearing it, Elyssa had slept long and deep in his arms. It had been a while since she woke feeling so good.

As Elyssa brushed her teeth, pictures of their night together brought a smile to her face and made her throb. It sucked that they'd met under these circumstances, but they'd have time once he got home.

Elyssa liked how tall he was, how athletic.

She'd traced her finger over his only tattoo that nestled below his ankle. It was a red arrow on a black disk about the size of a quarter. "Achilles heel?" she'd asked, hoping he'd tell her the meaning.

He answered her by saying, "I hope not." Then he dropped it.

Tattoos were often highly personal, so Elyssa had learned to lead someone to the conversation but not insist on the story behind it. Elyssa didn't share the meaning of her own tattoo with many people. It was a private commitment not meant for public scrutiny.

Bending over the sink to wash her face, Elyssa was thinking about the bruises on Xander's torso. "What happened?" she'd whispered. "This looks horrible." She'd bent and kissed a purple splotch.

"Boxing." He said it so matter-of-factly that she nodded and dropped that subject, too.

Elyssa unfolded a towel and patted her face and neck dry.

Boxing would explain his physique. Though it wasn't one of the sports she'd imagined when speculating the night before. Oddly, Elyssa wanted to scold Xander and warn him about the dangers of getting punched in the head too many times. Such a hypocrite, Elyssa scoffed. How many times had her parents taken her to her wrestling matches and later her rugby matches, and there her mom would sit in the stands with her eyes covered whenever Elyssa competed. Her mom wanted to be supportive of whatever Elyssa felt called to try, but the dangers were too much for her mom to handle. Elyssa's dad would wait until the all-clear, then tap her mom. The dangers passed, her mom would leap to her feet, shaking her fists, and cheering her.

Elyssa felt melancholy wash over her.

She missed her dad. And she wasn't sure that she'd ever forgive fate for taking him from her when she was so young.

Elyssa needed to call her mom. They hadn't spoken since Paris.

Was it odd that the thing she wanted to tell her mom—after all her adventures over the last few weeks—was about this guy she'd known for a couple of hours?

What could she even say? Mom, I met a guy with a gorgeous dog, a kind voice, and a condo near the Pentagon. What more could she add than that they had a fun conversation and she'd spent most of their time together having the best sex of her life?

Nope, she'd keep all of that to herself.

When she emerged from the bathroom, Elyssa saw Xander focused on his Henley that she had tucked fashionably into the front of her jeans.

He didn't say anything about it, but he looked pleased.

And then he looked conflicted. And then—yeah. The reaction was odd.

She was going to remind him that he had her contact info but decided that would sound a bit too needy. He knew he had it. He'd call if he wanted.

She'd respond if she wanted.

Elyssa couldn't fathom what was going on for him. Last night, he said he was single.

Maybe he lied? It did kind of look like guilt shimmering over his skin.

As she blinked at Xander, standing there in all his glory dressed only in those hiking pants that sat yummily on his hips, she wondered how they would say goodbye.

The timing was off; it already felt awkward. And her heart started racing.

Radar came over and booped her.

"Hey, buddy," Elyssa said, reaching down to rough his fur. "It was nice meeting you."

"Elyssa, do you have everything you need?" Xander's gaze turned worried. "Electrolytes?"

"I'm set." She adjusted her backpack. And scooped up her purse.

Yeah, super awkward. This vibe was so different than last night's. And she didn't need to figure it out. She just needed to leave.

Looking out the window as she shoved her feet into her boots, Elyssa said, "My car's here."

"I'll walk you," he said, moving toward his suitcase.

"Nope. Gotta go. Thanks for everything." She lifted a hand and gave him a finger wave, then slipped out the door.

My god, what the hell just happened? She wondered.

Cold feet? Self-preservation?

She felt like they had been in perfect balance, that there was a glowing future out in front of them. That she had taken the first steps of a new beginning.

And now?

Now it felt like she was falling from a circus high wire.

22

Sunday

Lumberjack, Alaska

THE LODGE HAD CLEARED the snow that had fallen overnight from the parking circle, but they were still on the far end of the sidewalk, working their way toward the lodge. Every time her foot went into the snow, it filled Elyssa's short boots.

There was a man on his snowmobile, and Elyssa wished he'd come over and offer her a ride to the car. Her legs felt like lead.

It isn't that far. This is fine. Elyssa encouraged herself.

The guy on the snowmobile fixed an unwavering, calculated gaze on her.

And suddenly, Elyssa's intuition yelled for her to get out of there. But the jolt of frigid air had sapped her of energy. She felt so weak and so tired that she wasn't sure what to do. This was the reason she needed to leave Alaska. The cold froze her veins.

While her heart was pumping with all its force, blood just wasn't circulating, and her eyesight was getting fuzzy.

If you sink into the snowbank, you'll die of hypothermia.

She turned to the lodge to see if it was closer than the car; either would be okay.

She didn't even think she had enough power to call for help, though she needed it.

The man on the snowmobile was heading her way. And Elyssa knew he meant her harm.

Knew it.

But Elyssa didn't have the capacity to move.

Coming closer, he revved his engine, then shot forward. As he drove by, he reached out and grabbed the wrist of Elyssa's free hand and kept going.

Elyssa's bags dropped from her shoulder. She was on the ground sledding along, thinking this guy was going to get her into the woods, and she'd never come out again.

Something in the self-preservation part of her brain kicked in.

She heard herself thinking in big, fat orange letters. *It's rugby. Get out of the hold.*

Adrenaline was her rocket fuel, and Elyssa morphed into her former self, a formidable athlete.

Pulling her knees to her chest, Elyssa reached her free hand up and clasped her trapped hand. Using that grip, she was able to pull her knees to her chest and swivel her hips to the side. With her feet on the side of the snowmobile, she shoved into her heels with all her might.

The man came flying off, landing on top of her, scrambling up, never releasing his grip on her wrist.

The snowmobile continued unmanned, coming to a stop yards away.

As the man dragged her toward his machine, Elyssa spread

her legs wide, then she pulled them together as quickly as she could in the snow, using the momentum to twist her over to face down. Her own clasped hand created a joint lock that broke his grip.

The man's face was a red snarl as he reached down to grab her again, and Elyssa pulled her leg to her chest to kick him away.

Suddenly, a streak of caramel and black flew through the air. Teeth clamped down on the attacker's forearm. Despite the heavy padding of his snowsuit, the man screamed in agony.

Barefoot and bare-chested, Xander scooped Elyssa's backpack and purse onto his shoulder, then reached under Elyssa's back and knees where she lay sprawled and spent in the snow. "Jeezis, Elyssa, are you hurt?" He rolled her into his chest as he stood. "Radar, detain," he barked the command as the guy got a knee underneath him.

Elyssa hadn't answered Xander. She had no idea if she was alright or not. This was all so alarming. In horrified fascination, Elyssa watched over Xander's shoulder as Radar dragged and shook the attacker until he was down in the snow, still screaming for help.

Xander scanned toward the parking lot. His focus landed on a black car, where a man stood with his hands on his head and his mouth wide in astonishment. "We've got to get you out of here." Xander slogged through the snow in that direction. "Elyssa, is that your ride?"

All Elyssa could manage was a nod, then she let her cheek land on Xander's shoulder.

The driver popped the back door open. "Wow, man, is she okay?"

Xander ignored the question. He laid Elyssa gently inside. Pushing her pack onto the floor at her feet, he said, "Elyssa, check, are you sure this is the right driver?"

The driver, standing wide-eyed, looked like he hoped he had failed the test, and Elyssa would be pulled back out of his car.

With a shaking hand, Elyssa handed Xander her phone from her zippered coat pocket.

Xander scanned the screen, then scrutinized the man, checked the license plate, and returned to her side.

He's barefoot and bare-chested, and it's negative ten.

Xander put the phone back in her pocket and zipped it shut.

The attacker was screaming in pain, but Xander's focus was only on her. He pulled her bottle from the side pocket on her pack, took off the top, and pressed it into her hand. "Drink it all."

She nodded and followed his command, so he would hurry up and get out of this weather.

Out of the corner of her eye, Elyssa saw Xander reach into his pants pocket and toss something surreptitiously onto the floor. He caught the driver's eyes, "You will get her to the airport safely and help her inside. If you don't, I *will* find you. Do you understand?"

There was a snarl of such blatant impending danger in Xander's threat that the man stuttered, "Yes, sir."

Screaming sobs of, "Help! Someone, please, help me!" rode the air.

And Elyssa was glad the attacker was suffering.

"I'm tracking you." Xander pointed a no-shit warrior finger at the guy, and all Elyssa could think was that he was going to get frostbite, and it would be all her fault.

Xander turned the power of his focus on her, swept her from head to foot, gave her a nod, then shut the door, tap-tapping the roof to let the driver know it was time to pull off.

She turned and watched Xander head back toward Radar and the assailant.

Who the hell was that Xander morphed into?

What the hell just happened?

When Elyssa spun back to face front, pulling the safety belt across her lap and somehow stilling her shaking hand long enough to slide the clasp into the slot, the driver stammered out, "Ma'am, it happened so fast." He shoved his car into drive. "I thought I was watching a kidnapping. That he'd pull you behind his machine like that? Shit, if he got you over the berm, you'd be gone. I got out of the car. I was coming to help, but then that guy came tearing out of his room. And that dog. That was some crazy shit." He pulled off his beanie and clawed his hand through his hair. "And his finger and that warning. He's tracking me? This is insane."

In the mirror, Elyssa could see the guy flushed bright red.

"That kind of thing doesn't happen." His laughter was a bubble of anxiety. "The only thing that's ever happened before is some lady's water broke, and I had to turn around and take her home so she could get her hospital suitcase." He glanced over his shoulder. "Should I go to the police department? The hospital? Do you need a doctor? There's a clinic about forty minutes from here."

"No, the airport," Elyssa's teeth were chattering, and she desperately wanted Radar.

"But you're okay?"

"I'm." She put her hands together as if in prayer, then breathed into her palms. "Wow, that was a lot. *He* was a lot."

"That he just buzzed over to you and grabbed you from his snowmobile? You must have been terrified."

Elyssa caught the guy's gaze in the rearview mirror and nodded.

But she had been thinking of Xander when she'd said that.

That feeling in his arms. The sacrifice of running out into the subzero temperatures. The sensation of being deeply cared for as she was cradled against him.

Elyssa had needed him, and he was there.

Her heart failed her, and she thought she was going to pass out. But when she didn't trust her body, she had oddly trusted Xander. Behind the orange words telling her how to save herself had been the conviction that she wasn't alone; Xander would be there.

Strangely, it seemed unfathomable that he wouldn't protect her.

But with Xander, it was like the temperature on the water tap running hot, then cold, then hot again.

That had started after they'd had sex.

She was in his arms, feeling perfectly content. She'd gotten out of bed to go to the bathroom, and when she'd crawled back in bed expecting the same sense of warmth, and—well, they were strangers, so what would she call that? Companionship maybe? The feeling was one of connection, but something had shifted. There was a sense of distance between them.

Did he regret saying he wanted to see her again? Regret asking for her contact information?

Just ghost me, then, whatever.

But then he raced onto the scene barefoot in only a pair of pants. It was *ten below*.

In his arms, she was safe.

When he was threatening the driver, all warrior-energy, scaring this poor stick of a man—Look at him, driving, Elyssa thought, with a constant flick of the eye to see if anyone was following them, hands so tight on the steering wheel that his knuckles were white.

What was that threat about?

She was, by anyone's definition, a one-night stand.

It was all she'd expected when she asked to see his room.

He was the one who asked for more.

She didn't need another pendulum relationship. She'd tried that. Married that. Divorced that.

Of course, Xander Belov was very different than Glenn Landers.

Elyssa needed to stop comparing everyone to Glenn and then running away.

This was all so confusing. Elyssa had never felt the things she'd experienced over the last twelve hours before in her life.

Xander was dangerous as hell. She felt his force at the moment of the attack, both his physical strength and the power he held over her heart.

This hot-to-cold business?

The hot was addictive, so the cold felt brutal. Not quite punitive, but something close. Is that how abusive relationships started off?

Well, Elyssa wasn't going to find out.

She wouldn't answer the text when it came in, she decided.

She was done. "I'm done," she whispered to her backpack.

Even with her abiding gratitude to Radar and Xander for her safety, that wouldn't change Elyssa's decision.

Xander Belov was quite literally in her rearview.

23

———

Xander
Sunday
Lumberjack, Alaska

Xander called Radar, and Radar bounded over, spun on a dime, and stood at attention by Xander's side.

The shithead didn't move to get up, but lay face down in the snow, sobbing. There was blood on his sleeve that told Xander that the guy thought he could get away from Radar.

The men, eating their breakfasts in the lodge, had at least taken time to grab their coats and hats before they ran outside.

Standing on one foot then the other, like the characters in that World War II movie he'd seen on the way to Bratislava, Xander staved off frostbite for the quick moment he needed to tell the men that the snowmobiler had tried to kidnap the woman.

As he signaled Radar and headed back to his room, the area men grabbed the guy up and took him back inside to call the police.

As far away from civilization as they were here in Lumberjack, that would be a while.

In his room, Xander first checked on Radar to make sure he wasn't injured in the takedown.

Radar, the miracle dog.

Xander didn't watch Elyssa walk away. His emotions were getting the best of him.

But moments after Elyssa walked out the door. Radar jumped onto the desk in front of the window, growling his warning.

Xander moved up to see what Radar had focused on. There was Elyssa, standing like a statue to stay out of the snowmobile's path. But the driver reached out and grabbed her wrist.

Radar through his body at the door to get out.

Xander was right behind him grabbing at the handle and dragging it wide.

Radar dashed out into the snow.

Elyssa did some crazy move, and the guy came sailing off as his machine continued forward. But as the asswipe fell, he wasn't done with Elyssa and kept her wrist in his grip.

It happened so fast.

So damned fast.

Blink of the eye.

Xander was racing forward, but Radar was a fur missile.

And now that the attack was over and Elyssa was heading toward civilization, Xander was on the floor of his cottage room, his whole body wrapping Radar in a hug. "Thank you. God, thank you."

Xander's shaking was part adrenaline, part hypothermia.

He climbed to his feet to do jumping jacks and warm his system.

As soon as he thought his temperature crisis had passed, Xander snatched up his clothes and dressed, then picked up his phone. He was shaking too hard to send a text – still part cold, but now also part fury at what might have happened to Elyssa. He slid the phone into his pocket to wait for equilibrium to return.

Someone tried to take her from him.

Could it have been the guy she'd called Gaston—the one with the hurt ego from last night?

It had to be local. It was the only thing that made any sense.

Xander needed to get on the road. He planned to catch up with Elyssa's car and shadow it, make sure she was safe to fly. He was worried about her heart.

Hell, he was a little worried about his own heart.

Seeing Elyssa in danger turned him into pure power. He was glad that Radar had managed the guy because if he had put his hands on him, Xander wasn't sure he could maintain his control. Xander couldn't save mankind from the Zorics machine if he were in a jail cell locked away for murder. And jail would be a hell of a bad way to ride out the Apocalypse.

With a quick scan of his room, Xander shoved everything into his pack and was reaching for the door handle when a woman's screams splintered the frozen air.

Primed by the attempted kidnapping, the entire lodge heaved out of their doors along with Xander and Radar.

The lodge staffer ran out of Eddie's room and stood on the walkway, looking around wide-eyed. Blood was all over the sheet she held in her hand.

Xander edged up until he could see into the room. It was Eddie's room. The sweater he'd worn the night before in the lodge lay on the floor.

Something violent had gone down. The blood on the sheet in the woman's hand was dry. Xander would say the event happened minimally an hour before.

"Put the sheet down. Step out of the room." Xander said

with calm authority that he wasn't feeling. "This is a crime scene."

Xander remembered the drunk at Elyssa's room at 4:30. He stepped past Orest's room to Paca's. There, he saw the door wasn't pulled all the way shut. Tapping the door open with his elbow, the scene here, too, looked like there had been a fight. A spurt of blood on the wall had trickled down and had dried to a deep brown. Xander thought it looked like someone got punched in the nose. On the ground at Xander's feet, blood droplets rounded the corner.

"Here too. Blood in the snow. Everyone, back away. Stay away. This is a crime scene." Xander pulled out his phone and recorded a video with footage of the room and the bloody trail, then stepped away to avoid contaminating the scene. He sent the footage to Finley, then dialed his number.

Finley answered with a groggy, "What?"

"Hey, man, sorry to wake you." He looked at his watch; it was after ten on the East Coast. Finley must have been burning the midnight oil. "We need an FBI team here in Lumberjack, Alaska, to investigate. And we need it now." Running through the sequence of events from the guy at Elyssa's door in the middle of the night up until that moment, Xander walked to the lodge, placed the key card on the desk, then headed toward his rental car.

"It snowed last night," Xander said. "In the fresh snow, you can see in the film that someone was dragged from Paca's room. I'm assuming Paca."

"Wait. Who's Paca?"

"Nickname for the squirrel researcher, Claude Burns." Xander spread his fingers across the screen to enlarge the image. Running the video through, he paused at the end. "Yup. In the video, I can see two sets of footprints, one on either side of the dragged feet. When that trail stops, there are snowmobile tracks over the berm and into the woods." He stopped and looked back at the room, then up to the sky. "Heading northwest. I didn't follow it out. I don't want to mess up the crime scene. And I'm not credentialed to interfere in a crime investigation."

With this new information, the chance that the attack on Elyssa was a local crime was down to zero.

But the why of it was beyond Xander.

Beeping the fob, Xander looked down at Radar, who had been pressed to his thigh, ready for the command the whole time. "Time to get going, buddy." They needed to leave before anyone with a badge detained him as a witness.

He needed to be with Elyssa.

If Xander thwarted the guy last night, and Elyssa saved herself again this morning, could they have someone going after her a third time?

Xander jumped Radar into the car, then climbed in behind him, sliding under the wheel.

While the engine was warming, he sent a text to Elyssa.

XANDER: **It's Xander. Checking on you. The luggage tracker I threw into the car tells me the car is heading in the right direction. Is that right? Are you physically safe? Are you emotionally okay? That was a hell of a departure. I'm in the car heading back to the city. I'd appreciate a call.**

HE EXPECTED her to take the time to read it, then she'd reach out to him with an update immediately.

But she didn't.

Did she even give him the correct contact?

Xander called Finley to run a check on the number.

While he waited for the information, Xander had the pedal down. But everything that had happened at the Lumberjack lodge had taken too much time. He'd never catch her.

The tracker was on the right road and nearly to the airport.

Xander didn't, in fact, know if Elyssa was in the car with the tracker. Someone could have gotten hold of her, and it was only the tracker that headed in the right direction.

Until Xander got eyes on, he wouldn't trust that Elyssa was safe.

He was flying down the highway when Finley called back. Xander tapped the call on speaker.

"Finley here. She gave you the right number."

"Did she do an advance check-in with her flight?"

"Affirmative. I know you're in the thick of it. I called our team, and they know everything you said to me."

"Good," Xander replied. "I'll call in when I have an update. Out."

Such a shitty twist.

There had been a connection between them. It was sublime. And then the revelation.

If the world didn't implode and Elyssa wasn't part of that effort, he hoped …

This wasn't the time for hope.

It was such a mindbender to think that something was actively brewing and ready to explode, a seismic shift that would shake the world into a new configuration.

Until it happened, it was all academic, all theory, all potential.

Xander's brain wanted him to think that he would wake up tomorrow, and the month after, and a year from now in the world as he knew it today. That he could live in a world where he met the woman who sparked his excitement, and they could learn about each other and grow their relationship with an eye toward the future.

Last night, when Elyssa was in his arms, he thought this was the first time that he'd been with a woman who wasn't just looking for a conversation and a stress-relieving roll in the sheets.

By design, he reminded himself.

Elyssa was the kind of woman who made him think about last calls, about hoping for ways to make things easier for her. He found himself thinking about how much he wanted the call where her car had broken down, and she needed him. He'd roar into the parking lot like some kind of suburban knight on a black steed.

The box was too heavy, and she needed him.

She had a bad day and needed him.

This was what *that* felt like.

It was a power that radiated from his core.

It always seemed cockamamie when he heard people on deployment lament that they weren't home to be the sword and the shield for their family. But he got it now.

For the first time, on an intimate level, Xander wanted someone to turn to him to ease their life. And their relief would be the reward.

How much did it suck that she was from the enemy camp?

Xander would take the blows from Bratislavan street thugs over these feelings any day.

Elyssa haunted him the entire ride.

What the hell had he done?

What in the *hell* had he done?

24

———

Xander

Sunday

Fairbanks, Alaska

He pulled into the airport lot and handed over the keys to the rental. Then he walked Radar to the woods because the poor guy hadn't had a chance to potty yet.

Xander, with his bags at his feet, leaned against a trunk with a racing mind.

Elyssa was a Kalinsky great-niece.

He simply couldn't believe it.

The look in her eyes, when he'd carried her through the snow to the car, told him her heart had been racing. He knew she must have been fighting for consciousness.

And yet there was trust in her eyes.

The phone rang, Xander dropped his gaze, only to feel disappointed that it wasn't Elyssa.

"Hiro, is Elyssa on her plane?" Xander blurted.

"It's delayed. I'll get to that in a second. She's checked in.

She's made her way through security. We saw her on CCV. She seemed okay," Hiro said. "And, hello."

"I need to get to D.C. We need to talk to her. Something isn't right with this picture and her role. I need to be on her plane."

"I figured. But that one's overbooked," Hiro said with something in his mouth, muffling his words. "I've got you on the next one out. Sending you the ticket."

Xander's phone pinged, and he checked the time of departure, confirming he had two seats, one for him and one for Radar. "Got it. Thank you."

"We couldn't get you the bulkhead, but I'm told the emergency aisle is next best. We assured the airlines that Radar was qualified to sit in those seats. They wanted to push back, but it was handled."

"I appreciate it, man. Radar does, too. Trying to get a dog body on a middle seat for that long haul would make everyone miserable. Do you have anything else for me?" Xander asked.

"We know why Orest is heading to San Francisco," Hiro said.

"He has a second leg. That's why," Xander said. "I'd lay money that he's hightailing it to Singapore."

"Bingo."

"What about two scientists who vanished and the attempt on Elyssa?" Xander asked.

"Finley and his joint task force are interfacing with Fairbanks FBI about the disappearances. We'll have a clearer picture once we know what the FBI finds in the woods."

"What's Adele doing? Is the Mossad coming up with anything helpful?" Xander asked.

"Does anyone ever know what Adele is up to? Actually, in this case, I do know," Hiro said. "She's on her way to Singapore. She wants to find out how the family is getting over to

Davidson Realm. And if The Family booked a boat for everyone, was there a date and time for departure? Adele thinks that once the Zorics are moved, it's say a twelve-to-twenty-four-hour time frame to take a last look at the sky and smell the sea before they descend into the chimney, and everyone else on God's green Earth descends into a hellscape of the End Times."

"Great imagery. Thanks for that."

"Adele told me Israeli intelligence working groups are stretched thin," Hiro said. "The regional dangers of today supersede the impending doom of tomorrow. She's the only one who is continuing on the Zoric case."

"I think our working group and the connections we had in place are the only ones who think the Zorics are a significant danger," Xander said.

"I've been told that my thinking is myopic because we've been working on this so long," Hiro's tone was a shrug. "My superiors, who were not my beloved AWG superiors, are telling me that I'm seeing the Zoric threat as bigger than it is."

"Do you believe that?" Xander asked.

"Do you?"

"I would have quit the hunt when AWG disbanded if I weren't terrified by what was coming." Xander reached up to tug the fur flaps on his hat down to cover his ears. "Ugly to admit, but there it is."

"I'm sitting here with a box of donuts in front of me, trying to smother my anxiety in carbs. I'm telling you, my hair is falling out as we speak. If we survive, I'm going to be fat and bald, but I'll also be a happy man. Okay, so back to Adele. We have a team in Singapore that will add Orest to their watch list if she's delayed getting there."

"Adele's in the air?"

"Yeah, even flying out of D.C., she should still beat Orest to Singapore," Hiro said. "Right now, Orest is at the Fairbanks airport with you. No idea why he headed out of Lumberjack around zero-four-hundred. And heads up, the pathologists believe that York got a hefty dose of palytoxin, but there's no way to prove it, which is the genius of using palytoxins. You don't want Orest to target you. We can't lose anyone else. Our team is small enough already. We've verified Orest checked in for the trip to San Francisco, and he's through security. Boarding was called."

"Go back. How's York doing?" Xander asked.

"Coming along. York told me that if he lived through open heart surgery to die in Armageddon, he's going to kill me."

"Sounds like he's rallying,' Xander said. "Did he give you the codes?"

"Not surrounded by the nurses, he didn't, and then he was out again. Crossing our fingers that York is conscious long enough that we can clear the room isn't a great strategy, but it's what we've got," Hiro said. "Listen, Orest boarded. Once he takes off from Fairbanks he has a seven-hour flight. It's a tight connection between landing in San Fran and taking off again. He doesn't have time to leave the airport for any side adventures, especially with that being an international flight."

Xander scanned the parking lot, watching as a car pulled up and a woman exited, reaching into the back seat for her baby. "You checked to make sure Orest didn't materialize another carry-on case?"

"We did," Hiro said. "He checked a suitcase. He had nothing more in his hands."

"He made it through security from D.C. to Newark with whatever was in the case. He was screened."

"We're aware. And interestingly, everything in that Newark carry-on must have been carefully chosen for its reaction to the acid because the entirety turned to a glob, then hardened into a rock."

"I wonder which researcher figured that out for him." Xander could feel his face turning red with windburn. He hated this kind of cold.

"Orest has a graduates degree in chemistry. He probably thought of it as a fun project to put that together."

"All right, that's out of my hands. I'm not tracking Orest," Xander said. "Tell me about Elyssa, what's going on there?"

"She's flying back to D.C. with a layover in Chicago."

Xander looked at his ticket information. It was a straight shot to D.C. "Do I get in first?"

"She beats you by like an hour and a half. With the flight mess out of Canada, it's possible that her layover will be longer than that. You don't have to deal with any of that. Once you're on, you take a nap and wake up on the East Coast, and you lose three hours, so your body clock should be good and misfiring from all the time zone hopping you've been doing."

"Hiro, I need to get to D.C. first."

"And how do you suggest we do that?"

"Delay her plane," Xander said.

"Delay the plane?" Hiro slurped his drink. "Okay, I'll bite. How do we do that, hotshot?"

"I don't know, call in a bomb threat?"

"I'd lose my job. You want me to make a bomb threat to an American airline? Are you out of your mind?"

"It could be less than that. It could be a call reporting that you suspect the pilot is impaired. They'd have to do something about that. Figure out another pilot to stick in his seat."

"We can't crap up someone's career," Hiro said.

"Would it really mess up someone's career? I mean, how? He takes the breathalyzer and a blood test, and if it comes back positive, we did a service to the passengers. If it comes out negative, and he looks confused that anyone accused him of drug use, then off he flies. The blood test doesn't take that long. It might give me enough time to get East Coast first."

"Keep talking your nonsense," Hiro said. "I'm looking into something other than blowing up the pilot's career."

"It's possibly a woman's life we're talking about. Look, we watch and see if the pilot has an issue. If they do, we send the airline's president a little note saying, 'Hey, the world was about to catch on fire, and we thought this was an easy remedy, our bad.'" It felt good to make up some plot line that might happen in one of the thrillers he liked to read, where a maverick hero might just get on the phone and pull crap like that and not suffer any consequences.

"You're making that joke because you're scared for Elyssa. I get that. Listen, about your first idea, the bomb threats, have you read the news?" Hiro asked.

"Something recent? I haven't opened a paper since I got to Lumberjack."

"There were bomb threats at Vancouver and Ottawa airports last night that are impacting some northern flights in the United States," Hiro said. "The Royal Canadian Mounted Police have the dogs in there searching every square inch. And since Elyssa is flying out of Alaska, I was looking up to see the impact on her flight. That plane was delayed in Vancouver. She may be in Fairbanks for a while. You might just get your wish and beat her to D.C."

Xander didn't respond.

Following Xander's long pause, Hiro asked, "What was that thought?"

"Bomb threat." Xander let that information trickle through his gray matter. "Far-fetched but ringing true."

"Keep going."

"Remember when you told me about Orest's flight time?" Xander watched Radar trotting around in a circle, trying to find the perfect spot to take a dump. "Why would he take a car at zero four twenty for a late morning flight to California? In my mind, he was up to something in Fairbanks. But what if it wasn't Fairbanks that was Orest's push out the door?"

"He had those plans in place the day before," Hiro said. "He mentioned it on his phone call."

"Do you have that readout on the whole conversation from the FBI?" Xander asked.

"No, I'll let you know when I do."

"Okay," Xander said, "Let's go through this. There were four people in their party, and three were impacted. Orest arranged for the three to be there and paid their way. He was very conveniently gone just as the attacks happened."

"We don't know what time the scientists went missing," Hiro said.

"But we do know what time they'd be discovered as gone," Xander grew more sure that his timeline was correct. "I told you that someone was at Elyssa's door right after Orest left, and Radar scared them off."

"Yes. Then a snowmobiler tries to drag her into the woods," Hiro said. "Let's move through that theory. Let's say Orest runs to stay out of the hands of the enemy or whatever, and that the group—and it would have to be several men—grab the two companions, Eddie and Paca. Then they go for Elyssa and miss. She wasn't in her room. They don't know where she is. They wait and go for Elyssa as soon as she pops her head out the door, and they've located her again."

"And they miss." *Thank you, Radar. I never would have gotten to her in time. I had no way to go after someone on a snowmobile. She'd be gone. Swept into someone's evil shitty plan.* He sent his thoughts in waves of gratitude toward Radar.

And Radar turned to catch his eye, giving him a single high-pitched bark.

Xander hadn't seen the full extent of the damage that Radar had done to the snowmobile guy as Xander grabbed his gear and ran to catch up with Elyssa, but he was bloodied, and the man was hitch-sobbing as the lodge men took him into custody. That picture gave Xander a sense of satisfaction.

"With a plane delay," Xander said, "they have one more shot at getting to Elyssa before she leaves Alaska.

"We don't have a why," Hiro said. "I mean, Elyssa is Orest's great-niece, which should be protective, unless, as you suggested, Orest was the target. And then there's a meat printer and a squirrel guy. How in the world do these things go together?"

"That's the million-dollar question," Xander said. "So, here's the theory: Orest believed someone was on his trail, and he thought he was in danger. He got out of Lumberjack at the absolute earliest point he could. He left the other three in his party because he thought they were safe. Or he might have thought they would be safer without him there."

"A benevolent Orest Kalinsky. That's an angle I hadn't considered. For a theory, it has potential. I mean, someone who was going after Orest might have missed their mark and decided to use the three people traveling with him as some kind of leverage. Do I think Orest is a caring person, and the leverage would work? I do not. But we can consider this scenario. I'm stuck on the part where you said, 'Bomb threat, far-fetched but rings true.'"

"The bomb threat isn't affecting Orest's flight. It is affecting Elyssa's. What better way to keep Elyssa in Alaska than to keep her grounded? They may make another attempt to take her."

"And you think Alaska is important?" Hiro asked.

"Yeah, I do. If they tried to take Elyssa from Lumberjack, then they have some structure in place here to deal with next steps. Would it be harder in D.C.? It would have to be."

"Following the timeline of your theory, someone figures out —which is easy enough to do—where Elyssa's plane is coming in from. And it's Canada? Give me a second."

Radar was wandering from tree to tree sniffing. And Xander was staring at the airport, wishing he could run inside and grab Elyssa into his arms.

Hiro was back in his ear. "Her Alaskan plane was coming in from Vancouver. And the Chicago plane is delayed out of Ottawa. Well, that's a hell of a lot of coincidences. The bomb threats were issued exactly ten minutes before loading time on the Alaskan-bound plane. Seems like a nice even number. It all lines up. But, like your crossing over the hundred-yard mark at the Newark airport—"

"A hundred yards?" Xander asked. "I thought you said a hundred meters."

"The computer measured it in meters," Hiro said. "It's easier to visualize in yards."

"Not the same distance, though. Someone setting a precise distance marker would use the metric system if they weren't from the U.S. The Zorics work in metric. It's just a detail that has no bearing in this moment. You were saying, 'like the hundred-yard mark.'" Xander put Hiro back to the thought he'd interrupted.

"Both scenarios could be happenstance," Hiro finished. "The airlines have rerouted a plane out of Oregon to take over the grounded Canadian flight. Elyssa's flight is delayed by two hours. There's nothing about the Chicago flight yet. The airports are probably hoping for a quick resolution. With both flights affected, you should beat her in."

"Yeah, I'm rethinking the situation. Do I want to beat her in?" Xander asked as Radar homed in on a squirrel. "Radar," he called, "leave it."

Radar sent him a look that said, "You're no fun."

"You got your fun this morning when you bit the bad guy. Leave it."

And Radar went back to sniffing the tree trunks.

"Hiro, listen, if the bomb threat was meant to stop the plane and strand Elyssa, and possibly keep her in Fairbanks, that means she could be here without any support. She's got POTS."

"And possibly muscles on her trail. You're right, we can't risk it," Hiro acknowledged.

"We have contacts with the airlines. Are there seats on my flight? Could someone from the airlines message her with information about the delays and offer to reticket her at no expense?"

"That would be easiest. Finley has a desk that manages that kind of thing. I'll call him now. I'll text you when I have something. In the meantime?" Hiro asked.

"In the meantime, I'm going to find a dark corner to stand in and guard her."

"You know Elyssa," Hiro said, "wander over and sit. Pick her brain."

"I think I'd frighten her if I suddenly showed up. And if I'm sitting next to her, I can't surveil the area. Better to be a shadow."

25

———

XANDER
> Sunday
> Fairbanks, Alaska

XANDER HAD SETTLED into his seat on the transcontinental flight. They'd be here for the next nine hours. Luckily, the elder sitting on the aisle seat was small, and she liked dogs.

The overhead pinged, and the flight attendant began her spiel about trays and seat backs in the upright position.

To learn a bit more about Elyssa's specialization, Xander was pulling up a book on tape about the future of food production in a warming world when a message dropped.

HIRO: **As discussed, Elyssa took advantage of the offer to switch to a different airline. She's boarded. Seat is in first class. Did you see her get on?**

. . .

XANDER: **Negative. I saw her get on the electric cart from her original boarding area. I hightailed it over here. Radar and I were first to board. I didn't want Radar crushed in the crowd. Took advantage of loading with special needs.**

Xander: **I can't see forward because they pulled the curtain between us plebes and the upper class. Her boarding was visually confirmed?**

HIRO: **Confirmed. Chicago's flight, BTW, was further delayed due to the Ottawa threat.**

Hiro: **Attaching an article for background.**

XANDER OPENED the link to find a newspaper article.

GLOBAL TIMES REGISTER
Alexandria, VA.

WHEN DOCTOR ELYSSA KALINSKY walked across the stage in New York City to accept the prestigious Hastings Award for Innovation in Agricultural Technology, she brought a tin spoon with her to show the audience. Holding it aloft, Kalinsky explained, "This was my great-grandfather, Heinrich Kalinsky's spoon. He carried it with him in his pocket the day he and his mother fled what is now known as Kalin Slovakia (the Slovak Republic during World War II). He was only five years old, but the stories of his early days of intense hunger stayed with him for the rest of his life.

.   .   .

THAT SPOON INSPIRED a different kind of journey, a journey of intellect and curiosity that caught the world's attention. Dr. Kalinsky, 27, while pursuing her doctoral degree, engineered Spoons of Hope, a modular, self-sustaining food production system capable of growing fresh produce year-round with minimal water usage and no soil. It is also animal- and disaster-resistant.

HER INNOVATION IS UP and running as a WorldCares pilot program in five East African food deserts, which were caused by changing weather conditions, overgrazing, political unrest, and an influx of refugees.

FROM A DIFFICULT PAST to a Hopeful Future

DOCTOR KALINSKY'S GREAT-GRANDFATHER, Heinrich Kalinsky, escaped the Nazi-occupied Slovak Republic in 1942. As German troops moved into the village of Kalin. Sadly, the family became separated in the chaos. Heinrich's father and brother were left behind as resistance fighters smuggled Heinrich and his mother out of the area. Mother and son eventually found their way onto a boat headed to the United States, where they had distant family members living in Pennsylvania. They arrived malnourished and unable to speak the English language. In high school, Heinrich worked on the family farm. Later, he opened his own grocery store, which he ran alongside his wife, Ruth.

GROWING FOOD EVERYWHERE FOR EVERYONE.

. . .

DR. KALINSKY'S Spoons of Hope pods are built on the idea of sturdy minimalism and are shipped to the sites where they are needed, snapping together like a children's toy without the need for tools. The design is intuitive, allowing the pods to be assembled without concern for language or literacy barriers.

"WHAT DR. KALINSKY has achieved is revolutionary," Dr. Carmen Brandywine, spokeswoman for WorldCares International, said. "In a world facing increasing dangers that lead to food insecurity, such as climate change and regional conflict, her work offers the possibility of a scalable solution, providing local populations with fruits and vegetables to help provide for the nutritional needs of people in crisis.

FROM LAB to Lives

IN A REFUGEE CAMP on the Syrian-Turkey border, Mohammed shows off his handful of tomatoes and cucumbers that he obtained from the movable farm. He said, "While we still wait for rice and lentils from the WorldCares trucks, we now grow our own herbs and vegetables to make the meals better for our health and happier for our minds. Happier for our hearts." Dr. Kalinsky visited a similar site in drought-impacted Ethiopia earlier this year. "I'll admit that seeing my concept in the field helping people made me cry. While this award is exciting because it will bring my design to the notice of more people, more organizations who may want to implement a Spoons of

Hope module, but the biggest thrill for me was seeing children eating the food that they grew through my system."

BACK IN KALINSKY'S LAB, her great-grandfather's tin spoon sits on her bookcase where she can see it and remember the human impact of something as simple and necessary as healthful food. The little girl who remembered hearing her great-grandfather's stories of starvation and trauma has now dedicated her life to reducing the number of children who might someday tell the same kinds of stories around their future kitchen tables.

XANDER READ the article three times, and it made absolutely no sense to him that this woman, who was part of the Zoric family through the Kalinsky bloodline, was on board with the Zoric plot.

No sense at all. None.

In this article, Elyssa was a world-class science hero.

Start with the name — Dr. Elyssa Kalinsky. The name on her driver's license was Elyssa Kalinsky Landers. Xander opened his photo file and looked at the picture he'd taken in his room in Lumberjack.

Kalinsky-Landers, hyphenated, he hadn't seen that in the dark.

Kalinsky was not her middle name, but a maiden name. Married.

Did Elyssa seem like the kind of woman who would have an affair?

There were no rings. The friends didn't make any references to her husband—or her wife—she could be bi—. But Eddie had frequently referred to his fiancé, Benny. Claude had mentioned his wife and children. And Elyssa had said nothing at all about her relationship status.

Married. Huh.

Not only had he slept with the enemy, he'd screwed somebody's wife.

He was going to Hell.

Before he realized that Elyssa was a Kalinsky, working with one of the architects who helped make the doomsday machine a reality, he would have read the article and recognized Elyssa in the journalist's words. He would have imagined all of that was true.

The hope that was sprinkled like pixie dust throughout the entirety of the article was the way that Xander had sensed her. Sunny, warm, self-sufficient, brainy, kind-hearted—Xander cut himself off before he added enthusiastic and flexible in bed. Under the circumstances, he wanted to distance himself from those memories.

Was all that a well-designed persona? Something that she showed the reporter and the men that she met when traveling far from home?

That was certainly a skill set that the Zoric family possessed: a smile on your face, a knife in your back.

She had given him the correct phone number. Would she have done that if she'd just violated her marriage?

There were all kinds of marriages, not everyone believed in monogamy the way that Xander did. He had never slept with a married woman—never slept with a woman that was in any kind of relationship before, and he didn't like the way that sat in his chest. "Tricked into immorality by the Zoric vixen," he muttered, and it felt like a false narrative.

Tradecraft 101: Never assume.

One could gather data and develop a theory, but to create a

narrative from the name on her driver's license was fallacious thinking.

Until he knew something definitively, he'd let that go.

Married or not, it didn't change the fact that Elyssa had used her doctoral studies to feed the world.

XANDER: **Is Elyssa working for WorldCares now?**

HIRO: **She runs her own lab. It's funded by the Carpathian Foundation for Scientific Advancement. Orest Kalinsky's foundation.**

SHIT.

Xander knew from Anna that Orest had been gathering science for William Davidson to use as he developed survival systems on Davidson Realm. And in Bratislava, Anna had specifically mentioned an interior vertical farm in the volcanic chimney.

Had Elyssa been working on that part of the Zoric escape plan the whole time? Was the foundation using the Spoon Full of Hope initiative to maintain international goodwill and encourage other bright and promising up-and-comers to sign up to pursue science? And would they know—did Elyssa know— that their science would lead to death and destruction for others while providing thriving-survival for a select few?

If they did know, it would take a certain level of duplicity that Xander could not put together with the evening he had last night with Eddie and Pacca. The ready smiles, the good-natured teasing.

Radar was the key.

Xander could be duped like every human being. Though he prided himself on being in the kinds of danger for enough years, with a wide variety of cultures, where language barriers meant he watched for the tiniest nuances that would lead to a better-than-average ability to read a person.

But still, Xander was fallible.

Radar, that was a different story. You can't fool a dog as smart as Radar. He could smell a bad guy a mile away. He'd had his eyes on that guy Elyssa had named Gaston. And that morning, when he saw the man get off the snowmobile, Radar was primed for the fight, standing on the desk and rumbling his chest as he looked out the window. Before there was any real sign that Elyssa was endangered, Radar had thrown his body against the door trying to get to her.

Radar had been hyper-vigilant and hyper-protective of Elyssa from the get-go.

She wasn't the bad guy here. Xander truly believed that.

He thought back to White's admonishment that he sleep, which hadn't happened. But White was right, Xander needed a clear mind. And this flight was going to be his chance to get some shut-eye for whatever came next.

With the arm up between their seats, Radar was curled up, his head resting in Xander's lap.

Xander put a protective hand over his best friend's head, closed his eyes, and passed out.

26

———

Sunday

Washington, D.C.

A buzz in his jacket pocket woke Xander. He lifted his head and wrapped a hand around the back of his neck, feeling how even that minor shift tugged at his knotted muscles. He hated to admit it to himself, but as he edged closer to forty, as he'd been warned by his fellow travelers down the military path, the hits felt harder and the recovery trail was longer.

It was difficult to admit that he didn't have the same body as when he'd joined up. But, too, Xander reminded himself, he didn't have the same mind either.

He'd learned valuable lessons.

He made fewer mistakes.

He developed a keen intuition from his days of walking around primed and ready.

Take Bratislava, Xander had felt danger riding the wind well before he was jumped.

And at the same time, he'd inexplicably labeled that sensation "Anna."

It *wasn't* inexplicable. He'd been betrayed a time or two.

Xander glanced down at Radar, who had shoved himself between the seats on the floor, belly up, paws tucked toward his chest, T-Rex-style, zonked out by the low rubble of the plane.

Xander reached into his pocket to pull out his phone and check the text message that had woken him. It was Hiro.

HIRO: **If we had the airline deplane you and Elyssa first, how complicated would that be given your seating?**

XANDER: **We need to be first off or last off.**

HIRO: **This is how it's going down. We have White with her CIA badge. She pulled Steve Finley in with his FBI badge. We have conference rooms set aside. We'll introduce ourselves and invite Elyssa for a chat.**

XANDER: **Radar and I need to be there for the entirety.**

HIRO: **Not entirety. I need to catch you up on the case, then you can go in.**

XANDER: **She has POTS, and this is a highly stressful situation. Let me show her my badge, walk her to the room,**

and leave Radar with her for comfort. I'll get my update, and she'll know that's what's happening. Her health and well-being are paramount. PARAMOUNT. You all will let her chill. I want salty food in there, electrolyte drinks, and a medic on hand but out of view.

Hɪʀᴏ: **That we can do. I'm watching your approach on my screen, just a few more minutes until they prepare the cabin for descent. I'd go ahead and arrange your things for a quick exit when an airline staffer comes to get you.**

Xᴀɴᴅᴇʀ: **Wilco**

Hᴇ sʟɪᴅ his phone into his thigh pocket, thinking there was more to text to prep the team, more that he could do to shield Elyssa.

With a sudden jolt, Xander dumped to the side.

Radar, suddenly awake, was scrambling and confused.

Xander reached across to grab the tactical handle on Radar's vest as he scooped and lifted his dog up. Thrusting his boot out, he caught the leg of the seat in the middle and pushed into it, bracing, as the pilot banked harder right.

While Radar tried to get his legs onto the seat, the elderly woman on the end was tipping into the aisle. As she grasped at the seat in front of her with one hand, she reached for Xander with her other hand, trying to keep herself upright.

Xander's right hand shot out as he grabbed the elder around the top of her arm and braced his abs to keep Radar and her in place.

An attendant stumbled for the empty seat on the aisle, one row forward of Xander. There, she buckled herself in. The person who had been in that seat was probably in the bathroom. A hell of a place to be.

This went on and on. It wasn't a jolt from rogue turbulence.

Xander was a trained pilot, flying himself into deserted mission areas. The only way this maneuver made any sense was that their pilot was attempting to avoid a sudden collision.

They were, after all, in D.C., where the military took taxi-like helicopter rides declaring mission secrecy and national security. While those regulations were stretched until they had the flexibility of a circus act, it meant that more and more frequently helicopters were in the air without proper authorization or adherence to procedures.

There had been crashes. And deaths.

Hadn't Hiro taken advantage of that system to get NASA information about Paca? Maybe this was a comeuppance for exploiting a self-serving system.

And with a bounce, the plane sharpened the tilt to an even more drastic incline.

Debris flew, overheads popped open, people screamed, and covered their heads as bags tumbled.

The plane continued its steep bank to the right as the nose lifted. Anything that wasn't secured was getting tossed around the cabin. A baby bottle rolled past.

What was happening to Elyssa? Was she buckled in tight?

The mother sitting at the far window, one row up, now lay against the wall, clutching her child as the dad did a kind of crazy plank over top of them, trying to both keep his weight off his family and serve as the shield, taking the assault of items as they came loose.

When Radar started pedaling his feet, Xander said in a calm voice. "I've got you, buddy. Come on now, you've been through stranger things in your training evolutions, jumping out of planes and fast-roping from helicopter platforms dangling from the clasps on my pack. This is a nothing burger for you."

His grasp on both Radar and the woman was suboptimal. Xander didn't have proper body mechanics; his levers weren't in proper alignment. As he twisted, his grip wasn't as solid as he wanted it to be. But his boot was in a pretty good position as long as that tilt didn't keep going and tip them upside down.

Then, all bets were off.

From the way the passengers' clothing dangled, Xander guessed they were approaching a fifty-degree angle far surpassing the thirty degrees allowed. Xander knew a thing or two about that, and the most frightening piece was that when the plane angles that sharply, the wings stop generating the lift to keep the plane from crashing to the ground. Maybe that was why the pilots were also angling upward to rev the engines in order to maintain loft and possibly give themselves a little recovery room.

Xander was at the emergency door. He'd taken the verbal oath that he was ready, willing, and able to pop that door open and help people get out. When the flight attendant looked at Radar with purse-lipped distaste, Xander said that he'd open the door and send Radar down the slide, then stay and help the others, as Radar was trained for that. His tactical vest with working dog patches helped flesh out the story. Though Xander knew that someone with authority had said to let it pass, she had not been down with that decision.

Never in a million years did Xander think he'd really have to help in an emergency landing.

As Xander fought both gravity and centrifugal force, he turned his head to look things over and make a mental map that he could perform without sight if they crashed and the cabin filled with smoke.

Xander realized he was expecting that eventuality.

He'd been through explosions before. He'd pulled through.

Xander's muscles were locking up along his back as he held the weight from a twisted position.

If he did paralyze his muscles into this configuration, he thought wryly, at least he could get the door open and maybe toss himself sideways down the slide out of everyone's way.

He sniffed, trying to detect smoke. Was the belly of the plane on fire from one of those damned Russian incendiary devices?

From this angle, all Xander could see out his window was blue. The passengers' bodies covered the windows below him.

No flames licked into view. No one was screaming fire. *Oheň* if he were in Slovakia.

Was this another communications dead zone, like Newark, where the towers couldn't tell the flight crew anything at all? At any minute, another jetliner could fly into their side. Was that what they were avoiding? A mid-air collision?

Xander wrestled his mind away from the possibilities. He could do zilch against any of them. All he could control was the three feet around him that included his dedication to the safety of the elder and his dog.

"Ma'am, I know this is uncomfortable. Are you doing okay?"

She lifted her head. "Okay," she panted.

Xander turned back to the door. If we crash, pull Radar onto my lap, let go of the woman, reach with my right hand to grab the bar, and with my left hand, run it along my knee to grab the release handle.

He kept that series of actions looping in his head—a survival mantra. If he were injured, he'd need to act anyway. When someone's injured, pragmatic steps are hard to reach for; clear thinking is gone.

Have a mantra, work that mantra.

Pull Radar onto my lap. Let go of the woman. Right hand to grab bar. Left hand release handle.

The husband across the way had dropped an elbow. And his wife was screaming for him to get off of her, that she couldn't breathe, and he was smothering their kid.

What the actual hell? Straighten it up, man.

Though Xander got it. His biceps and quads shook from exertion. He figured he had about a hundred-plus pounds per hand.

If you start something. You finish something. Xander was committed to keeping his row safe. But it would be nice if the pilot righted them soon.

Xander knew that the concept of time was useless in these situations. Absolutely f'ing useless. He had no idea, except for the fatigue in his muscles, how long the plane passengers had been dangling and screaming.

There was a roar of engine noise that freaked the passengers out. They shrilled their horror, not knowing what that sound could mean. The pilots were probably pulling out all their tricks to keep the plane from falling from the sky.

The fall would be shitty, but death would come quickly. And that's really the way Xander wanted to go. He wasn't big into suffering without a cause.

Whatever the hell was happening, the pilots in the cockpit were getting screamed at. The equipment alerted them to problems, sure, but it also breaks concentration and ups anxiety. Shaky hands on the control wheel, that was no bueno.

Xander was back to thinking about the loss of communication in Newark. Was Orest up to his tricks here? The thing that had created the communications blackout in Newark went through security with Orest Kalinsky. What if Orest put something in Elyssa's backpack?

But that would be putting his great-niece in harm's way. And the Zoric family was nothing if not deeply loyal to family.

None of this made sense. None of it did. And Xander would rather not leave this world in a state of confusion.

The old lady's armpit was sweating enough now that Xander's grip was getting slick.

27

XANDER

Sunday

Washington, D.C.

"THIS IS YOUR CAPTAIN. Ladies and gentlemen, that was extreme. Please stay in your seat. Tighten your belt. If you have sustained an injury, please pull the call sign above your head or have someone do it for you."

Pings brightened the cabin as people signaled their need for help.

"The situation is over. We received signals indicating that we were in danger of a collision, and I took extreme measures to protect lives. It was difficult for everyone. I want to acknowledge that. Our flight has been given priority to land. We will be met with support."

There was a buzz of static. The guy was probably giving himself a second to take a breath, gather his next thought, and wipe the sweat from his lips.

"When we land. It will be your inclination to want to leave

the cabin or move about, gathering your scattered items. I must insist that you remain seated while we assess and assist the injured. They are the priority. I am in contact with the tower. The instruments and all equipment on the airplane are functioning properly. The sound you are about to hear is our landing gear descending into place. We're all taking nice deep breaths. My copilot and I are in control. We will be down in a moment."

The sound of the wheels extending was overly loud.

Xander was desperate to get to Elyssa and make sure she was okay.

And White would say it was wrong of him, and he shouldn't get enmeshed. But here he was digging himself in a little deeper.

"Radar, find Elyssa. Go find her. Find Elyssa."

Radar hadn't needed to be told twice.

The woman on the aisle swung her legs out of the way as Radar squeezed by.

There was a stir from the passengers as the massive unaccompanied German Shepherd trotted toward the front of the plane. But honestly, after all that, what was the airline going to say to him?

Lifting up and leaning out, Xander watched Radar drop to the carpet and crawl under the curtain.

A taller man had been watching, then turned to catch Xander's eyes. "He's with a blonde," he called out.

Xander gave him a grateful thumbs up, then sat back down to tighten his seatbelt.

"Here we are, ladies and gentlemen, we're about to touch down. It's all going as it normally does. Ready? Here's the bump."

And despite the hand-holding by the pilot, there were still shrieks and gasps that rose, with an understory of soft keening and sobs from the passengers whose nerves had been wound too tight.

Xander bet that a whole new crop of flying phobias had taken root in the last few minutes of the nine-hour flight.

"Rolling to the gate now, everyone," the pilot used a soothing voice that responders developed to give the impression of control, to keep things calm and to steady nerves. "Almost there. Everyone will stay in their seat. The paramedics will go to those passengers with the lights on first. Everyone will be checked for injuries. If this causes you to miss your connection, service representatives will be available to ensure that you are cared for with the least inconvenience possible. And here we are. We've come to a stop. It's over."

There were a couple of people who gave a half-hearted applause.

Most people sat in stunned silence.

The old lady beside him reached over and patted his hands. "Do I ever have a story to tell the girls in my knitting circle on Tuesday." She pulled a phone from her bosom and snapped his picture.

"Yes, ma'am."

A woman in a blue suit with a photo badge hanging from her lanyard got on the plane and moved down the aisle to his row. "Mr. Belov, you need to get off now. Where's the K9?"

"Up front in business with Ms. Kalinsky-Landers."

"Quickly, sir."

Xander excused himself as he dragged his pack from under the seat in front of him and stepped over the elder.

She patted him on the butt as he passed by. "Thanks for the strong arm, young man."

"Yes, ma'am."

He moved forward, careful not to step on the debris.

The blue-suited woman lifted the first-class curtain and stepped through, leaving a gap.

Xander paused to see with his own eyes how Elyssa had come through.

Elyssa was in an aisle seat with Radar between her feet. His paws rested over her lap like a weighted blanket. Radar looked comfortable, which meant Elyssa had to be holding up okay.

She was kneading his velvety ears while she looked up at the staff.

"Ms. Kalinsky-Landers, while we do our assessments of the other passengers, would you mind stepping off the plane with your dog? We have someone to check on you in the boarding area."

Elyssa got up, and the attendant helped her get her backpack and purse from where they'd been wedged under her seat. "I've lost my phone," Elyssa said.

"I'll see if I can't find it after the others have deplaned," the staffer said.

"This dog belongs to Xander Belov." Elyssa looked toward the curtain. "I don't know …"

"Yes, Mr. Belov will meet you after you debark," the woman said, using a voice that suggested, "Stop stalling, get off the plane."

As Elyssa headed toward the exit, the first responders moved up the passageway.

Xander side-stepped out of their way and strode toward the boarding area where Finley was waiting for them with an electric cart.

"You made it. Listening to the tower exchange, for a while there I wasn't sure."

"Do you know the cause?" Xander asked. "Were comms working?"

"I was on the phone with White. She's finding out. We'll

have an answer for you probably by the time we get back to our rooms."

With Radar at her side, Elyssa made her way up the jet bridge, not looking at all surprised to see Xander standing with his hands on his hips. He was probably radiating concern, and he tried to tamp it down.

She looked okay. She was walking fine. She didn't grip the wall or Radar.

And Radar wasn't booping her or searching for help.

The look Elyssa shot him wasn't friendly.

Xander sent a questioning look toward Radar, and Radar lifted a single eyebrow as if to say, "What the heck, bro?"

So now, his dog was mad at him, too?

"You were on my flight," Elyssa said as she got closer.

"Technically, you were on mine," Xander rejoined.

"Okay. But you knew I was there. Or how did Radar know to come and check on me?"

She had him there. "Because he's Radar," Xander said.

"You just let him walk around the plane like that?" Elyssa asked.

"No."

Radar looked up to her, and Elyssa, in turn, scratched his neck and whispered. "You, handsome boy, are the best of all best boys."

Xander held out an open palm. "Elyssa, this is Special Agent Steve Finley, FBI."

Finley pulled out his badge wallet and extended it to her. "How do you do, Ms. Kalinsky-Landers?"

"It's Elyssa." She looked down at the badge, then over her shoulder, and saw that no one else was getting off the plane. She focused back on Finley. "Are you here because of the guy trying to grab me?"

"Yes, ma'am. My team needs to speak with you, please."

He held out an arm to herd her away from the plane as the attendant sent him a hurry-it-along lift of the chin.

"And you know Special Agent Finley?" Elyssa asked Xander, standing her ground.

"Elyssa, I'm on that team he just mentioned. I called Finley from Lumberjack and asked him to get the Fairbanks FBI involved."

"Yes, that man should be stopped." Elyssa turned. "Thank you, Special Agent Finley."

"Finley is good enough. Ma'am, if you, Radar, and Xander could come this way."

Xander looked down. "Radar, with Elyssa."

"He knows me by name?" Elyssa draped her hand over Radar's neck as they walked forward. "Smartest of all the smart boys. I will buy you all the bones that your heart desires. You're my hero, you know that, right?"

And Radar did know, because he wagged his tail as he ambled beside her.

Xander was glad that someone had thought to get the electric cart for Elyssa, which would be easier on her.

What wasn't great was that three Zorics were staring at them from where they were posted against the wall across from where the Alaskan flight was now unloading. That meant the Zorics had a way to read tickets and knew Elyssa had switched her plane.

The question was, were those men here to protect one of their own, or were they here to do Elyssa harm?

As Elyssa and Radar climbed onto a seat. Xander was able to surreptitiously get some video, hoping that if his actions didn't scare the three off, someone could track or apprehend them for questioning.

Once their electric cart was in motion, Xander tapped

Finley's shoulder, raised a brow of warning, then sent him the video.

From Finley's posture, he recognized the men. He sent out a series of texts as they rode to the secure room.

Once there, it was a short, silent walk from the main corridor, down a side hall. They stopped at a door where Finley knocked, then used his key card to let them in.

It was a typical-looking meeting room done up in man-made materials in blues and grays. But it had the advantage of being secure. A step down from a SCIF, but they could talk in here.

"Elyssa," Xander said, "this is Johnna White. She's with the CIA. And this is Suko Hiro with the DIA."

As his gaze swept the room, Xander was gratified that everything he'd asked to be in place was there, including a paramedic who was hanging out in a recess in the wall out in the hallway. Xander didn't think Elyssa had noticed the woman with her rescue equipment at her feet.

Elyssa cast her gaze around, then stared at the salty foods and electrolyte drinks on the table. When she plopped into a chair, Radar went to sit between her knees.

"Xander, now that Elyssa is here," White said. "Why don't we let her decompress? That descent was pretty intense from what I heard. And we need a few minutes with you in the room next door, to bring you up to speed."

Xander crossed his arms over his chest. "I'm not leaving Elyssa." Certainly not with the Zorics nearby.

"She can have Radar, right?" Hiro asked. "We're right next door. We'd hear if Elyssa needed support."

Xander considered that for a minute. "Let me talk to Elyssa, and I'll be right over."

The team left, snicking the door shut behind them.

"FBI, CIA, DIA, and you're on their team. Who do you work for?" Elyssa asked.

"The Defense Intelligence Agency at the Pentagon."

"You're a military spy." Elyssa hissed. "You told me you were an analyst. These are not the same things." She painted the word *spy* with so much disdain that it dripped onto the floor near Xander's boots.

"Are you sure that they're not? Spy. I mean …" Xander thought about it and, yeah, he kind of was a spy of sorts. He'd never thought of himself in that context.

"Spy. It's such a disconnect." She was kneading Radar's ears, and Radar was blissing out. "You have such a choir boy who loves his mother look about your eyes."

"I don't sing much, but I do love my mother. Choir boy?"

"Your eyes. You don't have trained killer vibes." Elyssa's frown was deep and heavy. "Have you?"

Xander's brows drew together. "Have I what?"

"Killed someone?" Elyssa's voice conveyed the "How dare you?" without her having to say it aloud.

"I was in Afghanistan for three tours," he said quietly.

"I am so confused by all this." This was her rugby face. Elyssa was fierce. "I'd never have slept with you if I'd known."

"Known what? That I work for the Pentagon?" Xander tried to step away from his DIA role, which seemed to bother her.

"That you were so dangerous." She pulled at the neck of his Henley that she was still wearing. And he wondered if she remembered what she had on. "I'm feeling an existential threat. Internal. I don't think you want to hurt me. But still, you'd think that I'd be able to sense that you're a killer. I can't trust my own instincts. I made such poor choices."

Killer. Xander had never thought of himself in that way, either. He was trying to line himself up with this conversation.

He could support her best—no matter what her role turned out to be—if he maintained rapport. "Your instincts?"

"I mean in bed."

Xander sat in one of the plastic chairs, so he wasn't looming over her. "I'm not particularly comfortable with the juxtaposition of being called a mama's boy one minute and then jumping to sex."

"I agree. Gross, right?" She drew in a deep breath. "Dangerous men tend to be selfish and self-absorbed." She slid her ring on and off her finger, and Xander let her sit with that thought, hoping she'd give him some insight. "I mean, there's a woman's truism about going to bed with a man for the first time, an orgasm isn't expected. My orgasms weren't expected last night."

Xander's mind was on the possibility that the Zorics had tried to down their plane, that someone had kidnapped Elyssa's friends, and there were Zoric goons in the hallway. But Elyssa had no idea why she was in this room, and so she was assessing the time she'd known him.

That made sense.

She was talking about orgasms.

Plural.

A smile spread across Xander's cheeks, then he forced his face into something neutral as Xander wondered why that seemed like a sticking point for her. It was as if the disconnect came from her belief that killers and spies were incapable of giving a woman an orgasm. And since she told him he was both a killer and a spy, maybe she thought she should have been left unfulfilled. And so, somehow, he was lying to her? Was that it? "What are we talking about, Elyssa?"

"Is this being watched or taped or something? Am I being interrogated?"

"Interrogated," Xander shook his head slowly, "No, we want to figure out—"

"Are you filming this?"

"Yes. But not because we believe you did anything wrong. But we do have some questions, and we want a way to go back and think about what you've said."

"Surely, this isn't about us screwing around. And it can't be about the guy grabbing me in Lumberjack because the White woman and the Hero guy are from intelligence agencies. Hero, that's a made-up name, right? Like, you originally called yourself Ender?"

"Hiro, H-i-r-o, not hero, h-e-r-o. Hiro is his last name."

"Intelligence agencies gather international information, right?" This was the Elyssa from the tapes he'd watched on Eddie's social media last night, with Elyssa's bare ass pressed into him as she slept. This was the woman who would take no shit from the competition. "Tell me why I'm here," she said.

"There appear to have been two attempts to kidnap you in Lumberjack. Someone tried to break into your room last night, but Radar alerted me because my room was right next to yours. We took care of it."

"That's why you were wearing pants," she said as if his pants had been a major question in her mind. "And I didn't wake up for that? Don't answer that." She held up a hand. "Answer this instead. Purposefully? You took the room expressly so you would be next to mine? That wasn't happenstance?"

This whole next chapter was going to be really hard on Elyssa, and Xander hated like hell that this was happening to her. He'd ease her in by mentioning her great-uncle now.

"Reservations were made for me. I was placed in the closest room available so I could get to Orest Kalinsky."

"Uncle Orest?" She startled and drew her chin back, genuinely perplexed.

"I had no idea you had a connection to him. Nor did I know that room was yours."

"Did you have sex with me as part of an operation? Like," she snapped her fingers, "what do they call it?"

"I don't know what they call it. But I had sex with you because I very much wanted to. My target, Orest Kalinsky, was asleep, so I was on my own time. I discovered that you were associated with him later." He let her have the smallest taste of what was coming, and he watched her reaction.

"Your *target*? You're going to explain that to me? You must be kidding if you think my Uncle Orest is someone a spy should watch. That's absurd."

"I'll have more information for you after my team brings me up to speed." He didn't like being called a spy. It sounded like someone without ethics who lurked in the shadows.

"But you knew I was his great-niece," she insisted.

"Not until after we were together."

"When they tried to break into my room?"

"Earlier."

"I had put my information into your contacts on your phone. Then, I went to the bathroom." She looked at her lap. "Well, that explains your shitty moodiness when I got back in bed, doesn't it?" Elyssa looked up. "Is this about drugs?"

"I wish it were," Xander said gently.

"That sounded ominous."

"I don't want you hurt." And Xander had never said a truer sentence in his life.

"Me neither. You think I might be?" Elyssa jumped up. "Whew."

Xander reached out to guide her back to her seat. "No sudden shifts, please. I know all of this is startling. For your safety, we have a paramedic right outside if you think you need someone."

Elyssa stared at the door, so Xander got up and opened it. "Ma'am?"

The uniformed woman lifted from the wall and took a step forward.

After he was sure that Elyssa had seen her support, Xander said, "Just making sure you were here."

"Yes, sir."

He closed the door and turned to Elyssa. "I need to get caught up on the case. I'll be right back."

"Before you go." Elyssa waited until Xander sat back down. "I hate being lied to, and you have to be lying. You slept with me because you wanted to manipulate me. It has to be that."

Xander placed a hand over his heart. "I would never do that, Elyssa."

"You knew who I was last night *before* you slept with me," she insisted.

Xander shook his head.

"You did. You must have. You must have done some research on me, too. You saw I was shaking and ordered nachos, and you placed the saltshaker directly in front of me that way. I didn't put it together because I don't live in a spy thriller. I'm a plant engineer. A plant plant engineer. I mean, I design plants for growing plants." She waved her hand in the air. "Never mind. If you knew about the salt, you already knew what I did for a living and had researched me enough to know I had POTS despite HIPAA."

"I didn't, Elyssa. Radar told me about the POTS. Listen, Radar was at a training facility in Oklahoma, and I was able to adopt him as my dog because he had been released from their service dog program. Radar is a great working dog, just not a good fit for a medical alert lifestyle. Now, how they train the service dogs is to start their puppy training in a family that does that as their good works in this world." He pointed to her wrist. "It's their little bit. Okay? Following?"

"So far. But you seem to want that to explain the salt."

"Though Radar was trained as a seizure alert K9, the family where Radar was puppy training had a friend who had POTS. That friend had a POTS service dog who would boop her on the leg when there was a change in the woman's blood chemistry. This service dog would assume a particular posture of concentration as she paid close attention to her handler. Radar learned that behavior when he lived in his puppy trainer's house."

Elyssa pressed her lips together like she wasn't buying this. And Xander needed Elyssa to trust him.

"The salt was pre-boop," she said.

"Yes, like I said, before the boop, which is the alert, the service dog's posture would change as she focused on her person. I recognized Radar's attention and posture when you were at the bar. This was when you were dealing with Gaston."

"That's not his name. I have no idea what his name is."

Xander grinned. "Gaston. That's marvelous." He caught her gaze. "That is such a Belle put-down. You remind me of that character."

"Do I? How?"

"I'll tell you later. Right now, you need to trust that I guessed that you had POTS because of Radar's behavior, and you were shaking and drinking electrolytes. I had a small inkling of how to help because of the way I saw that woman deal with her situation and how those around her supported her."

"But then you got on my flight and followed me here."

"Actually, you got on my flight. And I live here."

She looked around. "And now, I'm in a confessional in D.C., Xander. And I still don't know why."

28

—————

Xander
Sunday
Washington, D.C.

Thinking back to the complex series of events that Radar had processed through at Cerberus as they did the training evolution, Xander decided to let Radar manage Elyssa's room. And so, he simply said, "Radar, take good care of her," before closing the door.

He walked three paces to the only other door on the corridor, tapped, and was let in by White.

"Okay, Xander," she said, reaching out to touch his sleeve, "I didn't say anything about it in front of Elyssa, but what have you got smeared on you?"

Xander pulled the fabric around. "The lady sitting on the aisle seat was eating a tuna sandwich when we got the initial jolt, and she grabbed at me." He reached into the front of his pack and pulled out wet wipes to clean himself up.

"Tuna on a plane?" White asked. "Rude."

"Well, it seemed fishy." Xander's joke fell flat. "Planes first, what the hell was that?"

"Not the Zorics," Hiro said.

"Well, that's good, I guess." Xander tossed the spent cloths into the trash.

"I was tracking you in, for no good reason, and when you got over the Potomac," Finley pulled out a chair and sat, "your flight path became erratic."

"You don't say."

"Xander, it was stressful as hell," Hiro said. "I can't imagine how frightening that was, given the recent crashes in this area. And while our team uses sarcasm to deal, this time you have to let Finley flow through this information because we have a bunch to get through, and I don't want Elyssa to change her mind about talking to us and just get up and walk out the door. She owes us nothing. But we need her badly."

"Go," Xander said.

"White, why don't you take point on this?" Hiro asked.

"The traffic alert collision avoidance system, TCAS, is set up to enhance the pilots' situational awareness and is supposed to prevent mid-air collisions. When, for example, helicopters in D.C. are flying around without reporting to the tower, the tower can't watch how they interact with the airplanes. This backup system should help. When a situation is picked up by the system, it provides a warning and can also instruct the pilots on what to do to stay safe."

"And the TCAS told our pilot to bank hard right?" Xander asked.

"It told four airplanes to descend. One did descend because that plane had the space to do so safely. The other three, including yours, did not. Not seeing the threat but hearing from

TCAS that a mid-air collision was imminent, each pilot did what they could to save their passengers' lives."

"Heroic," Xander said. "What he did was off the books, and from what I could hear and see, he executed it masterfully. The guy was a fighter pilot for damned sure. What did we avoid?"

"Yeah, about that. You missed nothing. The TCAS gave false alerts because the Secret Service and the Navy were over at the Naval Observatory testing anti-drone technology."

"Despite the FAA warning them not to," Hiro grumped.

"The anti-drone tests were done on L-band, which is the same spectrum band as TCAS. It created ghost planes that TCAS tried to save you from hitting."

"Does everyone know about L-band and TCAS?" Xander asked. "I mean, given our Zoric mission and what happened in Newark, that seems like a vulnerability."

"And that's that?" Finley asked White. "Secret Service said, 'Whoopsie?'"

"They promised they wouldn't do it anymore," White scrunched her nose with disdain.

"It's getting to the point that I'm terrified to fly," Hiro said. "I'm taking the damned train."

"Obviously, anti-drone equipment needs to be tested, especially after Ukraine's genius attack on the Russian nuclear-capable bombers. But come on! Do it in a desert somewhere." Xander said. "It's pretty bad when you can't tell if you're getting dumped out of the sky because of a family of psychopaths, a rogue state, or just plain dumbassery. I'll be honest with you, when we were tilting over, I thought for a minute that one of Russia's magnesium incendiary devices made it past the dogs and I was about to get chargrilled."

"The private channels to Moscow worked," Hiro said.

White tapped the table in front of Hiro. "We think,"

Hiro turned to her. "They just got a conviction on four guys."

She tipped her head to show she was not convinced.

"All right. I don't need to know anything more about the plane. What's next? Let's start with the article Hiro sent me. It calls her Elyssa Kalinsky."

"Landers is her married name," White said, opening a file and handing it over to Xander. "She uses a hyphen, which probably didn't show up well on the driver's license when you were using a red light while doing your post-coital investigations from bed."

Xander ignored White's poke. Her sense of humor could be acidic. "Elyssa's married, then?" He kept his gaze studiously on the papers, which were genealogical tables dating back to the mid-1800s.

"Divorced," White corrected. "She was married for three years. Actually, and possibly interestingly, she filed for divorce the week after that article came out."

"Husband couldn't handle her success?" Xander asked. He picked up one stack and set it aside. The second stack had Elyssa's lineage.

"I didn't do a deep dive," White said. "Finley pulled her vital records and did a quick search of what's out in the public sphere. I was flipping through, so the dates stood out to me. Mostly because two months later, she signed a contract with Orest Kalinsky's foundation. She stopped working on the Spoons of Hope project for WorldCares, though her project is still active, and instead began working on a more ambitious project building vertical farms for Orest's foundation."

"What is all this?" Xander asked, sweeping his hand over the papers, just wanting the punch line.

"After your text, telling us you were sleeping with the enemy, our genealogists did a quick look-see. We've been mapping the family and their connections, and no one remembered an Elyssa in their research. The team compared Elyssa's family to the Zoric-Kalinsky family branch, and she is not on it. As far as we can tell, she's not even in the same forest. So, at least for the last five generations that they looked at, Elyssa has zero family ties to Orest Kalinsky," White said.

"Then why in the world would she call him uncle?" Xander asked.

"Your guess is as good as mine."

Xander put his fingers on the sheet. "And there's Medved' Zoric. We were in the field and not part of the analytical team, so let me make sure I understand. The genealogists followed all of these branches? They know the connections even of the people who are not in direct lines with Orest and Medved'?"

"They did. Elyssa's not in the Zoric line, and she's not a Kalinsky." White paused. "Let me rephrase. She is a Kalinsky. Elyssa's great-great-grandmother was born in Kalin and came to the US with her child, Elyssa's great-grandfather, Heinrich Kalinsky of tin spoon fame. Elyssa just isn't related to the Orest Kalinsky line. There's no possible way that they have any blood in common for at least six generations back on his side. Their families merely come from the same geographical area. But it's like saying everyone with the same last name is from the same family tree."

"Which you, in particular, don't want," Finley said.

"Me?" Xander looked up to catch Finley's gaze.

"She's also got some Belov on her recent family tree," Finley said as White reached out, shuffled the papers around, pulled one forward, and pointed.

Belov was a low branch on that family tree.

"F'ing hell." Xander pulled his hand down his face. "Did I just sleep with my cousin?"

"Man up," White said. "Just drop the F bomb already."

"Duty to a vow. So no," Xander said. "Did. I. Sleep. With. My. Cousin?"

"Same scenario as with Orest: Same name, no connection," Hiro said. "I looked because Habsburg jaw and all."

"Careful, brother," Xander said. "I put up with it from White because she can kick my ass. But I won't stand that from you. How do you know my family tree? Is that the typical way the DIA looks into its hires?"

"The DIA was involved in a case recently where the Prokhorov family tried to destroy Delta Force."

Xander nodded. "I read the files."

"One of the side players that isn't in that file was a guy Raine Meyers was tracking at that time, a guy named Todor Bilov."

"And I'm I related to that guy?"

"While you and Anna are from the same Bilov family, this guy was not. We had to look."

"Because you used Anna's family connections to infiltrate the Zoric family, you all thought I might have that kind of in?"

"You're grateful we looked before. It made it easy to let you know you're not sleeping with your cousin," Hiro said. "Which is a good thing."

Xander reached into his pack for his water bottle. His mouth was the Sahara. "The plane was a Secret Service goof-up. Elyssa doesn't have evil running through her blood. She and I aren't related," Xander said, unscrewing the top. "Next?"

"Onward then," Finley said. "I have information out of Fairbanks FBI and Foggy Bottom, and the two go hand in hand." He passed a page toward Xander. "This is the entirety of the box and Dr. Tapper conversation from Orest's phone call from his room in Lumberjack."

Xander took a swig of water before pulling the paper over.

"This doesn't edify anything. It's just two guys agreeing on boxes." Xander slid the page back to Finley.

"The box conversation makes perfect sense in terms of the criminal events that followed," Finley said. "It tells us that Orest Kalinsky was an architect in the kidnappings of Claude Burns, aka Paca, and Eddie Baylor, and the attempted kidnapping of Elyssa Kalinsky-Landers."

Xander accepted the map that Finley pushed his way.

"When the Fairbanks FBI got to the lodge, they were able to follow the foot and drag tracks out to a set of snowmobile tracks. They were able to follow the snowmobile tracks and map them before the next snowfall covered them over. They moved through the wooded area toward the northwest, coming out of the tree line at a small airport."

"There are airports all over Alaska," Xander said. "In certain areas, that's the only way to get around."

"The airport manager said that a man named Dr. Tapper arrived with three large boxes. He stored them in the hangar. When he left on his scheduled flight, he took two of the boxes with him, and the third was left behind. The FBI examined the box, and it contained folded blankets, a stack of pillows, and adult diapers. There was ventilation wiring around the lip."

Cold sweat slicked Xander's skin.

"Orest had to at least like Elyssa a little bit," White said. "She has tickets for a flight to Singapore on Monday."

"Why not just fly with him today?" Xander asked.

"That's not noted with the airline ticket counter," White said.

"We can ask Elyssa when we speak to her in a second," Hiro said. "I'm concerned about the line in the Lumberjack phone conversation when Orest said, 'Sadly, we must add the extra box. I had hoped to avoid shipping. Make sure Tapper has the file. This last box is the most important. There are to be no mistakes.' I am making the assumption that the last box was for Elyssa, indicating that Orest cared for her and took precautions for her added health concerns. And that, for some reason, Elyssa's getting to Singapore on Tuesday wasn't soon enough."

"It may be a clue as to their timeline," Finley said. "We're looking at hours to a day or possibly two before the event."

"Orest wasn't inviting her there as family. He was inviting her as a farm hand. She knows how to make the food supply work," Xander growled. "But damned if you're not right. This must be a clue about their time frame. Sometime before Tuesday. That's fast."

"He must like her enormously," White said. "Otherwise, I would think he'd just have her killed straight out. And it would be the easiest thing in the world given her POTS if he's carrying palytoxins."

Xander stopped breathing. His voice came out just above a whisper. "Why would he want her dead before the attack? Did she see something? Does she know something?"

"We have photos of her around plants—trees, bushes, foliage—from York's briefcase," White said. "We can't figure out their importance. AI doesn't know what they mean."

"They seem significant," Hiro said. "We'll ask Elyssa about them when we go in."

"Finishing up with the information of the kidnapping of the two men," Finley said. "There were a total of six men on the flight. The pilot, five men, two boxes. None of those five men flying as passengers matches the description of Eddie or Paca. The two cargo boxes were flown to Nome." Finley moved his finger from one red dot on the map to another.

"Isn't that the end of the Iditarod?" Xander stacked the genealogical pages and passed them back to White, then pulled the map closer.

"Not significant here. The two boxes were unloaded in

Nome and placed on a different plane, which flew them to Wales's airport. On this leg, it was only Dr. Tapper and *three* boxes. We have no idea what happened to the other four men. They got off the plane and left the Nome airport. And we have no idea why there was a third box or what that box looked like. There." Finley pointed to a small dot on the far west and well north of Nome. "That's Wales, Alaska. From there, the airplane refueled and then left again heading west."

"West?" Xander looked down to see water to the west.

"West," Finley tapped the map. "Lavrentiya, Russia. The pilot said his passenger held him at gunpoint and forced him to fly over the Bering Strait below radar."

"The Bering Strait separates Russia and Alaska at their closest point — a distance of around fifty-three miles," Hiro said. "It was a quick crime to planejack a ride to Russia and then send the pilot back." Hiro leaned forward. "Did you know that the Bering Strait is named after a guy named Vitus Bering? He was a Danish-born navigator who served the Russian Navy. And he's the first one to go up there and map the Strait. That was sometime in the 1700s. The Bering Strait was named in his honor." He sat back again. "I always thought that it was named because the compass bearing was north or straight up, and that someone spelled it wrong a long time ago. They just left it that way. Live and learn."

"Interesting," Xander said to Hiro, then turned back to Finley. "But the pilot made it back. He wasn't arrested in Russia and sent to the Gulag?"

"Everyone over in Russia seemed okay that he touched down. They unloaded the three boxes, and then Dr. Tapper told the pilot to go home. The pilot refueled, got back in his plane, and flew low to the water back to Wales. He said he was terrified that the U.S. Air Force was going to shoot him down. Now, going home was a bit more traumatic than his reception in

Russia had been. Fairbanks FBI had this all figured out by the time he landed. To be clear, the kidnappers weren't trying to cover their tracks, excuse that play on words. They're in the wind. When the pilot landed, the feds had a lengthy discussion."

"I'm sure. They believed his story?" Xander pushed the map back to Finley.

"Not entirely. Part of the problem was that he wanted to head to the bar instead of making a report," Hiro said.

"Maybe he needed a couple of scotches first," Xander said, thinking that was entirely reasonable.

"I think life's going to get a little tricky for him from now on," Hiro said. "For sure, he isn't getting a security clearance if he ever wanted one."

"Our theory of the case, then, is that Paca and Eddie were transported in those boxes, and the third box was empty because Elyssa's kidnapping was thwarted?" Xander's heart was squeezing down tight as he said that, though he worked hard to keep his tone neutral.

"We do. Dr. Tapper was the one who hired a flight out of Wales, and he's the one, according to the pilot's account, with the gun in his hand as they rerouted to Russia. Dr. Tapper had a slew of medical equipment with him, and we think that was to make sure Eddie and Paca didn't die along with whatever was in what I'm calling the fourth box. The third being in FBI custody."

"Orest Kalinsky all along," Xander turned to White. "Orest is a new player to me. I first heard his name in Bratislava when I talked with Anna. York was on your team. Did you all have a psych workup? How would that make any sense at all in Orest's mind? How would he even think up a stupid scheme like this?"

"If it worked, it's not so stupid," White said. "To Orest, this would make all the sense in the world. You remember, it wasn't that long ago that there was a bus filled with scientists who were taken hostage and hidden in an old World War II bunker under the mountains in—"

"Slovakia, somewhere near Bratislava." Xander exhaled.

"Exactly." White was moving her file folder back into her briefcase. "The kidnapper put the scientists on a drip and kept them unaware, so he didn't have to deal with them trying to escape. This is the same scenario, albeit more complex due to the flights. It was less complicated because they were planning for three scientists and whatever was in the fourth box."

"They planned for three," Finley said. "But Elyssa escaped thanks to Radar."

"I had a little to do with it, but okay, we can hand the win to Radar. My ego isn't involved here." Xander had meant a little self-deprecating humor. But his words sounded tone-deaf even to his ears. "Are Eddie and Paca just going to be in—what is it called—Lavrentiya, Russia?"

"Looking at air traffic," Finley said. "The Bureau thinks that a private jet flew out of Lavrentiya with a flight path that would take it toward Singapore."

"Can someone meet them in Singapore and get Claude and Eddie back?" Xander asked.

"Not if the jet lands directly on Davidson Realm, no," White said.

"There's enough space for a landing?" Xander asked. "When Anna showed me the overhead image, I didn't see a runway."

"Field landing," White said. "If it's a good pilot, yes."

"Okay, lastly, York," Hiro said.

Xander leaned forward. "How is he? Did you get the codes to his laptop and surveillance?"

"He's been given a paralytic cocktail because he's on a ventilator. No, we don't have access to his codes."

"What we have is this pile of photos from his briefcase," White handed him a file.

Xander rifled through. They were pictures of Elyssa. Just Elyssa. The back of each 8 X 10 glossy had a number. Each image featured a relaxed-looking Elyssa, sometimes smiling, sometimes not, against foliage. None of them were posed. She never looked at the camera.

"What is this? What does it mean?" Xander asked, handing them back.

"I have no idea." White stood. "Time to talk to Elyssa. Xander, what do you think of her vis-a-vis this situation?"

"I *think* she's a scientist who believed she was doing good work for the world. I wouldn't have slept with her if I ascribed any malicious intent to her. I'm not that needy." Xander stood. "I *think* she's courageous, and she'll do what she can if we are forthright with her. But what I *know* is that she has POTS, and it's disabling. If she's willing to help us, we need to protect her at every step."

"We'll give you that opportunity, Xander." Hiro patted Xander's shoulder as he passed behind him. "For now, let's go have a talk and see what she's willing to share."

29

———

Elyssa was lying on the floor with her head resting on Radar. She had been going over the years she had known her Uncle Orest. What had they talked about? The joy of life. Of food. Of tickling babies to hear them laugh. Of art and music, either of which could move him to tears of empathy. Uncle Orest had a warmth and an inclusiveness, a lot of worry for humanity, and a little good-natured scolding about her health and safety.

What in the world could Uncle Orest possibly have done that would bring the FBI, the CIA, and not one but two DIA officers to meet her plane?

The DIA meant it had something to do with military security, right?

And Uncle Orest did work with scientists all over the world.

There was a mistake. There had to be a mistake. Some kind

of circumstance that aligned Uncle Orest with someone or some act that was innocent on his part.

A knock at the door had her turning her head.

The group filed back in.

Xander came immediately to her side with his whole "ta-dunda-dun hero to the rescue" energy swirling around him as he crouched by her side.

Did she hate it?

No. Actually, quite the opposite. It was new to be the focus of that kind of attention. Elyssa could get used to it if it wasn't attached to some government guy who had her uncle in his sights.

With a lift of his eyebrows to ask permission, and a slight nod from her, Xander checked her pulse.

Elyssa loved his hand on her. But since they'd had sex, he'd been a constant source of internal conflict. Elyssa believed what he said about not knowing her before he bedded her. But still, he called Uncle Orest a target. *Seriously?*

"I'm fine. I was just more comfortable here." She accepted Xander's hand as she got up in stages. The government people found places around the table. Each one took out a business-style card and lined them up in front of the chair at the head of the table.

And that was the seat where Xander led her. He, then, reintroduced "the team."

As Xander sat down cattycorner to her, Radar lifted his head from the floor to see if there was a command, but none came, so he lay back down, curling into a ball.

"I'm sorry you were attacked," White said. She sounded sincere but no-nonsense. She was sorry bad things were happening, but that wasn't going to change the facts, and they were here about facts.

Elyssa decided she'd listen and answer because there was no reason not to.

"You should have seen her escape. It was the stuff of movies." Xander's voice was rich with pride. "I mean, Radar got to bite the bad guy, and that made his day. But the moves Elyssa used while she was getting dragged over the field were pure pipe-hitter shit." Xander turned Elyssa's way. "Was that a rugby technique?"

Pipe-hitter, Elyssa thought she'd heard that term in TV shows about special ops types. Everyone in the room looked like they could easily be in that category. These were the kinds of people that you could bounce quarters off their abs. Special ops spooks? Elyssa stared at Xander, thinking of his bruised body. Well, that made more sense, didn't it? He was on some mission, and there was a fight. Elyssa blinked away the emotions of pride and horror, turning to address the group. "That technique gets you up on your feet again when they're trying to drag the ball from your hand." Her voice was dispirited. They were obviously trying to show they were on her side because she'd need people on her side in the next few minutes.

"We want to talk to you about your Uncle Orest," White said, reaching into her briefcase and pulling out a file.

"Is he okay?" Elyssa whispered.

"Perfectly fine," White smiled. "He had a good flight to San Francisco."

"He's going to meet the family in Singapore," Elyssa said.

"What can you tell me about that?" White opened the file and pulled out a piece of paper.

"Just that he asked me to go with him. I couldn't go on the same flight because I'm an attendant at a wedding this week-end. I was going to join him, leaving on Monday."

White slid the paper her way.

Elyssa looked down at a copy of her plane ticket to Singapore. "Yes." She felt red rise, Eddie-style, from her neck to her hairline.

Xander was watching her like a hawk, primed to leap into action. She liked it and, at the same time, found it a bit overwhelming.

"Why were you going?" White asked.

"There's a family reunion, and Uncle Orest wanted me to meet them. And as a surprise, he said that he'd been building a prototype that I was developing. It's an interior vertical farm. And I guess the family has an island with a volcanic chimney." She licked her lips. "So, what is this about Uncle Orest? Apparently, you all think he's a bad guy."

"Have you always known him?" White maintained control of the information flow.

"No, there was an article in the paper about an award I won. And a woman came to see me. She said that she had read that article and wondered if she might ask me a few questions. I thought it was about my designs, but it was about my great-grandfather."

"This article?" White pulled out another piece of paper and laid it in front of her.

Elyssa looked down just long enough to identify it, then nodded.

"Do you remember the name of the person who contacted you?" White asked.

"Yes, it was a woman named Danika Zoric. And she had an older man with her named Radovan Krokov, yes, I think that's right. Danika said that she had family in Kalin, a city outside of Bratislava, Slovakia. And that they had family members who had fled the Nazis during World War II. Once the mother and son reached Pennsylvania, the family had lost touch. She said she thinks she knows my great-uncle, and his name was Orest Kalinsky." She'd been hoodwinked. As

Elyssa told her story, she saw how easily she had been manipulated.

"That was supposed to be your great-grandfather's brother? The one mentioned in the paper?" White asked.

"Yes. My great-grandpa's younger brother, Orest, had been a baby in diapers at the time my great-grandpa and his mother escaped."

"Your family told you the great-uncle's name?" White asked with a tip of her head.

"No, everyone called him 'Great-grandpa's brother' and not by a proper name."

"And you didn't ask your family when Miss Zoric approached you?"

"My only family who might know was my dad or grandpa, and they're dead. So, no." Elyssa felt so naïve. She fell into someone's design like a stone in the stream. *But what the heck? I mean, come on now.*

"And you were convinced that Orest was, in fact, your great-grandfather's brother?" White was walking this through like a lawyer, pulling a confession from the person on the stand.

I'm not culpable of anything, Elyssa reminded herself. "They had a scrapbook of things from the family. They showed me what vital papers were left. Not many. This was pre-computer, of course, and the Nazis burned the records hall. But they had pictures and their story … shit." She should just voice her conclusions and get them on the table. "You're about to tell me that he's not my great-uncle at all, aren't you?"

White caught Elyssa's gaze. "I am."

"But why would he lie?" Elyssa was staring at the wall, her face blank as she processed the news.

"We think that he wanted you to do research for him," White said gently. "And they thought that, given your philanthropic bent and your love for family, they could entwine you in both ways. That family simply enjoys manipulating people. It makes them feel superior and powerful." White tilted her head. "Also, Orest likes pretty things. He might have wanted to have a loving great-niece who smiled at him and doted on him."

"I did that. It's true." Elyssa swallowed, then sought out Xander's gaze and whispered, "I research food production applications. I don't know how I could have broken the law."

"You didn't. Elyssa, listen to me," Xander said, "you did nothing wrong. We just want you to know the truth, and we need you to help us."

"Because Unc—because Orest did something bad, didn't he?"

"Yes."

Elyssa licked dry lips. "Give me a category of wrong. Is he a serial killer?"

"Terrorist," Finley said.

"Terrorist? That's so crazy!" Elyssa gasped. "Terrorist? I was working on the problem of world food shortages. Orest believed—told me that he believed—that everyone should have access to delicious, nutritious food."

"It's an honorable goal, Elyssa," Xander said. And Elyssa got the distinct impression that he was trying to ease the first of many blows she was about to take. "Elyssa, we have some upsetting things to tell you. But if it gets too much, we can take a break. You have Radar. We have medical support just outside the door," he reminded her.

Elyssa flicked her gaze in the direction of the door, and for a split second, she considered walking out. But someone had tried to kidnap her, and if for no other reason than self-preservation, she needed to know why. And maybe they had that information.

"White, can you explain Elyssa's family tree, so she is very sure of the facts?" Xander asked.

White put some pages in front of Elyssa and walked her

through the genealogical information from Orest's family tree, then hers. She finished with the conclusion that Elyssa and Orest weren't related at all, and Orest had been lying to her the whole time.

"Not my uncle. But a terrorist?" Elyssa went numb.

"One of the worst people in the world," White's matter-of-fact tone was helpful. "And he's planning very bad things."

Elyssa dropped her hands between her knees and rubbed them together as if to generate heat. "Food things?"

"The food studies you were conducting and the systems that you designed were created specifically to keep Orest's family alive through a nuclear winter if one should occur," White said. "He and his family do not traffic in nuclear weapons. But *they* believe that there is a distinct possibility that the act of terror they're planning might result in worldwide dire consequences. If they are successful with their plan, there's a potential that a nuclear war would ensue. We need to stop him. And we specifically need your help to do that."

"Me." She put her finger on the genealogical page with her name. "Belov." Her eyes widened, and she fixed on Xander. "Are we cousins?"

"No. You and Xander are not in any way related," White said without hesitation.

Now that that was out of the way, the FBI guy next to White seemed to have the conversation baton handed to him.

"I'm Finley." He pointed to his card. "And as you know, I'm with the FBI."

She flicked her eyes toward Xander. "The FBI because the man tried to get me on his snowmobile this morning?"

"Elyssa," Finley said, "you escaped that event, but Eddie and Claude Burns—the man you call Paca—did not. They were kidnapped. We believe that it might have something to do with Orest going to Singapore."

Those were words sitting on the table. They didn't seem to want to go into Elyssa's mind. "But he left this morning." She flailed to make sense of this.

"And left you and his other two invitees in an Alaskan forest?" White asked.

"He had a family emergency. I switched my plane to leave Alaska early because I wasn't able to handle the freezing temperatures."

"How are you right now?" Xander asked. "Is there anything I can get you to make you more comfortable?"

"I'm okay. It's just a lot to take in. I introduced Eddie to Orest. Someone kidnapped Eddie? Dear god." She shook her head in bewilderment. "I didn't know Paca. Orest never spoke of Paca's work, just about his sled team in Alaska. You asked if Orest simply left us there. No, we had a plan. Orest would leave very early in the morning."

"Why didn't you go in the same car?" White asked.

"Because his flight was very early this morning, "Elyssa repeated. "He had to leave the cabins just after four o'clock to make it, and he wanted to sleep in the car."

White laid a paper in front of Elyssa, and she scanned over the copy of a plane ticket in Orest's name, from Fairbanks to San Francisco. White put her finger on the departure time.

"That was an hour after I was supposed to leave."

The room fell quiet, giving Elyssa time to process.

"He wanted to go without me. He left hours before he needed to." Elyssa looked at Xander. "How does that make sense?"

"We have pieces to that puzzle that tell us that Orest Kalinsky arranged to have Eddie, Paca, and you kidnapped." Finley let that information sit for a moment before continuing. "This morning, before your departure, Eddie and Paca were kidnapped from their rooms. Someone tried to break into your room as well."

"Elyssa was in my room with me," Xander said. "She left my room and was walking to the car when the assailant on the snowmobile was waiting on her path."

"Did you recognize him?" Finley asked Elyssa.

"No. The attacker was wearing a helmet," Elyssa whispered, her chest growing tighter. "The only thing I saw was that he was red-faced. He was angry."

"Did you recognize him, Xander?" Finley asked.

"I didn't wait around for that. I was following Elyssa to make sure she was safe."

"You followed me?" Elyssa asked. "Not just tracking me?"

"I got in my car as soon as I could and tried to catch you. Should your car have stopped, I would have been just behind you to help."

"I have a lot of questions about that," Elyssa said. "But I'm here to give you answers. I'm assuming that since you know about the kidnappings, you've saved Eddie and Paca, and they're okay."

"No, Elyssa," Finley said. "That's not what happened. Eddie and Paca were flown to Russia, and we believe they are now on a flight to Singapore."

"How does that make any sense? Why? Eddie prints meat, and Paca studies squirrels. No one is kidnapping Eddie and Paca for their science. No one is kidnapping them for money. Research scientists make little despite their high level of education."

"We don't have those answers," White said. "We think we know why they tried to kidnap you, though." White put a pile of pictures in front of Elyssa.

Elyssa picked them up and fanned through them. They were all pictures of her in gardens and parks.

She put them down and looked at Xander for a long time, then flicked her attention back to White. "There are only pictures of me. Orest didn't take them. Who was taking my picture?" She spun on Xander. "Was it you?"

"I met you in Lumberjack," he said evenly. "It was by happenstance. I knew nothing of you until that moment."

"You have these pictures, so someone you know took them?" Her gaze didn't waver from his. "But why?"

"Because," Hiro said with an edge to his voice that she hadn't expected, "you saw things without knowing the significance. Our guy, who took the pictures, knows what you know, but he's non-responsive in a hospital bed, so you, whether you like it or not, might just be the person standing between life-goes-on and nuclear winter."

"Stop it," Xander's voice was low and controlled, but no doubt there was a knife's edge in the base. "There's no need to frighten Elyssa. And given her medical situation, it's dangerous as hell to scare her." He lowered his voice, but Elyssa could still hear. "What if she ends up in the hospital like York? Then what would we do?"

"AI can't find this?" Elyssa asked, feeling like the room was sliding sideways. If humanity were picking a superhero to leap in and save the day, and somehow the spin of the dial had landed on her, well, the Fates made a pretty shitty choice.

Her body drooped forward.

"Elyssa?" Xander put his hand on her arm and lifted her from the chair, kicking it out of the way and guiding her body to the floor. "Give me a signal, paramedic?" He was steady as a rock.

Elyssa managed to shake her head. She hated the circus that came with public episodes.

Xander lowered himself behind her, letting her rest against him.

White came around and pulled Elyssa's legs out to lie more comfortably in front of her.

As soon as White finished that task, unbidden, Radar came and sprawled across her lap, acting like a weighted blanket that helped push her blood up toward her heart.

Xander lifted a hand, and White reached for an electrolyte drink from the table and passed it over.

After a few minutes, Elyssa felt well enough to speak if she stayed in Xander's arms with Radar on her legs. "Can I have the pictures, please?"

Elyssa could feel Xander's disapproval of her pushing herself, but he said nothing as White handed her the stack.

She switched to the next photo. "I was asking about AI searches?"

"It's a picture of you and a tree, Elyssa," White said. "We don't have the digital photos with embeds. There's no data on the prints."

She put her hand down on Xander's thigh. "You know who took these pictures."

"I believe so," he said. "And that person is the reason I went to Alaska. Again, Orest Kalinsky, traveling with Claude Burns, was my target. After Orest went to sleep, I went to the lodge to see if I could meet Claude, who is Paca, and there I met you. And you came over to speak to me, then Eddie and Paca came in."

She turned to the pictures.

"Elyssa, as a group, do these photos tell a story of some kind?" White asked. "What do these images have in common?"

"My uncle— This is surreal. I'm having trouble believing this is happening right now. What do these have in common?" She laid the photos beside her and knitted her fingers together. "Orest Kalinsky has an apartment in Paris. He told me that there was a convention in Paris, the topic of the conference was world cuisine and the new things we can anticipate in the next decade. I knew about it because Eddie was going to discuss 3D-printed meat. There are also cheeses that can be lab-made, under-ocean farming, and GMOs that allow food to grow in a new environment where the air is saturated with moisture, but the ground is dry. It's a new phenomenon that I anticipated and wanted to overcome with my own research of community vertical farms that could exist in any climate and survive any cataclysmic weather event, making them useful as emergency shelters as well."

"Orest told you about the conference," White said. "Did he attend?"

"He said that he wanted me to go, and he paid my way. He also asked me to hang out with him for the ten days before, as he did a bit of food touring, which we did. He was buying cider for the year for his family, and we were doing a little game for the children."

"Were the children with you? Any other family members?" White asked.

"No. Specifically, Orest wanted to go around Normandy sampling the ciders and ordering them for the family. I thought the family must adore cider because he was basically tasting and then ordering everything they had. I was worried that he was wiping out supplies for others."

"Where did he send the cider?" Hiro asked.

"That I don't know. Orest handed them a piece of paper. He was speaking in French, and my French is wobbly at best. I did what I had to get through my basic requirements in high school."

"These are all taken around Normandy?" Hiro asked.

"He met me in London. Orest was in London, and I had never been there before, so I flew there for a couple of days first. Then, we took the ferry from Portsmouth to Le Havre,

France, and worked our way back to Paris for the conference. One day, he invited Eddie to have dinner with us after we visited Versailles. I had been telling Orest about Eddie's discoveries in meat production, and Orest wondered if I could add that to the vertical farms. Orest invited Eddie to work with him, and I assumed that meant work with me on the Feed the World project, but Eddie had just signed a contract with NASA." She reached out and kneaded her fingers into Radar's scruff.

"Meat for the Mars astronauts," Xander explained.

"How did your uncle respond to Eddie declining the job offer?"

"He invited Eddie to Alaska. And he really sold it. I thought it was just my kindly great-uncle being overly enthusiastic." Elyssa leaned down and kissed the top of Radar's head and left her cheek resting there on his warm velvet fur, taking what comfort she could.

There was a knock at the door. Finley went to answer it and was handed a note. He read it and walked back to the table. He sat in a chair and leaned his forearms onto his thighs so he hovered near Elyssa. "Elyssa, do you know someone named Dr. Klara Westergren?"

Elyssa looked at the floor as she searched her memory, then shook her head.

"Dr. Westergren works in a lab that developed lab-grown butter and—"

"Cheese?" Elyssa lifted her head, sitting upright. "This is out of Seattle?"

Xander whispered, "No sudden moves, please," then eased her back into his arms.

"Yes," Finley said. "You know Dr. Westergren?"

"No. But Eddie was talking to Orest in Paris about cheese, and Orest asked Eddie to give him the name and contact information of the person Eddie knew who was developing the process. Oh shit." She clamped her hands over her mouth, muffling her, "Why?"

"She went missing two days ago. Her partner said that she went out to walk the dog. When the dog came home unaccompanied, a search was conducted. There is no sign of her anywhere."

"Seattle isn't far from Alaska," Elyssa whispered.

"Box number four?" White asked cryptically.

Finley's phone buzzed, and he quietly answered.

"Elyssa, drink." Xander touched her hand. "Do you need a break?"

"Yes, if I could have a minute." She'd gone clammy, and exhaustion weighed heavily over her body.

"Just before you take that break," Finely said, stretching out his arm to hand her his phone, "I have your roommate on the line. Tell her where your passport is and that she's to hand it to the FBI special agent at the door."

"My passport?" *Why in the world? Maybe to check my country stamps?* Elyssa accepted the phone. "Jen?"

"Elyssa, what's happening?" Jen's voice quivered.

"I'm sorry for the disturbance. My passport is in the center drawer on my desk, right in front. Can you give it to whoever is there?" Elyssa asked.

"Are you okay?" Jen whispered.

"Yeah, well, do I have a story for you. Just not now. I'll talk to you when I can. Okay?"

30

———

White made a call, and soon someone knocked on the door with a stretcher covered in pristine white sheets.

"I don't need to go to the hospital," Elyssa mumbled.

"No." White smiled. "But it would be good if you lie down for a bit. And this is much more comfortable than the floor."

White pointed to a place where the stretcher should be parked, then she walked to the door, effectively dismissing the first responder.

Xander got up from behind Elyssa and snapped his fingers to tell Radar to get off her lap.

Elyssa missed Radar's weight as soon as it was gone.

White unbuckled the straps on the gurney and adjusted the headrest to a comfortable elevation, then stepped aside.

Elyssa expected Xander to hold out his hand, but instead, he did a kneeling squat and scooped her into his arms. It was the stupidest, most girly sensation in the world, but Elyssa really liked it. She liked how it made her feel precious and cared for. Maybe it harkened back to the time when loved ones cradled her in their arms when she was a baby. Who knew? But it was true that it was wonderful. And she was a little sad it was over when Xander gently laid her on the stretcher.

"Do you want Radar back on your legs?" Xander asked, handing her a drink, then moving a bag of chips within reach.

"I would, thank you."

Xander lifted Radar into place, his hand on the tactical vest handle and another under his hind legs. Radar seemed used to it, lucky dog.

She should be mortified that that all happened in front of White when it seemed so intimate, *felt* so intimate. But Elyssa had zero energy to worry about such things right now.

Radar across her lap not only helped with Elyssa's blood pressure, but it also made her feel less vulnerable.

Xander had moved over to the wall and sat on the floor with his legs crossed at the ankles.

White dimmed the lights, then she too came to sit on the floor next to Xander with her legs stretched out in front of her.

Elyssa could see them both without strain.

"If you felt up to it, Elyssa," White's voice matching the calm state of the room, "I thought maybe you could ramble."

"Ramble." Elyssa tried on the word.

"I bet you've had a lot of thoughts come up since we've forced a paradigm shift onto you. We're grasping at straws as we figure out what's happening, and I'm afraid that our time frame has moved up to before Tuesday."

"Because Orest didn't have time to wait for me to fly there on my own, he was going to kidnap me." Elyssa paused. "But he bought my ticket. So that means he thought that if something were to happen, it would be later."

"We agree with that," White said. "So rambling, sometimes, in a stream of consciousness can allow your mind to offer up details that we wouldn't know to ask you about. How about you just start talking, and let's see where we go with that?"

"All right. I was thinking about other people's names that I might have mentioned in front of Orest. And if maybe my conversations put people in danger. Maybe Uncle Orest invited them to Singapore, like he did me. I can imagine that people are leading their lives and can't drop everything to go. I had to turn down his invitation. Is he just out grocery shopping for scientists? I may need what's in his brain? I may need what's in hers? With Paca, perhaps Orest thought, he's interesting, I might as well put it in my cart while I'm getting some meat and cheese."

"I don't think that's far off from the reasoning," White said.

Elyssa looked up. "I don't know what Orest wants. What is the goal of all this madness?"

"A return of the USSR," White said.

"Wait. What?" Elyssa's brows pulled tightly together.

"A return of the USSR, The Family has a grievance with the western world because their entire way of life was upended." White turned as Finley and Hiro came back into the room.

Elyssa hadn't seen them leave.

Hiro and Finley moved forward joining their teammates on the floor. Elyssa thought she should probably feel bad that everyone was sitting on the carpet. But they were adults and could make their own choices, so she let that guilt go.

"Elyssa agreed to ramble for a bit," White said.

They both nodded; it seemed like a tactic they liked.

"Here I go with my rambling. I get why Orest would want me. I even kind of get why they'd want the cheese scientist and Eddie. What I don't get is Paca. It turns out that because I did some consultation work with NASA on food, and Paca has been back and forth talking to them, we have someone in common. Belinda Hopkins. And in the pattern of rambling, I was thinking about Belinda because Orest had been very interested in her work with enclosed groups."

"It's so odd to want to go back to being the USSR," Elyssa said. "There's a word for that, *hiraeth.* I think it's Gaelic, maybe? It means nostalgia and grief for a place you long for but can never return to. Although it appears that Orest is doing his best to go back. But I was talking about Belinda, and the last conversation I had with her really sounds like it might apply here. She's part of an advisory group for NASA – seems all I talk about lately is NASA."

"For the Mars expedition?" Hiro asked.

"For over a decade, Belinda has been working on the psychology of confined groups. Astronauts are one kind, but also oil rigs, remote science installations, and submarines, things like that." Elyssa scratched the back of her neck. "Sorry, I feel like the kid who was just told she was adopted, and while mommy and daddy love me very much, they didn't make me." Elyssa grimaced. "No, that's not a great comparison. I don't really have one. Rug pulled from under my feet." She reached a handout. "I'm a big girl. I can readily admit that I am as gullible as anyone else. Naïve with a major case of wanting to be connected to a family. Which is why, when this amazing, warm, funny, supportive uncle showed up—no, he's an uncle-figure. An uncle-figure who apparently kidnapped one of my best friends—I easily accepted him at face value." She frowned deeply. "You told Eddie's fiancé, Ben, right? How's he holding up?"

"We didn't," Finley said. "This information is in a chain of authority, and I'm not at liberty to act. None of us in this working group is able to talk with him."

"Shit." Elyssa blinked.

"You were saying about your social psychologist friend?" White reminded her.

Elyssa stared at White, trying to remember why she'd even brought this up. "Yes, she's been talking a lot lately about understanding the problem with how American society is having an addiction crisis. I know everyone is a bit addicted to the algorithms on social media and what have you. But she said that there's a big chunk of the human race that has an addiction-prone brain. And that recent peer-reviewed A++ kinds of research studies say that revenge is addictive."

"What's this?" Finley asked.

"They did MRIs and found that revenge lights up the same space in the brain associated with other addictions, porn, drugs, gambling, and alcohol. Revenge, in these kinds of brains, releases dopamine to reinforce that revenge-seeking behavior. And Belinda said that in some people, the pleasure of the chemical reward means that the drive for the reward supersedes self-control and good judgment. There's this powerful 'happy brain', if you will, created in the presence of retribution. It can become compulsive and unhealthy. And, like any addiction, revenge addiction can both run in families and ruin families. I think anyone with two eyes can see that in the wild. White, you said that the Zorics have a grievance from their entire way of life getting upended. I'm imagining that the Zorics and Kalinskys are Russian mafia-type families. And if they have the genetic predisposition for revenge addictions—as mafia-type families often do—it sounds like they might be trying to OD. That's kind of scary."

"It's an interesting theory," White said.

"Yeah, well, Belinda says that grievance, the feeling that 'I didn't get mine' or 'someone took something away from me' is a trigger that pushes people with the propensity for revenge addiction to drug-seek. In this case, that drug is secreted when they can say 'gotcha!' It's the cruelty that's the point. There's an internal drive to see suffering, so the addict doesn't undergo withdrawal symptoms. This is physiological in nature." Elyssa scratched behind Radar's ears, then reached into her backpack to pull out an envelope of electrolytes. Shaking the crystals to the bottom before tearing them open, she said. "I mean, schadenfreude is a thing. And, for example, I'm thrilled that the snowmobile guy got some instant karma when Radar bit him. But what I'm talking about here is another level."

"Dr. Belinda Hopkins," White said. "You said peer reviewed, so this study is published?"

"Yes, and there was more to it, like, if the results of the revenge were short-lived, the person had to keep gathering personal grievances so that then they could have reasons to seek retribution, which, can I say, is a pretty messed-up way to live a life. And the vengeance can come by proxy like I got mine through Radar."

"Someone can take revenge on your behalf, and you'll still get the dopamine hit?" Xander asked.

"Like a whole family might all feel really good when one of their family members does something that makes people they don't like suffer. You don't need to be mad at someone specific; a group works fine. The addiction is obsessive-compulsive. The same as any addictive cycle: craving, tension, arousal, revenge (which is the drug hit), and around and around and around."

"Well, I can't see anything wrong with that hypothesis as it applies to the Zorics," White said. "That's the pattern we've been documenting."

"Maybe we just need to send the Zorics to a revenge rehab center with a twelve-step program to treat them for their addictions," Hiro said.

"Not saying it wouldn't be beneficial to them," Finley said.

"So as long as it's in a MAX security prison system where they're serving life."

"Looking forward to the dopamine hit of the perp walk?" White asked.

"I am looking forward to the world being a safer place," Finley said. "If I wanted a dopamine hit, it would be much more extreme. The family would be wiped off the face of the planet. Kidding." He pressed his lips out as if he was reconsidering what he'd just said. "Okay, only partially kidding. They've done a lot of bad things to innocent people, and I would like that to stop."

"Like what?" Elyssa whispered, still trying to put together that jovial, life-loving Uncle Orest was Orest Kalinsky, a terrorist. "If they did something really terrible, I would have heard about them, right?"

"The kinds of things they do? It's likely that they killed the power in a hospital and wiped out all of the medical records in Syria. It's likely that they messed up the instruments on the flight and disappeared a plane," Hiro said.

Elyssa paused her hand as the envelope emptied into her bottle. "Not possible."

"Completely possible." Xander reached for the packet and bottle, then finished pouring in the salts. After mixing the solution, he handed the bottle to Elyssa, pressing it into her hand as she stared at the wall.

She blinked, and she was back focusing on White. "I'm sorry, White, my ramblings didn't get me anywhere nearer to understanding why you have a fistful of my photos. But I'll let you know if I come up with anything."

"While we appreciate how hard these revelations have been today," White said, "there will be time to process it later. We are working on the Orest problem from various angles. The angle we need from you is to help us understand Orest's movements during your overseas visit. We're arranging tickets to get you back over to London. We're asking you to please go to London with Xander and retrace your footsteps for him, so we might be able to figure out what Orest was up to.

"You mean." Elyssa looked around the room, then shifted in his arms so her gaze landed on Xander. "She means now?"

"Now," Xander said. "That's why we were getting your passport."

"I don't have clothes." Elyssa could hear the bewilderment in her voice.

"We'll buy them." Xander reached out and rubbed Radar's butt. "We really don't have any time to waste. And frankly, you don't want to be in DC right now."

Her breath hitched. "Because you think the city is the target?"

"No. You are," Xander said softly. "Three Zoric family members were waiting for you when you got off the plane."

"You're a target," White said, "and we need to know why. So, I'm suggesting London. Finley, though, could take you into protective custody, if you prefer."

Rubbing the words on her tattoo, Elyssa drew her focus away from Xander, flicking it toward White. "I'll go to London with Xander. It's just I wasn't ready for this."

"Xander will be your point guy along with Radar," White said.

"Radar, are you sure?" Hiro asked.

"Radar is trained for electronics alert and found the case in Newark, I'll remind you. He's also a medical alert dog," Xander said. "He can wear the vest and go anywhere. He passed all his trials, he was only taken out of the program because he was too high-drive to make that his lifestyle."

Hiro touched his phone on speaker.

"Sir?"

"I need a service dog vest for a German Shepherd. I need it now. Lights and sirens getting it here. I'd go down to Sandra's office and borrow the one from her dog. Tell her it's an emergency."

"Sir."

And that line ended.

"Xander and Radar will be with you every step of the way, Elyssa," White said. "But we need you to be as specific as possible, not just location, but where in that location did Orest stand or sit. Do you recognize anyone? Do you remember speaking to anyone? Every detail. It's important. Do you have your phone?"

"No," Elyssa whispered. "I lost it when the plane dumped over to the side." She put her hands on her head. "Oh wow, you're asking me to get right back onto a plane!"

31

———

Elyssa

Sunday

Washington, D.C.

Xander shoved his carry-on into the bin above and then swung into his seat. "You seem to be doing okay."

"First class, a girl can get used to this." They were just words to say. Social convention.

"First class, yes." Xander looked around.

"Did they put us up here because the team was afraid I was going to die back in coach?" Elyssa asked.

"Bunch of reasons: last-minute flight, seat availability, Radar." He sat down and reached for her hand. "A lot has been thrown at you in the last couple of hours."

"Yah think?" Her brows went up to her hairline.

"I was checking in because outwardly, you seem to be handling it pretty well."

"I was betrayed," Elyssa said, liking that they were holding hands, liking the warmth and gentleness amongst the cold and cruel. "I feel betrayed. I've been in therapy since I got sick to deal with that subject."

"And that's helping you through this?" Xander asked.

Radar jumped down from his seat across the aisle and pushed into the space at Elyssa and Xander's feet, where he lay down and curled up.

Elyssa thought that Radar wanted to be with Mom and Dad and immediately pushed the thought away.

"Help me draw the parallel, here," Xander said.

"I was angry at my body for betraying me. My strength and my physical abilities were things I always counted on and believed were core parts of me. If my body could turn on me, then so could everything and everyone else. I took my butt to therapy because I was spiraling. There, I came to the conclusion that every aspect of my life that I perceived as solid could suddenly shift without warning. If I can't manipulate circumstances to make myself safer, what could I do? I have to own my responsibility for what my life looks like on the other side of the betrayal. I have to believe in my core that whatever gets thrown at me, I can handle it. It doesn't matter what the betrayal is, I can survive it and find a new way to thrive within the boundaries of my new reality. Orest Kalinsky is a betrayal of my love and esteem. I am pretty damned angry at the manipulation. And I hate this topic, so I'm going to change it to something else." Elyssa drummed her fingers on her knee. "Okay, got it. Let's play a get-to-know-you game, so I can be distracted from the takeoff. I want you to know that I'm being incredibly brave by getting on another flight in D.C. on the same day as the tip-over. We both are."

"Without a doubt. You've been brave for days on end." Xander lifted the back of her hand to his lips and kissed it. "How do you play your game?"

"You get a question, then I get a question. It has to be open-ended, and it has to feel intrusive if not downright embarrassing to ask."

"Wow. You really are a rugby player at heart. You grab the ball and drive it down the field, huh?"

"I said you get to go first," Elyssa shifted in her seat so she could better see him.

"Okay, today strangers came in and upended your life. Has it ever happened to you before that a stranger made a difference in your trajectory?"

"Yes. I left my husband because of a woman at the gas station," Elyssa said without hesitation.

"He was having an affair?"

"Not at all. Glenn was a good person. Good enough. But the scientific team I was leading had just received this major award. Huge. Something I had dreamed of and worked toward for years. And my team won. This is the article that White put on the table earlier."

"Congratulations! I read the article. That's amazing."

"Thank you." She smiled, then took a breath. "I told my family, and they did not say congratulations. They said nothing at all. When the article came out, I searched all over town trying to find the paper, which wasn't that easy. I finally found some at a gas station. And in case the other members of my team had trouble finding one, I purchased all five of the available papers. The counter lady pointed out to me that I had purchased five of the same paper, and I told her that that had been on purpose, because my name was in an article. She leaned forward and said under her breath, 'Uh-oh. What did you do?'"

"She thought you'd committed a crime or something?"

Elyssa shrugged. "I opened the paper and showed her my picture, then pointed to my name. 'That's me!' I told her." Elyssa's gaze fell to Radar as she remembered the scene. "This woman at the cash register picked up the paper and held it over her head, announcing my award to everyone in line. She said, 'This calls for some dancing.' And then she started singing. What a beautiful voice she had. As she danced behind her cash register, and the whole line of strangers was dancing too, all in celebration with me."

"Wow," he whispered.

"It was very wow. I was sobbing, I was so grateful. I am still so grateful." She pulled her hair to the side, tucking it neatly behind her ears. "But as I drove home, I realized that strangers lifted me up higher than my husband did. And I couldn't undo that in my head. As much as I love that woman in the gas station for her generosity of spirit, I guess I was also grateful to her because I was tired of trying to get Glenn—my then-husband—to tell me I was enough. That he was proud. I kept working for it, striving for it, and it was a waste of energy."

"What did you want to happen?" Xander asked.

"Honestly? I wanted him to sweep me into his arms and spin me around, throw back his head, and laugh with joy. I wanted him to set me on my feet and gaze into my eyes and say, 'You are amazing. What you've accomplished is incredible and will change lives.'"

"It is, and it will," Xander said with conviction. "What did Glenn say instead?"

"He said, 'Okay, good. I'm going to mow the lawn.'"

Xander just sat there and imagined what a gut punch she'd taken.

"Don't look at me with pity."

"This is incredulity with an overlay of aghast," Xander countered.

She pursed her lips and nodded. "The end wasn't a bang, it was the hum of a shutting garage door, and the buzz of the lawn mower. I went into town, found the newspapers, had my dance party, and then went home to pack a bag. That was pretty much that. Now, I live a poorer but very rich life with friends I love, doing things I love, both at work and for fun."

"Tell me about the fun things."

"No. It's your turn. I told you my sad story. You owe me something of equal weight. Or I am left as the pitiful one."

Xander laughed, and Elyssa read that laugh as nervous, maybe a bit bewildered, but he was definitely uncomfortable. She raised a questioning brow.

"I gave you a much narrower choice of topics," Xander said.

"Fair." Elyssa reached for her bottle and took a swig. "Got one. Tell me about your most excruciating dating fail."

He looked at her in silence, then rubbed his thumb over his chin. "I go out for dinners more than I date. When you say date, do you mean in a deep relationship?"

"Whatever you want to tell me about," Elyssa said.

"I have a group of friends, and the women in the group set me up for a dinner. They thought they had found this really great match for me."

"Checked all the boxes?" Elyssa asked. "Intelligent, attractive, interesting hobbies, successful career."

"Seemed so. But there weren't enough boxes on that survey."

"Uh oh. Not just a bad fit."

"Good fit actually." Xander was brushing a soothing thumb along the side of her hand. "I enjoyed myself on our one date. She suggested Chinese food, and then we went to the Capital because they were having a free concert, featuring buskers, and it was a lovely evening weather-wise. Yeah, all good. But by the end of the date, she was telling me that we were meant to be and started asking what I thought about where we should live when we moved in together. She thought we should consider the school districts. She wanted her parents to meet me."

"That's a lot for me to take in as someone hearing the story. I can't imagine what that felt like from your point of view."

"It felt like a win at first, to be honest," Xander said. "From the start, I was grateful to my friends for introducing us. Things were going well, and I could see that we had the potential for future dates. Then the red flags popped out in quick succession. It would have been so much worse had I been months in when I discovered that she wasn't—" He held his hand up, then let it drop. "'Sane' was what I was going to say, but since I don't want to misuse psychological words, I can't say that. But in my world, she's delusional."

"Present tense?" Elyssa asked.

"That I can't say. I haven't seen her in about six months."

"Go back. You haven't seen her, does that mean you decided to date her?"

"No. I told her I had a nice time, but I didn't feel like this was heading anywhere romantic. Best wishes. She smiled at me and said I'd change my mind, because she could feel it in her heart. It was just a matter of timing on my part, and she was patient. This was years ago. I was interviewing with the DIA."

"Okay. I'm stuck on the words 'I haven't seen her,' and I'm stuck on how your muscles contract when you talk about her. The way I'm reading that is that you're conflicted because you feel like you have to defend yourself against this woman, and at the same time, you were raised to never hit a girl."

"You're good at this."

She lowered her chin and raised a questioning brow.

"She never put me in a position where I felt defensive." He shuffled around in his seat. "She had a way to get under my skin because you're right," he turned to catch Elyssa's gaze, "if this were a guy, I'd have known how to handle things."

"*Mano a mano.*"

"We'd both understand the boundaries," Xander said.

"Yeah, well, picking out a house with a good zip code for schools on a first date says she's not great at understanding boundaries, even if you did know how to navigate them. What happened after that? She started calling you every fifteen minutes for days on end?"

"I told you we went out for Chinese on our date. Every time I was in that area, I'd see her out and about, which wasn't frequent, maybe every few months or so."

"A random 'we're at the same diner' kind of thing or 'she's hunting you down and stalking you' kind of thing?"

"Random." He looked over the tops of the seats, then scowled, paused, and shook his head. "Had to be random. Yeah, random. But the next night, say around ten o'clock, the doorbell would ring, and there would be a Chinese deliveryman delivering egg rolls. My address. Her name paying the tab."

Elyssa sucked in a long gasp. "What? From the date night restaurant?"

"Always a different place. I guess it was so I couldn't call and put my name on a do-not-disturb Chinese take-out list."

"Yeah, if some guy did that to me … And you're right, that doesn't seem to break a law. That would be hard to use in court to get a restraining order because you're not endangered. It is creepy. But this stopped months ago? Do you think she'll pop back on the scene?"

"I moved to my condo since then. So it might be the person at my old address who is receiving random egg rolls." He grinned at the thought, then let it fall off as his face grew serious. "Up until that point, I'd had zero interactions with someone like her. I didn't know the ins and outs of it. But I was hired by the DIA."

Elyssa shook her head. He was making a point that she didn't get.

"They do an extensive background check. I have to disclose everything in order for them to move me through my security clearance. I know they looked into her because they look into every nook and cranny of your life. They have security to maintain."

He rubbed his thumb over her "little bit" tattoo.

"It's not my turn, but I told you about my tattoo. Would you tell me the significance of yours?" Elyssa asked.

Xander slid down in his chair, so he was talking right near her ear. He had a way of speaking that seemed to hold the sound waves in tight, so that nothing said would drift off to some other interested listener. It felt very spy-craft to her. And it reminded Elyssa what this trip was all about. They were depending on her to remember which tree she stood under almost two weeks ago to save the Western world.

Her heart vibrated.

"It's the symbol for the AWG, the Asymmetric Warfare Group," Xander said. "Our job, before the group was disbanded, was to find the dangerous ideas that put our national defense at risk. We were looking for the ideas that pushed the envelope and were off the radar. And in that way, we found the Zoric plot years ago. But we didn't understand it. We still don't. We have pieces. We basically know the how and some of the ramifications. But we don't know the end event. We don't know what they've planned or why."

Elyssa shook her head. She couldn't contemplate that. Instead, she asked, "Finding dangers that were off the radar, is that how you named your dog?" She put her hand down between the seats to scritch Radar.

"Radar came pre-named," Xander said. "But I took it as a sign."

"Ender was your AWG name because that was your job to find the off-the-books kinds of dangers and end them?" she whispered.

"It was," Xander whispered back.

She squeezed his arm. "Will you end this one?"

"Me?" he shook his head. "I don't think so. Not alone. But for the world's sake, I hope like hell that together we can."

32

Elyssa
Monday
Atlantic Ocean

"Ladies and gentlemen, this is your captain speaking. I have received word that a major solar storm has caused a glitch in electrical activity. There are widespread outages that began in Morocco and Iceland and have now hit southern England, including our destination city, London. London is rerouting all international flights due to power outages and intermittent communications. Our plane will land in Paris, adding one hour and twenty minutes to our flight time."

Moans moved through the cabin.

"Once there, I cannot tell you what your next steps should be, as this is an unforeseen weather event, and we don't have a timetable for when the airports will be functioning again. Check with the company that provides you with travel insurance to see if they can assist you. We're sorry for the inconvenience."

Elyssa lifted her head from Xander's shoulder. "It's the Zorics, isn't it?" she whispered.

"Without evidence, I don't know. But my gut says it is."

"Have they done something like this before?" Elyssa asked.

"They interrupted communications between the tower and the planes in Newark just after your flight took off."

"I read about that. That's brazen. Did The Family know Orest was at the airport?"

"Orest is the one who did it."

Orest did it? Elyssa thought back to their flight out of Newark. She and Eddie had barely scraped through the door before they took off, and Orest had looked nervous. She remembered thinking he looked pale and a little sweaty. And she remembered thinking that there was a distraction in his eyes that wasn't typically there. Then he'd looked at his watch and said, "No, no, right now all is good. I had anticipated a slight delay. Perhaps not this long. But the benefit is that you made the plane." He'd anticipated a delay, so perhaps changed a timer on something? And the delay was longer than he'd considered, so he was at risk from his actions. Their plane should have flown out of range to the watch of a different tower. He only wanted other people to be endangered. Yes, his relief seemed to come when they were over the farmland, and she naïvely assumed he hated takeoffs, too.

Elyssa pushed herself up taller in her chair. "Did the Zorics tip us over on the way to D.C.?"

"No. That was the Secret Service, playing with a new toy. They're sorry. They won't do it again."

Elyssa frowned. "Huh."

"Yeah." Xander shifted his jaw as he nodded.

"They owe me a phone."

Silence fell between them.

Xander had his own phone out and was scrolling international news sites.

The entire country of Portugal had lost electricity.

In Spain, a patchwork of grids was still operating.

"We're almost to Paris, right?" she checked her watch. "If this is spreading, I'd like to be on the ground. Newark sounded horrific. Understaffed the way they were, and the papers said the people who worked in the traffic controllers had to take trauma leave, having lived through the chaos of a sky full of planes and no ability to keep them from plowing into each other."

Xander squeezed her hand, then released his grip so he could text.

XANDER: **Did you land? Are they getting on the boat?**

ELYSSA DESPERATELY WANTED to know what that meant and had a sick feeling that the boat had something to do with the family retreating to the island to escape the world on fire.

ADELE: **Yes. No.**

XANDER SLID HIS PHONE AWAY. "We still have time."

"What's their machine going to do to people? Is this it? An electrical outage?"

"Do I think that's it? No. I think it's stage one. They're wearing down people's reserves and good feelings. They'll stretch the rescue workers thin. They'll weaken the enemy before the strike. They'll affect the food systems as people use up their household reserves and eat their melting frozen items."

They were silent as they landed. There was no announcement of electrical issues here. Xander hadn't seen anything on the news, though Spain was now wholly without electricity, as were Greenland and Great Britain.

Xander carried Elyssa's backpack along with his own and a roller bag. As they moved through customs, Elyssa held Radar's lead. Over his tactical vest with its supply pockets, Radar wore a service dog vest with PTSD patches, American flags, and a pink name badge that read, "Dixie."

As soon as they were out the other side, Xander got a ping and a link to a map. He led them over to an exact spot in the airport between the men's room and a café.

A guy walked up. "Hey, there you are. Hiro sent me." He set a package down beside Radar. "Dixie, hi, Dixie," he crooned to Radar. "Such a sweet girl. Can I pet her?" Without an answer, he crouched down. "Not a good cover, man, when the parts don't fit the outfit." He looked up. "Hiro said he did what he could for you. In the bag, you'll find Euros. They'd prefer you leave the plastic in your wallet. Nothing that's lighting up a sign saying you're here, might buy you a little time. There are the coordinates for a London safe house." He stood, and his tone was barely audible. "Hey, man, I don't know what's going on, but you have a very angry family looking for your girl." He gave Radar a final scrub. "There's a boating service that can take you from Paris to Le Havre off their normal line. You're looking for Victor. He's been paid. From there, take the ferry. Pre-purchased tickets are in the bag. Get off in Portsmouth to start your retrace."

"England's got no electricity," Xander said.

"Not my care, brother." He patted Xander's shoulder.

"Good to see you. Hope you enjoy your stay!" He raised a hand to wave to Elyssa.

Elyssa picked up Radar's lead and the bag and wandered out the door with Xander. They grabbed a cab. "English?" Xander asked.

"Yes, sir."

"We have some time before our train leaves," Xander told the cabby. "Is there somewhere quiet we can go and get a shower, a nap, and walk to a meal?"

The cabby rubbed his brow.

Xander repeated himself in what sounded to Elyssa like flawless French.

"I have a friend with a room she rents," the man said in English.

"She takes cash?"

"We shall see." The man got on the line and spoke quickly in a language that Elyssa didn't understand.

"She says it's double for cash plus a dog, and she'll meet you there now for three hundred euros."

"That's fine," Xander said. "Thanks."

While the taxi driver concluded the call, Xander reached for Elyssa's hand, and they laced their fingers together.

Elyssa was afraid of saying the wrong thing at the wrong time, so she shut her mouth and waited to see what would happen next.

The place the driver brought them to was in a tiny court-yard. It was small, but clean and private.

"Elyssa, Radar hasn't had any exercise in a couple of days now, and that's not good for him. I need to take him for a run. Do you feel safe here by yourself?"

"Yes, I could use a shower and time to wash my hair. Do you think you'll be long?"

"That depends on Radar, about an hour. Then we can get something to eat and head over to find Victor."

He pulled out his phone and sent a text.

Xander: **Is the family on the boat?**

He laid the phone on the table while he went to use the bathroom and change into his running clothes.

When his phone pinged, Elyssa glanced over.

Adele: **No.**

When Xander returned, he read the message, then said, "She's in Singapore."

"Got it," Elyssa said. But this was a whole new world to her.

～

IT WAS nice to have some time to decompress with no one looking over at her to see if she was going to pass out on them.

Clean was a wonderful feeling.

Elyssa pulled her freshly washed and dried hair into a bun at the nape of her neck, then went to figure out her clothing situation with a towel wrapped around her chest.

Elyssa had four more days of panties because she always packed those into her carry-on like she was going to have dysentery and shit herself ten times a day. She picked out a pair that was both comfortable for athletics and made her butt look cute.

She was down to her only other pair of pants. They were good pants to have, though. Anti-microbial, so they wouldn't stink, anti-stain, water-resistant, fleece-lined. They were her favorites because they slid easily over her thigh-high compression socks, and nothing got bound up.

There were no clean shirts in her bag.

She was standing there in her bra, dressed except for the

question of what to do about a shirt, when there was a knock at the door.

"Me and Radar," Xander called.

"Yup."

He let himself in and shut the door behind them.

Radar's tongue hung long.

So did Elyssa's. *Look at him. Wow.*

And all Elyssa could think was that the timing was wrong. Yes, she wanted to have a relationship with Xander Belov. Yes, she wanted to spend her time getting to know him.

But how dare he show up in the End Times, distracting her like this?

It was really inappropriate.

Save the world, then—*then.*

Elyssa clamped her mouth shut and sent Xander a look of fury. "Goddammit. I don't want to fall in love with you until later." Elyssa scowled. "Stop it. Stop it right now."

"I … Okay." Confusion and laughter fought for dominance in his expression. "Could you be just a little more explicit?"

She gestured up and down Xander's body. "You're doing it right now, stop."

"Now?" Xander pointed a finger toward the floor. "I'm doing it now." He looked at Radar, then back at Elyssa. "Right now, I'm doing something that makes you feel like you're falling in love with me?" He wrinkled his brow. "I walked in the door after Radar's run. I'm covered in sweat."

She licked her lips. "Yes!"

"Covered in sweat makes you fall in love with me?"

"Obviously." She held her palms up and vibrated her hands at him. "Yes, sweat with the gorgeous dog looking like he would eat a bear for you."

"Eat a bear to protect you, yes." Xander pulled the towel from the neck of his sweatshirt, balled it up, and held it to his chest. "For me? He might leave me some leftovers, once he was full."

"Stop it!"

He lifted his brow. "Doing it again?"

"Self-deprecating humor. Glint of joy in your eyes."

"No joy then." He canted his head. "Some joy?" He held his finger and his thumb to show an amount. "A smidge of joy?" His smile was delicious.

Elyssa couldn't fight against a smile like that. The stress that she'd turned into, whatever this scene was, melted in the light of his smile. "Fine, a smidge of joy," she relented. "But this cannot be combined with sweat and an adoring dog. One component at a time is acceptable. Three is just mean." She wandered over and put her forehead on his chest.

And he wrapped her in his arms and dropped a kiss onto her hair. "Because you falling in love with me would be me being mean?" He rocked her back and forth.

"Thank you for understanding." And after standing there like that for a long minute, she lifted to her toes to kiss him. "Shower, please."

He released her and started toward the bathroom.

"Wait," she called. "First, I need to borrow a shirt."

33

———

XANDER

Monday

Paris, France

"YOU READY?" Xander asked, bringing his pack into the room.

They both turned as Xander's phone rang.

"Hiro, I'm putting you on speaker. I'm here with Elyssa. We're in a private space."

"The electrical outage is spreading into France."

"Do you have a local safe house for us, or should we follow the earlier plan to get to Portsmouth?"

"Let's see if you can get to the ferry before the lights go out," Hiro said. "Question, why Morocco, Greenland, most of England, Portugal, Spain, and now France, and not the rest of Europe? I'll answer that. If it were me, I'd want to see what happened. What safety measures were in place? How do people respond? Why would the Zorics take it in stages? I'm working under the theory that this is stage one, and it escalates from here."

"Agreed," Xander said. "They had to be careful about how they spread the attack. They couldn't be too close to Russia, so it couldn't include Poland. And not Germany because of U.S. installations and their military and weaponry," Xander said. "No need to put NATO on high alert. Just enough to test the theory. Nothing that would cause a societal meltdown. It's the same reason they chose Newark."

"Go on with that thought," Hiro said.

"Newark is close, they could budge over a bit and hit Manhattan. 9-11 is still a fresh trauma in many New Yorkers' minds." Xander was looking at Elyssa when he asked, "What would happen if New York's towers went dark like Newark's did?"

"Panic," Elyssa said. "Terror."

"Terror. Bingo," Hiro said. "It would be investigated as a terror attack, and the Zorics don't want the scrutiny. I checked my Aurora Hunter app, and there has been high activity on the sun. There was an alert suggesting that it could mess with our systems. The same alert that went out when Newark had their event."

"What if the call that Orest told Elyssa that he got—the one that he said was about a family emergency and he needed to get to Singapore—what if that was the family saying, 'We have the cover of a good sun storm. We're a go.'?" Xander asked.

"Checking your theory with data." There was a pause on Hiro's side, then "Elyssa, when did Orest say that he had to go to Singapore?"

"Let's see. We landed in D.C. I was packing for Alaska when he called and said I needed to go with him to Singapore after the start of the race. He didn't tell me a date. But I reminded him I had to fly home Wednesday at the latest to be in the wedding. When I suggested flying to Singapore on Monday, he seemed upset. More upset than I remember him being in the past, and he left to get a glass of water. I still thought he was going to be in Alaska to see the race leave Fairbanks. But the same day I got to Lumberjack, I realized I couldn't handle the cold, and I made arrangements to go home. Again, Orest asked me to accompany him to Singapore, where a crisis was unfolding. He told me he had changed his plans and was leaving in the morning. But so much has happened so fast across so many time zones that I can't tell up from down."

"Friday, you flew to Fairbanks," Xander said. "Saturday, you were in Lumberjack, and we met. Sunday, Orest flew to Singapore, and we flew to D.C."

"What day is it today? Monday?" Elyssa asked. "Yes. I was supposed to still be in Lumberjack today, all day Tuesday, and fly out Wednesday. Wedding stuff Thursday. Get back on the plane next Monday—Monday a week from now—and fly to Singapore."

"I was going through the information we pulled from Orest's phone. He doesn't use it for the most part. A text on Saturday morning," Hiro said. "It was a sun emoji, and it said see you Sunday-Tuesday."

"That's the cover story, the sun spots are creating havoc," Xander said. "That's pretty weak sauce. Is it working?"

"Europe is throwing it out there as the cause," Hiro said with a mouthful of something. "We think it's to keep everyone calm. But, yeah, it seems to be working. It's a good cover for the governments to offer the citizens an acceptable explanation. It's also good cover for the Zorics."

"But sunspots could be the cause, right?" Elyssa asked.

Neither Xander nor Hiro answered her.

After a pregnant pause, Hiro said, "Here's a question for you, Elyssa. Was Eddie planning on going by his lab during your layover in D.C.?"

"No," Elyssa said. "We were heading into the weekend.

Because he'd been gone all week, he didn't have anything running that needed his attention. He was going to go in after he got back from Alaska."

"Fairbanks FBI went by Paca's lab," Hiro said, "and it was empty. All his files, computer, and equipment are gone. Empty. Knowing this, Finley's team went over to check on Eddie's lab, and it had a huge bar bolted across the door and a "Do Not Cross" sign. Some information about contamination is available, along with a contact number that can be reached on Monday for further details. Upon further inspection, Finley's team discovered that the lab was also emptied. All of it. Everything. Same with the cheese lab in Seattle."

"They stole their labs?" Elyssa asked. "What did they think they would just set them up on their island and keep going? With the food research, it makes a little sense. But the squirrels? I mean, what the heck?"

"We're trying to figure it out, too," Hiro said. "What do you know about Paca's work? What did he say when you were there?"

"I know he's going to work for NASA to see if they can help the astronauts snooze through most of the trip. Do you think Orest thought that might be a good idea for his family?"

"White thinks Orest would find that an intriguing idea," Hiro said. "Orest is a brilliant man. Evil, yes. Crazy, yes. But brilliant. He can hire the right scientists to fix the problems that he foresees."

Elyssa said, "Here's an interesting thing Paca told us: When the squirrels wake up each year after their hibernation, they have to go through adolescence again, which sounds horrific. And each year during hibernation, they develop a kind of amnesia. They recognize their family and close friends, but they don't remember much more. Hibernation amnesia, in my mind, makes trying to hibernate astronauts headed to Mars a terrible idea."

"How far did Paca get with the astronaut hibernation, Elyssa? Did he say?" Xander asked.

"He had the designs and the science ready. He had done some work with large animal studies. Orest released Paca from his contracts to allow NASA to bring Paca in to get that going with human studies. But if Paca is like me, he would have been submitting his work to Orest all along. And Orest built my prototype without my knowing that he was doing it. He might well already have Paca's prototype built, too." Elyssa sank to the floor and reached her arms out for Radar. "Holy crap, he is batshit crazy."

"Agreed," Xander said. "Hiro, I'm changing the subject. You're seeing the news feeds from the affected areas. Are people panicking?

"Hardly," Hiro said. "It's like a national holiday. Everyone's out, looking like they're having a great time. Spontaneous street dancing."

"Okay, if you have nothing else, I'm going to end the call. Elyssa and I need to get over to the boat and head for Le Havre. What's the reason for a boat?"

"No CCV. We don't want anyone tracking Elyssa."

34

Xander

Monday

Paris, France

Xander had a backpack on either shoulder and his wheelie in one hand. Elyssa wasn't looking good. When he tucked his arm around her, she had no energy in her body.

He'd get them to the boat, and she could sleep for the five or so hours that they'd be on the water. Once they arrived in Le Havre, he'd come up with the next steps.

Radar stepped out into the courtyard, and as always, his keen gaze swept the area, his nose went up. This time, his body went rigid.

With his arm outstretched in front of Elyssa, Xander backed up against the wall. "Stay here a sec," he said. Signaling Radar to his side, Radar rounded into place, but his gaze was unwavering.

Xander slid down to see what Radar had fixed on.

Two men were climbing out of a car. The driver reached under his coat to the back of his waist and retrieved a gun. He looked directly at the archway into the courtyard, where the single room was situated. Then, he scanned the street, the buildings, and finally landed back on his cohort. They locked eyes. Their mission was a go.

How did anyone find them here?

Xander swung his gaze around the courtyard.

They were trapped.

His focus fixed on the wall ladder, a typical feature throughout France. They allowed people onto the roof for repair or snow removal.

"Elyssa," Xander whispered. "Can you climb the ladder?" If Elyssa could get up the ladder, Radar could climb second, and with his supply pack on his back, they could slip out of sight.

Elyssa looked at Radar, then at the ladder, touched her medical bracelet, and shook her head. The skin on her face looked lax as if even holding her normal facial expression in place was too much.

He pressed her back into the room, moving her as efficiently as possible. "Two men are coming up with weapons. If they get in, you get into the bathroom and lock the door. Leave Radar in the bedroom. His job is to protect you. You are not the mama protecting your puppy. He is a war dog. If you're in his way, you only make his job harder. Trust him."

"Absolutely," she managed, then put her hand on Radar's head.

"Radar, guard Elyssa." With that command, Radar expanded his chest, his ears up and rotating, his gaze keen.

Xander pulled the door shut, tested that it had locked, and was scanning the courtyard for weapons of opportunity—a cast iron chair, a wooden flagpole.

Assessing the usefulness of the ladder and rejecting it as a strategy, Xander's gaze slid to the archway between the buildings. *If it's good enough for a Bratislavan street thug, it's good enough for me.*

The goons waited on the other side of the street, watching traffic and looking for their break, unaware that they'd been spotted.

Xander pushed his hands into one side of the thick arch and kicked his feet up, pressing them away. He was surprised by how easy it was to get into this position. Hand then foot, hand then foot, he bear-crawled up the supports until his back curved with the ancient archway. The damp cold from the plaster radiated into his palms and up his wrists.

When Xander had been reviewing the effectiveness of this move, back in Bratislava, the goons' smiles and their uptilted heads had been part of the razzle-dazzle. They had meant for Xander to look up. They meant for him to be confused, for his brain to face something new that needed processing.

The traffic had cleared. The men crossed the street. They slowed on approach, each with a gun in hand, each weapon held in ready position against their chests. These weren't Bratislavan street thugs; these men were trained.

Just as Xander would do if he was stalking the target, the goons stopped under the cover of the arch to scan the surroundings before moving forward. But if he was flowing through a narrow passage like this, Xander would stack up with his team. He'd never do what these guys were doing, which seemed like some tactic they saw in a YouTube video or a poorly written movie scene. They stood opposite each other, each with their back to the wall, and they were going to peel off in opposite directions.

That might work if it were only Elyssa.

But the hell if it would work with Radar on the scene.

Xander was glad his dog was a silent sentinel. The less they showed their hand, the better. A bark could be easily traced. A bullet could be lined up, and the source of the sound could be eliminated.

For a split second, Xander questioned his decision to lock the door. Radar running onto the scene, evening out the numbers of fighters might feel like a good reflex.

But if they made it past Xander, Elyssa needed a weapon.

No, he'd set things up the best he could.

It was the guns in their hands that scared the shit out of him.

But since they held the pistols to their chests like that, yeah, this might just work.

Xander whistled a light, eerie set of notes.

The men looked up.

As soon as confusion filled their eyes, Xander merely dropped all two hundred and fifty pounds onto them, reaching for the one guy's head to push him down so Xander wasn't catching the goon's cranium in his diaphragm.

Did that. Hated that. Almost died from that.

It was a genius move.

One guy ended up face down with his hands trapped under his body. Xander's knee was on his back.

Xander shifted his other booted foot to the cobblestone, curling his toes under, ready to spring upright.

One goon managed to stagger to his feet, bringing his pistol around.

Xander gripped the barrel tightly. As long as Xander squeezed that barrel, the goon could exercise his trigger finger as much as he wanted. He wouldn't get a shot off.

Twisting his wrist, Xander wrenched the gun from the man's hand.

In order to heave the pistol up over the roof, Xander had to leave himself open to the goon's liver punches. Luckily, the goon was standing, and Xander was kneeling on his friend. The angle was shit for a good blast, and the punches landed on Xander's braced abdominal muscles without much damage.

The gun hit the roof with a thunk, then a skittering as it slid down the slate incline.

It must have caught in the gutter because the gun didn't clatter to the ground.

Two goons. One gun.

Xander brought his fist back around in a hook, hook, upper cut.

The guy beneath him was squirming, and there was a high risk that Xander would get rolled with an ankle lock.

There was still a gun in play underneath the guy.

Xander pressed his toes into the ground and came to his feet. In the micro-moment when his knee lifted, the guy shifted to rise. But Xander slammed his boot against his neck, then drew back and punched the standing goon, who had grabbed a fistful of Xander's belt, preparing to throw him to the ground. The punch landed, the goon's nose squashed flat under Xander's knuckles.

Blood spurted.

The goon's head snapped back, hitting the corner where the sides of the arch came together. The crack was hollow and resounded in the courtyard with a nauseating echo.

The man under Xander's boot had shuffled his knees under him, and he reared up.

This had all gone down in the blink of an eye.

Fluid devastation.

Pain and blood.

A sudden movement out of his right eye pulled Xander's attention away from the gun that now pointed at Xander's center mass.

Goon one wasn't in fact dead from the blow that should have at least knocked him out cold. He drew a knife from his pocket.

The chair and pole that Xander had clocked earlier were behind him.

Xander reasoned that the guy with the knife would come for him. The guy with the gun would pull the trigger only if absolutely necessary. Here in Paris, it would draw all eyes to the scene if there were a shot. The gun was there to incite fear. Maybe. Probably.

They wanted Elyssa.

And Xander had to assume they wanted her dead.

She knew *something*.

As the man gripped his knife with the blade running along the inside of his arm instead of pointed outward like an amateur, he'd lowered his body for stability and started the rounding tai-chi-like movements that would mask the setup for a strike.

The knife guy had to be seeing double. He had to be fighting with a concussion.

Xander pulled off his coat, wrapping it around his left arm to use as a shield since there were no trash can lids in the garden to readily snatch up.

Xander, too, was on the balls of his feet, keeping himself loose, swaying and curving his arms to-and-fro to hide his tactics. He used his footwork to position himself closer to his weapons of opportunity. A chair in his hand like a lion-tamer of old would be helpful right about now.

The man flipped the knife forward as he thrust out.

Xander skated his foot out to the side at an angle, using his height and the length of his arm to crash a fist into the man's jaw.

The knife guy staggered to the side.

The gunman stood solid with his weapon at point-blank range.

Xander needed to fight, but his being dead wouldn't help anyone.

Xander was weighing his options when a fierce roar startled his system, making him jolt.

The next moment, Radar was a streak of energy as he dashed forward, sailing through the air toward the gunman. His jaw clamped on the forearm, making the weapon fall to the ground.

Screams of agony ricocheted around them.

And there was Elyssa, lamp in hand, bulb and shade removed, bludgeoning the knife wielder, who was reduced to a puddle of clothes on the ground.

"Elyssa, stop. He's out. Elyssa, stop." He wrapped his arms around her and squeezed her into a hug. "Elyssa, he's out." She looked up at him, red-faced and sweaty, anger and tears in her eyes.

Xander called Radar off as he made sure that Elyssa was steady, then moved to the gunman. Grabbing the man by the collar, Xander twisted the gunman around until he was wrapped in the crook of Xander's arm. Xander squeezed his forearm to bicep, clamping down on the man's artery.

Xander knew the man had skills and could fight his way out of the hold.

But there was Radar, teeth bared, frothing at the mouth, rumbling his chest in warning.

Xander thought he, too, would choose a nap over the bite.

Xander dragged both assailants into the shadow of the corner and piled them up. Breathing. But out for at least long enough that he and Radar could disappear Elyssa.

Standing, panting next to their bags, Xander pulled Elyssa

into the crook of his elbow and planted a lingering kiss on her head. "You didn't listen to me," he whispered into her hair.

"You're not the boss of me," she said, leaning almost all of her weight on him. "And never will be." She was spent. She'd used everything in her to come to his aid.

"Agreed. Let's talk about being good teammates later. For now, thank you."

35

———————

ELYSSA

Monday

Paris, France

XANDER MUST HAVE DEVELOPED a plan while he was on his jog earlier.

Thank the Heavens she wasn't alone, blow drying her hair when those men had shown up and attacked Xander.

She had been terrified in the aftermath of the snowmobile. But seeing someone point a gun at Xander was an out-of-body, otherworldly experience.

With a bag slung over each shoulder, his roller bag in one hand and her hand in his other. They walked half a block to the hospital supply store.

He lifted his hand when he walked in, and Elyssa noticed his bruised and swollen knuckles.

Typing an amount into the computer, the cashier read the total, and Xander paid in cash.

The cashier rounded the counter with a wheelchair. It had a

nicely padded seat, and in the back, there was a large enough basket. Xander could easily slide his roller bag into it.

Still holding Radar's lead, Elyssa sat. "Xander, my condition isn't usually this bad. Just all the travel, and cold, and chaos."

"You're a super star and I'm in awe. I hoped this would take some pressure off."

"Thank you," Elyssa said as the cashier ran around them to the door and held it wide, Elyssa wondered what story Xander had offered this person.

Their next stop was three doors down at a women's clothing store. He walked to the shelf, pulled down a t-shirt, sweatpants, and a fleece jacket, and placed them in her lap.

Pushing the chair back to the area to try things on, Elyssa simply sat there with the clothes in her lap. This had to be some kind of ploy.

Xander was busy on the floor, pulling out a wand-like piece of equipment. Then, piece by piece, he meticulously went through every item in their bags, the clothes he wore, and then the clothes she wore.

Her boot lit up the wand.

Silently, Xander removed it from her foot and looked it over. Then, with a penknife, he worked on the liner. Elyssa wasn't great with the idea that he was digging into her sweaty boot. After a moment, he pulled up a flat disk that must have been in the heel cavity.

Cold washed through Elyssa.

She had brought those attackers to their room. She had put Radar and Xander in deadly peril.

She felt like she was cosplaying. It was like being in a movie without being given a script. None of this seemed real, despite the sights, sounds, and smells.

Meanwhile, there was Xander acting like this was his

normal, everyday life. And for all she knew, it was. Yup, he was just going about his business with no evident emotion about this at all. He retrieved a piece of gum from his kit, chewed it, and then pressed the tracker into the glob. Leaving Radar to guard her, he left the dressing area.

There was the tinkle as the bell jingled at the front door. A moment later, the bell tinkled again.

When Xander walked back into the curtained area, he was grinning as he said, "Now they're tracking a public bus, that should be fun for them."

After Xander performed a final sweep of every item they had with them and repacked, he wheeled Elyssa to the cashier and paid for her new outfit.

As they moved through the front door with the paper bag on her lap, she asked, "Did you buy me the outfit because you don't like me to wear your shirts?"

"The outfit was subterfuge," Xander said. "I love that you're wearing my shirt."

Their next stop was onto the Metro, heading toward Victor and the boat.

Neither of them had anything to say as they lightly swayed with a car filled with Parisians and tourists.

Elyssa was conserving what energy she could as she snacked on her pickle-flavored chips.

"Elyssa, we're the next stop." Xander released the brake on her chair and pushed it forward.

The subway lights blinked, then faded. They were in pitch black until Xander swiped his phone flashlight on.

Rolling to a stop, Xander said loudly enough for the car to hear, first in French, then in English, "Looks like the electrical outage made it to Paris." Xander reached for the door and pried it open. He jumped down. People around him were calling out to him, and Elyssa had no idea what they were saying, but

Xander's reply was in a reasonable tone. He seemed to be giving them information and explanations.

Heads were nodding. Xander reached for Elyssa and held her in his arms while two men got down and moved the wheelchair and their bags to the sidewalk that ran along the tunnel. Passengers held out their phone flashlights to provide light.

Radar jumped down from the car to the rails and then leaped up onto the sidewalk next to the wheelchair.

Xander set Elyssa down in her seat again.

Xander turned to see the men helping other passengers out. Once Xander got her chair rolling forward, Elyssa asked. "What's happening?"

"The electrical outages have been spreading across France, and my app showed them creeping closer to the city. I thought we had enough time to get to our stop and then some. There must have been a surge of outages."

"Damned sunspots."

"I told them that I wasn't willing to sit in a Metro for hours until some official came to get me off. As long as I was on the walkway, nothing could happen, even if they had a backup generator that would kick in."

"Well, as people see us leaving, they're getting the idea, too," Elyssa said.

"Good. I prefer to be lost in the crowd."

Xander and two other men from their same subway car carried Elyssa's wheelchair up the steep steps. Elyssa was both grateful and wanted to roll her eyes at the preposterousness of it all. It wasn't preposterous. If she were at home, she would have been in bed sleeping all day. Honestly, it had been two weeks of overexertion. And two days in a row, her brain had turned to big orange letters of insistence that she act to stay alive. And keep Xander alive. Who knew that was a thing her brain could do?

Xander was standing at a crossroads. "The boat is two

blocks that way. Believe it or not, we're still on time. We have about thirty minutes until we need to meet our helper. You need to eat."

"You need to eat," Elyssa said.

He pushed her up the road to a café where they read over the menu.

"English?" Xander asked the server.

"Yes."

"We'd like sandwiches and drinks to go, please." He turned to Elyssa. "Do you know what you'd like?"

"The Mediterranean, please. And the largest bottle of sparkling water you have. Two. No, three. Three of your largest bottles."

The server used his hands to indicate their size and a face that asked if she was sure.

"Yes, thank you."

Xander ordered his lunch and pulled out a chair to sit and hold her hand.

The eye of the storm, Elyssa thought, enjoying the calming sensation of Xander's thumb brushing over the top of her hand.

A pop dropped Xander out of his chair onto the ground as he reached out and pressed Elyssa's head down.

Was that gunfire?

Pop. Pop. Pop.

It sure sounded like gunfire. Had someone found them again?

Xander twisted to look around him, and Elyssa looked too. There wasn't really anywhere to go that didn't look easily shot up.

In one fluid motion, Xander released Radar from his lead and signaled him to his side. "Elyssa, hang on, this is going to be bumpy."

Pop. Pop. Pop. Pop.

They were moving.

Xander had the bags over his shoulders and was pressing her chair forward, running full tilt across the street, then over the sidewalk into the row of hedges and trees. He didn't stop. He didn't slow. It was like being on a wild amusement park ride through the branches.

Arriving at the ticket building outside the tourist boats' wharf, Xander burst through the door.

The man peeked up when the bell tinkled.

Now the strafing sound of gunfire was a constant ratatatat. It sounded like a war had broken out along the shores of the Seine.

Xander turned the sign to closed and locked the door. "Get back down." He pulled the blinds, so they had a couple of inches to see out, but mostly the interior was shielded from view. "If the glass breaks, this will protect the room from flying shards." He paused as he pulled down the next one. "It can't stop a bullet." He said it in English for Elyssa, then in French for everyone else.

"Has the world gone mad?" the head-looking guy said in heavily-accented English.

Banging at the door. "Jean Michel! It's me, Victor. Let me in."

"Let him in. He works here."

"Look first." Xander raised the shade.

"Yes. Yes. For sure, this is Victor."

Xander opened the door, and the guy stumbled in, dropping his hands to his knees and panting. "*Ca va.*" He raised a hand. "*Tout va bien.*"

Even from Elyssa's pitiful French, she recognized the words telling her everything was okay.

"What's happening out there?" The cashier asked in English. "Are you hurt?"

Victor looked at Xander and asked, "American?"

"My wife and I were vacationing." He made his voice sound defeated. "Paris in the springtime."

"So romantic," Elyssa added wryly.

"I am Victor," he sent a significant look to Xander. "This is Jean-Michel." He indicated the man behind the cash register.

Jean-Michel focused on Victor. "What did you see?"

"It's the adhesive factory. The popping is the sound of explosions contained inside the building. I saw firefighters there. They are running their hoses."

"Good thing the fire station is within hearing of the factory," Jean Michel held up his cell phone. "There is nothing. What could have happened to our cell connections?"

"Too many people touching base with loved ones all at once," Xander said. "It's best to text." He turned to Victor. "My wife," Xander said, "has a disorder that is exacerbated by big noises, public distress, all the things that are happening now. It's her heart. I'd like to get her out of town to Le Havre.

Victor nodded. "I can do it. I don't have a fancy boat, but I live on it. So, it has a couch for sitting." He looked at Elyssa. "You can lie down. I have a bed. I changed the sheets this morning."

Elyssa was numb and woozy. Just anywhere she could put her head in peace and quiet, without the need to fend off another assailant, would be amazing.

"Is it near here?" Xander asked.

"Yes. Yes. Just there." He pointed toward a covered window.

Victor walked with them as they made their way to the wharf and onto the boat.

Xander lifted Elyssa into his arms and carried her into the cabin, laying her gently on the couch.

"Seven hours from Paris to Le Havre." Victor put the two

backpacks near the cabinet. "I will have you there by dinner. On board, I have just gone shopping. I can make sandwiches, and I have fruit."

"Perfect, thank you." Xander turned to Elyssa. "I'm taking Radar to potty. I'm within hearing range just on the shore."

Victor had finished bringing the folded wheelchair and roller case on board when Radar trotted into the cabin, then jumped on top of Elyssa, covering her legs, pushing some much-needed blood to her heart.

36

Monday

Seine River, France

ELYSSA LOOKED OVER AT XANDER. "What do you think is happening?"

The hum of the boat motor, the peaceful countryside, and the gentle rocking. One could lull oneself into thinking that everything was good.

Xander swallowed down his bite of sandwich from the food that Victor had made for them before answering. "There's a word, *proizvol,* which means arbitrariness. There's the idea that the Zorics can do whatever they want to you. It creates a state of paralysis in society. Their actions are calibrated to feel like the consistent pressure of terror. There's another word, *prodazhnost,* which is close to venality. The Family, capital T capital F, used to do as they pleased when they pleased back in the days of the USSR. And that power was stripped from them. They want it back."

"What language?" Elyssa asked.

"Russian."

"The only thing I can add to that pot is a Polish saying: I found myself at the very bottom, then I heard knocking below. That's the way these last couple of days have felt, I keep thinking that something was bad, then I discover that there's worse and worse."

"In Russian," Xander said, "it becomes, 'There is no bottom.' For the Zorics, there is no limit to their depravity, sadism, and cruelty."

"And Orest just seemed to embrace life and love the simple things."

"I'm not saying he didn't enjoy those things," Xander said. "I am saying he liked cruelty just as much."

"I've been thinking about him and those pictures. Mainly, I've been wondering how I could ever identify a random plant that I once stood near. I considered my clothes. They were all items I had packed during my trip to London and France. I wish I had my phone because I could narrow down the day to the outfit."

Elyssa stared at the piece of peach resting on the side of her plate. "Do you remember when I told you we were doing a food tour and buying cider, but we were also setting up a game for the children?"

"You mentioned children, I remember that."

"See if this is interesting to you," Elyssa leaned back on the sofa and crossed her arms over her chest. "I was told that several of the families had decided to take a vacation in the area. The mothers wanted to use it as a learning opportunity where the kids didn't know they were learning. So, the mothers had put together a scavenger hunt of sorts, but it was nice because it wasn't just for their family. It was for anyone who wanted to play."

"Keep going."

"Yes, so it was basically geocaching. The kids would use maps and compasses, and some clues required them to have a basic understanding of local history to decipher the clues. So, reading and collaborating. Orest had these boxes. Inside, there was a notebook and a pen attached to a little chain. If someone found the box, they could write down their country and a little note of kindness for other families. There were toys, nice toys, and something—like a sticker or enamel pin—from the area. People who found the box could take a prize if they liked. And if they wanted, they could leave something behind. I had done that with my family when I was young. It was fun."

"Can you describe the boxes?

"They were about eighteen inches by eighteen inches, about five inches deep with a galvanized steel bottom to protect from rust."

"They were made out of metal?" Xander asked.

"Yes. They were really nice boxes. Quality design."

"Why would he need you?" Xander sat up straighter, his gaze very intense.

"I don't understand the question," Elyssa whispered.

"Orest invited you to Europe. He found an excuse that would entice you overseas, and then he had you go to specific places with these boxes. He needed you for something."

"He used me for something, you mean?" Elyssa frowned. "I am so damned naïve. My naïveté is going to be the downfall of humanity, isn't it?"

Xander reached for her hand.

"Why did he need me?" Elyssa shook her head. "I have no idea."

"Let's go through it," Xander offered. "Would you carry the boxes?"

"They were in the bag with our things. Sometimes, I carried it, and sometimes it was Orest."

"And when you got to a place he already knew where to place it?" Xander asked.

"He knew specifically where because he had a GPS, and he was very precise. Anally precise about the placement of the boxes, so the children wouldn't become discouraged."

"When you got to the X, you didn't just lay them on the ground, did you?" Xander asked.

"There was always something there." Elyssa stalled. "And that should have been my clue."

"Tell me that thought."

"There was always something there at that GPS point, like a bench or a stairway. That way, the boxes could be attached with a chain, so they weren't stolen, and they were out of easy view." Elyssa said. "Orest told me that the mothers had put the game together but how would a mother in Slovakia know the location of a bench in a French garden? I thought Orest was just an old man out trying to make the babies happy." She blinked at Xander. "What did I help him plant?"

"I don't know. I'm guessing elements of his machine."

"What does the machine do?" Elyssa asked.

Xander pressed his lips together to show that there were certain things they couldn't talk about when others might hear. "You were telling me that you were putting the boxes somewhere."

"Always something different. At the gardens in Étretat, for example, there was a trail that wound down the hill. There were various installations, so the garden appealed to all the senses. There were times when the garden flowered, for example, but in the seasons without blooms, there were perfume stations where you could breathe in an evocative scent. And there were sound installations. Sometimes you interacted with them, sometimes they were speakers making the sounds. It was at one of those installations, the smell or the sound, that we put the box."

"And it just sat there. "

"I'm trying to see where there's a pattern to the behavior. In each place it was easy to get to and on part of the path—no one had to rummage around or anything, but we chained them into place." Her gaze drifted toward the water as she remembered.

"Yup, that's what I'm looking for." Xander squeezed her hand. "Tell me your thoughts."

"We would call and make an appointment with the manager, explaining our plan. When we got to the site, we'd show them the box and the chain and how sophisticated and lovely the game component was. I told them where we wanted to put the box and informed them that we would be advertising the Normandy scavenger hunt, which would entice families with children to participate. We showed them the insides, so they saw that it was filled to the brim with lovely little treats. We, and by we, I mean I. I showed them the scavenger hunt website."

"Do you have the URL?" Xander reached for his notebook.

"No. It was on the flier I handed them so they could advertise it if they wanted to, and it was already queued up on Orest's laptop."

"And they let you put it in their garden or wherever?" Xander asked.

"Every last one of them did. But I was looking happy about a children's project, and there was Orest with his round tummy and pink cheeks, looking like he was an off-season Santa Claus."

"You're not the first person to point out that resemblance to me."

"Well, it's true. Between the two of us, it looked like what I described, a happy pair that was creating a children's experience for our family – and other people's families – to enjoy and perhaps to create new traffic to their site."

"And Orest didn't speak?"

"I know why," Elyssa said. "When Orest spoke in French, it was with a heavy Russian-sounding accent. I know it's Slovak, but most people don't have the exposure to distinguish it. With the war raging in Ukraine, a Russian-sounding accent would put people on the alert. And there was a significant disdain for that in Paris."

"No one in their right mind would allow a Russian to put something in their garden," Xander agreed.

"It wasn't always a garden. There were different types of places. All of them were of cultural importance, though."

"In Normandy? Was there anything put in the U.S. cemeteries?"

"No. Oh no. That would have been sacrilegious. I would have told Orest that. We did go to Sainte-Mère-Église. It's famous because on D-Day, a parachutist caught his chute on the steeple of the church, and he dangled there alive until the villagers could rescue him. We stayed in a chateau just out of town that had been there since the days of the Vikings. From there, we toured the cemeteries. We visited Colleville-sur-Mer, overlooking Omaha Beach. What a moving experience. And because Orest thought it was important, we also visited La Cambe German Military Cemetery. It's very near the D-Day landing sites." Elyssa paused, looking at her lap.

"What happened in that cemetery?" Xander asked softly.

"We stood by the grave of this guy named Diekman. He was the highest-ranking officer at the Oradour-sur-Glane Massacre. In that massacre, the entire village was gathered up, women and babies, old people, men, and women. People from the village. People passing by the village. The men were put in barns, and they had their legs shot. Then they were doused with gas and set on fire." Elyssa gave a whole-body shiver. "The women and children were taken to the church, and they too were set on fire." She raised her gaze to look at the ceiling. "Can you imagine the screams that rode the wind? Over six hundred people who were just living their lives. Humans can be monsters."

Elyssa sat with those images in her head. And she thought of Eddie. What was he going through? How cruel and horrible was that man that she had called uncle with such affection?

After a while, Xander squeezed her hand again. "That struck you. Why?"

"It was the one time that Orest told me about a specific person. And I remember him saying that had there not been Nazis, he would have had a father, a mother, and a brother."

"Which is what was in the article about you that was in the paper, the father and son were separated. The mother and older child escaped to the USA."

"Yes. So that was the story I knew. That made sense, that he sort of wanted to look the enemy in the eye. I remember I held his hand as he stared at Diekman's grave. Someone had left flowers there. And he was looking at the flowers, and Orest said. 'A man will do what he needs to do to support the cause he holds in his heart. And see there, the flowers? Somebody, all these decades later, believes that he did the right thing.' And then we walked away. He was comparing his upcoming actions with those of that evil man, wasn't he? He was feeling reassured. What will he suffer? He's old. He'll die soon enough."

"Elyssa, can you remember the names of places you left the boxes if I gave you a map? If we go there, Radar is trained to find electronics. You won't need to remember the exact spot. We can get to them and destroy them."

Together, they worked on the list. As she came up with a location, Xander pinned it on his off-grid GPS app.

He pulled the file folder of Elyssa's photos out of his back-pack and looked at the numbers on them. "These were taken by a man tracking Orest's movements. If he took a picture of each one where you placed them, on his phone, he'd have the GPS coordinates. His phone is locked, and we can't get in. But if that's what these photos are, then you're missing one box."

"I am?"

She looked back at the list of tourist attractions in Normandy.

"Not the cemeteries?"

"No." She scowled.

"Not the church with the parachutist?"

"No sacred places," Elyssa insisted.

"What about the chateau?"

Elyssa stilled. "Orest had decided that he wanted an apartment outside of Paris, not too far away. He wanted someplace easy to get to, but a sleepy place near the ocean where he could walk and have his thoughts."

"And where did he get the apartment?"

"At the chateau, Orest had an apartment in what was a side building. The nobleman built the building as a hospital for his men, and his descendants later converted it into lovely apartments. Orest also got a storage room in the turret of the castle. It's actually a bedroom that nomadic tech workers rent if they want to spend a month in Normandy. But that was so he could store some trunks that he had delivered to him."

"You saw the trunks?" Xander asked.

"I saw them from a distance. Workers brought them."

"In a truck?" Xander was obviously trying to contain his excitement.

"Van."

"How many?" he asked.

"Vans? Just the one. How many trunks? I saw three, but I

was simply walking by and not paying close attention. But that is odd, isn't it? Orest's apartment was on the first floor of the hospital. He had the trunks put in the castle turret, which is up four flights of narrow, rounded stairs. It's a lot even for me. I did it once to see what was up there, and that was it. I don't know that Orest could get up those stairs. But he said that he would have his assistant help him access the boxes when he traveled." The rugby side of her personality steadied Elyssa as she felt a surge of determination to conquer the field. "That's what we're looking for, isn't it?"

"I think so. We need to get to the chateau near Sainte-Mère-Église." He reached for his phone, and as he turned it over, it buzzed.

Swiping it open, they read:

Adele: **Xander?**

Xander: **Shit.**

Adele: **The ferry's loaded. They're under way now.**

37

Xander
Monday
Seine River, France

Xander had their captain heading them to a town that was on the road to Sainte-Mère-Église.

As Elyssa curled up to nap with Radar, Xander went up on the deck to get an encrypted satellite connection back to his team.

"Who's there?" he asked Hiro.

"White, Finley, and me."

"I think I have it figured out," Xander said. "I'm sending you a map."

He waited for White to say, "Received. What are we looking at here? It's like a wishbone."

"The point at the tip of the angle is the chateau outside of Sainte-Mère-Église."

"Normandy. You didn't make it to London yet," Finley said.

"I'm not going to London. I'm going to that vertex. Let me

explain what Elyssa came up with and see if you agree with my theory. First, though, we're out of electricity in France. Where has it spread?"

"Along the Baltic. Norway, Denmark, Sweden, and Poland," Hiro said. "But only along the Baltic and North Sea shores."

"The outages are not country-wide in those nations, right? And they're all west of Kaliningrad Oblast, the Russian exclave?"

"That's correct," White's voice was tight. "Russia's moving something up the Baltic, do you think?"

"The Russians could take advantage of the blackout by cutting communications cables in the Baltic. I wouldn't rule it out. But I don't think that's their goal." Xander thought for the first time in a long time that there was a glimmer of hope. He had committed to finding and destroying the Zoric machine. If he did that, then he was going off on his own, doing his own thing.

With his inheritance from all four of his grandparents that he'd split with his brother Adam, along with his military retirement, Xander was set to live a comfortable life, figuring out what made him happy for happy's sake.

He felt like he'd done enough; he could move on.

Tink had done it.

Scott had done it.

Unless the whole damned family went down, Anna would never be done. Never. She knew that when she signed up, but she signed up before she fell in love with Finley. And now she was trapped in her decisions.

Xander wondered if she had regrets.

Granted, without The Family, she and Finley may never have crossed paths.

Just like he would never have found Elyssa except for the evils of Orest Kalinsky.

"What was that?" White asked.

"What?" Xander looked around him, then back at the screen.

"That look on your face. It looked like you had a hopeful thought, but you let it slide into a scoff."

"I did. Didn't I? I remembered I was getting out over my skis. Let me tell you what I have. Let's call the left side ray 1. If you follow ray 1 from the vertex of Sainte-Mère-Église, you pass through five points in France and Portsmouth in England to arrive at Her Majesty's Naval Base Clyde in Faslane, Scotland."

"That's the only European dock where US nuclear submarines are regularly stationed," Hiro said.

"If you follow ray 2 from the vertex with five boxes—or points—in France and one in London, you land on—"

"Faroe Islands,' Hiro said. "We need to escalate this. We need to get to the president and get into the situation room. Excuse me, I'll be right back."

"What's on Faroe Islands?" Finley asked.

"We had a Virginia-class submarine up there," White said. "It bounces between Faroe and Iceland, it's up there for fears of Russian subs getting into the Atlantic Ocean because they can get situated off American shores and threaten cities like D.C. and N.Y. "

"Right," Xander said. "When we were at Iniquus, Adele mentioned that Orest was doing research into how the warming temperatures of the oceans were making it harder to hunt subs. That's been tumbling over in my mind. Last year, the waters off Florida hit record highs. Those waters curved up the East Coast making those waters warmer, too. It would take some time to move the subs from the Baltic across the Atlantic. Once the water warmed in summer, they could position, undetected, very close to shore. Strike range."

"Subs," White said flatly.

"Subs," Finley exhaled.

"Subs can communicate with satellites if they put up an antenna at periscope level," Xander said. "We know from back when they attacked Strike Force at Iniquus that the Zorics had the capacity to interrupt satellite communications. And we know that they can do that for whole regions. We also know that the Zorics just launched a communications satellite under the Iranian flag, put in place by Russia. I checked back in Paris. That satellite will be over the same area affected by the electrical outage starting at zero hundred Zulu time. It could well be that the Zorics have the capacity to stun—for lack of a better word—the other areas' satellites to make it look like an EMP while leaving their own satellite unaffected and able to guide Russian subs out of the Baltic."

"I'm following the reasoning," Finley said. "That all lines up."

Hiro was back in the picture. "I have a car coming to get me. They're putting everyone on alert. Give me what you've got. I'm headed in to talk to the joint chiefs, we need to be in motion, and I need to take them everything available."

"Bottom line, Xander, what do you see as the end goal?" White asked.

"Worst case in my imagination is that they sneak into the Atlantic undiscovered. There, they could position themselves off of D.C. or N.Y.C., where they could hold the United States hostage. Our administration would flinch. Of course they would. What choice would they have with millions of lives at risk?"

"We've had this dance before in Cuba," Hiro said.

"The devastation of a nuclear bomb," White said, "especially if multiple urban centers along the coast were targeted—not just D.C., what about Norfolk? What about Atlanta? Yes, our nation would be held hostage. I don't know how it works from there. But surely, it could change the world order."

"What if they weren't negotiating?" Hiro asked. "What if they just pulled up, launched the missile at close range, the bomb went boom, and the United States was facing its Hiroshima? And like Japan, terrified of who else might pop up and not knowing who sent the bombs and what could come next, what if not just the U.S. but the entire world capitulated?"

AFTER VICTOR LEFT them off at a village wharf, renting a car wasn't as complicated as Xander thought it would be. There was a mother who was willing to drive them to the chateau at Sainte-Mère-Église for a hundred euros. He didn't know she was going to bring her baby in the car seat, but at that point, the decision had been made.

When they arrived, Elyssa went to talk to Colette, the concierge who managed the chateau, explaining that she'd beaten her uncle in and didn't have the key to his apartment. Elyssa said she needed to retrieve a photograph from the turret room. Colette had no problems at all loaning her the master key until Orest arrived.

Xander made a quick dash through Orest's apartment with Radar conducting an electronics search, then they made their way to the side of the castle, entering through the back door and down the dark hall.

"The Gestapo were living here on D-Day. They have a swastika in the laundry room, and they have bullets in the walls where Americans came in to clear the leadership out of the area." She slogged her way up the staircase. It wound and wound up four flights of stairs, which were narrow and dizzying, and Xander understood why she didn't think Orest could get himself to the top.

Inside the rounded room painted periwinkle with white trim and a golden curtain at the enormous windows, Xander only took a moment to scan the room.

Beside the bed, six metal trunks were stacked in groups of three. So, more than Elyssa had seen go up.

"Radar, find electronics," Xander commanded.

Radar walked over to the trunks and sat down.

"Well, that was anticlimactic," Elyssa said.

There were no locks, and when Xander asked Radar to find explosives, he came up empty. So, Xander opened the first trunk, expecting the acrid smell of acid to fill the room, just as it had in the field in Newark.

It did not.

The trunks were filled with innocuous-looking components.

Xander did what his gut told him to do; he pulled out what he could grab and smashed them under his heel.

Elyssa joined in, but it was such an aerobic action that Xander didn't want her to do it.

"Elyssa, it would be faster if you could pull pieces out and throw them on the ground."

The first locker was completed, they hauled it to the side, then started the second.

When they got to the third, a car raced up the long gravel drive under the canopy of trees and screeched to a halt in front of the castle.

Xander was loath to leave his task. He looked around for a safe place for Elyssa to go. He knew that as soon as she heard those tires on the drive, her heart went into overdrive. She was not looking well, and Radar got up and booped her aggressively.

Then booped Xander for good measure.

Xander turned the enormous metal key in its old-fashioned lock.

As the men raced through the bright red castle door, Xander was leaning out the window, doing a head count. Three that he could see. He looked to the side and found one of those ubiquitous roof ladders.

And he hated every second of what came next.

He forced Elyssa out the window onto the ladder. Forced her hands to climb while holding her in place, getting her feet high enough that they were out of view of someone doing a quick look-see from the window.

"Xander, tie my hands together over the rung like when I held onto the snowmobiler, then put your belt around my waist to hold me to another rung if I pass out… I'm going to pass out."

Xander looked down the five stories to the gravel far below and felt sick to his stomach as he tethered her in place. Sainte-Mère-Église was known for the parachutist who had clung for his life to the steeple of the church while the Nazis fought below, and the irony was not lost on Xander.

Sliding back through the window, Xander pushed the trunks over to the door and stood them on end. If the tangos were shooting, at least they'd be destroying their own doomsday machine before they killed him.

From far below, footsteps pounded up the stairs.

Xander was able to pull Radar into the bathroom off to the side, out of line with the bullets unless they ricocheted. There, they lay flat on their bellies using the massive clawfoot tub to keep them safe.

Xander didn't understand a word of what the men were yelling. But at least the bullets had stopped. Now they were breaking down the door. A nice solid ancient door that didn't want to give way when they threw their shoulders into it.

He didn't want to be trapped without egress, so Xander opened the bathroom door, ready to face the enemy.

With a last thrust from the tangos, the turret room door slapped open, bouncing off the wall.

Radar made a leap for the gun hand of Tango One as he stumbled into the room.

Xander grabbed the hand of the one behind him, flipping the gun around and shooting the man in the gut. Tango Three roared as he ran into the room, snatching Xander off his feet and draping him over his shoulder like Elyssa had done back in the videos of her on the field. Tango Three raced toward the window. Xander had to have the guy by a good foot. Very quickly, he was able to switch things around. With the tango on his shoulder, and not knowing what else to do with him, Xander tipped him out the window.

It was a long damned way down.

Xander looked up to see Elyssa dangling lifelessly, and horror flowed through Xander's veins. Heart or bullets? Either was deadly.

Seizing the gun that had fallen from the hand of Tango One that Radar was subduing, Xander pulled it across his shoulder, then pistol-whipped the enemy. He was lights out.

Xander moved into the hall to find Tango Two. Though shot, Tago Two wasn't in danger of bleeding out as Xander had hoped, but up on his feet, looking for a way to attack.

Xander clocked that guy, too, telling Radar to guard the men as he went to rescue Elyssa.

Out the window and up the ladder in the twilight, the wind was strong here and pressed against him, rattling the ladder, making Xander wonder if it was well-maintained or if it was at risk of pulling loose, plummeting them both to the ground where Tango Three sprawled. Holding on one-handed, he pressed his fingers into Elyssa's neck at the carotid and found her heart racing. She felt conscious but unable to react.

Below him, the dark silhouettes of the castle inhabitants ran toward the bare-treed woods toward safety.

In the distance, sirens wailed.

Xander didn't know if there were more than just the three assailants who had breached the door, but he needed to get Elyssa to a hospital, even if they had no electricity.

Xander unbound Elyssa's wrists so that he could get her away from the ladder rung. Then bound them back together, slipping into the circle of her arms and into a cross-body hold. He took the belt from around her and the ladder. It wasn't long enough to go around both of them, so he looped it around her waist and thrust his arm through, catching it at his elbow.

Awkwardly, Xander took careful step after careful step until he was at the window.

A black-haired woman with a tear-streaked face reached for Elyssa's legs, pulling her in to the turret room. "I see this. I see her on the ladder. I come. I run as fast as I can," she said breathlessly, her bosom heaving as she worked to get Elyssa inside.

"Thank you so much," Xander was breathing heavily as he climbed through the window.

The woman must have been terrified to run toward gunfire and step over unconscious, bleeding men.

But her act of valor, in that moment, was balm to Xander's spirit.

Cradling a semi-conscious Elyssa in his arms, Xander followed the woman down the stairs to the front salon. There, he laid her on a brocade couch, hugging her tightly to him as Radar sat on her legs.

Xander's heart was a racing train.

The woman stood to the side, gripping the fireplace poker in her hands, looking like she was willing to jump and defend should the tangos make it down the stairs.

Suddenly, the lights stuttered, then flashed on.

The television blared.

Elyssa, too, was beginning to rouse when Xander's phone buzzed.

Xander grabbed it from his thigh pocket. "Hiro. What have you got?"

"I'm in the situation room at the White House. The lights are coming back online. The Pentagon reached out to our allied nations about the submarines. Sweden had detected submarine movement of four of the Russian nuclear class before losing capability. They sent a NATO warning via satellite to the subs, and Norway is, in real time, watching them turn. You destroyed the trunks?"

"Elyssa and I."

"Well, looks like you thwarted the Zoric attack. It was bad. It could have become catastrophic. The gratitude of a nation," Hiro said. "You did it."

"We did it for now," Xander said quietly. "You get that, right? They have the science."

Xander lifted his gaze as the police in SWAT gear swarmed into the castle.

Xander
Monday
Sainte-Mère-Église

"Xander," Anna gasped, looking pale and haunted as she stared into the camera on her laptop.

"Elyssa, this is my cousin Anna. Finley's fiancée, and the reason that we met."

"Thank you," Elyssa said.

"Good work. Much appreciation to both of you. It's hard to believe that it's over. And I mean really and truly over."

Xander knew that all he had done was buy them a short window of time. Months at most. The Zorics had the science to rebuild their destructive machine. And if what Elyssa was saying about the study of revenge addiction, the Zoric family would come at the world hard and fast. Xander wasn't sure how he could keep Elyssa safe. But right now, he was confused by Anna's tone, by how pale she was. So he just came out and labeled what he saw. "You look like you're in shock."

"That's putting it mildly. I ... there ... It ..." She put her hand on her forehead, then bent at the waist and blew out hard.

"Take your time, Anna. Sit down on the ground before you fall down."

She picked up the computer and sank to the floor. From the new angle, she must have her laptop balanced on her knees. "Adele just called from Singapore. There was an explosion."

"Breathe."

"The Family was on a ferry boat at what was late afternoon in Singapore, about the time you were on your boat in the Seine. That ferry was bringing The Family to Davidson Realm."

"An explosion?"

"The family was bringing auxiliary boats that held the servants."

"An explosion, Anna?"

"Adele had someone tracking The Family as they crossed so she would know when The Family landed and what happened next. They were set up like a fishing boat, and they were filming. I've seen the video." Her voice squeaked, and Anna clutched at her heart, much like Elyssa did when she was in pain. "There was a cigarette boat. It was aimed at the ferry and was going super fast. The video was very clear. Very crisp. On board, two people, dressed in full scuba gear, held underwater propellers. The driver pushed the throttle forward, aimed at the center of the ferry. Then the men jumped into the ocean. They went underwater and disappeared. But the speedboat." She gasped. "Oh god, the speedboat."

"Take a breath. Take your time," Xander said. "Is that a glass of water beside you? Take a sip."

"The speedboat was full of boxes. It went straight into the side of the ferry. And when it did, there was an explosion. It was so big that the blast wave flipped some of the pleasure boats that the Zorics were having shuttled over. The person filming was thrown backward, and moments later, he was back on his feet, filming again. He filmed as the captain of his boat made a circuit to pick up the living people in the water. Without much space, I guess that's all they could do. They left the dead." Tears were running down her face. "The live people from the water were the servants. Adele says her person thinks he got all of them."

Xander hugged Elyssa closer to him. He was trying to wrap his imagination around what Anna was saying. "The Family?" he whispered.

"Gone."

"How many are gone?" Xander asked.

"All gone. There's nothing left of the ferry. It exploded then sank. The speedboat was a bomb. The assailants didn't put the bomb on the ferry because the Zoric security team did sweeps to check for explosives."

"Gone," Xander's tone was hollow.

"Gone," Anna said.

Xander shook his head. He was looking for that drug-like sensation that Elyssa had described that addictive personalities experienced when they got their revenge. And he had cotton. He had smoke. He was numb. "That's stunning."

"Yes." Anna snorted and ran the back of her wrist under her nose.

"The babies and children, that's a tragedy."

Anna's face crumpled into a mask of pain. "Yes." She panted then sniffed. "All wiped off the face of the Earth except for the Zoric family members who are huddled in their Washington prison cells." She flicked her hand like she was trying to rid them of some substance. "I'm in shock. I don't know what to do with myself."

"Have you told Finley?" Elyssa asked softly.

"He was on the call with Adele. He's said he's getting on the first flight to come to me." A heavy breath and a grimace of deep pain. She panted and sniffed. "All those people. They were *people*."

"I know," Xander said soothingly.

"They were bad, terrible people, and for me, the death of many of them, this is a blessing—the biggest, most joyful thing. The most miraculous, wonderful thing that could have happened. It's such a conflict in my body."

"The families. I know," Xander said. "Anna, you're human. You ate at their tables, you cuddled their babies. It's a devastating blow, and you should not be alone. Tatiana. Can you go to Tatiana and stay with her until Finley gets there?"

"Uhm, no. No. I can't be around anyone at all. I can't put up a front right now, and I'd have to, the attack hasn't been on the news yet. This is such a horrible sensation. Half of me is jumping up and down, screeching with joy. Orest, Medved', and Melina all wiped into oblivion, never to hurt anyone again. The world is a far safer place without them. But Natasha was on the ferry, and she was always so kind. Criminally culpable but not death sentence worthy. Joy and horror are such strange bedfellows." Anna wrapped her hands around her ribs. "I think I might explode. Or vomit. Something. Hold on, it's White, I'll bring her on."

He waited a while.

Anna came back on the line. Her face was red and tear-streaked. "She sent Grey to support me until Steve can get here. Grey is pulling up now."

"The CIA has confirmed Adele's report?" Xander asked.

"White didn't have time for a conference call. I have notes. White saw the video and was able to verify its authenticity. Next, she said York is doing well and has been moved to a private room, and they expect a full recovery. So that's good news. She said to let Elyssa know," Anna pulled up a piece of paper. "Meat, cheese, and squirrel were all on a pleasure boat and survived without injury. They are on their way to the U.S. Embassy."

Elyssa crumpled in Xander's arms, and Radar, whining, crawled over, thrusting himself into her lap as she sobbed.

"So that looks like relieving news for Elyssa," Anna said.

"Absolutely."

Anna lifted the paper again. "White told me that Adele also had tape of exactly who loaded. I'm reading this from Adele. 'Medved,' Orest, and two hundred and forty-eight other family members boarded the ferry along with four ferry workers and six caterers. All two hundred and sixty souls are gone. The coffin has been nailed shut. Our job protecting the world from the Zorics is over."

And in the back of his mind, he wondered if Elyssa would have been on the family ferry had she gone with Orest as he'd asked. Had Elyssa's ethics in living up to a promise she'd made to a friend saved her life? Right now, Xander's heart was full to bursting. Just having Elyssa in his arms was euphoria. She'd survived the dangers. And so had Anna. "Anna, you're free."

"At what cost?" Anna looked to the side. "Someone's ringing my bell. Stay with me while I look out—John Grey's here," she called.

Xander kissed Elyssa's head as she lifted it to his shoulder. He smoothed the damp strands of hair out of her face and rocked side to side to soothe them both.

What a hell of a twist.

"Ender," a male voice said from off-screen as Anna found her place in front of the camera. "I've got some shit to tell you."

"Listening." *Bracing.*

"John Green was out in Singapore tag-teaming with Adele. While he was there, he caught sight of William Davidson without his family and wondered what that was about, so he kept an eye on him. William Davidson was at a restaurant overlooking the harbor and watched the family getting on the ferry."

"Any chance that was by happenstance?"

"None. Davidson had military-grade binoculars up as he watched in the exact direction of the explosion moments before it occurred. He continued to watch in that direction for approximately five minutes, then threw his head back and laughed so loudly that it brought the entire restaurant to a standstill. Green had no idea what the hell was happening. After Davidson sobered. He lifted the field glasses again and watched for quite a while. He received a single phone call that he put to his ear but did not reply to, then hung up. He paid his bill, and his driver took him to the airport. There he loaded onto his private jet and flew to his retreat in Tanzania."

"As the saying goes, revenge is a dish best served cold," Xander said. "It seems he ate his fill."

"Anna," Grey said from off to the side. "How are you holding up? Don't answer that. I can see you're struggling. Do you want me to light the fire and get you some tea?"

"Yes, please. I'm just saying goodbye to Xander and Elyssa."

"Well done, both of you!" Grey called out. "Heroes!"

"Goodbye, Anna," Xander said. "When you get home to D.C. The four of us—you, Finley, Elyssa, and I—are going to dinner to celebrate your freedom."

"At least from that threat," Anna said, "we're all free."

EPILOGUE

Elyssa stood in her bright pink dress that hung to her ankles and billowed in the wind. Her hand lay protectively on her rounded belly, where her daughter kicked her tiny feet.

Radar sat at her side, looking his regal self, wearing a service dog vest with medical alert patches and a tag that had his proper name.

And in the first row, front and center, Xander stood with their son straddling his shoulders, holding his ankles. "Look at, mommy, Eddie Ben. See her with those big scissors? She's going to cut the red bow, and when she does, we'll clap and yell very loud."

Elyssa sent her gaze around the hundreds who had gathered. "Good afternoon, all. I am Dr. Elyssa Belov the engineer who developed the science behind your project. I believe that food is a human right. I am incredibly proud of this day and of all the hard work this village has put into making your vertical farm a reality. My compliments to you all. Today, WorldCares opens its very first vertical farm and grocery store, designed to protect your community. In a natural disaster, there is enough room in the store to shelter everyone in the village. The cisterns will capture rainwater during the monsoon for use throughout the year, keeping fruits and vegetables healthy. And the mesh that covers the building not only protects the structure from flying debris in the case of a typhoon, but also captures any moisture in the air and allows it to accumulate into water droplets that are collected below, further insurance that a dry year will not leave you without sustenance. The farm is meant to be a gathering place for community and kindness." She stepped forward. "And with that, WorldCares declares that their first vertical farm is open!" Elyssa snipped with her ridiculously large ceremonial scissors.

The ribbon cut, and the cheers went up.

Elyssa stood there, her hand on Radar's head, looking at Xander with tears in her eyes.

Xander shouted out. "This calls for a victory dance!"

A woman in a bright-colored caftan stepped forward, and her rich voice rode the wind with joyful notes. Everyone who had gathered joined in the song as they danced their celebration.

Elyssa made her way into Xander's arms, "Thank you," she said laying her head on his heart.

And amidst the celebration, their family stood as a tight knot of love all doing their "little bit" of good.

THE END

I hope you enjoyed getting to know Xander, Radar, and Elyssa. If you had fun reading Radar, I'd appreciate it if you'd help others enjoy it too.

Recommend it: A few words to your friends, book groups, and social networks would be fantastic.

Review it: Please tell your fellow readers what you liked about my book by reviewing **RADAR**.

Discuss it! – I have a SPOILERS group on Facebook.

~

The Next Book in
The World of Iniquus Chronology:

Trusted Instinct
Cerberus Tactical K9 Team Charlie

*Make sure **Trusted Instinct** is added to your TBR list!*

WORLD OF INIQUUS NOVELS
IN CHRONOLOGICAL ORDER

Year One

    Weakest Lynx (Lynx Series)

    Missing Lynx (Lynx Series)

Year Two

    Chain Lynx (Lynx Series)

    Cuff Lynx (Lynx Series)

    WASP (Uncommon Enemies)

Year Three

    In Too DEEP (Strike Force)

    Jack Be Quick (Strike Force)

    Relic (Uncommon Enemies)

    Mine (Kate Hamilton Mystery)

    Deadlock (Uncommon Enemies)

    Instigator (Strike Force)

    Yours (Kate Hamilton Mystery)

    Open Secret (FBI Joint Task Force)

    Thorn (Uncommon Enemies)

    Gulf Lynx (Lynx Series)

Year Four

Ours (Kate Hamilton Mysteries)

Cold Red (FBI Joint Task Force)

Even Odds (FBI Joint Task Force)

Survival Instinct (Cerberus Tactical K9 Team Alpha)

Protective Instinct (Cerberus Tactical K9 Team Alpha)

Defender's Instinct (Cerberus Tactical K9 Team Alpha)

Danger Signs (Delta Force Echo)

Hyper Lynx (Lynx Series)

Danger Zone (Delta Force Echo)

Danger Close (Delta Force Echo)

Year Five

Fear the Reaper (Strike Force)

Warrior's Instinct (Cerberus Tactical K9 Team Bravo)

Rescue Instinct (Cerberus Tactical K9 Team Bravo)

Hero's Instinct (Cerberus Tactical K9 Team Bravo)

Striker (Strike Force)

Marriage Lynx (Lynx Series)

Guardian's Instinct (Cerberus Tactical K9 Team Charlie)

Beowolf (Iniquus Certified Cerberus Tactical K9)

Red Line (CIA Color Code)

Sheltering Instinct (Cerberus Tactical K9 Team Charlie)

Shielding Instinct (Cerberus Tactical K9 Team Charlie)

Year Six

Radar (Iniquus Certified Cerberus Tactical K9)

Trusted Instinct (Cerberus Tactical K9 Team Charlie)

Acting on Instinct (Cerberus Tactical K9 Team Delta)

Whiskey (Iniquus Certified Cerberus Tactical K9)

With more Iniquus novels to follow!

For the most up-to-date list, go to FionaQuinnBooks.com

ACKNOWLEDGMENTS

MY GREAT APPRECIATION

To my publicist **Margaret Daly**
To my cover artist, **Melody Simmons**
To my editor **Rossana Tarantini**

To the wonderful people at Chateau de L'Isle Marie where I stayed while researching this novel, with special gratitude to Jeanne for her kindness.
To my Street Force, who support me and my writing with such enthusiasm and kindness.
To all the professionals who shared their knowledge of working K9s, especially the various Virginia search and rescue teams.

Please note: This is a work of fiction, and while I always try my best to get all the details correct, there are times when it serves the story to go slightly to the left or right of perfection. Please understand that any mistakes or discrepancies are my authorial decision-making alone and sit squarely on my shoulders.

Thank you to my family for your love and support.

I send my love to my husband. Thank you for your driving skills and wonderful company as we explored Paris and Normandy for this book.

And, of course, thank *YOU* for reading my stories. I always smile joyfully as I type this sentence. I so appreciate you!

ABOUT THE AUTHOR

Fiona Quinn is a six-time USA Today bestselling author, a Kindle Scout winner, an Amazon Top 40, and an Amazon All-Star.

Quinn writes suspense in her Iniquus World of books; including Lynx, Strike Force, Uncommon Enemies, Kate Hamilton Mysteries, FBI Joint Task Force, Cerberus Tactical K9 Series: Alpha, Bravo, Charlie, and Certified Cerberus Tactical K9, the Delta Force Echo series, CIA Color Code Action Adventure, and now, an Iniquus cookbook!

She writes urban fantasy as Fiona Angelica Quinn for her Elemental Witches Series.

And, just for fun, she writes the Badge Bunny Booze Mystery Collection with her dear friend, Tina Glasneck, as Quinn Glasneck.

Quinn is a Canadian author rooted on the shores of the Atlantic where she lives with her husband. There, she pops chocolates, devours books, and taps continuously on her laptop.

Visit: www.fionaquinnbooks.com

COPYRIGHT